THE
ANTIDOTE
FOR
EVERYTHING

THE ANTIDOTE FOR EVERYTHING

KIMMERY MARTIN

BERKLEY
NEW YORK

BERKLEY
An imprint of Penguin Random House LLC
penguinrandomhouse.com

Copyright © 2020 by Kimmery Martin
Penguin Random House supports copyright. Copyright fuels creativity, encourages diverse
voices, promotes free speech, and creates a vibrant culture. Thank you for buying an
authorized edition of this book and for complying with copyright laws by not reproducing,
scanning, or distributing any part of it in any form without permission. You are supporting
writers and allowing Penguin Random House to continue to publish books for every reader.

BERKLEY and the BERKLEY & B colophon are registered trademarks of
Penguin Random House LLC.

Library of Congress Cataloging-in-Publication Data

Names: Martin, Kimmery, author.
Title: The antidote for everything / Kimmery Martin.
Description: First Edition. | New York: Berkley, 2020.
Identifiers: LCCN 2019030597 (print) | LCCN 2019030598 (ebook) |
ISBN 9781984802835 (hardcover) | ISBN 9781984802859 (ebook)
Subjects: LCSH: Sexual harassment—Fiction. | Transgender people—Fiction. |
Life change events—Fiction.
Classification: LCC PS3613.A7822 A58 2020 (print) | LCC PS3613.A7822
(ebook) | DDC 813/.6—dc23
LC record available at https://lccn.loc.gov/2019030597
LC ebook record available at https://lccn.loc.gov/2019030598

First Edition: February 2020

Printed in the United States of America
1   3   5   7   9   10   8   6   4   2

Jacket art: anatomy image © bauhaus1000/Getty Images;
scarlet flamingo flower © Florilegius/SSPL/Getty Images
Jacket design by Colleen Reinhart
Interior art: tropical leaves © wacomka/Shutterstock
Book design by Alison Cnockaert

For Philip Vernon, scientist, novelist, and library evangelist extraordinaire. So proud to call you my friend.

CONTENTS

PART ONE

PART TWO

PART THREE

THE
ANTIDOTE
FOR
EVERYTHING

PART

ONE

1

THERE'S NOTHING WRONG
WITH MANSCAPING

Most women did not begin their days by stabbing a man in the scrotum, but Georgia Brown was not most women. She'd risen as she always did at five o'clock, prepared her usual concoction of coffee and medium-chain triglyceride oil, and gone for a run. She loved the predawn streets of Charleston: absent the cacophony of tourists and the nuclear blanket of the sun, the air was usually quiet and cool, laced through with the tang of the sea. Afterward, a quick shower, a moment of meditation to try to tamp down the endorphins, a grooming blitz—hair in a twist, a smear of bright red lipstick—and she was ready to work.

Stab was the wrong verb, of course, but you didn't become a female urologist without a strong sense of humor. In any case, there was little humor in the scenario currently confronting Georgia in the OR, but at least she felt good about her role in it. Well—she felt good about saving a guy's life, not the unfortunate surgical procedure she'd been drafted to perform.

At first glance, the man splayed on the table in front of her appeared to be the kind of diabetic who, in another era, would have perished from a gruesome case of groin sepsis before reaching the age of forty. But now, thanks to the miracle of modern medicine, this man would live to fight another day. Granted, he might be fighting with only one ball—assuming at least one of his balls survived the infection currently encompassing his manhood—but surely losing a testicle or two was a small price to pay for regaining a life.

"Suction," Georgia said, as a geyser bubbled up from the incision she'd just made. "Thanks. Okay. Hand me the Bovie."

Though only his eyes were visible above his mask, the scrub tech—a dour, bearded guy in his twenties—communicated unmistakable, if silent, alarm. A floater, he usually staffed orthopedic procedures, but this patient had come in through the ER and wasn't on the schedule, necessitating a rearrangement of the ORs.

"I cannot believe I'm assisting in this mauling," he said finally, rolling his eyes as he placed a cautery wand in Georgia's outstretched hand. "Even on a fool like this guy."

"What?" She pointed the cautery in Evan's direction. "Why would you call him a fool?"

"C'mon, Dr. Brown. I guarantee he smokes, ignores his insulin regimen, doesn't fill his prescriptions, and probably doesn't even check his sugars. What did he think was going to happen?"

"Well, it's a safe bet he didn't think he'd lose his scrotum to necrotizing fasciitis," she remarked mildly. "That probably didn't even crack the top one hundred on his list of fears."

"Reap what you sow, though, Doc."

"I talked to him before the case," she said. "He's a night-shift manager at a convenience store, and he can't afford insulin, let alone glucometer sticks, which are about fifty dollars a box. So, you're right: he hasn't been checking his sugars in a while."

An uncomfortable silence ensued, broken only by the sizzle of the cautery and the *fwoompy* sound of the ventilators.

Evan retreated to familiar ground. "I can't believe I'm assisting in this case."

"Evan, if you drip sweat in my surgical field, I'm going to remove your balls too," Georgia replied, as cheerfully as possible. "Forceps."

"Omigod—are you actually going to remove—"

"No, just the skin and tissue around them. But a few of these guys do wind up with later removal of the testicles too. And he's going to need skin grafting for sure."

"Omigod. I can't believe I'm—"

"Suction," she interrupted. Best to nip this in the bud. Men could be so touchy about things like excision of the scrotum.

The room in which they stood was a nice one, as far as ORs went. Square and spacious, it boasted state-of-the-art equipment, everything gleaming like a TV hospital. Georgia had operated in some exceptionally dumpy ORs during her time, so she appreciated the clinic's facilities; everything was new, from the gargantuan office complex to the operating suites. The clinic, part of a large hospital complex founded by a church, combined doctors from more than twenty different specialties. It had been challenged in its initial days to attract patients to this budding suburb so far outside the city. But they'd offered good salaries, pulling physicians away from long-established practices in Charleston, and eventually the patients had followed. Now it had more business than it could handle.

"Dr. Brown," said the circulating nurse, a reedy, nondescript woman whose name always slipped Georgia's mind. "Your phone is blowing up. Do you want me to look at any of these texts?"

"Please do," she said, forcing her voice into false calmness. She'd left the security code off her phone for the explicit purpose of having the circulator answer texts and calls since Dobby, her rescue mutt, was at this moment at the animal hospital recovering from surgery. The irony of his particular ailment—a kidney tumor resulting in a nephrectomy—was lost on no one, save Dobby himself, of course. Waggy and loyal to a fault, he greeted each day with an exuberance bordering on mania. He wasn't perfect: at age three, he still occasionally gave in to the longing to chew on furniture legs, and he shed so much hair on the floor of Georgia's nine-hundred-square-foot house, it looked like an unswept beauty salon. Worst of all, he fetishized the smell of feet to the point where he couldn't sleep without cuddling one of her shoes, usually an expensive one, as nice shoes were one of the few things she was willing to buy brand-new. But, like every good dog, he loved unconditionally and enthusiastically. Georgia needed him in her life.

The circulator frowned, clicking through the messages. Georgia waited for at least five seconds before giving in. "How is he?"

The nurse didn't answer, so Georgia risked a look at her. Her expression had changed: it was, without doubt, the face of a person who did not want to answer the question she'd just been asked.

A ball of grief thudded into her stomach. "Just read it," Georgia whispered.

"Dr. Brown," said the woman, "I really think you should wait until later."

"Knowing is better than dreading," Georgia said stoically. "I'm done here anyway. It's fine."

"I don't—"

"It's fine! It's fine. Tell me."

The circulator cleared her throat. *"Dear Georgia,"* she read. *"Don't take this the wrong way, but it's over."*

Everyone stopped moving. Across from her, Evan stared at the wall with the suction tube held aloft as if he were a flash-frozen orchestra conductor in a blue gown; even the anesthesia people had gone still behind their curtain.

Now that she'd started, the circulator had evidently determined she'd see the mission through to completion. Before Georgia could stop her, she continued: *"I'm guessing you don't want to see me, so I'll stop by for my board if you leave it on the porch."*

"Hey," Georgia said weakly. "That wasn't what I—"

"If you want my advice, in the future—"

"I don't!" she yelled. She lowered her voice. "I don't want his advice."

"—you might try to pretend you don't know more than everybody else."

Dead silence. Even the patient, unconscious and ventilated, appeared to be holding his breath.

The circulator cleared her throat. *"One more thing,"* she read. *"You might also want to consider waxing. Or at least trimming."*

"Ouch," someone said finally: Debra, the nurse anesthetist, popping her head above the curtain. "That last part was . . ." She trailed off, defeated by the search for an appropriate adjective.

"It doesn't mean what you think it means," Georgia tried. It did mean what they thought it meant, actually, but she couldn't care less. Who had the time for extensive crotch maintenance? Or for pretending to be unintelligent? "Is there any way y'all could just unhear this?"

A chorus of assent filled the OR: *Absolutely! Already forgotten it! Unhear what?* She looked from face to face—terrible liars, all of them. Evan in particular wore the contorted expression you might see on someone trying to suppress a sneeze. Georgia waved a hand at him. "Go on, then," she said. "Let it out."

With a braying honk, Evan sucked in air and bent double. After a beat, Debra and the circulator started laughing too, followed by Georgia. She hadn't been all that into Ryan, to be honest.

"That's what I get," Georgia wheezed, "for dating a manscaped surfer."

"There's nothing wrong with manscaping," said Evan.

"Oh, here we go," said the circulator brightly, once she'd recovered. "This one is from your vet. Your dog is doing well."

Before Georgia could respond, the woman continued.

"And—let's see—an auto-reminder. It says don't forget your passport."

"Okay, yes," Georgia said, wondering if it would be possible to record a shrieking voice reminder set to play at a specific time, like a Howler from the Harry Potter books.

"Two more of those: *Don't forget your passport.* And this one: *Really, don't forget your passport.*"

"Passport, got it."

"And another one: you have a message from Dr. Jonah Tsukada. He wants to see you after you finish your cases."

"For what?"

"I don't know. All he said was, 'Karaoke. It's on, baby.'"

"Oh dear," Georgia said. Jonah, her closest friend, was currently irritated with her. Declining to sing with him tonight wouldn't help matters. Despite being unencumbered by the demands of a husband or family—or possibly precisely because she was unencumbered by the demands of a husband or family—Georgia seemed to take the least vacation time of anyone in the clinic. It had been over a year since she'd had more than a long weekend away from work. So when the clinic offered a stipend to attend a conference in the Netherlands—a multi-speciality program on physician efficiency—she and Jonah had decided to attend together, making plans to visit the Van Gogh and Anne Frank museums and also, at Jonah's insistence, the tulip fields, even though the season was completely wrong.

But the registration deadline had come and gone without Jonah signing up. There had been an issue with his stipend, apparently; the clinic wouldn't pay it. By that point, Georgia had purchased plane tickets and made a hotel reservation; she couldn't very well cancel the trip out of solidarity, even for Jonah.

"Okay, thanks," she said. "I'll call him when I'm done for the day."

"Wait," said the circulator. "He's typing something else."

Georgia broke scrub, nodding to Evan to finish packing the patient's wound. The circulator had drifted over to a counter along the edge of the room, where she was entering data into a wall-mounted computer. Georgia shed her mask, gown, and gloves, leaving her tangled red hair caught up in the OR cap, and retrieved her phone. Three blinking dots, indicative of an incoming message, filled the text bar; she set up at another computer to jot a quick note about the case. By the time she glanced at the phone again, the dots had vanished, replaced by a sterile message field. It wasn't until she'd left the

OR that the dots returned, followed in short order by a single terse sentence:

I think I am going to be fired.

~~~~~~

She called Jonah, let the phone ring through to voicemail, hung up, and called again. No answer. She tried texting: What do you mean? Are you ok? She was halfway to the offices of his family medicine practice when he texted back. False alarm. I'm ok. But something weird is going on with my patients. Will fill you in tonight.

Tell me now, she wrote.

No answer.

This was, of course, worrying, but at the same time, Jonah had a propensity toward exaggeration. Also: talk about burying the lede. How concerned could you be about losing your job if the first thing you mention in a text is karaoke night?

~~~~~~

Georgia and Jonah had been friends for seven years. He'd been a patient, one of her first, and after she'd resolved his urologic issue, he had invited her out for drinks. Ordinarily, this would not have been advisable: fraternizing with one of the penises. You needed a clear line of demarcation there. But Jonah was a dear: the bro genre of millennial, he offered everyone fist bumps and held an incomprehensible fascination with video games and had a thing for craft beer. He wore skinny pants and bow ties and styled his black hair like a Euro soccer star and occasionally descended into jealous fits brought on by having to compete with women for hot guys. They loved each other so much he'd joined a practice here at the clinic, enduring an hour-long commute and an office full of older partners who still seemed perplexed by him. Resolving to put her concerns aside until she could find out more, Georgia exited the double doors from the OR suite to head for her office.

Massive and institutional in appearance, the clinic held an OR suite, a pharmacy, a rehab facility, and offices for more than twenty kinds of specialists, but if a patient needed to spend the night after surgery, they got shuttled to the attached community hospital, where Georgia now headed to check on her last few inpatients. Late-morning sunshine streamed through the glass walls of the arched pedway to the hospital, refracting against the white ceiling. Half-blinded by the bright light, she could just make out a swaying row of palm trees outside. From her house near the historic section of Charleston, it took a good forty-five minutes to reach this utterly tasteful, utterly boring community a few miles outside the Charleston County line.

Her first two patients were routine. She saved the best for last: Mr. Fogelman.

Anyone exiting the bank of elevators would be able to tell which room contained Mr. Fogelman as soon as they set foot on the second floor, because he personified an unabashed confidence common to a certain kind of older man: booming voice, untended clouds of tufty ear hair—in short, total imperviousness to embarrassment. You had to love him.

"I got a new one for ya, Doc," he said, enthusiastically grasping Georgia's hand as soon as she came within grasping distance.

That was another thing about being a female urologist: you were confronted with a lot of penis jokes. Most of them were terrible, but occasionally one was right on the money. You might think patients would be reluctant to share such jokes with their own urologist, but you'd be wrong. Georgia heard them all the time.

"Hit me, Mr. Fogelman," she said, dragging a chair next to the bed with her free hand. Next to them, in an orange pleather cube appearing only slightly more comfortable than a block of cement, Mr. Fogel-man's tiny wife lay asleep with her mouth open. Georgia resisted the urge to check a pulse.

"What's that insensitive thing at the base of the penis called?"

She'd heard this one before but she didn't let on. "Tell me."

"The man!" He chortled. His chest shook as he laughed: it was impossible not to laugh with him.

"Aw, Mr. Fogelman," she said. "I'm sure you personally are among the most sensitive of men."

"I'm actually kind of a jackass, Doc. According to my better half." He gestured to Mrs. Fogelman, who, miraculously, opened an eye and croaked, "Yes, dear." Without opening her other eye, she eased out of the chair, tottered over to the bed, lowered the bed rail, nestled against Mr. Fogelman, and fell instantly asleep again, looking for all the world like a jumble of stick-covered skin. He lowered his lips to the top of her wispy white head and kissed her, winking at Georgia. "Isn't she a beauty?" he asked.

"She is," she agreed, trying not to think about the fact that Mr. Fogelman was dying of bladder cancer. Later today, he would be taking his final trip home from the hospital, this time aided by hospice. Both of them knew this was the last time they'd see each other, but neither of them wanted to acknowledge it; Georgia because she was afraid she'd cry, and Mr. Fogelman because there seemed to be no circumstances in which his natural bonhomie deserted him. Even now he was beaming through the pain and the drugs, his hearty face split by wrinkles of joy. He pointed at her.

"You're married, yes?"

"I'm not."

"You've got a fella, then."

"No," she said, and some compulsion toward honesty prompted her to add, "Not after today, anyway. I've been dating someone but he lost interest."

Mr. Fogelman's beam dissolved into outrage. "What? He's lost his damn mind. Who breaks up with a woman like you?"

"Plenty of people," she said, grinning, although in truth she was generally the dumper, not the dumpee. The downside—one of the downsides—of being a single thirty-six-year-old surgeon was the parade of people trying to fix you up with an ever-dwindling pool of single professional men, most of whom were single not because they hadn't met the right person but because of a glaring personality flaw. Possibly it indicated an abundance of pickiness on her part, but Georgia was perfectly comfortable being picky. She was not perfectly comfortable dating someone who said snide things about the pants size of the cashier at the grocery.

Mr. Fogelman, summoning up an uncanny ability to read her mind, nodded. "Don't even think about settling," he said. "A gal like you deserves to be cherished." Without disengaging her hand, he shifted in the bed to more directly face her, adding in a voice considerably more gentle than his usual, "You're the best, you know that, honey?"

"So are you," she said, redirecting her gaze toward Mrs. Fogelman in an effort to diminish the ache rising in her throat. "Call me right away if you need anything from my office. Don't go through the phone service, okay? Your wife has my cell number; just call me directly. I can come to you if I need to."

"I will, Doc." He traced the path of her gaze to the frail woman beside him. "I'm a lucky man: forty-eight years with an angel by my side. I know it's not going to be any better than this in heaven." Again, he brushed his lips against the snowy cloud of his wife's hair, and this time, finally, his voice cracked enough to reflect his age and his health. "Leaving her—" he started.

Georgia waited.

"Leaving her—" he tried again, his face still resting against his wife's head. He closed his eyes and cleared his throat, a harsh, haggard sound. When he spoke again, she could hardly hear him. "Leaving her is the only reason I'm afraid of what's coming."

The remainder of the day passed in the slightly surreal haze accompany-ing an epiphany. She did all the usual things: she performed a vasectomy on a grimacing man; she employed a green-light laser to photo-vaporize the prostate of a hedge-fund manager with trouble urinating; she spoke with a college soccer player and his weeping father about surgery to remove his cancer-ravaged testicle. She gave each of them her full atten-tion, focusing not only on the questions they asked but also on the ones they failed to ask, taking care to give the floppy-haired soccer player her special-patient email address so he could, at his leisure, write the ques-tions he could not bring himself to consider now. She placed a nerve-stimulating device in a painfully shy elderly lady, contemplating the yawning gap between social ease and the dysfunctional hell of being unable to control your bladder. Sure, people lauded their adorable pe-diatricians and their lifesaving cardiologists and the heroic last-ditch efforts of their oncologists, but you'd never experienced gratitude until you'd given someone the gift of continence. Not to mention the pro-found indebtedness of a man who could have sex again.

But throughout all of this, she kept reverting to an image of the Fogelmans, entwined in one another's arms, pressed by the narrow confines of the hospital bed up against the metal safety bars. Here death, the ancient, great, primordial fear, had been eclipsed by love. Her patient feared not dying, not pain, not a cessation of form and life and thought, but separation from the human being he loved above all others. What would that be like, she wondered, for another person to love you that much? And Mrs. Fogelman: Georgia imagined her face as she watched the sentience leave her husband's eyes, as his vital mind, so full of verve and dazzle, switched itself finally and irrevocably off. How did you withstand such a loss?

How did you find that kind of love in the first place?

2

THE TELL OF A LIE

Georgia stepped outside into a blast of warm air and an explosion of color. Reminiscent of Charleston's famous Rainbow Row, the stucco buildings comprising the clinic had all evidently been designed by a passionate admirer of tropical fruit, and they ranged in color from kiwi to papaya to banana. On top of that, someone had gone hog wild in the floral department, lining every walkway with a riotous profusion of ground-cover blooms.

An outgoing swell of hospital workers flooded the sidewalks, most of them striding with spry purpose toward the parking garages, a few trudging more slowly, burdened by exhaustion or a rough day or aching joints or who knew what. For once, Georgia moved alongside the slower crowd, lost in her thoughts of the Fogelmans. And Ryan, the guy she'd been seeing.

Ending things with Ryan was no tragedy—he was hot but dim, an ember of a human being. She'd known, subconsciously and probably consciously, that he offered no promise of long-term companionship, let alone the kind of epic soul-melding she'd witnessed in the Fogelmans. Still, it stung. The closest Georgia had ever come to marriage had been a passionate but dysfunctional engagement to a bartender named Angus, who turned out to be a serial cheater. Suddenly, she found herself craving an escape from the intensity of the day: a drink, some music, maybe something stupid and mindless on Netflix. She wanted to shut down.

She'd almost reached her car when she remembered: Jonah.

She'd just picked up her phone to call him when it rang. "George!" it squawked as she answered. She felt herself relax even as she brightened at hearing Jonah's voice. "Where are you?" he asked.

"Parking lot," she huffed, stomping up the final flight of stairs to the seventh level.

"Parking lot?"

"Doctors' parking garage at the clinic. I'm leaving work."

"That's sad. I've been done for hours."

"No, you have not."

"Fine. I've been done for *minutes*. Meet me out?"

She ignored this suggestion. "What was going on earlier? Why did you say you thought you'd be fired?"

"Momentary panic. It was nothing."

This was probably a lie—something was going on and he'd decided to ignore it—but there was no distress in his tone, so she let it slide. "Glad to hear it. But I have to get home."

"You want to go out and party. Got it."

"I need to be home to pack," she said. Jonah, endowed with galactic energy, was perfectly capable of working all day and going out half the night without suffering any apparent consequence the next day. Georgia was not.

"I guess you have to save Fun Georgia for Amsterdam," he said.

"Aw, Jones," she said. "Don't say that."

As a primary care doctor, Jonah made less than some physician assistants. He also staggered around under a hideous trifecta of debt: hundreds of thousands of dollars of student loans, the unbelievably costly expenditure of in-home medical assistance for his beloved grandmother, and a self-inflicted credit card issue stemming from his days as an underfinanced medical student. Georgia knew he couldn't justify the expense of an international trip without the stipend, and he knew she wasn't going to cancel because he couldn't go.

She tried a different tactic: "I'm very tired today."

"You can be very tired when you're forty. A single thirty-six-year-old person needs to mingle." At thirty-two, Jonah relished his status as the younger, hipper one, pointing out her elderly status at every opportunity.

"I don't—wait," she said, suspicious. "How did you know I'm single again? As far as you know, I'm still dating Ryan."

He laughed so loudly she had to hold the phone away from her head.

"Thanks for the sympathy."

"I'd be oozing sympathy if you needed it, you know that, but look at it this way: at least it wasn't a slow fade. You dated Surfer Dude for five minutes and it was obvious you weren't into him. You're just used to being the one who ends it. This . . . this is a blessing, George. Here, now. Let me see if I can put this in terms your generation would understand—that guy was a doofus."

"So, everyone knows, huh?"

"Surely you didn't imagine a story that good would stay confidential? *Tout l'hôpital.*"

"All of it? You heard all of it?"

He cackled again. "Don't worry, I hear the natural look is coming back."

"How would you—never mind." Suddenly, the conversation inspired her. "Anyway, I need to get home so I can mourn in private."

She figured Jonah would respect this: eating ice cream in unattractive pajamas, or whatever lame thing people did when they'd been dumped, but he was having none of it. "Nonsense. I'll see you in an hour and we'll discuss dating options for you."

"That's a hard no for me, Jones. I just want to pack and then crawl in bed. Alone."

"You gotta get back on the horse, George."

"It's been five minutes! No one gets back on the horse the same day they've been dumped. I'm in a refractory period."

A smug chuckle. "My refractory period is *literally* five minutes."

"No it isn't."

"Fine. You're the sexpert. I'll see you in a few."

"Do people like this? When you pester them nonstop?"

He played his ace. "It's the last night for karaoke before you leave me."

"Jonah!"

Both of them loved to sing. Georgia had a good voice, a kind of raspy smoke overlaid with honey, especially suited to bluesy songs. Even speaking instead of singing, her voice garnered plenty of attention from men, who seemed to associate it with a certain wanton quality: red lips blowing a stream of French cigarette smoke, black lace bras, sultry waves of hair, that kind of thing. When they realized it instead belonged to a physics- and machinery-obsessed, seventies-wannabe nerd, they tended to react with disappointment, even before they made the discovery that she was—literally—a ballbuster. You could appreciate why she had romantic problems.

"Dammit." She folded. "I'll be there."

"Excellent!" A clicking sound: the patter of a keyboard. He must have lied about having already left work. "Be ready to wail."

"I'm staying one hour," she said. "Max." She ascended the last flight of stairs, emerging onto the unroofed portion of the garage, which blazed with the heat of a thousand suns. Fanning herself with the edge of her white coat, she headed toward the far end of the deck. "Hey, Jonah?"

"Yeah?"

"Tell me why you said you might get fired."

The clicking sounds stopped. For a moment she thought he might have hung up, but then his voice puffed into her ear, hale and disingenuous. "Nothing. Some hassle from the suits."

"What kind of hassle? From who?"

He ignored the first question but answered the second. "The Cheerio."

She stopped walking. John Beezon was the chief human resources officer for the clinic. People referred to him as The Cheerio because he signed all his emails with his job acronym—CHRO—rather than his name. This nickname was a bit of a misnomer: Beezon was about as cheery as a tarantula.

"Jonah. What did he do?"

"Don't worry about it." He still sounded untroubled. "I'm going to stop by before I go and see if I can get this sorted out."

"Get what sorted out?"

"Nothing. I don't know. A bunch of patient no-shows for appointments."

"Wait, what?"

"I'll handle it. You go get gorgeous and I'll see you soon."

She reversed course, spinning on one heel to face the stairwell again. A low pattering of voices emanated from Jonah's end of the phone, followed by the sound of him greeting someone, muffled as if he had his hand over the phone.

"I'm coming to his office too. I'll be there in five minutes," she said, but it was too late: he'd already hung up.

~~~~~~

Swanning into the HR offices, where everyone still seemed to be working, she put her game face on. Nodding with regal composure at a couple of agitated reception people as they tried to wave her down, she bypassed a little cluster of cubicles. Fact: if you assumed an air of authority, people often wouldn't challenge you. Plus she still wore her white coat, potentiating the notion that she was very busy and important. After a short chase, the reception people gave up, and she entered the depths of the HR department, heading for Beezon's lair.

Revealing the utter lack of imagination of its owner, Beezon's office had been decked out in time-honored middle-management style: a desk veneered in faux-oak laminate; a creaky utilitarian swivel chair; an uncomfortable couch composed of right angles. A framed portrait of Beezon resided on the desk in a prominent spot. After one glance at it, you recognized his kind: a classic underdog prone to short-sleeved dress shirts and an occasional experimental mustache.

Neither Beezon nor Jonah was in the room, so Georgia plunked down in the swivel chair, idly leafing through the books and magazines. These ran the gamut from the boring gibberish of financial journals to the pontificating bureaucratese of HR manuals. Did he ever read anything for fun? On the one hand, one should not judge a man based on his taste in workplace reading materials—he undoubtedly kept the good stuff at home—but on the other hand, she was talking about Beezon here. She tried and failed to imagine him engrossed in a copy of Colson Whitehead's *The Underground Railroad* or Khaled Hosseini's *A Thousand Splendid Suns* or Zadie Smith's *White Teeth*. She couldn't even fathom Beezon having the intellectual curiosity to check out internet porn, let alone literature.

She turned from the small stack of books and nudged the mouse of Beezon's computer. To her surprise, the black screen of the monitor instantly gave way to the white background of an email: Beezon's computer was not password-protected, a striking lapse for a human resources officer in possession of sensitive material about employees. Any thoughts she might have had about not reading the document vanished when she saw the words typed across the top: *Confidential: re Jonah Tsukada, M.D.*

One sentence in, Georgia realized a showdown of epic proportions loomed in the future, because someone—the as-yet-unknown author of the email—was trying to make the case that Jonah was a substandard physician. This was bullshit; Jonah's clinical skills were exemplary. Even his patient satisfaction scores—the dreaded Press Ganey surveys, which were often utilized as revenge by patients for factors beyond a physician's control—were top notch. The key, Georgia thought, was his authenticity: he loved his patients with the kind of fervor that wasn't easily faked. People knew when someone was shining them on and when someone genuinely cared. Jonah genuinely cared.

In the early days of their friendship, Georgia'd once seen him, an hour after his office hours ended, walking with a man through the exit to outdoors. Curious, she'd followed them. Dressed in an assortment of ill-fitting garments, the man gave off the emaciated, matted air of someone down on his luck; with his grimy skin and his ratty coat still damp from an earlier rain shower, he hardly seemed like the kind of company she'd have expected a fastidious, fashionable man like Jonah to keep.

They passed the porticoed entrance and then the parking lot, heading for a small natural area adjacent to the hospital dotted with a few hydrangeas and a solitary bench. By now, a frisson of worry struck her; was Jonah being coerced somehow? But his body language didn't reflect alarm. He ambled along with unmistakable ease, making animated hand gestures, even once placing a light hand on the man's shoulder. She came to the conclusion that she should stop spying. This must be a relative or something personal. It was no concern of hers.

Just as she turned, though, Jonah and the man took a seat on the bench and Jonah raised his arms to draw a series of rectangles in the air, his slight chest rising and falling with each exaggerated inflation and exhalation. Perplexed, Georgia turned back. After a moment of watching, she got it.

Jonah was teaching the man breathing techniques to manage anxiety.

Much later, she'd asked him about it, and he'd responded that the man was a homeless Army veteran. He had panic attacks, Jonah said, bad ones; and he'd taken to coming to the ER on a regular basis when they got overwhelming. Jonah, who'd encountered the guy during a volunteer shift at a free medical clinic, started meeting with him once a week to teach him meditation techniques.

Shaking her head at the absurdity of someone trying to imply that Jonah was a bad physician, she returned her attention to the document. She'd had only a brief moment to view it—long enough to read the first paragraph—when footsteps sounded in the hall immediately outside Beezon's door. She shoved herself backward from the computer, grabbing and opening an HR manual off the desk as if she were reading it.

One of Beezon's underlings stuck her head in the door. She wore a timid expression and profoundly unattractive glasses, steel-framed and masculine, like Georgia's dad used to wear in the 1980s. Right away Georgia felt compelled to put her at ease.

"Hi there," she said, surreptitiously lowering the manual under the table. "I'm Dr. Georgia Brown. Are you looking for Mr. Beezon?"

"No," the mouse squeaked. "I was looking for some paperwork."

"Well." Georgia opened her arms in welcome. "Here's his stuff."

The woman crossed to the desk, prompting an awkward moment of reshuffling as Georgia scooted out of her way so she could access a desk drawer. Her intimidated expression didn't alter, even though she could not have failed to notice that Beezon's computer monitor was still on and displaying a document Georgia had no business seeing. She kept her eyes averted, both from the screen and from Georgia. Working as an administrative assistant for Beezon must wreak havoc on the nerves.

The mouse found whatever she'd been seeking and straightened up. Beezon's computer chimed with an email and it belatedly occurred to Georgia that perhaps Jonah had run into him elsewhere.

"Have you seen Dr. Tsukada?"

Georgia expected her to say *Who?* Instead, she grimaced. "I'm sorry, I haven't."

"What about John Beezon?"

On this score, she looked more relaxed. "I think he's left for the day."

Georgia looked at the computer's clock: it was five thirty. Outside the room, she could hear the unmistakable sound of things winding down: the thud of chairs being shoved under desks, voices murmuring, heels tapping down the hallway. Retrieving her phone from her bag, she sent a text to Jonah: Where are you?

No answer.

The mouse, hovering near the door, was looking at Georgia expectantly but could not seem to work up the gumption to kick her out. She wanted to stay and root through Beezon's computer, but that would require lying to this poor soul, not to mention the questionable ethics involved. Reluctantly, she stood.

"Okay, thanks," she said. "I'll try him later."

The mouse nodded, grateful that she was leaving without a fuss. She checked her phone again. Nothing. Where was Jonah?

Suddenly it came to her: perhaps they were in one of the conference rooms. A long corridor, carpeted in an industrial-grade shade of barf, led to a set of double doors opening to the outside. For reasons no one fully understood, all the conference rooms were housed in a small annex across the patient parking lot, necessitating a slog across the scorching pavement whenever anyone called a meeting, which, with this many doctors and administrators milling around, was hourly. The mouse followed Georgia as she zipped across the lot toward the employee parking garage.

Halfway across, something caught Georgia's attention. She slowed and squinted against the angled sunlight: two people were turtling their way across the black tarmac toward the boatlike grandeur of an ancient maroon Oldsmobile. It took a moment longer than it should have to recognize them since something seemed to be off in their pacing, but eventually she got it: it was a patient of hers named Frieda Myers Delacroix and her companion, a much younger man whom she knew only by his first name, Andreas.

Frieda Myers Delacroix—everybody called her by her double first name, Frieda Myers—was an aging Southern queen who'd reached a point in life where she felt perfectly content to be her most authentic self in public. In Frieda Myers's case, being her most authentic self meant using feminine pronouns, even though her physical anatomy at birth had been male. The nature of her urologic issues was such that she saw Georgia often, but she sought out Jonah, her primary care physician, even more frequently. Known around town for her impeccable manners, she sent thank-you notes in beautiful cursive, hand-delivered by courier after each appointment.

Her face vacant, Frieda Myers appeared to be mustering her dignity as she plodded with straight-backed stiffness toward her car. Andreas trailed her with uncharacteristic reticence, his hands wrung together in front of him. They reached the car and Frieda Myers fumbled a bit as she tried to manipulate the key into the lock, her hands visibly shaking even at that distance. Still trailed by the woman from Beezon's office, Georgia had just taken a step toward them when Andreas looked up and saw her.

She faltered at the raw fury on his face. He opened his mouth as if to speak, but instead of saying anything, he sliced his hand across the air in her direction in an unmistakable gesture of disgust. His movement must have caught Frieda Myers's attention; now she looked up and spied Georgia too. In contrast to Andreas, Frieda Myers appeared depleted: an old balloon of a person. For a moment her gaze locked with Georgia's before some reserve of control within her shifted and a single sound escaped her: a hoarse, abbreviated gulp. She turned back toward the Oldsmobile.

Wincing at the sound, Georgia started toward her but once again was felled midstep by the death rays emanating from Andreas. "Miss Delacroix," she called. "Is everything okay?"

Andreas raised a trembling finger at Georgia. "You leave us alone."

After another futile attempt at unlocking the car, Frieda Myers, her shoulders hitching, opened her hand and allowed her keys to drop to the pavement. Andreas, his handsome face distorted with distress, stood behind her whispering something into one of her wattled old ears, and eventually she bent and retrieved her keys and Andreas opened the door for her and they got in and drove away, very slowly, as if the car had transformed into a motorized wheelchair.

Georgia turned to the mouse, wide-eyed. "What in the world was that about?"

Her eyes darted. "I don't know."

You didn't need to be a psychologist to recognize the tell of a lie. "You do know," Georgia said. She concentrated on her voice: firm, but nonthreatening, persuasive. "What's going on?"

The mouse capitulated, her shoulders lowering as she released the information. "I think a lot of Dr. Tsukada's patients have decided to leave the clinic."

"What? Why?"

"I don't know," she said. "I heard there have been problems with his care."

3

~~~~~~

THE PRECIPICE DIVIDING
THE LIVING FROM THE DEAD

The next morning dawned clear and cloudless, one of those sensational autumn mornings when it was neither too warm nor too cool. Still slick and salty from her run, Georgia eased into the kitchen to fire up the French press, letting the coffee brew as she showered. She missed Dobby: the house felt sterile without his happy panting and the prancing click of his toenails against the floor.

Jonah had canceled their karaoke plans last night, texting her a few minutes after she'd left the clinic to say he'd changed his mind about going out. Concerned at the brusque tone of the text—so different from his voice a few minutes earlier—she'd driven to his house, way out in Folly Beach, but he hadn't been home.

This was not unprecedented. Jonah had a habit of going dark when something big was going down, but usually this related to the throes of a new relationship. Occasionally, however, it portended something more ominous: a plunge into depression. Jonah suffered from periods of depression, from time to time falling into an unforeseen pit of black misery. When it happened—sometimes triggered by actual events, but sometimes without warning—his characteristic resilience and chipper personality vanished, replaced by a grim fatalism. He could not see that he'd ever return to normal. He could not even appreciate that there had ever been a normal to which he might return. He saw only darkness and hopelessness, a world robbed of light and meaning and purpose.

Lately, however, he'd been happy. He'd had a string of months—a year or two, probably—without depression. It had been long enough that the memory of the last time had faded, relegated to some washed-out corner of her mind. Things had been so good for him, she could almost convince herself those episodes had never happened at all.

Almost.

She took her coffee to the front porch, a pleasant space just large enough for two wicker chairs on one end and a hanging daybed on the other. As the sky lightened, she stared up at the pale blue porch ceiling, almost mandatory in this section of Charleston. *Haint blue*, the Victorians had called it, convinced the watery color would deter unruly spirits from entering the home. Vengeful specters from the afterworld ranked low on her current list of worries, however. She needed to start packing. Gulping the rest of the hot coffee, she stood and walked back into the house to find her suitcase.

Converted from an old carriage house, her little dwelling was comprised of one all-purpose room with a sleeping loft. As you might expect, the kitchen/living area space was compact, the kitchen tucked neatly under the loft, which vaulted up to a tall, arched ceiling. The short walls in the loft were lined with bookshelves, separated by both genre and color, so she could easily identify and reach her science books, her well-worn Bible, her biographies and histories and geopolitical texts, along with a smaller contingent of steampunk science fiction and a clandestine smattering of literary romances. It was like sleeping in the middle of a crowd of friends.

The distance between the couch and the kitchen was four steps. When the space was renovated, the designers had inserted all sorts of clever little storage areas and space-saving hacks, basically providing Georgia with a grown-up version of the childhood hidey-holes she'd inhabited all over the college campus in Kentucky where her father had taught. She came home each night to the safest, coziest, most perfect space in all of Charleston. Flowers and potted plants dotted a small, enclosed garden off the back of the house, next to her workshop; Dobby had a dog door so he could zip in and out while she was at work; one wall in the living room was entirely covered with blown-up photographs of Georgia and Jonah and Dobby, all of them—including, seemingly, the dog—appearing young and carefree. She pulled her suitcase from the closet, taking in her perfect little haven, and not for the first time wondered if maybe she should cancel her trip.

~~~~~~

Charleston was a world-class city, thronged with five million visitors a year, but it didn't boast an extensive international airport. Georgia's flight to Europe was scheduled to depart early in the afternoon from Charlotte, North Carolina. After a three-and-a-half-hour drive to the airport, the second leg—a flight to Frankfurt, Germany—was scheduled to be in the air for eight hours and forty minutes, followed by a train to the Netherlands. After a last gulp of coffee, Georgia finished dressing, loaded up the car, and hit the road.

Midmorning, she pulled over at a gas station deep in the backwoods of South Carolina. The day was clear and breezy and sunshiny, enhanced by flowering trees and chirping birds and all manner of glorious wildlife. Even the acres of pestilential sorrel weeds surrounding the station looked pretty in the morning light, rippling in red waves across a series of barren cotton fields. As she waited for the gas tank to fill, Georgia grabbed her phone, and its screen lit up with an accusatory stack of blue rectangles: texts from Jonah.

Heaving a sigh of relief, she opened the first one and saw an empty blue bubble. Clicking through all of them in rapid succession, she discovered they were all the same. She'd be baffled, except Jonah had done this before. It was his version of a butt dial: he sat on his phone while it was open in text mode.

At least she knew he was alive.

She immediately texted back, to no avail. Possibly he had fallen asleep on top of his phone. She tapped out a message asking him to call her just as a shiny car pulled alongside hers on the other side of the gas pump. A man got out, dressed in an incongruous business suit, his gaze flitting across the island to check her out. After a lingering glance at her breasts, he strode off into the station, ostentatiously clicking the lock button on his Mercedes. Well, really: did he think she was going to burgle his car? *Humph*-ing to herself, she plunked the nozzle back in the gas pump, jumped in the car, and drove off.

Ten minutes down the road, she found herself stopped at the world's longest traffic light, inexplicably set at the juncture of two potholed roads in the middle of nowhere. At one corner, a giant Confederate flag crackled in the wind. Both sides of the road were double-laned, although there wasn't another car to be seen for miles. She'd no sooner made this observation than the car from the gas station roared up beside her, its eight-cylinder engine shrieking in dismay at the abrupt stop. The driver had a cell phone wedged between his shoulder and ear, his steering hand occupied with a cigarette. He barked something into the phone and leaned in the direction of the driver's-side door. The window glided down and the stump of his cigarette, still glowing red, flew out of the car, pinging off the side of her car before hitting the road. As an afterthought, the man, still talking, tossed a crumpled white paper bag after it.

This was too much. Without thinking, she banged open the door, flew around the back of the car, scooped up the cigarette butt and the trash, and tossed it back through his open window. "You lost something," she shouted helpfully. The man, his mouth hanging open, stared at her for a moment. This provided a critical few seconds for her to return to her senses. Belatedly, it occurred to her: the kind of person with no qualms about using the world as his personal ashtray might not have any qualms about shooting an obnoxious eco-do-gooder in a Prius. She'd better haul ass.

He decided not to shoot, thankfully, although he did tailgate her for a couple miles before honking away in a cloud of angry fumes. She grinned sheepishly to herself; she hadn't even left the state of South Carolina and already she'd broken a promise to Jonah not to piss anyone off while she was gone.

~~~~~~

The plane began a slow taxi forward as it turned to align with the runway before thrusting itself aloft, engines roaring. "We're blasting off!" a child shrieked happily.

They ascended to cruising altitude, the ground beneath them transforming from an urban tangle of roadways and buildings to a soothing patchwork of green circles and rectangles. Around her, everyone settled into their routines: high-maintenance types blowing up their little inflatable neck pillows, businessmen retrieving laptops and headphones, moms doling out Cheerios and electronic games encased in bright plastic covers. Opening her computer, Georgia connected to the plane's Wi-Fi, thinking she'd watch a movie, but then changed her mind and decided to read. She opted for *Cryptonomicon* by Neal Stephenson, which she'd been longing to read for months despite its imposing length.

She was several hundred pages in and had lost all track of time when a faint electronic crackle issued through the air. A woman's voice echoed through the cabin.

"Is there a doctor on the plane?"

Seven otherwise innocuous words, striking fear into the heart of every physician. Like "Quick, can you bring me a whole bunch of paper towels" and "Omigod, where's the plunger," the implication was obvious. Some phrases just herald disaster. When you thought about it, it was surprising there weren't more medical disasters on planes; certainly it was surprising there weren't more psychological ones. Sealing yourself in an aluminum tube and zooming up to the outer reaches of the troposphere and the lower reaches of the stratosphere, sailing through the jet stream at speeds of six hundred miles per hour, where the temperature might be -60 degrees Fahrenheit and the windchill might be -120 degrees Fahrenheit—well, that was not natural.

As the call for a doctor went out again, Georgia allowed herself a few furtive glances around in case a random ER doc was about to spring to the rescue. She was a passionate believer in helping your fellow man—or woman, as the case might be—but she had to admit, chances were slim this would be an issue related to her specialty. How many people had a urologic emergency on an airplane?

"Here!" yelled the woman next to her, a bleached blond twenty-something-year-old in a bedazzled T-shirt, waving her arms energetically. "Right here."

Georgia turned to her in surprise. A few seconds later, the flight attendant appeared at the end of the row, regarding the woman with a similarly dubious look. "You're a doctor?"

"I'm a dancer."

"Thank you," said the flight attendant, baffled, "but we're looking for a doctor."

"*She's* a doctor," said the woman, triumphantly pointing to Georgia's carry-on bag. The flight attendant's eyes followed the woman's finger, landing on the bag, where *Georgia Brown, M.D.* was stitched at the top. The flight attendant pivoted, her eyes drifting from Georgia's high ponytail to her giant rhinestone hoops to her clothing: a threadbare green T-shirt, emblazoned with the words *Foosball Wizard*; a maroon smoking jacket; flared orange pants; and a pair of Lucite-heeled sandals. The flight attendant consulted a list in her hand. "Any chance you have your medical license with you, ah, Dr. Brown?"

"No one carries their medical license around," said Georgia.

"What seems to be the problem here?" A wiry older gentleman made his way up the aisle, all irascible eyes and ferocious hair and stubble: Gregory House, personified.

The flight attendant relaxed. "Are you a doctor?"

"I am Dr. Magnus Doellman," said Gregory House.

"Oh thank goodness, we have a situa—"

"I am a herbologist. But I volunteer frequently at the hospital."

The flight attendant faltered, torn between two evils. By now, the people in the rows of adjacent seats had awakened and were eying the spectacle, turning around in their seats. A scrawny guy in a beanie raised his hand. "*I'm* a herbologist too," he said, prompting his friends to collapse in helpless guffaws. Dr. Doellman glowered.

The flight attendant eyed Georgia again. "What kind of doctor are you?"

"A urologist," she said emphatically; the flight attendant needed to know what she was getting here.

Apparently urology trumped herbology in this particular emergency, because the attendant nodded. "Okay," she said. "Please come this way."

~~~~~~

They walked past two dozen rows of people glued to their electronic devices until they reached the rear galley, where the sprawling form of a man filled the floor. Someone had laid him out perpendicular to the aisle, his head in the kitchen area and his large feet, shod in a polished pair of wingtips, near the jump seats. With one look, Georgia knew: this was bad. In medical training, the first thing they taught you was to answer one question: *Sick or Not Sick?* Not Sick covered a lot of territory, from legitimate but non-emergent medical needs to a whole bunch of asinine things for which people routinely showed up in hospital ERs. In med school, she'd seen—they'd all seen—people for dumb complaints all the time: zits, paper cuts, emergent requests for liposuction.

On the other hand, you had the Sick People. These were the MIs, the septic patients, the ones with blood vessels full of clots or lungs full of fluid or kidneys full of toxins, hovering at the precipice dividing the living from the dead. From an academic standpoint they were interesting, but they also held a peculiar disastrous power: they possessed the potential to take you with them, metaphorically speaking, if you made a mistake. And sometimes they took you with them, literally speaking, as in the case of certain neurotoxins and infectious diseases.

It was apparent to even an untrained eye that this man belonged in the Sick category. Georgia stretched a hand toward him and he stared at her with the vacant panic of a mole, beads of perspiration dotting his flushed forehead.

Aside from his sudden impairment, he looked healthy, as far as she could tell. She gripped his shoulders and leaned her ear against his chest: his heart rate hovered in the 160s, way too fast; his breathing sounded shallow, but without sounds indicative of pneumonia or asthma. Examination of his abdomen revealed no bowel sounds; also no distention or apparent tenderness. Enormous black orbs swallowed his irises, so she couldn't discern his eye color; peering into his mouth, she observed a dry, caked tongue, without any swelling or redness in the back of his throat.

The flight attendants offered a brief rundown: he'd seemed flushed but fine as he boarded, but he'd begun to look a little strange as the flight took off, becoming heated and restless as the miles piled up. The attendants had proceeded cautiously; he hadn't been rude or disruptive, but they had all seen plenty of personality disorders manifest themselves mid-flight. As the flight progressed, though, it became clear this was not an intercontinental freakout brought on by alcohol or anxiety; by the time they'd cleared the landmass of Greenland he was confused, followed by outright hallucinations and a brief, terrifying seizure. Following their in-flight protocols for medical emergencies, the attendants had contacted a physician on the ground, who'd directed them to obtain vital signs and enlist the help of any doctor who happened to be on board.

The man let out a feverish yelp as a flight attendant dabbed his head with a wet, rolled washcloth held by silver tongs. Frantic, he clawed at the skin beneath his eyes, flopping like a banked salmon, his nails digging into the soft tissue of his face.

Georgia forced herself to think, sequentially and logically, through a differential diagnosis as the flight attendants strained to hold the man down. One possibility seemed more and more likely here. Otherwise healthy male, with sudden agitation and mental status changes? Not sepsis: the attendants reported his blood pressure as high, not low. No reported history of head trauma. Even though he looked red and had scratch marks on his arms, there were no other signs to indicate anaphylaxis, ruling out an allergic reaction.

This had to be drugs.

She lowered the pitch of her voice. "Cocaine? Meth?"

The older flight attendant, still gripping the man's forearms, swung around. "I really don't think so."

Georgia had to admit this man didn't project the aura of the typical meth head. Even though currently he could best be described as delirious, he was clean-cut and well-dressed, with the look of a businessman. But with stimulants, you never knew. An insistent little clanging at the periphery of her consciousness began to intensify as she regarded him. She'd forgotten something, or there was something she'd overlooked. She kept thinking of nursery rhymes, which made no sense. Nursery rhymes? But the thought wouldn't go away.

For a moment she found herself hung up on the image of Alice in Wonderland chugging the potion that sent her sprouting like a sequoia toward the heavens. Did Mystery Man drink something in the hopes of getting . . . bigger? But this wasn't quite it. Not Alice, not the Queen of Hearts, not the Cheshire Cat. It was . . . the Mad Hatter.

Now she knew why she'd been reminded of nursery rhymes; it was a mnemonic they'd learned in med school for the symptoms of a particular kind of toxicity: anticholinergic poisoning. *Red as a beet, blind as a bat, mad as a hatter, hot as a hare, full as a flask, dry as a bone.*

Red as a beet: flushed skin. Check.

Blind as a bat: dilated pupils. Check.

Mad as a hatter: raving and confused. Check.

Hot as a hare: warm to the touch. Check.

No way at the moment to assess the fullness of his bladder—*full as a flask*—in order to ascertain whether he suffered urinary retention, but it seemed a reasonable assumption. The last one—*dry as a bone*—threw her, however. His mouth was dry, certainly, but she thought again of his damp forehead, and her certainty diminished.

Anticholinergic people were never sweaty.

As she watched, the pretty flight attendant dipped her washcloth in a basin and swiped the man's forehead again, creating a shiny rivulet of water snaking down his temples. He wasn't sweaty! He was wet. For a second, a flush of self-congratulatory excitement swamped her: she hadn't studied this stuff since medical school, and somehow she pulled this diagnosis out of her ass? With great effort, she resisted the urge to shout *Eureka!*

"Help me," she instructed the attendants, rolling the patient onto his side in order to pull off his sport coat and button-down. "We need to undress him; he's overheated." To the older flight attendant she added, "Can you open the plane's emergency medical kit? I need an IV kit and a bag of saline. And some kind of sedative."

The flight attendant jerked a metal box open. "We do have IV equipment and saline," she said, "but our kits don't contain sedatives."

"How about we commandeer some from the passengers?" Georgia asked, yanking the man's shirt off. "I'm sure there's plenty of Xanax on board."

"How would he take it? We can't get him to drink anything."

Georgia paused to give this thought. "There might be a mom on board with rectal valium for a kid's seizures."

The younger flight attendant, battling the man as she tried to remove his pants, looked up in alarm. "Say what?"

The other flight attendant took control of the conversation. "Rectal valium is a nonstarter," she said firmly.

With the man's outer layer of clothing shed and the white cotton T-shirt he wore underneath yanked up, they all noticed them at the same time: several small round patches affixed to the skin under the man's shoulder blades.

"What are those?"

Georgia pulled them off and inspected one. *Gebruiken als nodig is voor braken.* The writing on them was in a foreign language—she guessed German or Dutch—but they were likely a brand-name form of scopolamine, a common anti-nausea medicine in European countries. Another thought occurred.

"I need to see where he was sitting. Quickly."

The flight attendants eyed one another. "He was sitting in first class," one of them offered. Georgia looked toward the front of the plane and then down at her patient; first class was a long way off. "How did you get him back here?"

"When it became obvious he was getting sick, we asked him to move," said the younger woman, a freckled strawberry blonde. "He was getting kind of belligerent, so we lined up a couple ABPs to help."

"ABPs?"

"Able-Bodied Passengers." Like medicine, aviation apparently had its own set of confusing acronyms. "We don't want to leave someone combative near the cockpit, so we generally move them back here if we can."

"I'm sure the pilot appreciates that. Is there any way I could ask him a question?"

The flight attendant smiled sweetly. "Her. Captain Lucke. And yes, I can convey anything you need to her."

"Okay," said Georgia. "Let me check out his seat first."

The flight attendant complied, leading her to the first-class cabin, where ice tinkling against real glass broke the swishy hush of the plane's ventilation system. The passengers who weren't knocking back cocktails had donned their complimentary masks and gone to sleep in their fully reclining seats. The attendant gestured to a window seat occupied by a stout older woman dressed in black. The aisle seat—presumably the guy's seat—was vacant, and an array of objects littered the flat area on the seat divider: a tablet, a crystal glass, some of those weirdly appealing little bottles of alcohol, a round white ceramic dish full of nuts. None of it was what she sought. She thrust her hand into the pocket on the back of the seat in front of her, feeling her way past the linear edges of the airline magazines and the smaller flat expanse of a barf bag. At the bottom, her fingers curled around something crinkly. She hoisted it into view.

A small rectangle: divided by perforations into smaller squares, the metallic coating on them peeled back to expose several empty spaces that had at one time each held a pill.

"Diphenhydramine?" asked the flight attendant, reading the back of a foil pack.

"Yep," she said, giving in to an inappropriate surge of elation as they hustled back to the rear of the plane. "Benadryl! This must be anticholinergic poisoning."

She explained her theory: somewhere, the man had gotten ahold of prescription medicine patches for nausea. For whatever reason, he put on too many of them—either he forgot he had the first ones on when he added the others, or he held a "more is always better" philosophy, or maybe they weren't working so he tried more. In any case, he didn't remove them once he reached the airport, and they probably caused him to feel itchy. So he took diphenhydramine—generic Benadryl—to treat the itching, and he took too many of those as well. This would explain why he got much worse after the flight took off: Benadryl and scopolamine were both in a class of medicines that inhibited neurotransmission at a certain kind of receptor. In large quantities, they could cause these kinds of symptoms.

In tandem, they looked at him as Georgia finished: eyes wide, flared nostrils, teeth clamped in feral ferocity. He whipped his head from side to side. "Where exactly are we right now? Can we land?" she asked.

In answer, the attendant gestured to the flight-tracker screens in the galley. They were heading northeast along the great circle route between the eastern seaboard of the United States and Frankfurt, Germany, currently placing them over the middle of the Atlantic Ocean. Landing was obviously not an option.

"Okay," Georgia said, hoping she sounded more confident than she felt. "Treatment for anticholinergic poisoning is largely supportive. Although I think there is some kind of antidote. I'm not a toxicologist, of course, but I'm hoping he'll do much better now that the patches are removed."

She took what action she could: after a discussion with a physician on the ground, she cobbled together a treatment plan, systematically proceeding through a checklist of available options. She stayed in the back with him; he was dead weight, so snowed that he'd sprawled out diagonally across the galley floor, limbs flung akimbo with the confident, space-snatching thoughtlessness common to most men and all small children. He snored, too: throaty reverberations that shook his entire body.

By now, the plane had gone dormant; overhead lights out, engines droning, no one moving. Georgia sat on the galley floor, her back pressed against the metal of a cabinet, feeling the soothing mechanical vibrations of the plane's innards through the floor. After what felt like an eternity, she'd almost fallen asleep when something jarred her into full consciousness.

Her patient's snores had stopped. As she watched, he rolled onto his side, facing her, and opened his eyes.

4

FELIX CULPA

MARK

Mark McInniss looked up to find the proportions of the world had shifted in some fundamental way: sizes blown out of whack, angles off-kilter, surfaces entirely wrong. He blinked and looked again. An institutional-appearing gray cabinet stretched above his head toward a distant ceiling. He could not figure out where he was: in a bunker of some kind? A . . . jail cell? His head throbbed as if he'd awoken from a world-class bender, so this last thought, though frightening, was not impossible.

As his vision began to resolve, he realized he must be on an airplane, although his position, lying supine, seemed to indicate a problem. Confusion swamped him, along with a dawning awareness that he must have somehow made an ass of himself. He whipped his head to the side and then relaxed. He must be in first class, in a reclining seat. A very uncomfortable, very hard seat.

A light hand gripped his forearm. "Are you thirsty?" said a woman. Right away, he liked her voice; if her words had been script, they'd be one of those looping, artistic fonts you see on placards and memes. A warm voice, musical and smart and slightly hoarse. He stretched his neck to see who it belonged to, but an alien object in his mouth dis-

tracted him: a baked rock, etched with salty, hardened cracks, had replaced his tongue. He tried to speak but could manage only a raspy
bark.

The hand retreated from his forearm and returned bearing a cup. It
was exquisite; nothing in the history of humanity had ever felt as good
as the sensation of this cool liquid rolling down his tongue and along
the sandblasted gorge of his throat. He raised his head to guzzle it, not
minding as it splashed down the sides of his face. As his thirst abated
and the water puddled in the hollows of his collarbones, it occurred to
him he must not be wearing a shirt. He looked around, discovering he
was stretched out along the floor of the galley, his shirt and pants and
shoes missing.

So. Quick summation of his circumstances: he was lying half-naked
and groggy on the floor of an airplane. What the hell was going on?

He wanted to ask the water-bestowing angel, but before he could
force the words past his newly restored tongue, his head lolled back,
felled by an immense gray mist of fatigue.

~~~~~~~

The next time he opened his eyes, things were marginally clearer. He
was flying back to Europe from the United States. He knew he hadn't
been feeling well as the flight took off, but he couldn't quite remember
why. Apparently he'd done something stupid, assuming, of course, that
whatever had happened to him was personal in nature and not the result of having been conked on the head by a terrorist or hit by a suitcase during a cabin depressurization or some other random event
beyond his control. For a hopeful moment he considered these scenarios, but quickly rejected them. As best he could tell, the rest of the
plane was behaving normally, which would be unlikely in the face of a
major disaster.

None of this mattered now, however, because a woman's face hovered into view just above him, riveting his attention. It was an arrest-

ing face, not quite beautiful, from the apex of her wide jaw to her small, slightly rounded nose to her curved forehead. It was also an animated face, the wide amber eyes alight with intelligence and curiosity and energy, rimmed with a beautiful band of brown, complementing her coloring: dark red hair, skin dotted with light brown freckles. He resisted the absurd urge to reach up and trace the swell of her cheekbone.

"Hi," he said, trying to mask his confusion with an air of confidence.

The woman smiled. "Hi."

A long while passed and Mark realized he must have dozed off. Absently, he wiped a crust of drool off his lower lip with his shoulder. "Wazz—whass your name?"

"Georgia. What's yours?"

"Mark," he said. At least there was one thing he could answer. Emboldened, he picked up her hand. "Not married," he observed. What? Where had that come from?

"That's right," she said, in a slightly cooler tone.

With some effort, he heaved himself up onto his forearms so their faces were level. "What are you doing later?"

A tinkly laugh burst out of her. "Are you hitting on me?"

"No," he said automatically, before honesty forced him to reconsider. "Yes."

"Well, this is . . . unexpected."

This was a good beginning, especially considering that he'd been unconscious a few minutes ago, but progress stalled as he tried to think of what to say next. Flopping his head back down, he noted a few more details of her appearance: the flat, almost imperceptible glint of a tiny nose ring, unadorned fingernails, a blue bandana wound around the cloud of rust-colored hair. A few minutes passed in peaceable silence while he tried to puzzle out why this woman in particular would have been assigned to mind him.

"What happened to me?" he managed, finally.

She perked up. "Anticholinergic poisoning," she said, sounding pleased. "You've been out of it for many hours."

"What? What the hell is that?"

Her gaze was intent. "Where did you get the patches you were wearing on your back? They have instructions on them, but they're not in English."

"Patches . . ." he began, confused, but then a spark of memory ignited. "Oh! Yes. They're for nausea; I gave them to myself." She opened her mouth and, anticipating her question, he spoke again. "I spent yesterday on a boat."

She grinned, one cheek rent by a deep dimple. "I was actually going to ask why you were wearing so many of them. Did someone tell you to put them all on?"

"Oh! No, obviously that would be a ridiculous thing to do. Uh, I don't know—I'm not sure, actually—how many of them was I wearing?"

This time she laughed. "A bunch," she said. She began talking—something about Alice in Wonderland and poisoning and whether or not he'd been sweaty—but it was too difficult to follow, so he let his mind wander. Eventually she stopped and waited for him to say something. He tried to think of an intelligent question.

"So I poisoned me? It wasn't someone else?"

"I'm pretty sure it was you," she said, grinning. His stomach, which had been roiling with the ferocity of a tropical depression, produced an audible rumble. She stiffened. "Uh-oh."

"Take cover," he managed. When the vomiting ended, he let out a feeble gasp or two, sounding even to himself like an extricated fish in its final throes. Eventually he recovered enough to assess the damage, which was worse than he'd thought. He'd barfed on her feet.

"It's okay," she assured him. Her shoes appeared to be constructed out of some clear material, reminding him of Cinderella's slippers. She slipped one off and sponged it down, flicking away a bright pink oblong that appeared to be an undigested Benadryl. "People have vomited worse stuff on me," she said. "This was mostly water."

"I'm sorry," he groaned.

"I bet you'll be feeling much better now. They're going to transport you to the airport's medical facility when we land, and I'm pretty sure you're going to be fine."

"Okay," he said, a bit uncertainly. An idea struck. "Would you like to have dinner?"

"No," she said. Before his disappointment could register, she added kindly, "It's nearly morning."

"Yes, I realize that," he said in a sudden surge of clarity, "but here's my motto: *carpe diem*."

"*Carpe diem* is your motto?"

Another long pause while he searched for a word: the art of conversation seemed to be returning to him in fits and lurches. Then: "Yes."

"But *carpe diem* is a bit overused as a motto, isn't it?" she asked, her body easing from its rigid posture of a moment ago. She handed over another drink of water, and this time he managed it neatly.

"I have losh—lots—of mottos, actually," he said, "but I try to tailor them to the situation."

She gestured toward the nearest acrylic window in the wall of the jet, through which they could see an oval of dark sky. "In that case, technically, I think you mean *carpe noctem*," she offered.

His eyebrows rose in appreciation. "You speak Latin?"

She tilted a freckled hand back and forth in the universal gesture for so-so. "I'm a doctor. I don't speak Latin so much as use it to keep other people from understanding me."

A doctor. She didn't look like Mark's idea of a doctor, but it explained why she'd been drafted to rescue him. "In that case, I exchange my motto for a better one. *Felix culpa*."

"*Felix culpa*? Happy . . . Guilt? I might have to look that one up."

Mark decided to go for it. "Before you do that, I want you to know I'm very serious about the dinner. Or breakfast. I'd love to see you again."

Her face went still for a second, so subtly he wondered if he'd imagined it. But no, he was a good judge of faces: for whatever reason, she didn't want him to ask her out. His gaze slid to her hand again. She'd said point-blank she wasn't married. Was she gay? He didn't have the most functional gaydar in the world but he wasn't clueless either; he felt certain she was straight. She must not find him appealing. A wash of warmth colored his cheeks. "But of course," he said, "you must already have plans."

"It's a nice offer," she said, her expression softening at his embarrassment. "Thank you, I'd love to grab some food once you're, ah, medically cleared, if there's time."

"Of course," he said, stupidly. He could not think of anything else to say.

"So, my turn to ask about you," she said, picking up the conversational slack. "What's—"

She paused as another face appeared above them: thin eyebrows angling precipitously toward one another, a bow of pursed lips. A flight attendant. "Thank you so much for your assistance, Doctor." She leaned down, thrusting out a bony hand to clap his caregiver on the shoulder. "I think he's doing well now, and we're beginning our approach into Frankfurt, so do you mind returning to your seat?"

"I don't," said Mark's new friend, "but I'm going to accompany him to the airport clinic when we land. Assuming that is okay with you," she added, looking at him.

"It is," he said, pleased. He watched as she made her way down the aisle toward the rear of the plane, turning midway to direct a glance over her shoulder.

With her departure, he took stock: his head ached and his body felt battered, and a heavy drowsiness still suffused him, but his mind felt much clearer. Even under the best of circumstances, he tended to tolerate jet lag poorly, usually spending the last portions of long flights in a drooly stupor, not quite able to sleep but not firing on all cylinders either. He tried to look on the bright side: at least on this flight he'd gotten plenty of rest. His thoughts swerved back to the woman who'd been caring for him and a strange sensation shot through him. By the time he'd identified it as interest it had already been replaced with a sense of loss. No matter how attractive he found this woman, the chances they lived near one another were slim. Still, though: you never knew.

5

THE SCIENTIFIC AND MATHEMATICAL EMBLEM OF CHANGE

Georgia watched through her neighbor's window as the plane touched down onto a gray tarmac in Frankfurt amid skies the color of a stainless steel refrigerator, everything glinting silver from the shrouded rays of the sun. As soon as the wheels hit the runway, the army of drowsy passengers mobilized, unbuckling their seatbelts in clear defiance of airline policy as they leaned toward the aisle in preparation to fight their way out. Georgia contemplated muscling through the throng to reach the paramedics who'd been called to meet the plane, but it was useless; her seat was in the middle of the plane, and both aisles had jammed with people the instant the plane came to a full stop. She decided to catch up as soon as she exited the jetway.

She staggered off the plane, her legs limp from a combination of jet lag and depleted adrenaline; naturally enough, she'd planned to sleep on the flight instead of running an airborne ICU. As she navigated the corridor to the airport, she looked for a stretcher, but her patient was long gone, no doubt whisked past in a special line for emergencies.

How had she forgotten about customs? At this hour in the morning, the enormous space resembled the inside of a disturbed beehive, people swarming all over the place, a billion buzzy languages clogging

the air. She'd also missed the handout of the obligatory immigrations
form during her time tending to the sick man, forcing her to step out
of line to obtain and complete it. By the time she cleared customs and
immigration, nearly another half hour had passed, and all she could do
was hope he was still somewhere within the airport complex.

The airport's medical clinic turned out to be surprisingly sophisticated. More of a compact emergency department, it was equipped with
trauma rooms and a small operating room, X-ray capabilities, an ultra-
sound, and even a laboratory, according to a pamphlet at the desk. Also
a quarantine station, which made perfect sense in an airport. More
than twenty thousand people a year sought care here, averaging to over
fifty a day. This place was hopping.

She tried bluffing her way back to the treatment area, identifying herself as "the physician from Flight 704," but a pinched-face receptionist
took one look at her and directed her to wait in a seating area. She took the
opportunity to check her phone: no new messages from Jonah. After that,
she waited. And waited. After reading an array of useless magazines, she'd
just stood and walked out of the clinic when her phone buzzed. Jonah!

Sorry about all the butt-texts.

Easing out of the flow of traffic, she fired off a reply. What's happening with your patients?

Four cancellations, three more no-shows.

She waited for more but apparently that was it. She sat down hard
on a gray, stiff-backed bench.

So where did you go last night?

She stopped, confused. Had it been last night or the night before?
What day was it now in the States?

Three dots appeared in the message screen, followed by more words.

I went for a drive. I'm really sorry I bailed on you.

This made sense; Jonah often went for a drive when he was upset. Still, he could have at least called her.

Why?

I don't know. The office staff is acting weird.

Why didn't you call me last night?

I'm sorry. I called Deanna. She said to get more information and then allow time to process before I respond. Talk when you get back?

We can talk now! she wrote, but, after a delay, Jonah replied that he was still in clinic. Georgia slumped back against the gray seat. Should she call him anyway? She had a lot of faith in Deanna, Jonah's therapist, whom she knew from volunteering at the county's free medical clinic. A lovely woman with purple ombré hair lightening to a pale lavender at the tips, Deanna was the sort who brooked no nonsense: she called you out if you dissembled or equivocated, but she never failed to deliver an impression of confidence in her patients. Jonah had been seeing her for over a year, since his last bout of depression. Georgia rose from her slump. With Deanna at his back, Jonah would be all right.

She hoped.

Upon her return, if anything, the airport clinic looked even busier than when she'd left: the waiting room chairs were all occupied and a man in a feathered fedora stood at the check-in counter, arguing in vociferous German with the receptionist; behind him stretched a line of people. An unexpected melancholy washed through her; Mark had probably been discharged already, or transferred to a hospital. She took the first step back toward the terminal, stopping when her phone buzzed again with a text, this time from an unfamiliar number.

Felix Culpa.

Felix Culpa! She realized she'd forgotten to look up the Latin phrase on the plane. Hurriedly, she opened the phone's browser and typed it in, receiving an immediate hit from an article in the online magazine *Mental Floss*:

Felix Culpa: a felix culpa is literally a "happy fault."

Hello, she wrote back. How are you feeling?

Mortified.

Don't worry about it, she typed. Someone is always overdosing pretty much every time I fly.

A moment of radio silence, then: Can I call you?

Sure.

The phone rang a moment later. "So I'm curious," she said. "How much do you remember?"

The voice on the other end, scratchy and slightly sheepish, hesitated briefly before answering. "Not much. I called to apologize."

"Think nothing of it."

"I'm embarrassed. I generally prefer to meet people when I'm not sloshed on the floor of an airplane. I understand you had to, er, undress me."

"Well, not fully undr—"

"Horrible. You're probably traumatized. I am so sorry."

"How are you feeling?"

A rumbling locomotive sound: it was his laugh. "I'm fine. I've gotten more IV fluid and medicine and a lecture from a very stern medic about how I should check with a functional adult in the future before I make any medication decisions. At this point I'm suffering mainly from humiliation."

"I'm so glad. I mean, I'm glad you're fine, not that you're humiliated."

"It was worth it," he said, and with a start, Georgia realized she was hearing his voice directly. Looking sideways, she found herself staring into someone's groin. She tilted her neck farther.

It took a moment to register that the man in front of her was the patient from the plane. This was the first time she'd seen him upright. The molish dilation of his pupils had receded, so it was also the first time she could make out the color of his eyes: a nice, light, clear hazel. Also—regarding him in a nonclinical frame of mind for the first time—she noticed his features. Dark, short hair, doubtless smooth and stylish under normal circumstances but ruffled up in little peaks right now; straight eyebrows, cutting a fine horizontal swathe above each eye; a longish face with a straight, longish nose; pale skin, with the faint gray undertone of incipient stubble along his chin and jawbone. It was an intelligent face. Georgia had dated every possible kind of human in her thirty-six years, and while she tended to gravitate toward the roguish sort—creative misfits, musicians, entrepreneurs, and eccentrics of all stripes—she did appreciate a smart man.

The man—Mark, he'd said his name was Mark—straightened up to his full height. His ability to sneak up without her noticing became even more impressive as a couple of things dawned on her: first, he was extremely tall, probably at least six foot six, and second, under his gorgeous jacket he wore paper clothing.

"What happened to your clothes?"

"My pants," said Mark in a wry voice, "are apparently still on the airplane. Along with my shirt."

Georgia nodded, recognizing the disposable garments common to medical clinics everywhere. "Are they releasing you?"

"They weren't keen on the idea, but as I'm obviously human again, I don't see how they can stop me. I'd love to figure out what happened to my bags so I can get out of these ridiculous paper scrubs before I endure another social catastrophe. And I've missed my train."

Georgia had missed her train too, of course, but it seemed rude to bring it up. And she was not in a hurry, anyway; she didn't have to be at the conference until the following day. "I'll go with you to the baggage claim area before I catch my train," she said.

After Mark had been formally discharged, they made their way through the wide corridors to the baggage claim, to a room to change and freshen up, and then toward the regional *Bahnhof*—train station—conveniently located within the airport terminal via a bunch of long connectors.

"I'd like to pay for your ticket," Mark said. "I bet you missed your train because of me."

"Oh, you don't need—"

He waved aside her protestations. "It's the least I can do. Plus, I have an ulterior motive: maybe I can wait with you. Where are you headed?"

A brisk group of backpackers surged around them on both sides, isolating them in a little air pocket of their own. "Amsterdam," she said.

"Really?" A delighted smile. "I live there." He bounded toward the ticket counter, each of his strides equaling two of a normal human's. She trailed him, only to discover the next open train to Amsterdam didn't leave for another four hours.

Mark turned to her, guilt etching across his smile. "Ugh," he said. "I'm so sorry."

"Don't be sorry."

He nodded, shoulders slumping, before moving to the next counter to rebook the seats. He returned in a few moments looking more cheerful. "This way," he said.

"This way to what?"

"There's a fine airport bar in this direction. I have you pegged as a bourbon drinker."

"I am," she said, impressed, "but I don't think you should be drinking."

His grin returned to full wattage. "At least let me buy you breakfast."

The cafe, of course, was modern in design: backless leather stools, bright pools of light spilling onto blocky white tables, an ascetic-appearing tile floor. Georgia held her glass aloft and considered the swirl of caramel-colored bourbon. Having grown up in Kentucky with her father, a bona fide genius and a stern bourbon aficionado, she took drinking seriously. This was good stuff; she was impressed at the depth of this little bar's bourbon reserves. If someone had told her yesterday she'd be toasting with a shot of Weller in a random airport bar with a recovering poisoned man after saving his life on an airplane—well, she could not quite imagine what her reaction would have been. Delight? Amazement? Confusion?

If Mark's face was anything to judge by, he was similarly taken aback by the turn of events. Catching her studying him, he tilted his water in her direction. "Cheers," he offered. "Or maybe I should say 'prost.'"

"Proost," she said agreeably.

"This has to be one of the strangest days of my life."

"Mine too."

"Okay," he said. He took a giant swig of his water, so she downed a correspondingly large swig of her bourbon. Maybe not the best idea, but she'd earned it.

The Weller tasted fabulous; smooth and warm, with an ass-kicking little jolt at the end, even better than the surprisingly good pastry she'd ordered along with it. This was airport food? "I misspoke a bit when I said I had a question," Mark was saying. "I've got several, actually, and I'm ashamed I'm just now asking the first one, given that you rescued me on the plane." He paused.

"Proceed."

"This is awkward, but it's only going to get worse as time goes on."

"With a buildup like that, you've definitely got my attention."

Mark's clear eyes shone with something that looked suspiciously like mirth. "I realized I already know a lot about you—you're a doctor, you're a bookworm and a science geek, you're a bit of a rogue but you're lonely, you—"

"Whoa," she interrupted. "Hold up. Obviously you're aware I'm a doctor, but how do you know those other things?"

"I'm paying attention. You have not one but *two* novels and a biography sticking out of your shoulder bag. Only a dedicated book junkie would carry that much weight around."

"Okay."

"The science part: the biography is Nikola Tesla, and there's a novel by Neal Stephenson. And then there's your tattoo."

"You saw my tattoo? Which one?"

He nodded. "A delta. I saw it on the plane, when your pants leg rolled up a bit." He paused, adding, "I wasn't purposely staring at your ankles or anything."

She must have looked dubious, because he went on. "Okay, yes. I was looking at your ankles. They're very nice."

"No, it's just most people think I have a tattoo of a triangle. Or if they recognize it as a delta they think it's a sorority thing."

"The Greek letter delta," he said. "The scientific and mathematical emblem of change."

"Correct. *And* it's the differential operator given by the divergence of the gradient of a function on Euclidean space."

He stared, his mouth slightly ajar. "The Laplace operator."

Her turn to be impressed; she'd never met anyone who didn't look at her strangely if she started babbling math jargon, let alone anyone who could actually comprehend what she was talking about. "You know about the Laplace operator?"

"I was a math major; how do *you* know about the Laplace operator?"

"My father was a college math professor. So, yes, I have a lot of reasons for liking the delta symbol. What about the rest of it?"

"The rest of the Greek alphabet?"

"No, the rest of what you said." She waited, embarrassed, but he still looked puzzled. "That I'm a rogue or whatever."

"Ah," he said. "Well, it's no great feat of deduction to figure out you like bucking expectations. You're a doctor but you've got a tattoo, and—"

"Lots of physicians have tattoos."

"Be that as it may, you've got a tattoo and you dress like you're in a folk band, and—"

"Not a *folk* band, a—"

He held up a hand. "But the real clue," he said, "is that."

He pointed to a round button pinned to her shoulder bag, which sported a picture of Will Ferrell dressed in a wig, makeup, and a weird outfit. Printed across it were the words *ANTI-ESTABLISHMENT: SO HOT RIGHT NOW.*

"Ah," she said. "yes." They each had another sip of their drinks. The silence suddenly felt oppressive; she was still burning to know what it was about her Mark had identified as the tell of a lonely person. Did it waft off her like the stale odor of the bread she'd found in the back of the pantry last week? Were her aging ovaries emitting a man-repelling sonar ping? No, she decided. All of that was ridiculous. First, she hated when people yammered on about ovaries, and second, she wasn't the kind of person who conveyed—or even felt—desperation, even when perhaps she should. She tended to err more on the side of overconfidence.

But that didn't mean she wasn't lonely.

"That last bit," he said, in a softer tone, "about you being lonely. I made that up."

"Why?"

"Possibly it was projection."

She considered this. "Are you lonely?"

"Well, sure. Sometimes. I work too much. But I was mainly glad you're not with anyone."

A fine flush of pleasure crept up her neck. "I see. What sort of work do you do?"

Two identical and longitudinal rents appeared in his cheeks as he smiled. "I'm the CFO of the European branch of a venture capital firm based in California. Most people find my job to be incomprehensible or boring, so I usually don't bang on about it too much. How about you?"

"Back up a second. I don't even know your full name."

"Mark McInniss." He held out his hand, and she set down her glass to shake it. "Expat American, math dork, and reader, so as you can see, we have a few things in common. Okay, now that we've been formally introduced, on to my question: what kind of doctor are you?"

"Nope," she said. "I'm gonna make you guess my specialty."

He chewed thoughtfully. "Hmm," he said. "I'm a great guesser, so I'm likely to get it right on the first try. Give me a second." He set his fork down and massaged his forehead. "Pediatrician."

"What? No. Why would you think that? Because I'm a woman?"

"Yes. But not because I'm sexist. I mean, I hope it's not because I'm sexist. It's logical; there are more pediatricians than most other specialties, and most pediatricians are female."

"Yeah, but no. Try again."

He stared at her, with the same intent look he'd worn on the airplane. "ER doc."

"No. But that's a good guess, because deciphering what was wrong with you was very ER-ish. I'm still impressed with myself."

"Proctologist."

"No! And they're called colorectal surgeons. But you're getting warmer."

"Proct—wait, colorectal surgeon is warmer? I think I give up."

"I'm a urologist."

"Neurologist?"

"No, UR-ologist."

"Georgia Brown the urologist," he said. "What an interesting job."

She straightened, gratified by this approval. Most people tended to detour down a predictable conversational path at this point, wanting to know why in the world she'd chosen to be a urologist, or if it bothered her patients that she was a woman, or most commonly, an incredulous appraisal of her tattoos and her nose ring and the fiery halo of her hair, followed by a couple unsubtle questions about whether or not she'd found medical school to be difficult. Mark's mind, though, had wandered down a different track. He settled back in his seat, his arms across his chest.

"Did you ever consider another field? Something nonmedical?"

"Sure," she said. "Architecture, physics, even divinity school or philosophy at one point. I also worked as a car mechanic in college."

"That's quite a range of interests. You don't often see science geeks pondering a religious career."

"That's a widely held misconception, that science and religion are incompatible," she said. "And if you're Southern and religious, everyone assumes you've got the brainpower of an amoeba and you fit in socially somewhere to the right of Attila the Hun."

"Am I to take it that you're smarter than an amoeba and to the left of Attila?"

"Yes," she said.

"That's intriguing," he said, giving away nothing of his own beliefs. "And you wound up as a doctor instead of a theologian or a car mechanic."

Even though he hadn't inquired directly, a compulsion to explain her specialty choice took hold anyway. "I went into medicine because I liked the idea of alleviating suffering. But I didn't know which specialty to pick, and the thing is, urology was a process of exclusion. I knew I wanted to be a surgeon of some sort; in surgery you can actually fix things, and I love fixing things. But I didn't really dig on intestines, so that let out general surgery; and all those dainty little tweezers they use in head and neck surgery struck me as too doll-like; and orthopedics made me feel like a construction worker. I even tried to wear a hard hat to the OR one day to rod a femur, but my attending at the time had an underdeveloped sense of humor." To illustrate, she assumed an expression incorporating both vapidity and hostility. "Transplant and cardiovascular are cool as all get-out, but the lifestyle can be grim. By the time I sorted through it all, only urology was left, and I thought it was the most interesting of the bunch anyway: it incorporates both medicine and surgery to treat a wide range of illness. Plus I kind of like being a woman in a dude's world; there are only about a thousand female urologists in all of America."

"I imagine you must mourn the loss of your ignorance in some respects."

"Wha—oh, you mean I know too much about men?"

He jerked his chin: a portrait of mock gravity. "The loss of the masculine mystique."

"Well, you've got that right. Mystique is in short supply when you do what I do. And actually, romance is in short supply when you do what I do. Some dudes are not anxious to date a woman who interacts with penises for a living."

"Occupational hazard, I suppose," Mark said diplomatically, adding, "and are you traveling for business?"

"Yes. You?"

"Yes. I go back and forth between the states and Europe frequently. California and the research triangle in North Carolina, mainly. This is not exactly going to heighten my appeal, but I often work seven days a week. I haven't had a decent date in so long I can't remember the last one. I've never had a date with anyone who saved my life before, or with a doctor, or, for that matter, with a smart redhead."

She thought about this; it was rare for a man to acknowledge he was on a date, even one that was more clear-cut than this one. She decided she liked his lack of pretension. "Does that mean," she said finally, "you've had a date with a dumb redhead?"

"I've had a date with every dumb redhead in Europe. Please don't deny me the opportunity to improve on that. Let's have dinner tonight in Amsterdam."

The words *dinner tonight in Amsterdam* held an undeniably exotic ring. "Yes," she said. "Okay, yes. I'll have dinner with you tonight in Amsterdam."

"That's perfect." He took down the last of his water, setting it back on the little table with a clunk, before glancing at his watch and then at her. "I should vomit on women more often, apparently."

She grinned. "I've been barfed on by worse people."

6

THE PSYCHOLOGY OF ATTRACTION

By the time they reached Amsterdam, after what surely had been history's most epic conversation between two strangers on a train, Georgia realized two things: first, it had been years, if ever, since she'd met someone to whom she felt such an instant attraction, and second, she had a strong desire to cancel her hotel reservation. She was in the midst of a mental rearrangement as they waited at the station for a ride—maybe they'd just skip dinner, maybe she'd abandon the conference registration altogether—when Mark picked up her hand and said, "You'll come with me?"

She'd been booked into a depressingly American-sounding hotel with attached convention facilities, so she'd been pleased to hear Mark lived in a posh and ancient area of town called the Jordaan. It wasn't his apartment, he explained as they got in the car; the flat belonged to the head of his company, a guy named Rolly who apparently traveled so often he had apartments in several European cities. Amsterdam, obviously, but also London and Munich and Basel, Switzerland. She hadn't thought of any of those places as biotech hotspots, but Amsterdam alone housed many such companies, including one of the first to launch a gene therapy product.

They stopped in front of an old building overlooking the canal, its brick facade dotted with windows. "It's gorgeous," she said.

"I moved here from California for what was supposed to be two months and now I've been living in this flat for two years," he said, unlocking the front door and stepping into a vestibule dominated by an intricately carved staircase. "And it never fails to impress me. It's light and airy and full of horrendously expensive modern art. The one drawback"—he grasped the handle of her suitcase and started up the first flight—"is that it lacks an elevator."

A seemingly endless number of stairs led them to the top floor, where he flung open the door to the flat and stepped inside. "Home sweet home," he said, looking over his shoulder. *"Welkom in Amsterdam."*

But she didn't follow him in. To her surprise, somewhere between the first floor and the fifth floor, following his tall form up the stairs, she'd turned into a walking cliché of lust: weak-kneed, flushed, gripped with an all-encompassing desire. She studied Mark, the entire length of him, ending at his face, which had turned quizzical as he waited for her. "Come here," she managed, leaning against the grayish green wall of the landing, her voice rasping into the stairwell.

It took him only a second to understand, and even less than that to cross to her. He had to lift her in order for their faces to line up; his eyes, looking right into hers, had gone dark. He held her around the waist, his hands spanning her hipbones and her ass, her hands grasping the sides of his face.

Georgia had long been interested in the psychology of attraction, her mind a repository of useless research conclusions about what cranked up the dial on the sexometer. She knew about the impact of an easily visible ocular limbal ring on the perception of attractiveness (good), what color women should accessorize with if they want to attract men (red), and the impact of internet porn on the relationships of newlyweds (bad). She understood symmetrical faces connote beauty, so much so that you could measure the distances and the ratios between certain facial features on a woman and predict, without ever looking at her,

whether or not men will find her desirable. She knew about phero-
mones and how sociocultural status impacts relationships and whether
or not people are attracted to people who looked a lot like them (they
are). But some chemistries were indefinable. Mark's face, which you
might or might not regard as handsome, was to Georgia compelling
beyond all measure. His scent almost knocked her out; she nearly lost
her mind at the angle of his jaw. Why this man? What did he possess
that so many others did not?

Whatever it was, it rivaled some form of induced chemical ecstasy.
She'd never tried cocaine or heroin, not wishing to become one of the
unfortunates who suffered an arrhythmia or an overdose, but Jonah's
friend Jace—one of those people whose threshold for stimulation was
considerably higher than average—had tried everything there was to
try. He'd reported back: a really good drug was like really good sex.
These words didn't do justice to either drugs or sex, she thought now,
as her overwrought senses verged on meltdown. Mark ran his hands
through her hair, pausing over a tangle near the back of her scalp, and
then he pulled her inside and she forgot everything.

〰〰〰

Afterward, as she lay on her side, cocooned against him in a limp daze,
his words drifted over to her. "How was that?" he asked.

With effort, she flopped over to face him. "Fishing for compliments?"

"Yep."

"I've had better."

"You have not. Try again."

She laughed. "Well, then. I'd say it was like the earth shuddered on
its axis and the heavens screamed in ecstasy and the universe immo-
lated itself in a great celestial ball of flame and a chorus of angel voices
cried out as everything faded to black. How was it for you?"

"I've had better."

She thwacked him with her pillow. "You have not."

He closed his eyes, granting her the opportunity to study his face in the bright wash of light from the windows opposite the bed: the fine, long bridge of his nose; the curving fringe of his eyelashes; the black arc of his eyebrows against the cool white of his skin. He opened his eyes, drinking in her absorption. "I'm certain I have never known anything better," he said softly.

A thrumming kicked up in her chest, low and sultry, like the bass note in a blues song. Sometimes—many times, actually—when she found herself relaxing into unguarded happiness with another person, some perverse part of her psyche would kick in, alerted by the opportunity to throw shade on her bliss: her own personal little relationship troll. When things were going well, this troll would stick a quivering snout out of his lair, assuring her *This won't last* or *Something will go wrong* or *You'll be sick of him in a month.* She didn't understand it; she was not a cautious person. It was a mystery why she often deliberately stalled out of relationships before they began.

But she experienced no such negativity when Mark draped his arms around her. "Ah," she said happily. And sleepily: within minutes she felt her eyelids dragging down. She gave in to the urge to sleep, her last conscious sensation a new and entirely wonderful feeling of contentment.

~~~~~~~

The contentment was still there when she woke. They'd both slept hard, waking up in a state of disorientation to find it was the middle of the night. Mark turned on the light and she laughed at him: he sported a deep furrow across one cheek where he'd apparently been attacked by a seam in the pillow.

"You don't look good either," he told her. "I've never seen such an acute and catastrophic case of bedhead."

"Please do not appropriate doctor vocabulary when addressing my looks."

"Or what?"

"Or I'll be forced to talk like a business dork."

"Oh God, no. I'll behave."

She wanted to keep up the banter—she knew lots of bizspeak from a short-lived entanglement with a stockbroker last year—but a sudden realization struck her: she'd forgotten to text Jonah.

She scrambled to the side of the bed, patting around for her bag. Her phone, once she found it, was dead, leading to more fumbling for the charger. Once it revived, a new bout of text messages and missed call notifications exploded across the length of the screen like a little shower of popcorn. She scanned them quickly, but they were innocuous messages, the kind Jonah sent her twenty times a day: someone too good to be true had reached out to him online; his next-door neighbor, plumbing the depths of bad taste, had painted his house a shade that could only be described as Booger Green; a confusing series of texts that turned out to be a plot synopsis of the Netflix adaptation of Caroline Kepnes's novel *You*. Georgia mentally checked that one off her watchlist, since Jonah had just given away all the surprises. She debated whether to text back or to call: at this hour, he'd likely still be asleep. She sent an apology, telling him she was safe and fine and asking him for a status update as soon as he'd heard more about why his patients were leaving. As an afterthought, she tacked on an admission that she'd decided not to stay at the conference hotel, stating she'd found a more authentically Dutch place but neglecting to mention the authentic Dutch place came equipped with a man.

Glancing at the man in question, she saw Mark had rolled back to his side. She started to get back in bed when an avalanche of needs struck: she was starving, thirsty, and in danger of imminent bladder explosion. Obviously she'd rather keel over from dehydration than wet the bed in front of a dude, especially right after a romantic interlude. Mumbling that she needed the restroom, she leapt up.

And stopped in awe.

Whoever had designed this apartment in Amsterdam had possessed a clear vision and an apparently unlimited budget. Even if you weren't into mid-century modern, the room in which she stood was spectacular: a fifty-foot expanse of warm, wide-plank floors, boasting a bank of floor-to-ceiling windows overlooking the canal.

Despite her urgency to find the bathroom, she paused for a moment to take it in. Gauzy linen curtains rippled from the ceiling, presumably flooding the room with natural light in the daytime, but currently framing an aerial view of an army of bicycles parked on a dark, cobbled streetscape above the fluid black of the water. Partitions subdivided the space into functional areas: a bar separated the sleek kitchen from the lounging space, stuffed with Arne Jacobsen Egg chairs and funky chaises and huge, arcing lamps. Bright, trendy art graced the white walls; enormous banana leaf plants in silver pots dotted the floors. Only the bathroom, with its stand-alone tub just visible from where she stood, had doors.

She looked past the table to the blackness outside. It struck her that all these lovely expansive windows were currently showcasing a view of her naked ass, so she scooted along. The smooth wood floors of the main room gave way to cool marble in the bathroom. She didn't turn on the light—there was enough ambient moonlight from an oval window to make out the fixtures—but she did take the time to nudge the heavy wooden door closed. She might have just leapt into bed with a stranger, but she did have some sense of propriety.

Ordinarily, you would not find Georgia and the phrase *leapt into bed with a stranger* in the same vicinity. She sometimes boasted (complained) to various friends about her single status, but in truth she was a serial monogamist who often lapsed into celibacy owing to a poor playing field. Even including the shorn surfer, she hadn't met any intriguing men in ages.

Everyone believed marriage rates were declining, but marriage rates in her particular demographic group—educated women—were actually rising. Her friends from medical school were all married: Zadie, a cardiologist, and Emma, a trauma surgeon, both lived with their husbands and kids in Charlotte; Hannah was an ob-gyn in California. She alone, among her female peers, fretted about the ever-dwindling pool of functional spouses out there.

So now, as Mark called out from the bedroom, no doubt wondering if she'd fallen asleep on the toilet, something in her automatically responded to the sound of his voice. This clang of interest, this little surge of . . . *pleasure* zoomed through her synapses, lighting her up. You couldn't force that feeling, and you couldn't fake it.

If you were lucky enough to find it, you recognized it right away.

~~~~~~

In the morning, the apartment was even prettier: infused with sunlight, bright and crisp. Seated at a high desk fashioned from some sort of shiny metal, Mark hunched over a laptop, his forehead crunched in concentration, chewing on a pencil as he pecked. She watched him until he looked up and saw her.

"Good morning," he said, the pencil falling out of his mouth.

She pointed out the obvious. "You can't type."

"You are correct." He replaced the pencil and mumbled around it. "I refused to take typing in high school because I was concerned that if I knew how, people might ask me to type things."

"What are you working on?"

"It's a bit boring. I'm lucky enough to work with some of the most original and innovative minds on the planet, but all I do is push the money around." He closed the laptop with a snap. "Anyway, good news and bad news. Which do you want first?"

"Well, I like to end on a high note, so let's start with the bad news."

"Right. The bad news: I have to head to Munich."

A surge of ridiculous dismay enveloped her at the thought of him leaving. "What's the good news?"

"I don't have to go until the weekend. So—I'm free to hang out with you until then, except for a meeting here and there. If, uh, you'd like."

Yeah, she'd like. Mark evidently picked up on that, because he walked over and gave her a kiss. A smooth warmth, like liquid sunshine, poured over her, producing a fizzy feeling. She wanted to stretch and purr, like a cat.

Mark kissed her again, and then pulled back. "You know, you have—" he began thoughtfully. She waited for the compliment to land. She had what? She had glorious hair? She had an aura of sexy brilliance? She had an irresistible mind?

"—the most devastating morning breath," he finished. "I was going to offer you a coffee, but maybe you want to brush first."

Oh.

~~~~~~~

Four days later Georgia found herself slumped at the edge of a metal folding chair in a vast meeting room, filled with physicians in various stages of terminal boredom. She, however, was not bored. Like Eloise, the impish six-year-old heroine of children's fiction, Georgia believed that getting bored represented a character flaw. One should always be able to entertain oneself; that was what creativity and imagination were for.

Her lack of boredom at the moment had little to do with either creativity or imagination, however, and plenty to do with fear. Or rather, imagination was involved, but not good imagination. This was *bad* imagination.

She hadn't communicated with Jonah in three days. He'd called her and texted her and even emailed her, but she'd managed to miss all of the calls and most of the texts. She had tried calling him back, but truth be told, she hadn't tried as hard as she could have. And of course she had texted, but when she did, he hadn't responded. She had no idea why so many patients of Jonah's were canceling. She had no idea what Jonah's mental state might be. And now, she had no idea where he was or what he was doing, because the last time she'd heard from him had been more than twenty-four hours ago.

The time change wasn't helping matters any, but most of the problem had arisen from her preoccupation with Mark: since meeting, they'd spent nearly every moment together.

Thinking of Mark was considerably more pleasant than worrying about Jonah. They'd spent the last few days doing all the touristy things: jogging in the Vondelpark, drinking beer on canal tours, gazing at art in the Rijksmuseum and the Van Gogh Museum and the Stedelijk Museum. Every night they stayed up until the wee hours, drinking and talking in atmospheric cafes and courtyard gardens, wandering hand in hand along the beautiful bricked streets like the stars of a picturesque rom-com. They went heavy, delving into science and politics and religion and philosophy, but also discussed their favorite TV shows (him: *Breaking Bad*, her: *The Office*), and whether or not it was acceptable to serve ham at Thanksgiving (her: yes, him: no). They talked about their jobs: his concerns that his company might be on the verge of a world-changing discovery without having adequately prepared for said discovery; and her concern that Jonah was in trouble at work.

She'd have skipped the conference altogether but for a dutiful prick of conscience. The clinic had paid her a stipend, so she was attending the conference. Glancing up from a presenter droning something unintelligible about value-based modifiers, she spied a woman from Charleston in a row ahead, a physiatrist—a rehab doctor—named Darby Gibbes. Extending her leg to its utmost length, Georgia poked the back of Darby's heel with her toe.

Darby looked up, startled. She'd tucked a pencil into her fair hair, which, when combined with the pair of tortoiseshell glasses sliding down her delicate nose, gave her a cerebral air, like a lab scientist. Darby was tiny and wispy, as delicate as a glass bell. Georgia knew her only because they'd started running together last year after they'd discovered they both liked to go at the same pace at the same stretch of beach near Darby's house in Isle of Palms. She was pleasant and bland and Southern to the core, the kind of woman who pulled back her daughters' hair with bows so enormous they looked like they might take flight and pull off the child's head. Outside of their occasional get-togethers to run or in the doctors' lounge at work, she and Georgia had never spent much time together.

"Want to bail?" Georgia mouthed.

Darby scribbled something on the edge of her conference schedule and passed it back to her. *Lunch as soon as this is over?*

I'll meet you outside afterward, Georgia wrote back and passed the program up. Glancing up at the speaker, who was now gesturing toward some sort of complicated flowchart on reimbursements systems, she hastily gathered up her stuff and mimed apologies to the people seated between her and the exit.

The venue, like all conference venues everywhere, was a cavernous hotel, bland and homogenized, with acres of abstract-patterned industrial carpet. Same folding chairs and white-clothed tables, same accordion panels dividing the spaces into smaller breakout chambers, same bitter coffee on pushcarts. Georgia wandered through the hotel's main artery, studying the placards on the doors in case any of the upcoming sessions sounded more enticing.

"Georgia."

A short distance away someone standing in a clump of men beckoned to her. She squinted: one of her partners, McLean Andersen. McLean sported brown hair sticking up in an honest-to-goodness cowlick, and that, combined with round blue eyes and a smattering of freckles, lent him the look of an earnest little boy, even though, as the clinic's newest board-certified urologist, he couldn't be less than thirty-one or so. "Hey there," he said. "Haven't seen you around."

"Oh, I've been around," she said vaguely, adding, "Fun city."

"Too much fun," agreed McLean. "Have you been to one of the 'coffee bars'?"

"Have you?" she asked, surprised. McLean looked too wholesome to be a pothead. Then again, he did have sort of a mischievous look to him.

"I refuse to answer that," said McLean, "on the grounds that it may incriminate me. Hey, Buck!" he bellowed suddenly. A stocky man in a blue sport coat—presumably a physician or an administrator of some kind—ambled up, munching on a flat pastry.

"Andersen," he said.

"Georgia, this is Kyle Buckley," McLean said, "our rival. Just signed with Palmetto. We trained together."

"Oh yeah," she said, realizing he was one of the new urologists at a hospital across town. If beefy, pugnacious guys were your thing, Kyle Buckley could probably be considered handsome. Short and barrel-chested, he was built like a keg on sticks, but he balanced that with wide-set blue eyes and nice teeth and a smooth helmet of brown hair. "Nice to meet you."

Kyle Buckley nodded to her and turned to McLean, punching him lightly on the arm. "Heard you guys have some shit going down at your clinic."

"What?"

"I heard the juice has just been walking out of the med rooms on its own."

"Wha—oh, you mean the missing drugs. Yeah." McLean nodded unhappily; ever since last year, when a nurse at the clinic's urgent care had been found dead in a bathroom with a tourniquet around his biceps, they'd all been alert to the problem of illicit drug use among clinic employees. Now, apparently, it was happening again: the drug counts on some of the more dangerous controlled substances had come up short several times in the last few months.

Kyle's mouth opened, displaying overly white teeth. He leered in her direction. "It's not you, is it, babe?"

Georgia blinked. "What? No, of course not."

He kept his eyes on her for a beat too long, then returned his attention to McLean. "Probably a chick, though," he said. He eyed Georgia again, his oily smile back. "Uh, no offense."

"Excuse me?" she said.

"Whoa, ease up off me, babe." He turned again to McLean and winked. "She looks like the fun type."

"I am standing *right here*, dude," Georgia said. She took a step forward, keeping her eyes locked on his.

He backed up, raising his hands with an expression of exaggerated calm, as if trying to defuse a hysterical person. "Sorry, Red. You looked like you could take a joke."

"Kyle," said McLean, "don't be a jackass. Why do you always have to irritate women?"

"It comes naturally, man." He shrugged. "Sorry. I digress. I was golfing with one of your docs a while back and he said your clinic is getting ready to fire some doctor. Maybe drug abuse."

"Which doctor? And what's the guy's name?" Georgia asked slowly. "The one you heard this from?"

Kyle's wide face lit up. "I don't know who's getting fired, but I heard it from a guy whose name, literally, is Dr. Right."

Georgia's breath caught in her lungs, sticking there with a heavy, inert feeling, as if she'd inhaled water instead of air. She managed to produce a small sound, but fortunately Kyle didn't seem to require a response; he'd already spied someone else he knew down the hall.

"Let me apologize," said McLean, oblivious to the change in the atmosphere as Buckley left. "He's a fraternity brother of mine and, as you can tell, he never progressed beyond the *Animal House* mindset."

"WTF, McLean." She knew she had to sound normal or she'd arouse his suspicion, but her voice came out wrong; too high. "That guy is single, right?"

McLean's eyebrows shot up. "Don't tell me you're interested."

"God, no. I was just hoping he's a lonely virgin."

McLean laughed. "He's married and his wife is a very patient hu-man being." His smile died, replaced by a look of puzzlement. "Who was he talking about? Could he have meant Donovan Wright?"

She studied him: his round eyes were guileless. "Have you heard anything about anyone being fired?"

"Nothing. You?"

"No," she said. "What about the drug thing?"

He shrugged, but his face was pensive. "There are always rumors, but . . . is something going on with that family medicine guy? Jonah somebody?"

Another hitch in her breathing. "Tsukada. Jonah Tsukada. He's a friend of mine," she said.

"Oh. Well, I don't know, it's probably nothing."

Suddenly a rumble filled the hall: the session had ended. Both of them took a step back to avoid being trampled by the egress of freed physicians. Georgia spied Darby traipsing down the hall in her direc-tion; she'd be at their sides in another thirty seconds. She touched McLean's sleeve.

"Are you saying the missing medications have something to do with Jonah?"

He held up a hand. "I'm not. I don't know anything. Somebody said he was the topic of an executive committee meeting and they were also discussing the missing medication issue. So I don't know if those two things are related. I shouldn't have said anything. Sorry."

She wanted to ask him more, but Darby had reached them. Her head tilted, she was rooting around for something in her handbag and did not appear to have gauged the tone of the conversation yet. There was a brief silence as they waited for her to look up. "Ah!" she said, raising her cell phone clutched in a triumphant fist. "Crisis averted. I thought I lost this!" She looked at them for the first time, her gaze shifting back and forth. "Y'all okay?"

"Sure," they both said. Georgia shifted her balance. "Everything's good."

McLean took a slight step backward, hands jammed into his pockets. "I'm meeting some people for lunch. Catch you guys later?"

Georgia gave him a dude-punch on the shoulder. "If you hear anything else," she said, careful to keep her voice light, "about any of that, will you tell me?"

"Of course." With a polite nod to Darby, he walked away.

Darby regarded Georgia with a bright look. "Hear anything else about what?"

Georgia watched the little cowlick at the back of McLean's head recede through the crush of conference-goers until it vanished from view. "Nothing," she said, shifting her attention to Darby. "Let's go."

They walked through the large central corridor of the hotel to the lobby and out through the main doors to the street, where the clattering sounds of pedestrians and cyclists and even a few cars filled the air. Darby made polite, innocuous conversation as they walked, not requiring much in the way of response, so Georgia's mind drifted to Jonah. She pictured his intense black eyes and crazy hair and his unending variety of facial expressions, and it struck her again: she'd been a crappy friend. She should have texted him back more often. She should have tried harder to reach him instead of wallowing around in a moony trance over a man.

"Aren't you friends with Jonah Tsukada?"

Georgia almost stopped dead in her tracks. Was Darby a mind reader? "Why do you say that?"

"Have you talked to him since you've been here?"

"Not really," Georgia admitted. "Do you know him? Why are you asking?"

"I do know him. Sometimes we have mutual patients. And I'm asking because"—Darby brandished her cell phone—"there's an article about him in the paper."

"There's *what*?"

She nodded, searching the phone, eventually landing on the website for the *Post and Courier*, Charleston's newspaper. Georgia had to resist the urge to snatch the phone from her hand as she read the headline: *Patients Involved in Dispute with Local Clinic.* The gist of the story, while somewhat muddled, was this: several patients had written the health reporter for the paper, complaining that they'd received letters telling them they needed to find a new primary care doctor somewhere else.

This would have been a nonissue—there were lots of legitimate reasons a healthcare provider might ask a patient to seek care elsewhere—except for one thing. The doctor in question, Dr. Jonah Tsukada, was not leaving his practice, was not overscheduled, and in fact, when contacted, claimed to have had no involvement in sending the letters.

The patients weren't leaving of their own volition.

They were being told to leave.

"I've been hearing some rumors about Jonah," said Darby.

Her tone held the hesitancy of someone congenitally unable to say anything that could be construed as negative. From what little Georgia knew of her life, it seemed conventional and comfortable. She had three little daughters and an adorable husband and a beautiful home situated at the end of a long tunnel of Southern oaks, their ancient old arms stretched across a roadway encrusted with heaping tendrils of Spanish moss. On their runs, she'd spoken enthusiastically of subjects of little familiarity to Georgia: potty training, the Junior League, her volunteer efforts at the same fundamentalist megachurch that had founded their medical clinic.

Georgia stopped walking. "Tell me what you've heard." A stray gust of wind rattled along the sidewalk, whipping their hair into their faces. Across the street, a swinging sign on a shop caught the wind too, flapping back and forth like a great black bird beating its wings.

"I heard . . ." She hesitated, an uncomfortable grimace on her face. "I heard there's some kind of investigation of him."

"You don't know details?"

She shook her head. "The guy I heard it from didn't mention any specifics."

"Who?"

"It was one of the doctors on the executive committee at the clinic. Donovan Wright; do you know him?"

Everything around Georgia—the cobblestone street and the painted doorways and the gray, portentous sky—entered a state of suspended animation, dimming and blurring at the mention of Donovan Wright. She stood frozen for a second or a century or who knew how long until she roused herself with a mental slap.

Scanning the street, she grabbed Darby's arm. "I'm hungry," she said, nodding in the direction of a little pub or something that appeared to be a possible food source on the opposite corner. "Want to try over there?"

If Darby was surprised by the abrupt change of subject, she didn't show it. "Of course," she said with good grace. "I'm hungry too."

7

THE SEVEN STAGES OF GRIEF

After lunch, Georgia made her way back to Mark's flat, finding it clean and sunny and empty, the gauzy curtains standing sentinel at the windows like a set of tall gossamer angels. It was hushed in here; no mechanical humming or clocks ticking, no voices rippling across the still air. The thick walls of the old house blocked any sound from the street; not that there was much of that anyway. The Jordaan was a quiet part of town, less plagued than other areas by raucous red-lighting college boys or stoned tourists, but now the serenity of the place irritated her.

Jonah's last email, text, and phone call had all been more than twenty-four hours ago. He was not responding to messages. She thought again of the newspaper article and felt a dangerous pressure building up in her bloodstream, but she didn't know what to do to release it. She kicked at one of the beautiful dining chairs and stubbed her toe. Here she was, primed for action, and stuck with nothing to attack except a herd of smug Danish modern sling-back chairs the color of a polished acorn.

She drifted to the kitchen, where a bottle of bourbon rested on the counter, a red bow intact around its neck. Perhaps Mark had bought it for her. Rooting around in the cabinets, she extracted a crystal glass and added a few cubes of ice, enjoying the civilized little clink of the ice against the glass. The amber wash of the whiskey swirled against the curves of the cup, lit by a beam of sun from the tall windows opposite the kitchen.

She wasn't normally a daytime drinker, but what the hell. She'd just carried her glass over to a massive furry beanbag across the room when the door to the flat opened: Mark. He wore a perfectly fitted charcoal suit, paired with a sharp-edged white shirt and a ruby-red tie, his face shining with a kind of calm vitality she'd come to recognize as his default expression. He looked happy.

"Georgia!" he said, and then, taking in her face, "What's wrong?"

"Come over here," she said, downing her shot. He crossed to her and flopped onto the chair, redistributing the contents of the beanbag so she suddenly shot upward a few inches, prompting her to emit a startled squawk. "That was fun," she said. "Do it again."

Obligingly, he started to stand, but she put a hand on his shoulder and pulled him into her. He smelled like safety: clean and somehow strong. "This looks so uncomfortable," she said, unraveling the knot of his tie and pulling it free. She unbuttoned his suit jacket and the top few buttons of his shirt, and then, with escalating urgency, the rest of the buttons. She'd dressed today in a slippery one-piece halter pantsuit with a silk scarf tied at her neck, and she inhaled in a rush as Mark reached a hand toward her throat and untied the scarf. She had to clench her teeth to keep her mouth from falling open as a sudden surge of heat flooded her face. Mark traced her lips with his finger and then pulled the length of silk from her neck.

"Let's have some fun with this," he said.

〰〰〰

After, she lay in bed with her head on Mark's bare chest, her hair snaking down his abdomen in a mess of flaming streaks and whorls. He stroked her back with his free arm, staring up at the ceiling, where a wide-bladed fan spun in lazy revolutions.

"Have you ever noticed that in every Hollywood sex scene ever, there's always a slow-moving fan in the postcoital wrap-up shot? All we need is a cigarette and some sultry music."

She smiled.

He smiled back but then turned serious, raising a lock of her hair and wrapping it around his finger. He twirled it a few times and let it fall. "What happened to upset you today?" he asked quietly.

She could see her phone from here: still nothing from Jonah. She didn't know if she had the energy to answer Mark; the combination of the adrenaline-fueled conversations at the conference and her solitary whiskey-fueled rumination and the sex-fueled romp with Mark had left her in a state of dreamy, depleted lassitude. "I don't know," she said.

"It's okay; you don't have to talk," he said, stroking her back again. "But the offer stands: I'll listen anytime you need it."

"Thank you." She closed her eyes, then raised her head, confused: the light in the room had changed. It took a moment to realize she must have fallen asleep. The warm air, the soft whir of the fan, the soporific effects of the bourbon and the sex; all of them had combined to lull her into unconsciousness.

She was alone in the bed. Mark stood, his back to her, reaching for his clothes. "Where—" she croaked. She cleared her throat and tried again. "Where are you going?"

He turned and smiled; a beam of light falling across the bed caught him flush in the face. "Hey, Sleeping Beauty."

"Sorry about that. It's been a thousand years since I had an afternoon nap."

"I wish I could stay with you. I have meetings for the rest of the afternoon, and then a dinner with an investor. I could meet you after, for a drink or dessert, if you want." He eyed her. "Although maybe you don't need any more to drink."

She laughed. "Thank you for the bourbon." She could see the bottle from here, a bottle of Colonel E.H. Taylor, still wearing its jaunty ribbon. "I love this brand. How did you know?"

"The day we met, you asked the server in that bar in Frankfurt if they had it."

"It was my dad's favorite." She squinted at the label. "It's not easy to find, even in the States; it's kind of obscure unless you're a hard-core aficionado."

Mark stopped dressing and sat down on the bed. "You mention your dad a lot," he said.

"My dad was the best," she said. "He raised me in this literature-soaked nirvana where all I did was drift around the campus where he taught. I read a book a day and I had hidey-holes all over the university where I stored my treasures, and my dad and I ate the same meal for dinner every night for ten years because neither of us liked cooking, and no one made us cook, so we didn't. But then—my dad died, and in college, I had to get a job to support myself."

Mark's voice was quiet. "What happened to him?"

She looked past him. "He died of bladder cancer," she said.

Mark picked up her hand and she remembered she'd told him her selection of urology had been a process of exclusion, as if she'd randomly stumbled upon it instead of pursuing it as part of a deliberate plan to attack an enemy. He gripped her fingers tighter, enclosing her entire hand inside his large one.

"And your mother?"

Georgia didn't know what had happened to her mother—she'd disappeared when Georgia was little—but she wasn't in the mood to out herself as an orphan. The only person who knew the story of her mother was Jonah.

"She's not in the picture," she said, "and so I lived with my dad until he died."

She waited, afraid Mark would start hammering her with questions about her mother, but instead he traced a line from her fingertips up her arm to her shoulder and down to her chest, alighting just at the apex of her heart. "Take off another week and stay with me. Come with me to Munich."

Returning to reality sounded about as appealing as bathing in a tub of raw sewage. For a fleeting moment Georgia considered it: blowing off her responsibilities and extending her vacation. But she had to return, and even more than that, she didn't want to get too happy.

"Look—" She stretched out an arm, inadvertently striking him in the chest. "I'd love to. But I can't."

"So," said Mark, standing and reaching once again for his pants. "That's a no for Munich?"

She nodded. "I'm sorry."

Spurred by a sense of atonement, she made her way around the bed to where he stood, wordlessly working her way up his shirt buttons in a reverse striptease until they were all closed. Meeting his eyes, she tucked his shirt into his pants and slid his belt around his hips, buckling it without once looking down.

"Georgia," he groaned. "I know you think you're helping, but having a beautiful naked woman put my clothes *on* is the worst thing that's ever happened to me."

"You don't have to go," she whispered.

"I'm trying to decide if it's potentially worth the loss of zillions of investor dollars to throw you back on the bed."

She waited.

"I lose," he said, and he picked her up.

~~~~~~~

With renewed energy, she roused herself from Mark's apartment, rode a rented bicycle to the park, and went for a run, only to discover afterward that her bicycle had been stolen. She'd left it—a gearless, rust-encrusted beast with fat tires—at the edge of a path in the Vondelpark, and either she'd forgotten to lock it or it had been attacked by a thief enterprising enough to carry wire cutters, because it had vanished. She sighed and resigned herself to walking the three kilometers back to the apartment in the Jordaan.

As she made her way along the path in the Vondelpark, a light late-afternoon rain pattered at her face. She trudged along, getting wetter by the second. It had rained often this week, with low banks of clouds sweeping in from the sea, unleashing on the arched bridges and the canals and the long, elegant rows of houses. Everyone here seemed used to it, even though no one used a car in the Jordaan. In Amsterdam, bicycles ruled. No matter where you wanted to go—both in the city and in the countryside—a dedicated bicycle path could get you there.

The rain let up just as she reached Mark's building. A low-slung ceiling of clouds remained, but the reinvigorated sun emerged, backlighting the five-story stone structure and casting a sheet of rosy rays onto the water in the canal. The apartment building rose up in an infinite line of conjoined houses with pointy triangular roofs, fronted by a little strip of sidewalk; beyond that stood one of the ubiquitous lines of parked bicycles, and then the wide green canal. Just along the canal edge floated a line of anchored boats.

As she drew closer to the door, she saw someone waiting on the stoop; her hands flew to her mouth. It looked like . . . but it couldn't be. She still hadn't told Jonah where she was.

"George!" said Jonah grandly, opening his arms wide. Dressed in a slim-fitting two-piece twill suit, he could have passed for a high-powered young executive. "Fancy meeting you here!"

"Jonah?"

"Oh my God, George, have you forgotten me already? Yes! *C'est moi!* In the flesh!"

"How did you get here?"

"Sweet pea, it might have escaped your notice but it is *misting* out here, and I'm wearing my Brioni. Can we have this conversation indoors?"

Jonah stepped in front of her, but she could tell he wasn't actually angry. An eruption of joy bubbled up from . . . wherever it was feelings bubbled up from. Resistance was useless. "Jones!" She tackled him from behind in a bear hug. "Oh! I have so much to tell you."

"Off the Brioni, you deviant," said Jonah in a muffled voice. "Let me at least get up the stairs before you attack me. Which floor are we on?"

"The fifth."

"Naturally," Jonah huffed as they climbed, but his eyes were welling. He swatted at his face clumsily, like a bear. "I was destroyed when I couldn't reach you," he said in a small voice. "I thought maybe you died."

"Oh my God, I am so sorry, Jonah. I—I tried calling you after I was off the grid for a few days, but I thought—here, let's get you inside. How are you? How about a drink? I have plenty of—Jones? What is it?"

"Shut the front door," shouted Jonah, standing stock-still in the middle of the large open room comprising the bulk of the flat. She obliged, slamming the door behind them before realizing Jonah meant it euphemistically. "What. Is. This?"

"This," she said, gesturing proudly, "is my friend's bedsit."

"My ass," said Jonah. "This is no bedsit." His head swiveled, followed in slow motion by the rest of his body, till he'd done a full three-sixty. "One hundred K," he pronounced. "Easy."

"What?"

"Somebody spent at least a hundred Gs on the decor in here, probably just on the art alone. Oh my sainted aunt. Is that macaroon thing a Will Cotton? George, what is going on? Are you a kept woman?"

"No."

"I googled the Jordaan, sweet pea." He removed his shoes and set them by the door. "You can't get into this part of town anymore unless you're a hedgie or a Saudi or something. You call me from the airport or somewhere and then you disappear without a word—"

"Technically, I did share words—"

"—an email with thirty-three words to be exact, I counted them, and—"

"—and I texted—"

"Twice." Jonah advanced on her, wagging a finger. "You texted two, maybe three, times. I texted you *seventy-seven* times before I realized you'd been abducted and killed."

"That's not ri—"

"And"—he stabbed her in the center of her chest with his still-extended finger—"now after I've been through all seven stages of grief—"

"Five—"

"—seven, because my grief has extra stages, I find that you are not abducted and killed, you are just ghosting me. You are ghosting me while you party down in freaking Amsterdam in somebody's mega-posh apartment."

"I can explain. And also you have to tell me how you found me. I didn't even know I was going to be staying here."

"I called the office and asked your PA for your address."

"Liar. He has no idea where I am."

"Geo-tagging in social media?"

"Not possible. I haven't opened my Facebook account once since I've been here."

"I knew it." Jonah fanned himself with both hands.

"And Instagram. And Twitter. I told you: I'm off the grid. So stop lying. How did you find me?"

Jonah's outraged expression battled with a sly smile. "You spill first, babe."

She beckoned toward a mohair-covered daybed, strewn with cashmere throws in various flaming colors: fuchsia, orange, lime. "This could take a while. Why don't you join me on the divan? I'll make cocktails."

"This thing looks like a crayon factory vomited on a cotton ball," he said, but, obediently, he removed his suit jacket and flopped onto the mohair concoction. "Oh, that's nice," he admitted. Propping himself up on an elbow, he surveyed the apartment again as she bustled around the kitchen preparing drinks.

"Okay. Spill it. How did you find this place?"

"It belongs to the head of some business group in California," she said, handing Jonah a Kentucky Mule in a copper cup. He gulped it down and handed it right back, so she went to make another. "I met their CFO, Mark, on the plane."

In a petulant voice: "Mark?"

She settled next to Jonah on the divan. "I'll tell you about him in a minute. He's letting me stay here. I'm really sorry for ghosting you, Jones." A swell of shame rose in her gut: with all his debt, Jonah could not afford the exorbitant expense of traipsing across the globe after her. Not to mention she'd left him in the midst of whatever evil shit was going down at work.

"Jonah, I'm sorry," she said again, despite the inadequacy of the words. She lay her head in his lap. "Do you want to fill me in about the clinic?"

"No, bitch." Jonah stroked her hair lovingly. "Not right now."

"I mean it. I am melting in remorse for being so hard to reach."

"Well," said Jonah, validated. "Go on."

"You suffered through no fault of your own, despite being the finest friend, and the, the . . . *handsomest* individual ever to grace the planet. If you'll find it in your heart to forgive me, I swear I'll mend my ways. I'll be the most devoted, the most grateful—"

"Okay, I forgive you," whispered Jonah. He leaned forward to plant a kiss on her forehead. "Just please don't ever do this again, G. I've never felt as bad in my life as I did when I thought you were dead."

"I won't," she said, adding softly, "Are you okay?"

He leaned across the divan to seize an orange mohair-covered pillow and tucked it under her head. "That's better," he said, flexing his legs. "You have an absurdly heavy brain."

"I know," she said immodestly. She reached up and poked the underside of his chin. "I'm serious. Are you okay? I keep hearing weird things."

Jonah directed a baleful stare at the wall. "Look," he said. "Let's talk about this later, okay? I'm only here for a long weekend, and I want to forget about everything and have some fun."

"Okay, babe," she said. "I know you spent a fortune to get here. Can I float you some of it back?"

"Absolutely not, George. This is worth a little more debt. Let's go party."

"Look," she said, seized by sudden awkwardness. "About tonight. It seems I am, somehow, sort of involved with someone. I know that's a lame excuse, so I'm not even going to . . ." She paused for a second as she debated how to describe Mark. A hookup? A love interest? The most intriguing man she'd met in years?

Jonah, meanwhile, had fixated on the middle of her sentence. "What did you just say? Involved with what?"

"Involved. With a man. I met a man. I know this seems abrupt, but we really hit it off. I haven't been to the conference as much as I should have."

Jonah sat upright, dislodging her. *"What?"*

"First you tell me how you found me," she said, "and then I'll tell you about him. I met him on the plane on the way over."

"Were you sitting next to him?"

"No, there was an emergency and I saved his life."

Jonah's mouth fell open. "Somebody had a urologic emergency on an airplane?"

"No, you dope. I possess other medical knowledge beyond urology. As a matter of fact, this man had been poisoned. Oh, and he's handsome and smart and rich."

Jonah nearly choked in an effort to get out too many words at once. Georgia held up a firm hand. "You first."

Jonah flung up his arms in surrender. "I used Find My Phone," he admitted. "You have the world's stupidest iCloud sign-in, George, it took me thirty seconds to guess it. I didn't think of it until you'd been dead—until you'd been gone—for a day or two, but then I did, and I watched your phone. It kept coming back to this address."

Georgia blinked, impressed at his resourcefulness, but then checked that: Jonah had mad computer skills. She wondered if he'd been reading her email.

"I am NOT reading your email," said Jonah, reading her mind.

"Okay."

"I'm not. Or I'd already know you'd found love."

She'd better cough up some information. "I didn't say I'd found love, exactly," she offered, launching into the bizarre story of how she'd met Mark, when, right on cue, her phone rang. For a beat neither of them reacted, and then they both lunged for it; Georgia because she knew it would be Mark, and Jonah because he saw Georgia perk up and came to the correct conclusion about who the caller might be. She moved first but Jonah's sprightlier physique got him there a fraction of a second before her.

"Hello!" he crowed into the phone. "This is Georgia's friend Jonah. And who might this be?"

Leaping off the divan, he crossed the room in a couple paces, planting himself on the other side of the partition dividing the bed area from the living area. Georgia feinted to one side and then flung herself in the opposite direction, but Jonah wasn't fooled; he scooted around his side of the divider, staying a few feet ahead of her. He *mmm-hmm*'ed and grinned as Mark spoke, at one point erupting into a small but excited shriek.

"Gimme the phone," Georgia hissed.

"Oh really?" drawled Jonah, bounding away from her. "Oh really? Tonight?" He trilled in delight. "I'm wide open."

"Mark!" she shouted. "Mark, can you hear me?"

"Bahahahah," said Jonah. He snickered at her, merrily skidding out of reach again. She plunked herself back down on the divan in capitulation, battling a moronic, creeping smile as she listened to him talk. After several more minutes, he handed over the phone.

"So, that was Jonah," she said.

"So I gathered," said Mark. "He's charming."

"You have low charm standards, apparently."

"Nonsense. I can see why you like him. He thought you were dead, you know."

"Don't you start too."

"Sorry. Listen: my meeting is running long. I'm going to be another couple of hours. But I'd love to meet you for a nightcap if I can." His voice betrayed a hint of uncertainty. "Is that okay?"

"As long as you don't mind Jonah joining us. I'll make reservations and text you."

"I've been hoping I'd get to meet him."

She hung up and looked at Jonah. "Well," she said, "looks like you'll be meeting Mark tonight."

8

BADASS GANGSTA AMNESIAC

Jonah's eyes glittered. "I can't wait to meet him. Congrats on finally renouncing this abstainal shit."

"What are you talking about? I was just seeing somebody."

Jonah raised a fist and dramatically extended his fingers, one by one. "Kari. Lazaro. Jackie. Biff. The hot Scottish one who proposed to you, what's his name, Ian?"

"Angus." Georgia paused; her relationship with Angus had ended right around the time she met Jonah, and it was possible she had understated the impact the implosion of her engagement had had on her. "And you're just making stuff up. There was no one named Biff."

"Angus! George, I've seen pictures and Angus was *en fuego*! You could have settled down with that guy and instead you squashed him like a grape. I'm feeling like I should try to establish some solidarity with Mark so he doesn't go into this thing ignorant of the trail of prospective spouses littering your past."

"Jones, forget Angus. He was a pig. And Ryan dumped me, not the other way around. I'm not exactly the runaway bride."

"You drove him away."

Wisely, she chose to ignore the bait. She hadn't consciously done anything to run Ryan off—it wasn't her fault if he couldn't sustain an interesting conversation—and if anyone had deserved to be squashed like a grape it was Angus, but getting into that now would be pointless. If you engaged him head-on, Jonah was as tenacious as a viper, but she knew how to handle him. Like a wayward toddler, he responded well to redirection.

"Hungry?" she asked brightly, not bothering to wait for a reply. Jonah was *always* hungry. Feeling energized, almost zippy, she grabbed her cell phone to make a reservation at a restaurant in the next neighborhood that came highly recommended by locals.

"We have some time until they can seat us, but we can grab a drink on the way," she said. "Go for a walk?"

"Coffee bar," whooped Jonah. "I'll freshen up!" He ran to the bathroom and returned a few minutes later with his black hair resculpted, his dark eyes obscured by metallic aviators, his top three shirt buttons undone, and his jacket tossed over one shoulder.

"You are so gorgeous, Jones."

"Stop fawning. You know I've had a lifelong wish to visit a coffee bar in Amsterdam."

"Leading the way," she said. In truth, she felt a little frightened of the coffee shops, having heard some horror stories. Coffee shops in Amsterdam, as *tout le monde* knew, served not coffee but weed. Pharmaceutical-grade weed, from the warnings she'd received: every American expat in the country had a graphic tale of bumbling into a coffee bar expecting a mild appetite enhancer *à la* the marijuana of the 1990s, only to awaken three days later in the red-light district with vicious rugburn and shaved eyebrows. She'd just have to be very careful about what she ordered, and more to the point, what Jonah ordered. They both had a tendency to overdo things.

"Are you sure you want to do this?" she asked as they neared the closest coffee shop to the apartment, an unobtrusive green-paneled storefront with absolutely no signage indicating what it was, other than the name, written, thankfully, in English: BOTANICAL DEFENSE LAB.

"They're not allowed to advertise," she added, as Jonah doubtfully side-eyed the exterior.

"When in Rome, George! I'm all in. It's legal and it's no worse than a couple Kentucky Mules, *n'est-ce pas?* Do you think they were aiming for the color of bud with all this drab paneling?"

They stood in the front of the shop, intimidated, as their eyes adjusted to the dim interior. A few people sat at little metal tables, their posture languid, pecking with desultory interest at laptops. Some kind of frenetic music—it sounded like Swedish hip-hop—pounded in the background. A wide bar ran the length of the back wall, behind which stood a scrawny guy in an apron. He was the antithesis of languidity, hammering away at the air as though he was under attack from a flock of invisible biting insects. After a moment, Georgia realized he was playing the air drums; either that, or he was having some sort of unusual seizure. In any case, he didn't appear to be stoned.

"Where's the menu?" whispered Jonah.

"I think you have to ask for it," Georgia whispered back.

"Menu, please," said Jonah to the seizing weed dispenser, who whirled sideways, lurching himself over to a shelf under the counter, where he extricated a plasticized piece of paper. They studied it, bewildered; nothing on the menu—hundreds of items—had a comprehensible description.

"I think it must be like the Kentucky Derby," said Jonah, "you just pick a horse based on the name." To the counter guy: "I'll have some Badass Gangsta Amnesiac. Please."

After a confusing interlude in which the counter guy kept pointing to something written in Dutch on the back of the menu, they finally understood they needed to specify a delivery route: rolled or bong. They opted for bong, afraid the Dutch guy would expect competence at rolling a joint, which neither of them possessed, and then realized after they'd been handed a baggie full of drugs and an oddly shaped blue plastic contraption that they would need to purchase a lighter.

Adjourning to a small metal table, they messed with the bong until they figured it out.

"I feel nothing," Jonah said. "I think we just got ripped off. He could probably tell we were tourists who can't tell the difference, so he gave us a forty-dollar bag of oregano and kept all the ganja for himself."

"No, that's—"

"Do you feel anything?"

Georgia eyed the empty bong. "Not really," she admitted.

"Okay," said Jonah, standing, "let's bolt. I don't feel baked but I do feel hungry."

He held the door, ushering her back out onto the street. She stepped onto the curb, alert for any change in perception, but the curb remained reassuringly solid. "Which way do we head to get to the restaurant?" asked Jonah, both hands splayed against his flat stomach.

"I think it's that wa—yahhhhh." A percussive *thwoomph* echoed through her body, signaling some seismic change in her temporal-spatial awareness. The world suddenly went cattywampus, everything slightly askew. Also, she had the dizzying sense that her head was very, very large.

She peered anxiously at Jonah, who peered back at her, equally concerned. Oh God, it must be true. Her head had exploded. By contrast, Jonah's head seemed to have shrunk to tragically small proportions, cemented on the end of his stalky neck like a nearly consumed lollipop. She reached out to touch him and flinched backward as a bike whizzed by.

"WHAT WAS THAT?" shrieked Jonah, grabbing her. He whipped his diminutive head in the direction of the departed bicycle, the whites of his eyes showing underneath his irises. Some clinical portion of her brain whirred to life to diagnose his condition: Microcephaly with Thyroid Storm. Also possible dementia. Damn, she was smart. She reverted to layman's terms, preparing the explanation she'd offer him: Crazy Shrunken Head with Associated Glandular Problem. *Not good,* she'd say wisely, *not good*. She looked at him again. Something about the way he was tossing his little head around reminded her of Mark; for a second, she was awash in nostalgia. Lovely, lovely Mark, with his terrible poisoning problem on the galley floor. So helpless.

A daisy chain of bikers blurred by. "INCOMING," screamed Jonah, cowering with his hands above his head. "WE HAVE TO GET OUT OF THE LINE OF FIRE."

Georgia was the picture of calm. "Sure," she said. "We'll just go to the restaurant, as planned. We can regroup there."

"FALL OUT," barked Jonah. He marched off in one direction as she drifted in the other. He pivoted, coming after her. "This way," he hissed, looking over his shoulder.

She stared at him in surprise. "How do you know?"

"Keep your head down," he said. "Or I'll notify the relevant authorities." Embarrassed, she reached up to her giant balloon head, but there was no containing it as it floated along. She cringed. She could feel the webby vascular supply of her central nervous system glowing with the raw energy required to maintain such pure intelligence. Her worries and inadequacies disintegrated in a puff of smoke, subsumed by her brilliance.

They headed off, Jonah skulking and Georgia alternating between a dreamy traipse and a nervous lurch. After they'd walked for an indeterminate amount of time—minutes? hours? eons?—it occurred to her that Jonah, their leader, could not possibly know where he was going, since she'd never told him the name of the restaurant. Also he did not speak Dutch—nor did she—and furthermore, Jonah, who tended to get lost even on the familiar streets of Charleston, had never been to Amsterdam before. She reached for his arm and he instantly whirled around.

"WHAT WAS THAT?"

She recognized, with her fearsome intelligence, that this was a phrase she might shortly find wearisome. However, it was important to stay unified. "We need to regroup," she said.

They found a doorway and huddled, clutching one another desperately, peering out at the closest street sign. The rain had started again, pelting sideways in bullety little bursts that were not conducive to Jonah's mental stability. "If only we had a map," she said, forlorn. "I don't want to die in this doorway."

Jonah smacked his tiny head. "A taxi!" he shouted. "They're usually conflict-neutral and they'll recognize the name of the rendezvous." He marched out to the edge of the street and stuck out a confident hand. A bike raced by and he screamed, running back to the doorway. "I'm afraid we're *gonnahaftahoofit*," he said, panting.

She narrowed her eyes, suddenly suspicious. Was that a street name? Or Dutch slang for *about to die*? Since when did Jonah speak Dutch?

"We are going to have to hoof it," he said, enunciating each word exaggeratedly.

"Well . . ." Georgia didn't want to admit she had no idea where they were; Jonah was relying on her. "Right." She nodded, hoping to look knowledgeable. "By any chance, did you pick up a map at the place?"

"Did I pick up a map from the weed store?"

"Yes."

"No. But why don't you just look on your phone?"

Her phone! She pulled it out of her bag, delighted to have rediscovered her external brain. Wise though she might be, no one person could possibly know everything. There was so much . . . *stuff* . . . in the universe, so many facts and natural laws and bodies of accumulated knowledge, so many twinkling frozen nebulae and exploding, dying stars, so many eerie forces and bizarre quantum worlds that even she could not . . . she could not . . . where was she going with this?

"Georgia?" Jonah waved a hand in front of her face. "Where are you?"

Where was she? She looked around. There was something strangely familiar about this doorway, with its swinging wooden sign . . . she scrunched up her cheeks, pursing her lips, sounding out the words on the sign. *Boh-tan-i-cal-De-fenz-Lab.* Through the window she could just make out a blurry octopus flailing behind a bar.

"Jones," she said. "I think we are still at the coffee shop."

~~~~~~

The restaurant, when they finally reached it, glowed like a spaceship through the deepening gloom of the wet evening. Warm light spilled from the large plate glass windows overlooking the street, through which they could see animated diners raising wineglasses and twirling forks, leaning toward one another across tables laden with an array of unidentifiable but mouthwatering dishes. Even through the glass, a wash of sound reached their ears; the buzz of a hundred conversations, the clinking of cutlery, a little throb of jazz. Jonah stood with his nose almost pressed against the glass, staring at the oblivious diners with a childlike yearning. "It looks so nice in there," he said.

"Yes," Georgia agreed dreamily. "So nice."

"We could go in there and eat food too," suggested Jonah, a tentative note marring his voice. Somewhere between the Botanical Defense Lab and their present location, his delusional military paranoia had ebbed, replaced with a docile acquiescence Georgia found even more unnerving.

"Okay," she said, motioning to him. "Lead the way."

Once again, Jonah proved to be a poor leader. For a while he stood rooted, watching people eat, but when he finally roused himself to action he couldn't find the door. The big windows extended along the entire storefront, broken at intervals by small staircases—three or four steps—leading to landings between the windows. Immense old doors topped the landings, but when Jonah rattled the tarnished brass handles, nothing happened. They were locked, or they were decorative, or possibly they had nothing to do with the restaurant and opened into somewhere else. Georgia and Jonah retreated back down to the sidewalk to ponder their options. Perhaps one of the windows was actually a door?

This idea held promise, but after they'd furtively pressed their hands all over the glass, trying to find some hidden release, they had to admit they were stymied. They'd begun to garner some odd looks too, from people inside who were clearly wondering why two freakshows were standing outside groping the windows. How had all these people gotten inside when there were no doors? Frustrated and hungry, they positioned themselves in front of the central window, huddled together for warmth.

Another couple, hands entwined, glided past them and disappeared. Georgia returned her attention to the window, fixated on someone who'd just been presented a plate of steaming food. A moment later, the couple from the street reappeared inside the restaurant, shedding their overcoats and shaking the rain off their boots. The woman tilted her head back and laughed at something her companion said, revealing a row of even, white teeth. Georgia felt faint with hunger.

"The next time someone goes by, we follow them," she said. "Okay?"

"Okay!" Jonah said agreeably. He looked delighted to have a plan.

They waited, shivering. After a million years had passed, another couple finally materialized out of the mist, and Jonah sprang to attention. The couple strode past, unsuspecting, murmuring in Dutch. They passed all the windows and all the faux doors on the landings, reaching the end of the restaurant without going in. Georgia deflated in savage disappointment. These people were headed somewhere else.

Except they weren't. As they passed the last window, they vanished from the street. Jonah and Georgia looked at one another, befuddled. They sped up, hurrying to the spot where the people had disappeared, and discovered to their astonishment a narrow alley opening onto the street a few feet from where they'd been standing. Easily visible, just around the corner, a large door was just swinging shut.

"We tell no one about this," she instructed Jonah with a fierce look.

"What happens in Amsterdam stays in Amsterdam," he said cheerfully.

His paranoia had totally vanished now, along with his nervousness, and he seemed to be in an expansive mood. Despite being late for the reservation, they were seated quickly, and in no time at all, they were feasting on a smorgasbord of items selected at random from the Dutch menu, Jonah barely chewing as he happily recounted the many deficiencies in Georgia's love life.

"Angus, now," he said. "I guess I do remember why you had to rid yourself of Angus. That was unfortunate, to say the least. But did you have to ditch Murph? And Mortimer? And Coop?"

They had definitely entered phase two of being stoned: Georgia's sides ached from laughing. She'd always known Jonah to be something of a raconteur, but now she found herself bowled over by his wit, his charm, his ferocious intelligence. It was as if he'd opened his mouth and a stream of jewels poured out, his words transforming into sparkling gems of every variety: diamonds, emeralds, sapphires, rubies, pearls. They glittered in the air, small precious words, each shining with razor-faceted brilliance. She marveled at her luck in finding this friendship, this remarkable individual, this rare, rare treasure of a man. Never in the history of humankind had a conversation been so scintillating, never had a mere mortal spun such tales of bravery and insight and hilarity and poignancy. How perceptive he was about her! If only he'd been managing her social life all this time! She ached to tell him of her adoration, but she, by contrast, had become somewhat tongue-tied. No matter: rarely could she get a word in edgewise. Still, she managed to convey to Jonah something of the last few days with Mark: how, whenever he wasn't working, they'd drifted about the city, visiting parks and galleries and museums in the mornings, spending the afternoons in bed in a rapturous haze, supported by the shocking intimacy that had arisen and consumed them both despite her reservations. Or at least that's what she hoped she was conveying. Jonah was so excited it was hard to tell.

A server appeared, bringing another round of drinks. Jonah tossed back his, but Georgia took her time, treating herself to small decorous sips. The last thing she needed today was more alcohol, plus she wanted to prolong this evening, this moment, this mood. Across the table, Jonah's face was shining, colored by his high spirits; his black eyes sparkled. He leaned forward, elbows resting on the table. "I love you, George," he said.

"I love you more," she managed.

He signaled in the direction of the waiter. "Check's on me."

"No, of course n—"

He held up a hand, imperious. "I insist. It's the least I can do."

"The least you can do? I'm the one who owes you. Something's going down at work and I left you."

As soon as the words left her mouth she regretted them. Why had she reminded him of his job when he'd been so happy tonight? Her brain, still somewhat impacted by the drugs and the alcohol, promptly conjured up a pleasant vision in which she hit the pause button, freezing them both in their current states. She followed this action with a couple juddering strikes at the rewind function until she'd unspooled time, back to the perfect moment before *I left you* had fouled the air. Voilà!

Jonah shared no similar vision. Having finished his own drink, he reached across the table for hers, draining it in one gulp. "Ah," he said. "You had to come, George. Bad timing and all that"—he waved an arm around vaguely—"but I truly didn't want you to cancel your trip."

"I should have planned for you to come too. I should have paid."

"I wouldn't have let you spend the money."

"Nonsense." Rather than bring up Jonah's lack of money, she mentioned her surfeit of it. "I have plenty."

Jonah perked up, energized by the mention of their long-running argument over the remuneration of surgeons versus primary care doctors. "Yeah: I know what I'm making and I'm sure it's about half of whatever you're making. Which makes sense, when you think about it: I treat the entire individual over their entire life span, from cradle to grave, head to toe, inside and out, heart and soul, and mind and body. And you treat penises. Priorities."

"That's unfair," she said, but she gave him a fond smile. Jonah had a point, but he knew as well as she did there was more to her job than penises: urology was a platform incorporating both medical and surgical treatment of multiple diseases in the young and the old, and both males and females. Not to mention her extra years of residency.

"I can still pay for your trip."

"No," he said, thrusting out a mulish lip. "I have my pride."

"Would your pride allow it if I paid for dinner?"

"That would be acceptable." He looked around for the waiter. "As long as it's on you, I may have another drink."

"Dude. You are going to float out of here."

He waved his glass at the server and turned back to her, lowering his voice. "Should we talk about it?"

"Talk about what?" For a confused moment she thought he was alluding to his alcohol intake.

"My patients. The clinic."

"Oh! Yes. Yes, I do want to hear about that."

He stared with moody absorption into the dregs of his drink glass. She waited, afraid he'd change his mind if she prodded him. Behind him, the rest of the restaurant carried on as if things were fine, everyone serenely engaged in the aggressive act of living. Eventually Jonah sighed and twisted sideways in his seat.

"Well," he said. "I found out what they're doing."

9

THE MUNITIONS OF THE GAY ARMY

She thought of Frieda Myers Delacroix, the trans woman she'd seen leaving the clinic. "The clinic is getting rid of all the transgender patients, aren't they?"

Jonah jerked his head: *Yes*. "At first, they kept it on the down-low," he said, his back straightening. "But now the whole thing's blowing up. It's become obvious most of the patients being asked to leave are trans. A few others too, including a couple of my gay teens. But all of the trans patients are gone."

Jonah's medical practice was the kind of group where your doctor knew you, literally, inside and out. He'd been made for this sort of thing: by nature gregarious and inquisitive, the professional opportunity to be all up in everyone's business suited him perfectly. As he often reminded Georgia, his patient population ran the gamut from squalling newborns to non–ambulatory old people. He sometimes saw patients after hours if it suited their schedules better, and he stopped by the nursing home once a week, his visitations so invigorating that the home had eventually hired a meditation specialist to try to settle everyone down after his departure.

But as good as he was with adults, Jonah's special gift was teenagers.

About half his practice consisted of either angsty heterosexual teens or members of Charleston's young LGBTQ population. Adolescents flocked to him: the ubiquitous Charleston blondes, the sort with social pedigrees and bright clothing, but also a more anguished crew—the black-clad, multiply-pierced Goth clichés; the cutters; the eating-disordered, with their weaponized clavicles jutting up, bladelike, through their shirt necks. And, of course, the gay and transgender and nonbinary kids, not to mention the gay and transgender and nonbinary adults. They, more than anyone else, loved him.

"What reason are they giving these patients?"

"None. They're just told they need to find another provider. The letter implies I'm leaving the practice, so people started asking me about it. I went to the scheduler and checked to see who all had gotten letters, and, yeah. Sure enough, everyone getting a letter is queer. And they're kicking all the trans patients out of my practice for sure. Every single one of them is gone."

"Jonah, what does Beezon say about this?"

He didn't respond. A throaty sound escaped him as his hands rose and encountered a twin set of tears coursing their way down his cheeks, followed by a look of horror flashing across his face. With a grunt, he pushed aside his chair and bolted from the table.

She'd never seen Jonah cry, at least not full-on, with actual falling tears. She'd seen him angry on occasion, and he got agitated on a near-daily basis by virtually everything, but the sight of him crying left her bewildered and aching. Their check hadn't yet been delivered, but she wrenched a wad of American bills from her bag and flung it on the table, hoping it would be sufficient to cover the bill.

She rose, taking a step in the direction of the restaurant's bathrooms—presuming that's where Jonah had gone—then sat again. She couldn't very well blunder into a men's bathroom, especially in a foreign country. She hovered for a moment, fretting, until a cascade of concern forced her to her feet again. To hell with waiting.

First: some reconnaissance. She checked out the women's restroom.

To her relief, it was a single room with a toilet and a door that locked, rather than a multi-stalled communal space. She exited, and, trying to project the air of a non-pervert, listened at the door of the men's room. Total silence. Hoping Jonah hadn't bolted secondary to a bout of genuine GI distress, she tried the door. It was locked. She knocked again.

No answer.

She knocked a third time. This time there was a brief hesitation, followed by a chirping voice: "Be right out!"

"Jonah," she said, keeping her voice low. "Let me in."

The door creaked open an inch. Jonah's face, streaked and blotchy, peeked out. She handed him a breath mint from her bag, the only comfort item she could manage under the circumstances. Jonah regarded her with a half-sorrowful, half-quizzical look.

"I wanted to help," she said. "Pickings were slim." A tear formed at the corner of Jonah's eye, and before she could stop herself, she dabbed it. "Here, now," she offered. "I'm no ophthalmologist, but you seem to be having some kind of facial leakage problem." Easing the door wider, she stepped inside. The bathroom was tiny and ancient: walled in stone, with a mottled mirror and one of those U-shaped European toilets.

"Ah," he mumbled. "Thanks. Lacrimal duct malfunction, I think."

"Maybe you should see someone. It's kind of a social issue, isn't it, to lose control so spectacularly?"

For a second she thought this had been the wrong thing to say. Suddenly, inexplicably, Jonah grinned through his tears. "Shut up, George."

"Ah, that's better! For a minute I was worried you were experiencing an emotion. It's unlike you."

"I'm good."

She shifted, lodging a hip against the small sink. "Do you want to talk?"

He nodded. "I do, but thinking of this is not the best way to get myself under control. Hold up." He spiraled a hand through the air, fanning his face. "Whew. The more I try to banish her, the more she keeps swimming up in my mind."

"Who?"

"Frieda Myers Delacroix."

Georgia nodded, and then, recalling the details of the weird encounter with Frieda Myers in the patient parking lot, nodded more fervently. "Is that what triggered Beezon? Did Frieda Myers proposition the mayor in your waiting room?"

"Nobody propositioned anybody. Beezon told me they'd been getting complaints about 'him,' that some of the other patients were finding the waiting room to be an uncomfortable environment when 'he' was there. He also said some of the clinic employees felt they were compromising their beliefs by taking care of 'him.' Oh, and you'll love this: it's not even just the queer patients. They're talking about a clinic policy allowing providers to stop providing birth control to female patients, because that also compromises the beliefs of these same employees."

"What?" Georgia yelled. "What? I haven't heard anything about this."

"You will, I guess," he said. "I heard it's coming. Anyway, Beezon asked me to 'adjust my patient population.' I asked him how in the world I was supposed to know—no, how my *scheduler* was supposed to know—if somebody was undesirable when they called to make an appointment, and he gave me this prissy look and said it might be obvious from their voice. I said hell no. He said fine, he'd talk to the scheduler about it himself.

"It turns out they told Frieda Myers she's no longer welcome at the clinic. Andreas called me. She hasn't gotten out of bed since they booted her."

"She's my patient too," Georgia cried. "They can't just ban her."

She stopped talking. Two bright spots of red on Jonah's cheeks highlighted his skin, pasty and stark against his black hair. She reached a hand to his face.

"Jonah. How does this even make sense when they know you're gay yourself? Plus, it's illegal."

For the first time she saw incredulity flare in his eyes. "Nope. Nope, nope, nope, Georgia, it is in fact perfectly legal in our state to refuse medical care to someone because they're transgender or gay. For that matter, it is perfectly legal to fire someone because they're gay."

"That can't be ri—"

"It is right, because I called my lawyer to confirm as soon as I left the room. They have every legal right to do this."

"You have a lawyer?"

"Yes, and as soon as Beezon said he dismissed Frieda Myers I informed him and those Dementors who work with him that I would gnaw off my own arm and eat it before I'd be a party to any more discriminatory patient firings. Furthermore, I said, he could anticipate the wrath of hell descending upon him if my patients did not receive a full apology and an open-armed invitation to return, and I told him I have a vicious, brilliant, ruthless attorney who is fully prepared to kill on command."

"Good."

"Yeah. Except that's a lie: Terz"—one of Jonah's friends, a patent lawyer—"has a friend who does some kind of discrimination law, but no one in their right mind is ever going to refer to Stewie as a killer. Unless he kills by talking people to death. But anyway."

"How did Beezon respond?"

"Let's just say he successfully contained his unease at the threat," Jonah said. "If anything, he looked thrilled. And he countered with a bluff of his own. Or at least I thought it was a bluff."

"And?"

"He gave me a totally putrid choice: either I inform certain patients I can no longer care for them because doing so would violate the moral standards of the practice; or I can inform *all* of my patients I can no longer be their doctor because *I* have violated the standards of the practice. We're meeting again sometime next week so I can give them my decision."

"He literally spelled out which patients?"

"Sure," he said, running a hand along the length of his face. "The ones like me."

If you possessed some degree of power, there were a million subtle ways you could harass a gay man who worked with you. You could leave the room every time he walked in; you could, in his presence, audibly muse about the train-wreck lives of certain gay actors, or the pedophilic tendencies of gay priests; you could offer ostentatious displays of interest in everyone else's spouses and significant others and dates, but never mention his. Or you could ramp it up a notch: take away his assigned parking space; claim budget cuts require him to share his PA with two new physicians; assign him to some bullshit committee that meets at seven o'clock on Friday nights. None of this could be traced to overt homophobia; all of it was easily explained away. You could cut, and cut, and cut, until you forced him out. And if he was stubborn enough to stay? Then you could fire his patients. And you could do all this, without worrying you'd go to jail or pay a fine, because it wasn't uniformly illegal in the United States to discriminate.

To Jonah, this wasn't a personality conflict or a partisan thing or a manifestation of sexual politics. In his case, adhering to the guidelines of someone else's religious freedom meant two things: he would lose his job, and his patients would lose their doctor. Unable to think of what to say, Georgia pulled Jonah to her, wrapping her arms around him until he dropped his head onto her shoulder. They stood, silently, until someone, muttering in incomprehensible Dutch, began banging on the door.

~~~~~~

By the time they made it out of the bathroom, they'd regained their composure. Their table had been cleared during their absence, but the server caught them to say he'd already poured another drink; did they still want it? Jonah carried it to the bar, an ancient piece of carved wood next to a fireplace. It was cozy and comfortable, the polished wood of the bar shining in warm yellow light from sconces and the hot, flickering light of the fire, and after a few moments of silence they did what they always did when something was bothering them: laugh about it.

"You know, I don't think Beezon has thought this through," Jonah said. "You really do not want to rile up queer folk."

"Or what?"

"Or they will unleash upon you a volley of witty insults on Twitter."

Georgia nodded wisely. "Death by a thousand tweets."

"And if that fails, they will create memes."

"*Lacerating* memes."

"And GIFs."

He started to say something else about the munitions of the gay army but paused mid-word, staring over Georgia's shoulder. She sensed a presence before turning to catch sight of him: Mark, at the door to the restaurant. If they hadn't been so messed up, surely they would have remembered earlier: he'd been supposed to join them. The table, set for three, had reflected his absence, and even the waiter, she now remembered, had made some allusion to waiting before they ordered. But none of that had registered; the two of them, in their self-absorbed, drug-addled stupor, had simply forgotten about him.

Walking in their direction, Mark hadn't spotted them yet, which gave them the opportunity to study his face. As he drew closer, Georgia could make out his attentive, interested expression.

Jonah's eyes widened. "That's him, isn't it?"

"That's him."

"My stars!" Jonah whispered excitedly. "He's forty feet tall."

"Lower your voice," she hissed, but kept her gaze on Mark.

Jonah looked at her looking at Mark, and then swiveled in his seat, a hand on his hip. "Well, well, well."

"What?"

"I'm surprised he hasn't burst into flame. There're, like, twenty smoldering holes in his chest from the way you're looking at him."

"Jonah, shut up right now."

"I'm serious. What is this look on your face? I've never seen it before."

"Jonah, I would hate to have to destroy you."

He raised his hands in mock surrender. "Okay, okay. I'll behave. But I am *highly* intrigued."

Mark looked up and saw them. "Georgia!"

"Hey," she said, unable to hide her pleasure as he approached. Jonah stood to greet him, politely bowing his head before raising it up. And up. Georgia watched as he and Mark sized each other up, in the midst of the subtle jockeying that occurs whenever any two men meet. Jonah, who stood two inches taller than she did, now had his head tilted nearly all the way back as he regarded Mark.

"This is my friend Jonah."

"I've heard so much about you," said Mark. "I'm Mark McInniss, Georgia's new friend."

"Jonah Tsukada," Jonah said, adding after a beat: "I'm her beloved."

"Is everything okay? You guys look a bit tired."

This comment was aimed at Georgia, but Jonah's hand fluttered by his bloodshot eyes. "I'm so sorry," he said. "Too much ganja. I seem to be somewhat . . . dampened."

She wrapped an arm around him. "We hit a bar before dinner."

"It was gruesome."

"Awful. We got lost, and then there was an incident—"

"—with the door of the restaurant—"

"—and then we got a little emotional . . ."

"I see," Mark said, a perplexed look on his face as they all took seats. Georgia and Jonah did that to people sometimes: the syncopated rhythm of their speech, their obvious closeness, the unadulterated fun they had in each other's company—all these things had bothered previous boyfriends of both of them, even though neither of them, of course, could possibly present as a romantic rival. But Mark didn't seem threatened, just alert. He shifted his attention back to her.

"You're easy to spot, Red," he said, cupping a hand at the base of her scalp, his fingers trailing through her hair. "Even if you weren't wearing a lot of sparkles."

She smoothed out her hair and then her sequined halter.

Jonah imitated her, brushing back his silky, inky hair. "Did you know eighty percent of the world has black hair?"

"Jonah is half-Japanese," Georgia said to Mark, as if this explained anything.

"I'm half-Irish," Mark said, pointing to his own dark hair, and then, gesturing to her: "Where do you think you got your red hair?"

"Autosomal recessive mutation on the MC1R gene, probably."

"Okay!" Jonah clapped his hands together. "Enough chitchat. Let's go out. Mark? You in?"

Mark stood, pushing back his chair and extending an arm to Georgia. "Absolutely."

They glided through the restaurant and into the cool night. The intermittent rain had eased, and in place of the low clouds hung a massive golden moon. Soft moonlight mingled with the glowing orbs of the cast-iron streetlights, flicking effervescent daubs of light onto the dark water of the canals and illuminating everyone's faces with an alien radiance. The ancient bridges, the cobblestone streets, the couples strolling arm in arm— all of it combined to produce an atmosphere of such romanticism it felt almost contrived, like a scene in a Hollywood movie about Amsterdam.

They ambled along in no particular direction, Mark offering cheerful getting-to-know-you conversation and Jonah exercising previously undemonstrated powers of discretion, in that he failed to mention any of Georgia's prior romantic debacles as he shamelessly prodded Mark for personal information. She listened with interest: she and Mark had engaged in several of the obligatory *tell-me-about-your-life* chats one tends to engage in on dates, but they hadn't gotten to the point of exchanging complete biographies. However, Jonah failed to unearth anything outrageous, extracting from Mark stuff she already knew: he'd been born in a middle-class home in Cincinnati, he'd attended business school at Duke University, he'd never been married.

As they moved farther from the restaurant, the noise and light increased, little by little, until eventually they found themselves standing near a conglomeration of streets throbbing with a carnival atmosphere. The moon, chastened, retreated behind a wall of neon.

"Oh," she said. "The red-light district."

"Yep," said Mark. "I guess you have to see it at least once, right?"

An alley reared up in front of them. This was where romance and ambience came to die, apparently, replaced by some sordid, businesslike approximation of lust and at least ten thousand dopey, gawking tourists. Catching up to Georgia, Jonah picked up her hand and squeezed it as they passed the lighted showcases of the prostitutes. To their right, a young woman with coarse blond hair and broad Slavic cheekbones appeared on the verge of dying of boredom, standing in her underwear in her glass-walled cubicle, aggressive hipbones jutting out all over the place, a cell phone to her ear. Jonah studied her.

"I'm not feeling it," he said.

"You're gay, Jonah."

"So? I appreciate beauty in all its forms, as does any man. But I also appreciate a little more, you know, *joie de vivre*."

"Or at least consciousness," Georgia agreed. The prostitute, expressionless, had closed her eyes. She appeared to have fallen asleep, still on the phone.

"I leave in two days," Mark said into her hair. They'd wandered a short distance away from Jonah, but she could tell from the shift in his posture he could hear them perfectly.

"Ah," she said.

"Come with me."

"Mark," she said. "You know I can't."

"You can't what?" Jonah asked, wandering over.

"Mark has a business obligation. He wants me to join him in Germany."

"Paris, actually," Mark interjected. She turned to him, wide-eyed. He turned up his palms. "Slight change of plans."

"I can't," she said again. "I have to be back at work this week."

Intensity lit up Jonah's features. "You can," he said.

"Excuse me, Jonah—"

Jonah thrust up a palm to silence her. "You can, and you know you can, and what's more, you want to," he said. "You could cancel your cases for a few days. Don't ruin things."

"I can't do that; people plan their entire lives around their surgeries. It wreaks twenty kinds of havoc to cancel last minute."

Jonah started walking. After a moment of confusion, Mark followed him, sensing an unexpected ally. Behind him, Georgia started walking too; they traipsed along single file until Jonah whirled around, bright-eyed and fiery. "Me!" he said. "I've always wanted to go to Paris!"

Georgia glared at him. "I don't recall anyone inviting you."

Jonah looked pointedly at Mark, who paused, bewildered. "I'd love to take you to Paris, Jonah?" he said.

"All settled," trilled Jonah. "Thank you, Mark, I'd love to come."

"Georgia?" Mark tried. She looked down.

He picked up her hands. "It's okay," he said. "It's really okay. I understand and I admire your dedication to your work. Of course you can't just pick up and leave." Still, she stared at the ground. He went on: "Jonah and I will enjoy ourselves." He paused. "On a trip to the single most romantic city on earth."

"Hot damn," said Jonah, eyes shining. "I'm going to Paris."

"That's not going to work, you two," Georgia said, but despite herself, she smiled.

"No, it's fine," said Mark. "I've always pictured myself, windblown and glamorous, atop the Eiffel Tower with . . . Jonah. I just didn't know it."

"We'll tango by the Seine at night! Have croissants and cappuccinos in alley cafes for breakfast! Drive around in a vintage Citröen!"

"Gaze at the Cézannes in the Musée d'Orsay."

"Sing the blues in a wine cellar!" Jonah wiggled his hips seductively. "Stroll the Left Bank in matching berets!"

"Buy ancient books in Saint-Germain-des-Prés."

"We might even get engaged in the Temple Romantique!"

Mark held up a hand. "Okay, now you've gone too far." A constellation of smile wrinkles bracketed his eyes.

"Excuse us for one moment, please, Mark?" Jonah barked. He stormed over and yanked Georgia to the edge of the street.

"Don't be a damned fool," snapped Jonah. "Men like this come along *never*."

"I have surgeries. Plus, there's no way I'm leaving you again right now."

"I grant you permission."

"I'm glad you approve of Mark, even though, I must point out, you just met him. But you of all people know canceling days of work would create a monumental shitshow. I can't do it. Not to mention what it would cost." She shook her head. "Plus, I need to come back with you. You're not going to be facing this alone." She put her arms around him and drew him in. "No man could ever compete with you, Jones."

"Thank you?"

"You're welcome."

"Then what was this? A fling?" He gestured in Mark's direction, who, mistaking the movement for a wave, waved back.

"I don't know," she said. "He lives here, so I don't know where it could go, anyway."

"Bullshit. You can fly here again, you know. He can fly to Charleston. All is not lost."

"Well, of course," she said. "I could fly anywhere. But I only met him a week ago, so I'm not exactly ready to plan a wedding. We'll just take it slow, and—"

"Oh balls," said Jonah. "You're going to do it to this guy too? This guy?"

"Jonah, you are in no position to give anybody relationship advice."

"He's perfect for you. You can't see that?"

"You met him twenty-five minutes ago, Jonah. How would you know?"

"I'm a keen judge of character. Plus, I just—I wasn't kidding when

I said I've never seen you look like this. You are thirty-six years old, George, and you are shriveling before my eyes into a withered, sexless heap of dust. You should jump on this while you still have some flower left."

"Flower?"

"I thought that was how women referred to their fertility."

"No one refers to fertility that way. Are you sure you're a doctor?"

"It's not a medical term," he said haughtily, "it's slang. The hipsters say it, I think. Anyway, I am trying to help. You need to trust me."

"Jones," she said, lowering her voice as much as possible. "I do trust you, and I love you, which is why I'm coming back for your meeting."

Jonah's face crumpled a little, but recovered before she could be certain she'd seen it. "That's a beautiful gesture, George, but it's misguided. Beezon thinks you're an even bigger menace to society than I am."

"Yeah," Georgia said. "He's right about that."

"Fine, come back," said Jonah. "I'd love to have you with me." He sighed, then knocked his shoulder against hers. "But please: try not to make them any madder than they already are."

PART

TWO

10

APOCALYPTIC SCORN

Georgia awoke every morning of her first week back in Charleston disabled by jet lag. Everything was an effort: getting out of bed, forcing herself to go on her run, eating and showering and dressing. She'd previously disliked her long morning commute, but over the past few days, having discovered it was the best time of day to talk to Mark, she'd been enjoying it.

This morning Mark answered right away. "Hey there," he said, and she smiled at his voice. "How was last night?"

"Busy," she said. She'd had to take two extra call shifts to make up for having been gone, so she hadn't had time to recover from her fatigue.

"Tell me what you did."

"Well, let's see. Yesterday at work I spent the day in the operating room, whacking kidney stones, fighting strictured urethras, wrestling a few problematic prostates." These procedures had technical names, of course, but there were times in this career when Georgia felt it more accurate to employ the language of battle when describing what she did. "And then I was on call, so I spent half the night in the OR, trying to extract a bobby pin from some guy's urethra."

"Wha— Oh my God. I don't know how you do it."

"I'm used to it," she said, unsure if he meant staying awake all night or removing weird objects from intimate body parts. "But to tell you the truth, I'm running on adrenaline today. This afternoon is Jonah's showdown with human resources."

Every day over the past week, more patients had been dismissed from Jonah's practice.

"I know," said Mark, in a quieter tone. "Will you call me afterward? And tell him I'm thinking of him."

"I will," she promised.

Inside the clinic, she headed for the lounge. Turning the corner, she spied Darby Gibbes, wearing a silk flower-patterned dress, chatting with a clump of rehab people. As Darby looked up and noticed her, she flashed a neatly manicured hand and detached from the group. Georgia caught up to her.

"Hey there," said Darby. She motioned toward the group she'd just left with a sideways jerk of her head. "I just heard something."

Georgia's antennae went up; it wasn't like Darby to dispense with pleasantries. "What?"

"It's about Jonah Tsukada," said Darby. She gave Georgia a meaningful look, presumably based on their conversation in Amsterdam. "They're saying he violated some sort of ethical guidelines."

"What? Who's saying that?"

"I don't know exactly who; you know what the hospital rumor mill is like. But that's not the worst of it."

"What could be worse than that?"

"You know those missing medicines?" started Darby. She went on, but Georgia lost the rest of her sentence as something caught her attention; a herd of white coats entering the corridor from an outside door. The surgery team. There were at least eight of them, mostly men, mostly tall, but two women tailed the group; one with a blond ponytail and the other a young black woman, her hair swept back. The ponytail she recognized as a nurse practitioner. The other woman was unfamil-

iar, probably a medical student on a community-hospital rotation shad-
owing one of the surgeons.

"Excuse me, Dr. Gibbes?"

Georgia turned to see one of the fifth-year surgery residents regarding Darby, taking in her little heart-shaped face and her tiny ballet flats
and her carefully curled hair. She looked back at him, wearing her
baseline face: accommodating, trusting, eager to please, despite the fact
that as an attending, she outranked him in the hospital's hierarchy.

"Room 117," he said to her. He had bright blue eyes and a build
that managed to combine stockiness and grace, like an agile receiver
on a high school football team. "Mr. Drake, in rehab."

"Yes?"

"Did you . . ." The fifth-year paused, leaving a momentary conversational thud in the air. No one met his eyes as they waited for the rest of
the sentence. "Did you remove the staples from Mr. Drake's incision?"

She was still clueless. "Oh! Yes."

"I see. You consulted us on this guy and then you took it upon
yourself to intervene in a surgical patient's postoperative care, because
you're the expert. Do you still expect the surgical team to follow him,
or were you going to perform his next procedure too?"

No rustle of movement from the team. Even the air went still, as
the smile left Darby's face.

"There were instructions on the chart to remove the staples on
POD"—that was postoperative day—"fourteen."

"Did the instructions say for *you* to remove the staples?"

Darby's brow knitted together but her voice, clear and sweet, re-
tained its unmistakable sincerity. "There was no specificity as to who
should remove the staples. So we paged your team for clarification but
didn't hear back. That was two days ago, so we removed them on POD
fifteen. The incision is closed and healing nicely without any sign of
infection or dehiscence. As I hope you've appreciated." She paused,
and then added, with no apparent guile, "And I hope that was handled
appropriately."

Another silence.

Then: "I received no such page." He looked to his team. "Did any of you receive a text about 117's staples?"

One by one, the team members shook their heads. Darby looked back and forth between them, her lips parted slightly. She began blinking.

"In that case, I think—"

"Excuse me?"

Everyone looked: it was the young woman on the team. She had a genial expression dominated by wide, lively eyes. "I received the page, sir," she said.

If looks could kill, the entire planet would have detonated and settled into a smoldering ruin. "You received a page and you failed to answer it?"

Without a trace of fear: "Yes, sir. I mean no, sir. I didn't answer it because I didn't know who was supposed to remove the staples and I didn't want to assume. So I asked Dr. Dalton"—she gestured to another man in his late twenties, whose name badge read *J. Augustus Dalton III, M.D.*—"and he said he'd handle it."

J. Augustus Dalton III, M.D., who twenty seconds previously had denied knowing anything about the critical matter of staple removal in a rehab patient, now mirrored his chief resident's apocalyptic scorn. "No such thing happened."

"It did," said the medical student, unruffled. "Remember, we were in the cafeteria and you said, 'It's like these physical therapists have an alarm telling them we're about to eat,' and I said—"

"—physiatrists—" said Darby.

"—Yes, thank you, *physiatrists*, and I said—"

"Enough!" said Dr. Dalton. Georgia regarded him: with stringy brown hair and a thin, slightly lopsided face, he hadn't been particularly appealing to begin with, but now his eyebrows were lifted, cheeks reddened, a crazy gleam in his eye. "This never happened!" He looked at his chief, appealing. "She's lying."

"I am not lying," said the medical student calmly.

The chief readjusted the glare of his indignation onto her. "Have you no respect for your team? Dr. Dalton is your superior."

"I do, sir, but I didn't want you to hold this doctor"—she gestured to Darby—"accountable for our misfire. Even though it sounds like the staples were removed properly."

"What's your name again?" snapped the chief, despite the fact she was wearing a visible name badge, same as the rest of them, and despite the fact that she'd probably been on this rotation for at least a full day.

"Glory," said the student. "Gloriana Miller."

"Well, Glory-whatever, I'd say you just earned yourself an interesting evaluation from Dr. Dalton here. Right, Dalton? Did you know the third-year resident helps with the med student course grades, Glory?"

"No, sir, I didn't know." A lesser medical student would have crumbled to ash by this point, but Gloriana Miller, chin up, stared straight back at him with powerful impassivity. He blinked first.

Caught up in this ridiculous drama, Georgia startled at the touch of a hand on her shoulder. She turned her head and found herself staring directly into the expressionless gaze of Donovan Wright.

Anyone observing would have to have a keen eye to see past her calm exterior; she kept still and didn't change her expression. Internally, however, a nuclear dumpster fire consumed her, accelerating her heart rate from zero to sixty—or more accurately, from sixty to one hundred—in an instant; dilating her pupils; sending her sweat glands into hyperdrive.

Donovan Wright: an anesthesiologist, known around the clinic for his meticulous care in the OR, but also for his habit of parking his Ferrari square in the middle of two spaces in the doctors' parking lot to avoid acquiring a door ding from an inferior vehicle. Before she'd known him, he'd come across to her as both bland and bombastic; a dime a dozen, as far as male doctors went—your basic golfer in a white coat. The most notable thing about his appearance was the unearthly hue of his eyes; they were so pale they reminded her of icebergs.

"Hey there," he said, gripping her shoulder tighter. "How's it going?"

With a final squeeze he released her arm. Without thinking, she dropped her face into the crook of her elbow as if to shield her expression from the group. Taking in a shaky breath, she lifted her head again, willing her features into blankness. She managed to take only one step away from him before the blade of his voice caught her in the back.

"One moment," he said. She looked at him, but he was looking at the chief resident. For the first time, she noticed the guy's name badge: *H. Jonathan Ramsey, M.D.* What was with the surgery team referring to themselves by first initial? Maybe she should start calling herself *G. Maybelle Brown, M.D.* instead of Georgia.

Some of H. Jonathan Ramsey, M.D.'s cockiness had begun to wither under the unrelenting stone-faced stare of Dr. Wright. He shifted to the side a bit. Like children observing a fraught parental interaction, the rest of the team turned from Wright's face to his and back again as they waited for the storm to hit.

When he finally spoke, Donovan's voice was all the more devastating for its icy quietness. "Apologize," he said to Jonathan Ramsey, "to Dr. Gibbes."

Ramsey's blinking increased in tempo. "What?"

"You heard me."

For a moment it seemed Ramsey might defy him. Despite the fact that Donovan Wright was the head of the anesthesia department and therefore a powerful figure around the hospital, he was not a surgeon; he had no direct jurisdiction over the surgery residents. The two of them remained locked in a mortal stare-down until, suddenly, Dr. Ramsey bit the dust.

He turned to Darby, his sculpted cheeks and well-cut jaw now subsumed by an unattractive blotchy redness spreading up from the hollow of his throat, highlighting a bit of stubble on his Adam's apple. "I'm sorry," he mumbled.

"Dr. Gibbes," said Donovan, still in the same tone, "is an attending physician. You might be a chief, but you're still a resident. Dr. Gibbes deserves the same level of respect I'd expect you'd display to me, or to anyone for that matter, whether they're the head of a department"—he gestured to himself—"or a patient or a part of the cleaning staff. Is that understood?"

Everyone nodded.

"Ladies," said Donovan, tipping his head to Darby and Georgia and the medical student, who'd drifted over next to Darby in silent solidarity. "I have to get to a meeting." He stalked off down the hall, the reproached team drifting in his wake like a shape-shifting amoeba, nearly running into one another when he stopped to add, over his shoulder, "Nice to see you, Georgia."

Before she could respond, he'd gone.

Darby unfroze, her eyes enormous. "What in the world just happened?" She leaned in the direction of the departed surgery team, so close Georgia could see a tremble in her lower lip.

Georgia reached for Darby's shoulder. "Honestly. *Staples?* What a dick."

"That was sweet of Donovan, though," said Darby. Her hand fluttered, birdlike, by her hair. She smoothed it down, running her fingers through her shiny curls, succeeding only in mussing them.

Georgia jammed her hands into her pockets to hide their trembling. "You know him?"

"He goes to my church. His dad golfs at Wild Dunes with my dad. He's nice."

"He's not nice," Georgia said, her voice coming out too soft. Darby looked up, startled out of her preoccupation about the encounter with the surgery chief.

Hastily, Georgia deflected before Darby could query her. "Well, I think I'm gonna see if anybody on the surgery floor looks like they're begging for staple removal. Catch you later?"

It was lame but it worked. Darby smiled. "Thanks, Georgia. See you later."

Only after she'd disappeared down the hall did Georgia relax, allowing her breath to unfurl from a brittle knot in the center of her chest. She stared for a moment in the direction of the departed Dr. Wright, trying to will her mind into blankness.

~~~~~~~

Jonah was still seeing patients when she reached his practice that afternoon. Normally she'd have chatted with his office staff—she liked them, especially the women who worked the front desk—but today it occurred to her that someone in this office had complained about how intolerable it was that transgender patients were receiving medical care. She felt something shift and harden in her throat as she stalked past the front desk, entering Jonah's private office.

Although Jonah admired an aesthetically pleasing room, an inborn sense of interior design did not rank among his talents, so he'd hired someone to deck out his office in swank tweeds and nubby grass cloth. Should he have spent money on this? Arguably, no. But it was hard to take issue with the immense pleasure he took in this space: he liked it so much he'd been known to sleep here on nights when he worked late.

If she strained, Georgia could hear his voice from an exam room down the hall. She couldn't make out the words, but the cadence of his speech—calm, reassuring, knowledgeable—was clear. A higher-pitched voice alternated with his, speaking faster, a note of anxiety clearly audible. The voices established a pattern—*anxious, calm, anxious, calm*—until the anxious voice gradually lost its strident sound, slowing and softening. Then there were only low murmurs and, finally, the sound of a door swinging open. Georgia stuck her head out of the room in time to see Jonah ushering a woman into the hallway. Everything about her had faded with age: her dishwater-colored eyes, her once-brown hair, even the veiny ropes on the backs of her hands. The two of them had reached the end of the hall when she stopped. Her voice was quivery and sweet. "Thank you, Dr. Tsukada," she said.

With some hesitation, she lifted her arms and enfolded Jonah in a brief hug.

"It's been an honor to take care of you, Mrs. Eads." Still focused on his patient, Jonah hadn't noticed Georgia yet. "If you change your mind, I'm here. Anytime."

The older woman looked at him a final time. Then she pushed open the door to the waiting room and was gone.

Jonah stood for a moment, watching through the glass. His erect posture loosened slightly, a slump appearing in the line of his shoulders. Finally, he turned.

"George," he said. A tired hand flashed in the direction of the waiting room. "Sorry about that. I'm running late."

"What happened? Surely she's not one of the patients being told to leave? She looks like a little old church lady."

"You've got to stop making assumptions based on appearance, G," said Jonah, reviving a bit at the opportunity to needle her. "She's as queer as they come."

"Oh," Georgia said, chastened. "Oh, I'm sorry. I'm an idiot."

"Just kidding," said Jonah, grinning wickedly. "She's a little old church lady."

"Oh," she said again. "Okay, you got me. But why is she leaving?"

"Apparently," said Jonah, spinning in the direction of his open office door, "it just dawned on her that her physician is living a sinful life. She's conflicted. She doesn't want to leave; I've seen her through a number of problems she felt were inadequately treated elsewhere. Plus, I know she's lonely—sometimes I think she makes up physical symptoms just so she can come in here and have another human being hear her voice." A tender look crossed his face.

Georgia followed him into his office, watching as he shrugged off his white coat and placed it neatly on a hanger in the closet. "So why is she going?"

"When she read in the newspaper that I might be aligned with the devil, she asked her minister what to do," said Jonah, "and he told her to distance herself from sin. So she came in to find out who I'd recommend she see now."

"Ugh. What a—"

Jonah cut her off. "She's torn up about this; she didn't want to do it."

"So you comforted her because she was upset she's leaving you."

He offered a guileless smile. "Yeah. Basically."

In contrast to his usual immaculate style, Jonah appeared a bit off today. His bow tie drooped; a tiny shred of food clumped between his upper incisors. Georgia had planned to ask him about the drug rumors to which Darby had alluded, but on second thought, that appeared to be a poor idea. Why get Jonah agitated right before a meeting in which it would be crucial that he kept his calm? He might not be displaying any feistiness at the moment, but that could be a good thing.

"Well," she said, taking his arm. "Out of the frying pan, into the fire. Let's go see Beezon."

11

A DANGEROUS POINT OF COMBUSTION

As they neared the glass-walled enclosure of the clinic's conference room annex, they could hear voices: Beezon's drone, mingling with the clipped consonants of the clinic's chief medical officer, a stringy, blade-nosed physician named Claude Reiner. For all his haughty angularity, Claude was an attractive man, or he would have been if he possessed a shred of animation. He'd always reminded Georgia of a starved cowboy, weathered and masculine, with eyes so light they were opalesque. Both of them were seated with their backs to the door, and to their left sat a stubby man she didn't recognize. Even from behind, he radiated waves of importance, so he was probably the legal counsel for the medical practice, or maybe some kind of HR crisis person. He held a fat stack of papers in his hands. As her eyes traveled to the end of the table, Georgia blanched. Next to the lawyer, his head turned slightly in profile, sat Donovan Wright, tapping a ballpoint pen along the edge of the conference table in repeating staccato bursts.

Jonah, sensing her sudden apprehension, gripped her hand. "You don't have to come in."

"Of course I'm coming in. Unless you don't want me."

He squeezed her hand tighter. "You know I want you."

"I'll try not to embarrass you. Anyway, you know who really needs to be here: your lawyer."

"My lawyer agrees with you," said Jonah, "but I'm still hopeful I can work this out on my own. Maybe not with Beezon," he added quickly, seeing her opening her mouth, "but there are other people who might be persuadable. I think it's worth a shot. Once they know I'm lawyered up, everyone will get hostile."

Georgia tried to stifle an attack of nerves. "I can't remember what you want me to say . . ."

"George, I got this," said Jonah, flinging open the door and stepping inside before she could continue to second-guess him. The men all turned at the intrusion. Georgia tried not to look directly at Donovan, but even in her peripheral vision she could sense him, his posture straightening as he caught sight of her.

Beezon didn't bother to stand as they entered—a bad sign—but instead cleared his throat. "Dr. Tsukada," he said, and then, to Georgia: "Dr. Brown?" His eyes drifted to the tiny, tasteful glint of silver against her nose.

Last month, the HR department had outlawed unconventional adornments of any sort: visible tattoos, nose rings, and headscarves, as well as any sports jerseys not supportive of Beezon's alma mater. Georgia didn't wear sports jerseys—or headscarves, for that matter—but in addition to her nose ring, she did have a few discreet tattoos. Beezon might be on stable ground with the nose ring ban, but she was fairly certain the Civil Rights Act made it illegal to forbid religious garb like headscarves.

Pulling off the hideous cafeteria-style hairnet she still wore from her last in-office procedure, she crumpled it into an airy blue ball and launched it over Beezon's head in the direction of a wastebasket. In unison, they all watched as it fell about three feet short and unraveled itself back into a hat. "Beezy," she responded.

His officious air tightened into something else: poorly restrained dislike, maybe, or that justified look people got when provided with an opportunity to rationalize whatever malignant crap they've been secretly longing to do. He cast a glance to his left, where Claude perched, almost languidly, on the edge of his chair, and then on to the lawyer, and, finally, Donovan. For a moment, Georgia could not imagine why he would be here, and then remembered: he was the head of this year's executive committee.

Avoiding his end of the table, she took a seat next to Jonah. Beezon cleared his throat again. "We're here to speak to Dr. Tsukada, Dr. Brown."

"I'm aware of that." She made an ostentatious show of settling in the chair, her heart galumphing at an unseemly rate.

"I asked Dr. Brown to attend with me," said Jonah. In contrast to her fidgeting, he appeared composed, his voice calm, his hands folded in front of him.

She sat on her hands to hide their shaking. "I'm here to show my support for Dr. Tsukada," she said. "But not only that. Some of the people you're banning from the clinic are also my patients."

There was a brief silence as Beezon looked at Claude, who in turn looked at the important-paper man, who pursed his lips. He offered a dour nod to Claude. It seemed they'd have to accept her position as Jonah's second in this duel.

"This meeting serves as a follow-up to discuss clinic policies regarding our moral code of conduct," said Beezon.

"I'd like to say something, if I may," said Jonah. He leaned forward, shining with goodwill. "I recognize we may have some basic disagreements when it comes to what constitutes a moral code of conduct. But all human beings deserve medical care. I respectfully request that those patients who have been instructed to leave our clinic be welcomed back."

"No," said Beezon.

Jonah waited a beat but apparently that was it. "No?"

"No," Beezon said again. "Moving on—"

"Wait. What is the rationale for dismissing these patients?"

Beezon issued the slow, tolerant sigh of a parent dealing with an irrational toddler. "Dr. Tsukada, we've been over this."

Jonah blinked. His earnestness had begun to deflate a bit, but his voice was still calm. "First, *Do no harm*, right? It is harmful to our patients to refuse them care."

"They are perfectly free to seek care elsewhere. Furthermore, this decision is out of our hands." A self-satisfied nod. "This is coming from the hospital, which does not condone certain therapies you've been providing. Going forward, we will no longer be able to accommodate transgender patients. We are not legally obligated to enable medical care contradicting our moral code, especially of patients attempting some kind of unnatural transformation."

In unison, every eye in the room shifted in the direction of the red-bricked monolith across the pedway. Like the clinic, the hospital had been founded by the fundamentalist megachurch across town to which many of its employees, including Beezon, belonged. An urge to respond rose up from Georgia's gut, prompting her to clench her teeth.

"They can't always seek care elsewhere," said Jonah. "Many of my trans patients have complex medical needs that few other doctors treat. Plus, this is the only hospital and the only clinic in this county. Some of these patients don't have the means to get all the way into Charleston, and there are often long waits to get into a medical practice as a new patient. Not to mention that they'd likely be charged more or have to go out of network."

"Interesting that you brought up paying more," said Beezon. "You do not have the authority to waive your fees to your patients—it defrauds the clinic."

Jonah, recognizing he'd made a tactical error, backtracked. "Okay, but what about the issue of the patients having difficulty finding a doctor who will see them? It should not be legal to be able to refuse to provide medical care to someone on the basis of perceived immorality." He paused. "Or to fire someone on the basis of perceived immorality."

The third man perked up. "I assure you it's quite legal," he said to Jonah. Definitely a lawyer, then. "You signed a morals clause."

"This violates the World Medical Association's oath of ethics. And the AMA's position. And it's un-American."

Beezon motioned to the important man, who handed Jonah a piece of paper from his stack and began to read aloud, presumably from the contract he'd signed when he joined the practice. Georgia cast her mind back to the day she'd accepted her own job offer, but didn't remember noticing, let alone parsing, a morals clause. Could they have added it later?

"If the physician, Dr. Jonah Tsukada, commits any act or becomes involved in any situation or occurrence which brings said physician into public disrepute, contempt, scandal, or ridicule," the lawyer read in an emotionless voice, *"or which justifiably shocks, insults, or offends a significant portion of the community, or if publicity is given to any such conduct . . . the practice shall have the right to terminate."*

"So you want to terminate me too," said Jonah. His hands drummed the table in front of him. "Let's be honest."

"You had a clear-cut choice," said Beezon. "Adhere to the expectations of your employer, or not."

"It's kind of two birds with one stone, isn't it? You get to get rid of all the undesirables at once."

"If you say so." Beezon smirked. "You're the first, certainly, to test us on this policy. Whether or not others follow you is up to them." He directed a glance at Georgia.

Ignoring him, Georgia regarded Jonah with some wariness. In contrast to a few moments ago, everything in his posture had shifted: his unnaturally straightened back, the blurred vehemence of his hands, even the energized lick of his hair. She recognized he was nearing a dangerous point of combustion. She hesitated, uncertain if she should intervene or not, but also uncertain how much longer she'd be able to remain silent. She should have insisted that Jonah bring his lawyer. This seemed like the sort of situation requiring a precise understanding of the legalities. Maybe she should get Jonah out of here; either one of them losing their shit in front of a hostile lawyer could not possibly end well.

She reached for his hand. "Let's go," she said quietly. "Your lawyer can follow up."

"No," said Jonah. "I think there's more to say."

Beezon made a little moue of encouragement. "Be our guest."

"He wants you to keep talking," she said to Jonah in the same low voice.

Jonah stood, and for a moment Georgia thought he was about to commit some epic blunder, but he bowed slightly and stepped back from his chair. "Dr. Brown is right. I think this meeting is over." He turned to her. "Thank you." He pivoted back toward Beezon. "For the record: I do not agree to the dismissal of my patients. And if you tell even one more of them they can't come back, I'll sue the clinic for every dime it has."

The lawyer's head sprang up. Midforties, appropriately besuited, boring haircut: he was perfectly cast for this role. In ten minutes, if Georgia tried to recall what he looked like, all she'd be able to picture would be a charcoal tie and an expression of smug neutrality. "Dr. Tsukada," he said, and paused for dramatic effect. Once satisfied he had the room riveted, he continued: "You will not sue."

Jonah, who had nearly reached the door, stopped. "Just try me," he said.

The lawyer continued, unruffled. "You are legally prohibited from bringing a lawsuit."

"What?"

A thin-lipped smile. "No one ever reads their contracts, do they?" He shook his head in mock dismay at the mass ignorance of the American workforce.

Suddenly, Georgia realized where this was going. "Actually," she said, "I read my contract. In full. Including all the indecipherable fine-print bullshit you guys cram in there. And there wasn't any mention of a forced arbitration clause. Or, for that matter, a morals clause."

"It wasn't in your initial contract," said the lawyer. His gaze sharpened as he regarded her. "You agreed to both those clauses and other terms of agreement after responding to an email sent by the clinic regarding your yearly educational stipends. You were required to click a box indicating your acceptance of the terms."

"What?" howled Jonah. "When?"

The lawyer: "The email containing the relevant clauses came several years ago."

Georgia waved a placating arm at Jonah. "The timing is a separate issue," she told him. "What this gentleman is saying now is when we responded to an email a few years back, we had to agree to mandatory arbitration for any workplace disputes as a condition of continued employment."

"That's correct," agreed the lawyer. His expression shifted to one of careful contemplation. He exchanged a sidelong glance with Donovan Wright, who was frowning.

"What the hell is mandatory arbitration?"

Both Georgia and the lawyer began to reply to Jonah at the same time, but she barreled over the guy until he hushed. "It's a condition of employment stating that instead of suing to resolve a dispute, we have to let an assigned person—or a group of people—decide who is right. And their decision is binding; you cannot appeal it. Plus, you'd have to pay a large fee even to initiate the arbitration, and if you lose, they might make you pay the clinic's legal fees."

Jonah asked the obvious question. "Who picks the arbitrator?"

Everyone looked at the lawyer. He smiled again. "The clinic has preselected the arbitration company."

Both Beezon and Claude wore the same expression: *So there.* The lawyer's smile had faded to an expression of watchful anticipation. Georgia looked past him at Donovan Wright. In contrast to the other men, he didn't appear smug; he stared at the table, a frown creasing his forehead.

Jonah opened the door, then turned back toward the room. "I want the names of the rest of the patients you plan to contact."

"Not a cha—" Beezon began. The lawyer cut in. "We are not legally required to provide that," he said.

"Guys. I think it would be kind to provide this," Georgia said.

This stymied everyone for a moment: in the entire history of the legal profession, apparently "kind" had never come up. Beezon recovered first.

"No," Beezon said. He turned to Jonah. "You have a clear choice. You can support the clinic's policies on moral conduct, or you will no longer be employed."

Georgia couldn't hold back any longer. "How can you presume to tell a physician how to treat his patients? How can you presume to tell a physician *who* he can treat? Are we really facing a situation where administrators decide who is worthy of medical care and who isn't? Because this affects every single doctor and patient in this clinic."

"Dr. Brown." Beezon leaned back in his seat and folded his arms. "If you'd like to insert yourself into this discussion, I'm sure we could afford a brief detour. You and Dr. Tsukada seem to share a . . . reputation . . . when it comes to attracting certain kinds of patients." He paused, almost smiling. "And weren't you involved in a patient death last year?"

At the reminder of the worst episode of her career—a wound infection following a relatively simple procedure—Georgia's feet went numb. It was startling, how quickly the body could manifest a physical reaction to words, which were, after all, not bullets or swords but rather a jumble of sound.

Jonah leapt to her defense. "Infections happen. It wasn't poor care on her part. And there was no bad outcome for the clinic."

Beezon acknowledged this with a supercilious tilt of his head. "Not such a great outcome for the patient, I'd imagine."

Georgia cast her eyes to the table. Jonah was correct—there had been no lawsuit—but only because she'd had such rapport with the patient and his family that they refused to even contemplate suing her or the clinic. Even now, today, she could hardly bear to think of it.

"That's an entirely separate issue," she said, forcing a note of calm into her voice. "The point here is that you do not have the right to deny our patients medical care."

"That's exactly the point," said Beezon. "We do have the right. And you have the same choice as Dr. Tsukada: you can comply with our policies, or you can leave."

Jonah crossed his arms. "It comes to this: if you fire my patients, I'll walk."

"Jonah," Georgia said. She reached for his arm. "Don't quit. I'm not sure you can go to arbitration in that case."

Jonah jerked his arm away from her, trembling. "Fine. If you want me to stop seeing my patients, you'll have to fire me."

John Beezon leaned forward, making eye contact with the lawyer, who offered a curt nod. He passed a set of papers to Beezon, who in turn handed them to Jonah. "This is your employee termination letter. There is a checklist of items for you to return, and as of now, your access badge has been disabled. This packet contains information about COBRA compliance and your last paycheck."

Despite everything, Jonah looked dumbfounded. "You already did all that?"

"You've been given prior warnings. We had hoped a reasonable accommodation on your part could be made to comply with the policies of the clinic, but we had plans in place if you were unwilling to do so. Which, today, you've stated explicitly you are unwilling to do."

Beezon decided to chime in: "Not to mention the other concerns about you. You'll be hearing from us about the rest of it."

For a moment Jonah simply stared at them. Then, without looking back, he swung around and stepped through the door. They listened to his footsteps fading away until the door swung closed.

A strange sensation tethered itself around Georgia's ankles, seeping upward in a rope of ice and fire. Her fingers went cold and her cheeks flamed. She gave herself a moment to gain self-control, remembering the way the lawyer had looked at her a moment before. Spouting off about the arbitration clause had been a tactical error; it would be better for the time being for this crowd to underestimate her. She stood to follow Jonah, but Beezon grabbed her arm as she passed by him, causing her to shift a bit off-balance as she recoiled from his touch.

"Dr. Brown, let me be clear: we will be in contact with you regarding your own performance as a physician in this clinic."

Georgia didn't reply.

The lawyer piped up. "If you'd like to pass this along to your colleague, Dr. Tsukada is welcome to participate in an exit interview. Afterward, we will reconvene for a meeting with the executive committee"—he motioned to Donovan Wright, who nodded blankly—"and we will present any recommendations to the board as to severance. If Dr. Tsukada chooses to contest his termination, he has the option to initiate arbitration."

The room quieted, anticipatory schadenfreude written on the faces of Beezon and Claude and the lawyer as they waited to see if Georgia would make a stink. She pictured it: their cheeks elevating in smug satisfaction at the rising pitch of her voice, tinged with that note of inevitable feminine hysteria; maybe a hint of heaving bosom; and tears, of course. Or maybe they expected volatility: the throwing of things more substantial than an OR cap, spit-encrusted f-bombs descending on the landscape of the conference room as everyone ducked for cover, perhaps a slap or two. After all, she was not only a woman, but a red-headed one.

"Very well, then," she said, gritting her teeth into a parody of a gracious smile. She offered her hand to Claude, the CMO, the ostensible ally of physicians, who stared with sudden absorption through the conference room windows at a stream of passing vehicles. She turned next to the lawyer, who shook her hand with a noticeable lack of enthusiasm. She ignored Beezon, who pulled out a cell phone.

Donovan, still standing next to her, cleared his throat, reminding her that he'd been mute throughout the meeting. She had the impression he was about to speak, but the lawyer beat him to it. "A quick reminder to pass on to Dr. Tsukada," he chirped. "The contract also contains a restrictive covenant, which means he may not seek employment as a physician within one hundred miles of Charleston for a period of two years."

"I'm sure he's familiar with the non-compete clause."

"Good."

She swiveled to address Beezon. "Why is this happening?" she asked.

He raised his hands in a *Who, me?* gesture. "No one is dying," he said. "Dr. Tsukada could have made a different decision, but he chose what he chose, and we chose what we chose. Not to mention we have other informatio—"

The lawyer interceded before Beezon could say something terminally stupid. "Dr. Brown. I assume you are close with Dr. Tsukada. Who is his legal representation?"

"I'll tell him to get back to you on that."

She'd almost reached the exit when another thought occurred.

"Beezon. Do you know a patient named Frieda Myers Delacroix?"

He flicked his eyes upward; the sign of a positive tell. But Claude, who hadn't spoken once up to this point, suddenly took up the mantle on this one, swiveling in his seat to better view her. Unlike Beezon, his face gave away nothing; he might as well be a stone carving, he was so self-contained.

"I know who he is."

"What happened to her after you got rid of her? Did she find another doctor?"

Claude didn't blink. "Not to my knowledge," he said.

12

~~~~~

THE UNITED STATES OF GEORGIA

MARK

He'd just fallen asleep when his phone woke him up. It took him a second to recognize the sound: the distinctive staccato trilling of a FaceTime call. Rolling to his side, he grabbed the phone and swiped it on, holding his breath during the slight delay as the picture established itself. Then Georgia's features swam into focus, her forehead and nose magnified by the angle of the phone into elongated blobs. Perhaps it wasn't her best look, but upon seeing her a swell of pleasure engulfed him nonetheless, until he realized she'd be unlikely to call him this late his time unless something was wrong.

"Georgia," he said. "What happened?"

He'd had a long week, mainly spent drilling down into the financials of a company that Rolly, the CEO of their firm, wished to acquire. The vast majority of this sort of work was tedious: analyzing balance sheets, trying to discern hidden liabilities, teasing out overvaluations in assets. While he wouldn't exactly describe these tasks as enchanting, they were satisfying enough. Or normally they were. But this week, since Georgia had left, he'd been restless and blue and—uncharacteristically for him—bored with his work.

"It's Jonah," she said. "They fired him."

She spent the next ten minutes recounting the events of the day. Mark listened, occasionally interjecting to clarify something but otherwise remaining quiet, allowing the story to pour from her. He fought to keep his face impassive as she spoke, not wanting to distract her with his shock that such a thing could be happening in the present day.

"Are they going to fire you too?" he said quietly, once she'd finished.

"I don't know," she said. "Maybe."

"How's Jonah taking it?"

"I have no idea," she said. "He vanished after the meeting."

He listened to her for a few more minutes, her voice growing more agitated as she talked about the patients who were being forced to leave the clinic. Before he could ask another question, she abruptly switched gears.

"Didn't you tell me you have some pretty good IT guys on staff?"

"We're a biotech firm based in California, Amsterdam, Munich, and Hong Kong. We have nothing but computer geeks. Well, and science guys. And, you know: finance guys."

"I don't need a science guy or a finance guy," she said slowly, "but I might have a question for one of your computer geeks. I'm still thinking about it."

"Is it something to help your patients? Or Jonah?"

She moved the phone closer to her face, briefly transforming her eyes into two bulging fishbowls, before the view shifted again. She'd set the phone down, presumably propped up against something, and settled back against a couch. From this distance, he could see the fine bones of her face and the hollow at her throat and just a hint of the swell of her breast, moving subtly as she breathed. She'd pulled her hair back into a knot and secured it with two crisscrossing chopsticks. He was overcome, suddenly, with the urge to pull them out and watch her hair tumble down her back.

"Maybe," she said. "I have an idea."

"Want to tell me?"

"No," she said, and her expression changed. "You're better off not knowing."

He hesitated. "That doesn't sound good."

She offered a small, sad smile. "So do you know somebody or not?"

"I'll put you in touch with Olin Dortch. He's basically a computer himself."

"Thank you, Mark," she said.

"Georgia?"

"Yes?"

"Fair warning: Olin can be a little weird."

"I'm a fan of weird. You're possibly the first normal guy I've ever dated."

"I can't decide if that's good or not. Plus, Jonah warned me that you're hell on men."

To his relief, she laughed. "Only if they deserve it. And really, I haven't dated anyone seriously in a long time. I had a dry spell in med school, where any attempt to sleep—let alone date—was met with lit- eral bloody carnage, and then I was engaged to the world's biggest narcissist, and then I was a surgeon with a real jo—"

He blinked. "You were engaged?" He thought about their long talks in Amsterdam, trying to recall the exact structure of her words as she'd described her past to him. "To who? Angus? I thought he was just a boyfriend."

"Angus? Yes, well, the boyfriend phase preceded the fiancé phase. He's neither one now, as you may have noticed."

"What happened?"

"Nothing. Nothing unusual, anyway," she said. "He had this strange aversion to monogamy, as it turned out. He also found my career choice unseemly: all the cock-doc jokes, maybe; or maybe it was that time I shared too much detail about how sex can cause penile fractures. Any- way. He's happier now. And I've learned I'm not great at relationships."

If this loser Angus had been standing in front of Mark at the present moment, he'd have been tempted to punch him in the head, despite a lifelong commitment to nonviolent conflict resolution. Having been raised by a man who'd knocked him around plenty, Mark had vowed never to raise a hand to anyone in anger himself, but surely an exception could be made in this case. He pictured this satisfying image for a moment and then wrested his thoughts back to a more productive zone. "Georgia," he said. "I was hoping to come see you in a week or two."

She took a moment to answer and, immediately, doubt assailed him. Perhaps he was making much more of their fling than she was. Plenty of applicable adjectives existed to describe the notion of thinking you might have a meaningful thing with another person after such short time: *premature, foolhardy, delusional*—take your pick. He had a gallon of milk in his refrigerator older than whatever this thing was he had going on with Georgia. (Granted, cleaning out the refrigerator was not his forte.) And it wasn't as if they'd discussed it: when they'd been together those seven days in Amsterdam, neither of them had mentioned the future. They'd delved into the past, sure, but their shared experience had existed mainly in the realm of the present. It hadn't even been a representative present: they'd been enveloped in a bubble, wandering the streets and museums and landmarks of Holland, more or less free of responsibility.

Still, Mark had the sensation Georgia understood him in a manner few people ever had. It was embarrassing, actually, how much he'd enjoyed himself with her. He might as well have opened up his skull, unfurled a tangle of neurons, and exported the contents of his mind into another body, so great had been his ease in her company.

Mark had never considered himself overly competent with women. High school, a dim and tragic period in which he had ceaselessly mourned the death of his mother, was best forgotten. He'd graduated a virgin, which in ordinary circumstances might have embarrassed him, but in the throes of his prolonged, bewildered teenaged bereavement, the fact that he wasn't scoring barely registered.

His mother had been named Earla but everyone called her Early. The nickname suited her; she had been prompt, arriving for everything with time to spare, but also with a sparkly, resolute cheer that added luster to even the most mundane events, like picking Mark up in the afternoon carpool or attending the incessant, stultifying, sweltering baseball practices of his older brother. Early's luminosity defined her. Her expression, at least in Mark's memory, shone with perpetual delight: the face of a mother gazing with adoration upon her son. It wasn't until she died that Mark realized no one would ever greet his arrival with that expression again.

In their family, Early had been both the sunshine and the glue, lighting up and drawing together her taciturn husband and her introverted sons. After her death, they fractured like repelled atoms, shooting farther and farther away from one another until they barely cohabited the same universe. His brother, Todd, a good athlete, coped by turning with single-minded determination to the pursuit of a baseball scholarship; and his father, Ed, a gruff and basically vile alcoholic, coped by pursuit of Old Milwaukee beers at Nan's, the closest thing they had to a neighborhood bar in their particular section of suburban Cincinnati, ignoring everything his shattered sons did. It had been a lonely, sad adolescence.

Things got better in college. Mark had an affinity for numbers; by the time he graduated, he'd taken as many upper-level math courses as he could and somehow had gotten himself admitted to the Fuqua School of Business at Duke University. Despite—or maybe because of—his geekiness, he appealed to a certain subset of girl there, the sort who appreciated a subtle Handsome Nerd vibe. Of course, most often, his vibe resulted in his being "friended," but he still had racked up a halfhearted girlfriend or three by the time he graduated.

No one would claim this track record as one of overwhelming success, but, all things considered, Mark wasn't complaining. Or at least, he hadn't been complaining until lately. Now, at age forty, a few insidious doubts had begun to worm their way into his consciousness. He was reasonably interesting and reasonably handsome and unreasonably tall; shouldn't he be committed to somebody by this point? He didn't know exactly what he sought in a woman—until now, he hadn't come across it—but it wasn't any of the women in his past. Personality-wise, they ranged across the spectrum: some of them were breathy-voiced dingbats and some were sharp-eyed social climbers and some were ultra-ethical angry vegans, or whatever. It didn't matter. He liked them—he tended to like everyone—but he didn't feel any overwhelming pull toward any of them.

So it was with total surprise that he'd realized he felt something more for Georgia, despite the fact that they'd only just met. She hadn't reared up and slapped him when he'd kissed her in the hall outside his flat. In fact, she'd kissed him back, so hungrily and with such abandon that it was only with Herculean effort that he had been able to tear himself away from her to get inside. Even getting through the doorway in that state had been no small feat either; never in his entire life had he experienced such lust.

"Look," she said, breaking into his reverie. "It's time."

"Time for what?"

"Time for me to warn you what you're getting into here. I do not have a gift for maintaining relationships. Some might say I'm a deeply flawed human being."

"As opposed to the many perfect women out there?"

She leaned toward the screen, blowing up her nose again. "I just want it on the record: my dating game starts out strong, but usually by the end of it, the man has been reduced to a sniveling heap. You need to know this up front."

"*Caveat emptor*," he said.

"That's exactly right," she said, smiling. "Buyer beware. You're assuming the risk that I may fail to meet expectations or have defects. You've been warned."

"So why do you do it?" he asked. His hand reached toward the screen and he pulled it back. "Destroy these poor men? I'm assuming they don't deserve it?"

"No, Angus aside, they're mostly pretty nice," she admitted. "I mean, occasionally one turns out to be a jackass, but the majority of them have been decent guys."

"So what happens?"

"I don't really know," she said. "Jonah says I need to spend a little time working on the United States of Georgia."

"Meaning?"

"Meaning he thinks I have a hard time reconciling my emotional state with my logical state, or something like that. The part of me who wants a functional relationship continually gets taken down by this control freak who is afraid to get too close to anyone."

She said it lightly, as if Jonah had been overthinking things, but in truth Mark knew exactly what he'd meant because he'd experienced something similar himself. He recognized that the fault for his unmarried status should be assigned to him, since, in some perverse and ultimately self-defeating mechanism, he'd been known to lose interest in things if he thought he liked them too much. He wanted to protect himself from the pain of losing people, so he lost them intentionally.

Even thinking about this now activated some subterranean warning system in his mind: he worried mentioning this aloud to Georgia would jinx him. In one way, this was about as dumb as it was possible to be; there was no malignant cosmic force hovering above his head, alert for the faintest sign of happiness in order to squash it. But in another way, it wasn't so stupid. For the first time since losing his mother, he truly cared what a woman thought of him.

"I'll take my chances," Mark said.

"Anyway," she said. "That's my stupid hang-up. I'm sure you have plenty of preferences when it comes to women."

"Not really," he said. "I like smart women. And funny ones. There's only one absolute deal-killer for me, and that's women who wear purple lace bras. I hate those."

"I'm guessing there a story there . . ."

"Yep." He could feel himself grinning sheepishly. "Let's just say it involves a humiliating incident from my youth and leave it at that."

"I don't own any purple lace bras, so you should be safe. Anything else?"

"No," he said. "Oh, wait, yes; there is something. Dishonesty. I guess that's the only thing I truly can't abide. I don't want to be with someone who lies or who hides something major from me. Ever."

He was quiet for a second and shook himself. "Anyway. There's a story there too, but you don't want to hear it."

Softly: "You know I do."

His mother's death had come as an earth-shattering shock. Out of a misguided urge to protect her sons, Early had hidden her illness from them, and, wrapped up in the blinding narcissism of adolescence, Mark had failed to register her weight loss and weakness and near-constant nausea until it had been too late. One day he came home from school and she was simply gone.

This event—a pretense that everything had been fine, followed by the tragic, brutal, unanticipated loss of a parent—left him with a life-long horror at the possibility of being deceived; deception, in his young mind, became inextricably linked with crushing grief. But this wasn't a conversation he could face via a transatlantic data cable. He'd talk to Georgia about this in person.

"Later," he said, softening the word with a smile at her.

"Whatever it is, I'm sorry. So: no lace bras and no lying. You're safe with me."

He laughed. "I didn't say no lace bras," he said. "Just no purple ones."

13

THE DELECTABLE ONION

In theory the temperature should have cooled—it was mid-October, after all—but the air, devoid of an ocean breeze, baked her the moment Georgia set foot outdoors on Saturday morning. Jonah had texted her that he'd "gone out for a bit" and he'd stop by afterward. He didn't say where he was—maybe his favorite coffeehouse near his home in Folly Beach or one of the parks—but her money was on a sail. Maybe he'd taken his boat out at sunrise, tacking through the swells until his arms ached. Or perhaps he'd gone for a drive. He often did this when something plagued him; filling up the tank and driving aimlessly, crossing the Ashley River and paralleling the coastline toward Kiawah Island and Edisto Beach. She pictured him behind the wheel, music throbbing, the odometer on his boxy old Volvo clicking off the miles until finally he looked up and realized he was halfway to Savannah, at which point he'd turn the car around and head home. He'd drive carefully; he'd be safe.

She hoped.

If ever a situation called for peeling out of the parking garage, yesterday afternoon had been it. She'd left the meeting, staggered to the garage, and fired up her Prius—or rather, she pushed a button on the

Prius, which started without a sound, thus depriving her of the satisfaction of revving the engine and screeching out in a fit of macho indignation. Instead the car had drifted like a giant innocuous bubble down the spiral of the garage, hovering briefly on the edge of the roadway before she was able to gun it to pull into traffic.

Rolling down the windows, she'd allowed the swampy humidity and carbon dioxide–laden exhaust fumes to seep into her lungs. It barely registered as uncomfortable, however, because she was generating plenty of hot pollution of her own. She felt the self-control she'd summoned during the meeting explode and then contract, transforming into a knot of incandescent fury lodged somewhere in her skull. It wouldn't have been surprising if it had blown out of her ears in a volcanic eruption of steam, like a choleric cartoon person, lifting her off the ground. She thought of the expression *seeing red*. In her case, that was literal, and it wasn't just because her hair was falling across her face.

You didn't hurt Georgia's friends.

Her friends—especially Jonah and her far-flung med school friends, Emma and Zadie and Hannah and Anders and Rolfe and Landley—were her family. She didn't have any other family. She had never had siblings, but once she had a father, and while her upbringing could only be described as unconventional, it contained all the essential elements: safety, unconditional love, lots of math and science. She'd grown up wild and self-reliant and free but there also existed within her a fierce, protective loyalty.

Now, stretching for her run, she thought again of the plan she'd begun to devise. It wasn't fully formed, but the germ of an idea had sprouted, nurtured in some dark recess of her mind, quietly growing and expanding and blossoming, its tendrils drifting ever forward, biding its time. She tugged at it a little, but it remained stubbornly tethered, not quite ready to tease out.

But even if she figured it out, she'd face an uphill battle convincing Jonah. Although there was no way to reinstate Jonah's patients—or his job—on the merits, she knew he'd balk at doing anything not strictly aboveboard.

Somehow, she'd just have to convince him.

~~~~~

Jonah showed up just as she returned from her run. He stood at the door, jiggling his key in the lock, a cardboard cup holder with two steaming coffees wedged between his hip and the door. Inside, Dobby, who was home from the animal hospital but not yet quite recovered enough to run, was losing his canine mind at the sudden miraculous appearance of not one but *two* of his people. His hoarse yelps filling her ears, Georgia hurried forward to assist Jonah with the lock.

"Peace offering," he said, handing her a cup as they stepped inside. "I'm sorry I didn't call you back yesterday after the meeting."

Georgia knelt to scratch Dobby behind his ears, then set her cup on the floor and hugged Jonah's knees. "It's okay, babe," she said. "I'm used to your ways. How are you?"

Jonah flopped onto her futon couch. He tended to sit in one of two postures, depending on his mood: straight-backed with legs either crossed at the ankles or wide apart in a traditional manspread. Today he was manspreading, which she took as a good sign. She slumped on the edge of the futon next to him.

"All things considered, I'm good," he said. He took a sip of his coffee and winced. "Crap! This swill is yours."

They switched cups. Jonah took his coffee black, while Georgia preferred hers doctored up with cream and foam and whatever syrupy monstrosity the coffee place offered. "So?" she said.

"So, I am trying to reconcile myself to the possibility that I may have to move out of state."

She sat bolt upright, slamming her cup down hard enough to shoot a little jet of foam out of the opening. "No. I thought you were going to talk to your lawyer!"

"I talked to Stewie as soon as I left. He spoke with the clinic's attorney, who said they're going to enforce the non-compete."

"They can't do th—"

He held up a hand. "George, they can. It's pointless and it's vindictive and it's completely legal. They can keep me from joining another practice anywhere within a hundred miles of here, which not only wrecks my career but means there's no chance my patients can come see me in another practice. And the firing itself is legal. On 'moral' grounds. Stewie said because the clinic is a privately run practice, they're in the clear to use the religious exemption. Their argument is that since homosexuality is condemned in the Bible, I'm condoning immorality by facilitating a gay- and transgender-friendly lifestyle in my patients." He paused. "To say nothing of my own lifestyle."

She bristled. "I've read the Gospels," she said, pausing, "word for word, and I feel strongly Christ would not have said to me, 'Suffer unto the gays urinary retention; but everybody else can see the urologist.'"

"Right."

"I mean, that's definitely not the Christian way. Have these guys even read the Gospels? How can this be the message they're getting from church?"

"Georgia." Jonah snapped his fingers in front of her face. "I need you to stay calm."

"This does not represent Christianity to me!"

"Right. Focus. My lawyer. He's researching the precedents. But, like I said, we don't have a strong case right now. The courts have been upholding religious liberty laws. Furthermore, there's the issue of that thing I apparently signed saying I can't sue. Stewart says even if we can get around that, we aren't likely to win."

"Because . . . because . . ." She searched for a delicate way to phrase her concern. "Because they suspect you're the one stealing drugs?"

"What the actual fuck, George! No."

She tabled that line of inquiry. Of course Jonah didn't have a drug problem and of course the clinic would like to blame him instead of whoever did.

"So is Stewart advising you to let it go?"

"No," said Jonah. "He thinks we should play to lose."

"What? Why?" She thought of Jonah's precarious finances and repressed a shudder. Surely his lawyer would not take a losing case just for the fees?

Jonah looked at her, deadpan. "To appeal it."

"But wouldn't you just lose the ap . . ." She trailed off. It came to her: the lawyer wanted to make it a cause célèbre, probably with the intent of forcing a change in the law. A revolving series of images rose in her mind: backs being turned, insults and counter-insults; social media slurs, Jonah dodging herds of camera-toting journalists. Or worse. She could tell by Jonah's face he understood. "Are you okay with that?" she asked quietly.

He looked down. "I don't know. I'm a private person."

She almost laughed; Jonah was about as private as a Kardashian. He told everyone his business, whether they wanted to know or not. But then she looked at him again and wondered how his insubstantial shoulders would fare under the weight of a world of scorn. He must have sensed her thoughts, because he straightened and met her gaze. "I'll be fine."

"No," she said. "Listen, I've been giving it some thought. I think we can overcome this discrimination before it has to get legal. We still have options."

He blinked, suddenly fierce. "I love you for saying 'we.' But I know you, George. Maybe you should take a step back. I don't want to burn down the clinic or anything."

"Burning down the clinic would be a last resort. Joking!" she added hastily at his alarmed look. "We could organize a petition at work; I'm guessing most doctors would disagree with administrators deciding who qualifies for medical care and who doesn't."

"You think?" He pointed a finger at her. "Because we already let insurance companies do that."

He had a good point, but she'd built up too much of a head of steam to derail. "I know people will be furious the clinic is firing you."

He picked up both her hands. "I think you may be overestimating my appeal. It's pretty unlikely there's going to be an angry mob when news of my firing goes public. Some people might be mad, of course." He paused. "And then again, some people will celebrate." Seeing her crestfallen expression, he added kindly, "A petition is a very good idea to try, though."

She felt something give way in her chest. "You wouldn't really move away, would you?"

"I don't want to." He disengaged his hands and stood. "I'm seeing Stewart next Friday at four thirty. Is there any chance you can come?"

She consulted her phone. "My last case of the day is at three o'clock. If the OR isn't backed up, I should be able to meet you." She leaned in and kissed his forehead. "Next Friday. It's a date."

"Let's do this," Georgia said to the OR team. Regarding the helpless young man lying before her, she placed her gloved finger in his right hemiscrotum and pressed upward, angling toward his inner pelvis, until she felt the circular opening of the inguinal ring to mark her incision.

Her assistant passed a scalpel. Georgia dissected down through the subcutaneous tissue, cauterizing the wound as she went. While she couldn't exactly describe the removal of a testicle as joyous for anyone, she had to admit she loved her time in the operating room. Surgery was mechanical and technical—both things that appealed to her—but there was a beautiful creativity to it as well, one she missed whenever she was away from it for any length of time. It was a well-rehearsed,

intricate dance of flesh and bone and blood and steel; a ballet performed with the hands. In front of her, small wisps of smoke arose
from a living landscape; her fingers flew in the spotlights, weaving
slender filaments of silk.

This was a sad case, yes, but not a long one. And it wasn't so sad,
really, when you considered that the small series of movements she'd
just performed had rearranged the future for this young man; instead
of dying from the slow cellular hijacking of his body by a bunch of
rogue cells, he'd almost certainly go on to a full and lengthy life. Or, at
least, he'd go on to a full and lengthy life as it related to his cancer; she
wasn't making any guarantees that he wouldn't get fried by a lightning
strike on the way home from the hospital. But she'd done her bit.

She thanked her team and headed from the OR to the waiting area,
where her patient's wife, a young woman in a tank top and torn jeans,
knelt, praying, in a corner of the room. A group of people, probably
family, surrounded her. She moved toward them and she didn't even
have to speak. They saw her smile and erupted.

This was among the more gratifying things about the practice of
medicine; who wouldn't leap at the opportunity to tell a family member that their loved one would be okay? Talk about a rush of goodwill
and gratitude and happiness. If Georgia could somehow capture that
feeling and dole it out when things were tense, she'd solve the world's
problems overnight.

~~~~~~~

They were early for the meeting with Jonah's lawyer, so they sat in a
corner of the waiting room, Georgia thumbing through her email and
Jonah thumbing through a pamphlet entitled *We Can All Be Philanthro-
pists: How to Plan Your Giving*. After a moment he flung the pamphlet
away and let out a long, exaggerated sigh. "I'm nervous as hell."

She squeezed his hand. "Try reading something else."

He leaned against her shoulder. "What're you reading?"

"The *Bulletin*. Have you seen it this week?"

"Hardly," grumped Jonah.

"Whoops," she said. "Of course you haven't."

The *Bulletin*, the clinic's weekly email newsletter, was an HR-generated, fluff-filled collection of useless links that tended to focus on things like recipes for sweet-potato casserole and chummy exhortations to get your steps in by taking the stairs instead of the elevator. It was supposed to promote health and morale, but instead sounded like it had been written by a bunch of goobers who'd escaped from a 1950s women's magazine.

"Please tell me there isn't something about me in it," said Jonah, sitting up to scan it, adding, after a moment, "Or you."

"Listen to this." She began to read aloud. "All over the country, 'unfulfilled' housewives are encouraged to abandon the well-being of their husbands and children in order to seek a 'me-first' career."

Jonah's face contorted, although she couldn't tell whether this reflected horror or glee. "What the hell is this?"

"Keep listening," she said. "It gets worse. 'One acquaintance of mine, after outsourcing her family's needs all day, rushes home from her job each evening to prepare dinner. Because she arrives only moments before her husband, she's developed a sneaky technique to misdirect his attention away from the lack of progress in the kitchen. She quickly sautés an onion, allowing the homey aroma to suffuse through the house. Thinking a wholesome family dinner is imminent, he settles down to enjoy a moment's peace. Naturally, he's surprised to be served hastily assembled tuna fish sandwiches.'"

Georgia switched off the phone.

"As a man," Jonah crowed, "I feel for the guy. He thinks he's getting a delectable onion for dinner and instead the bitch hurls a can of tuna fish in his face while he's trying to relax with the paper. No wonder there's outrage. Who wrote this? Beezon?"

"Some 'parenting expert.' It's old. The *Bulletin* linked to it today under a section called *Managing Stress: Your Job and Your Family.*"

He widened his eyes, no doubt inferring from her icy tone that he'd better tread carefully. "Well, at least it has gifted us a new term for chauvinists. Henceforth, they shall be known to us as Onions."

"The question is," Georgia said, "if the children have been suffering all day without their parents, why is it okay for the dad to come home and ignore them while he waits for his onion?"

Jonah eyed her, an evaluative look on his face. Since it was becoming more and more evident it wasn't in the cards for her, Georgia didn't like articulating it, even to herself, but she did want a child. She wanted a child badly. A baby, sure: a cooing, rosy, round-cheeked angel who would gaze sleepily around and then curl up, buglike, on her chest; she could handle that. She didn't want colic and diapers and relentless shrieking demands for food, but she understood, in the abstract, that those things were part of the bargain. Her fantasies of an older child, however, were more sharply drawn. She'd be a mini Georgia: long auburn hair with wispy tips; skin so freckled it looked tan; smart, tough, a genuine smart-ass. Georgia would explain things to her and she'd listen, her little head cocked, and then she'd ask astute questions. They'd read books, hike mountains, tinker together in the backyard to build machines. They'd be confidantes.

Jonah's thoughts had drifted in a different direction, his eyebrows knitting together in a sad frown. "My mother didn't work. And it sure wasn't because she wanted to be with me."

"Mine either," Georgia said, more sharply than she'd intended. Jonah swung his head around to look at her. It took only a few seconds for his gaze to soften into comprehension, followed by an expression Georgia truly despised: pity.

She hadn't spoken to her mother since she was five. She'd disappeared from Georgia's life, utterly and irrevocably, without so much as a written note. Because Georgia had been so young, she didn't remember everything, of course, but for a long time—or some period of time that seemed long in her childish mind—she'd thought her mother was coming back.

"What's the latest? Does Stewart think arbitration will help?"

She knew he knew she was changing the subject, but he accepted her avoidance with grace. "He does not. He says every time he talks to the clinic's attorney, he gets the feeling a great black cloud of vultures is gathering overhead, preparing to pluck out my eyes."

"Stewie said that?"

"Yeah. No. He didn't phrase it like that, because Stewie was born without imagination. But I got the gist: he thinks arbitration won't get my job back. Or my patients back."

"What's your next move?"

"I don't know; that's what we're strategizing about today."

A door across the room opened, revealing Stewart's receptionist. "He can see you now," she said.

~~~~~~

The offices of Stewart Hessenheffer, Esq., were exactly as Georgia had imagined them: traditional and boring, full of leather-bound law volumes and dark-grained imitation Regency furniture. Fittingly, Stewart himself was traditional and boring, with a thin nondescript face, colorless hair, and an affectless droning voice. If you wanted to be charitable, you'd describe him as the perfect secret agent, because he was so hard to remember. If you didn't—and not to cast any aspersion on his lawyering skills—you might reasonably observe that Stewie was less likely to impale you on the razor-sharp spear of his legal prowess and more likely to talk until you keeled over. But what did Georgia know about lawyering? Maybe boring people to death was a legitimate legal strategy.

She made a mental note to find out how Stewart had wound up with a preponderance of discrimination cases. It wasn't a stretch to picture him as an estate attorney or a corporate lawyer, but the practice of discrimination law called to mind someone more along the lines of a fiery young person of color from the ACLU. Maybe he liked playing against type.

She'd no sooner thought this than she remembered Jonah had mentioned meeting Stewart in his gay poker group. She looked at him again with more than a little embarrassment. Lost in her reverie over Stewie's appearance, she'd spaced during the last portion of the meeting. They were seated around an oval mahogany table, Jonah and Georgia on one side, Stewart on the other, and he'd been talking steadily, finally finishing with some questions about the members of the executive committee.

"Donovan Wright," Jonah said. Georgia tensed, an involuntary reaction, and then cringed again at the fact that even his name had power over her. "I think he might be an ally."

"He's not an ally," she said, so sharply both men turned to look at her.

"I mean, I know he's not a proponent of gay rights or anything like that, but I think he might be persuadable that I should be rehired."

"Based on what? He's scum, Jonah."

"I did a little research. He has a gay cousin."

"So what?" Her voice had kicked up a few notches too many and she tried to dial it down. "Everybody has a gay cousin; they just don't all know it. Maybe he hates his cousin. He probably hates his cousin. Leave him out of this."

"We can't leave him out of it." Jonah, baffled, raised his voice. "He's on the executive committee. I already left a message about setting up a meeting with him."

"No," she cried. "No, don't do that."

Silence. Both Jonah and Stewart were staring at her, Stewart with polite puzzlement, and Jonah with an expression of dawning comprehension. She rushed to fill the silence. "Never mind. Meet with him if you want."

"Stewart," said Jonah. He pushed his chair back from the table and stood. "Would you mind giving us a moment?"

Stewart, nodding assent, gathered up a few papers from the table and slipped out of the room. The sound of Georgia's breathing, fast and ragged, filled her ears. She concentrated on trying to slow it as Jonah walked around the table, gently rotated her chair, and knelt in front of her. He picked up her hands. "Tell me," he said.

14

FALSUS IN UNO,
FALSUS IN OMNIBUS

Almost six months ago, there had been a code at the clinic.

It had been awful, a tragedy. The cheerleaders at a local high school had been performing a maneuver called a pike basket toss, and even though this was a fairly routine stunt, something had gone wrong. The girl who'd been flung into the air had been dropped, or missed her catchers, or somehow landed incorrectly. Georgia'd never been clear on the specifics, although apparently a viral video of the event existed, providing entertainment for the legions of ghouls out there who got their kicks from watching a beautiful sixteen-year-old break her neck.

The girl had been transported to the biggest trauma center in Charleston, where she'd remained for more than a month, through spine-stabilizing surgeries and multiple evaluations. By the time she'd transferred to the rehab facility at the clinic, it seemed conclusive: she was unlikely to walk again, and, even more devastating, would have only limited use of her hands.

Georgia had the bad luck to be present when the girl coded, because she'd been called on a neurogenic bladder consult. It was near the end of the day, and she walked into the room with no warning of what she'd find: a young girl, so slight that her immobile limbs and torso barely created a rise under the sheet, her face dusky from lack of oxygen, her blue eyes staring sightlessly ahead. It took a moment to sink in: evidently, Georgia had bungled into the room just ahead of the Grim Reaper. She found herself so unprepared for the sight of imminent death that she stood for a full five seconds before screaming out the door for the nurses to bring a crash cart.

The code, too, had gone spectacularly wrong. As the first physician present, Georgia knew she'd have to run it until someone more competent arrived, and that made her nervous as hell because, while she could start CPR like a boss, the main intervention this girl needed, immediately, was defibrillation and an airway. Georgia hadn't intubated anyone in years; it wasn't something the training for her specialty emphasized. With shaky hands she attached a pulse oximeter to one of the child's icy blue fingers as one of the nurses grabbed a defibrillator and another started chest compressions. Georgia had to hold the mask to the girl's face tightly, with two hands, because her chin was so tiny the air seeped around it, but even so, it wasn't doing any good. Her oxygen levels weren't rising. Weren't there any respiratory therapists nearby?

Georgia realized she was going to have to try to intubate her.

A tremor rattled her hands as she attached the curved blade of the laryngoscope to its handle. Even had she been confident in her ability to place the breathing tube in the girl's trachea instead of her esophagus, this was going to be difficult; because of the injury to her spine, Georgia couldn't simply open her mouth and yank back her neck to get a good view. A nurse's aide wheeled a black, snaky contraption into the room, setting it next to the crash cart. Georgia recognized it as a fiberoptic scope—a tube with a camera on the end of it, which would allow visualization of the structures in the girl's throat without tilting her head—but she didn't know how to turn it on. She reached for it anyway and yelped in relief when someone appeared beside her and took it from her hand.

Donovan Wright. Without a word, he took over, and within thirty seconds, the tube was in place and connected to a ventilator. For a brief, intense second their eyes met. Georgia held the precious tube in place while he secured it with tape and she mouthed her gratitude: "Thank you."

By now, chaos gripped the room: people churned at the bedside, wielding defibrillator paddles and starting IVs; discarded equipment wrappings littered the floor; bloody gauze was crumpled atop rickety metal Mayo stands. From outside, an eerie, whooping wail of grief: someone in the girl's family must have arrived.

The code kept going. Georgia switched places with the valiant but exhausted nurse who'd been doing chest compressions, her arms aching at the strain after only a few moments. No one wanted to call it, especially after all the indignity and pain this child had endured in order to cling to life. So they kept at it, doggedly compressing and zapping, forcing air in and out of her lungs, sending shots of epinephrine through her sluggish bloodstream, until someone finally bowed to the inevitable and called it. Georgia felt arms wrapped around hers, holding her back from performing any more compressions; she had not realized they'd been shouting at her to stop.

"Time of death," said a voice behind her, "six seventeen p.m."

~~~~~~

The thing was, the outcome of the code had not been her fault. If anything, it had been preordained; the girl had probably been without oxygen for a significant time when Georgia found her. Rehab patients weren't on telemetry, and this girl had been doing well, her youth and her otherwise good health working in her favor, so she didn't have eyes on her every second. Usually one of her parents stayed with her, but that day her mother had stepped out; Georgia never did find out why. And yes, it was tragic, and yes, it was normal to feel stunned and distressed after a code—especially when they weren't a daily part of your job—but she barely knew this child. She'd met her only once before. She had done everything she could do to try to save her, and, thanks to the timely intervention of Donovan Wright, she hadn't screwed anything up.

So why then, once it was all over, had Georgia staggered out of the room until she landed on an empty corridor, pressing one cheek and then the other against the cool cinder-block wall, her legs trembling with such violence they could not support her? This was not the doctorly way to react. This was not even the Georgia way to react. But something about the juxtaposition of what she'd expected to see—an engaged, expressive patient—and what she'd actually seen, the buggish eyes, the gaping mouth, the blue skin, had thrown her, as had her desperate panic when Georgia'd thought she'd kill the child by screwing up her breathing tube.

She'd had a case go wrong last year and her patient had done poorly, and it had haunted her in a way she'd never have anticipated. She could not bear the idea that she'd almost harmed someone again.

She wanted to cry, and she hated to cry, and that made her angry. So she sat puddled on the floor, up against the wall, in her stupid little seething pile of emotions, and she didn't hear the footsteps.

She didn't actually stand, or at least she didn't think she had, but suddenly she found herself supported by another body.

"I've got you," someone said, somewhat roughly. Startled out of her reverie, she looked up and found herself facing Donovan Wright.

This took a few seconds to process. Although they had very little in common, over the past year she'd developed an easy camaraderie with Donovan. Their interaction in the beginning had been limited to a couple banal pleasantries, including some pointless chitchat in the surgeon's lounge one day while waiting for their respective cases to start, during which he'd shown her a picture of his family, naming his four blond sons with obvious pride, but not naming or mentioning his blond, pallid wife; and one longer, slightly heated discussion a few months later related to whether or not people living in Charleston had any business being fans of the Carolina Panthers. The football argument had broken the ice, though: after that, he sought her out from time to time in the lounge or in the cafeteria during their limited minutes of downtime, mainly to talk about sports or clinic gossip, or, on a couple awkward occasions, a complaint about his wife.

It wasn't unusual for people to think they were better friends with Georgia than they were; she didn't know why, but something about her face or the way she dressed seemed to give people the impression they could unload on her. She didn't mind—she was happy to listen to anyone who needed it—but even so, Donovan Wright didn't interest her. He was fundamentally a boring guy; she'd spent her life seeking an antidote to men like him.

Therefore, she had no reason to ever think she'd one day find him grinding himself against her in a remote hallway in the rehab center. At first, before she realized what was happening, she was grateful: she interpreted his presence, even the fact that he'd hauled her to her feet, as an attempt at comfort. Or maybe he wanted comfort himself; she'd seen him at the end of the code, his blond hair damp, his neck pink and blotchy. He did not look good.

But then: his hands were roaming her breasts, pressing against her back, clutching her ass. She gasped in shock.

Her gasp didn't calm matters down any. Misreading her reaction as lust instead of horror, Donovan lifted her off the ground, simultaneously groping the rest of her body with what seemed to be twenty-five tentacled hands. His lips, thin and rubbery, smacked against her neck. "Wait," she said, "no," but he carried her about five feet down the hall and nudged open the door to a supply closet lit by a flickering fluorescent tube.

"Donovan," she said. "Stop."

"Georgia," he breathed. "That was— Oh, God."

"No. I'm not—"

His mouth smashed into hers. She tried again to say something but the only sound she could produce was an underwater *wohhh*. Nausea surged up from her midsection. If she vomited into his mouth the only option left would be death from instant mortification; the thought of regurgitating her sushi dinner into someone's open throat was so repellent it almost produced the exact circumstance she wanted to avoid. She wrenched her head to the side and, in desperation, clamped her teeth together. Donovan seized the opportunity to start gnawing on her neck with his rubbery lips, smashing her back against the ridge of a shelf. She felt him pawing between her legs, tugging at the zipper on her pants. How was this happening? Her ability to articulate thoughts vanished, even in her own mind. She raised an arm, and, with great strain, shoved his face off her neck.

"You little tease," he breathed. His pupils were tiny pinpricks.

She had to get away. But in an irony worthy of an O. Henry story, she had morphed into one of the rehab patients, aphasic and disoriented. She tried and failed to command her legs to move. All other sensations had been eclipsed by the urge to vomit. She began to breathe through her nose, ragged desperate breaths.

"Mmm, mmm," said Donovan. Sweat slicked his forehead; it oozed from his temples onto the side of her face. His breath, fetid and revolting, mingled with hers. With a mighty effort, she shoved him, hard enough that he staggered back a step or two. Seizing the opportunity, she lurched to one side, just outside his reach.

"No," she said. "Donovan, no."

He stared. "I thought—" For one fleeting second he looked bewildered and vulnerable, like a child who's been smacked, who didn't know, even, that getting smacked was a thing. She'd already reached an appeasing arm toward him, feeling bad, she supposed, at his embarrassment, or maybe even feeling some vestigial flush of feminine guilt for rejecting someone who wanted her, but then his face changed again. His small pupils darkened even as the white space around them expanded, giving him the look of a creepy cartoon owl. "Are you kidding?" he said.

"I'm sorry—" she began, and then stopped. What the hell was she sorry about? She hadn't asked to be groped in a supply closet. She started to say more when she traced the path of his eyes to her chest and realized he'd ripped her shirt open and pushed her bra up. Face flaming, she grabbed the edges of her shirt and pulled them together.

"You're *sorry*?"

"Please don't—"

His eyes flashed; all she could see was a rim of icy blue. Before she could finish her sentence he'd thrust up a hand, gesturing backward with such blazing fury that she flinched, even though the swipe of his arm had been away from her. "What was all this about, then?"

"All what?"

"You've been coming on to me for months."

Her mouth fell open.

"And I just saved your ass in there. What about that? Was that nothing?"

A feeling of shame swamped her that she had not wanted to be the one to try to intubate the girl. Some rational part of her brain insisted that this was wrong: she was not an ER doc or an anesthesiologist; being competent at intubating people was not part of her everyday job. But the rational part of her brain, subsumed by a great tide of adrenaline, could not get any traction.

It was stifling in this closet, even if hurt and accusation hadn't been emanating from him, poisoning the atmosphere. He opened his mouth as if to speak, then abruptly closed it, reaching up with an angry finger to flick off the lights in the closet as he kicked open the door. He was gone before Georgia could react, the door slamming behind him, hard enough to rattle the shelving full of toilet paper rolls and thin white hospital towels. She leaned against the vertical support beam of a shelf and slid to the ground, her breath exiting her chest in a keening bark.

She lowered her head to her knees and rocked.

~~~~~~

By the time Stewart came back into the room, Georgia had resigned herself. She couldn't keep the ugly episode between her and Donovan a secret. Now that she'd breached the dam by telling Jonah the entire story, it would surely become easier to tell other people.

And the more people who knew, the more the story would change. People had no qualms about rendering judgments on events they didn't witness and didn't understand; for most, reality was filtered through perception. She'd cease to be herself and become a symbol, an emblem of the culture wars, an embodiment of a belief, someone you supported or hated. What had actually happened, and her reaction to it, would become irrelevant.

In retrospect, all she could think was that the code and its terrible aftermath must have disarmed her, somehow opening up her skull and applying an iron to her brain, searing out all its ridges until nothing remained but featureless white noise. It seemed as if the assault had happened to someone else. That fit with her memories of the event too: when she looked back on it, her vision flickered like a strobe light, revealing in pulsating shiny bursts a woman doubled over in a closet; not her, though, not her, not her.

It was still hard to believe. If you had told her before this happened that someone would feel her up in a hallway at work without her consent, she'd have told you exactly how that would go down: her professional devotion to testicles notwithstanding, she'd kick him in the balls as hard as she could, and then, for good measure, she'd spit in his face. Georgia did not think of herself as some pliant good girl who worried about hurting normal people's feelings, let alone someone who worried about hurting the ego of a blustery alpha-male doctor. She generally didn't care that much about what people thought of her, unless they were people who mattered to her. But still, if he had apologized, if he had said he misunderstood or read the signals wrong or was overwrought in the aftermath of the code—anything—she'd have let him save face. But instead he transfigured his embarrassment into toxic anger and blamed her.

People thought they knew how they'd respond in that situation? They didn't. It didn't happen with academic forewarning and a couple of cool heads. For instance: Georgia'd have definitely counted herself among the people who thought sexual assault should be reported. She might be a bit roguish in the way she dressed, and you could credibly accuse her of a progressive slant on issues such as the legalization of drugs (yes, they should be legal, and no, not because she had any personal desire to party down all the time), but she was not soft on crime. She had a keen sense of right and wrong. She had a conscience. She didn't condone liars or thieves or people who ripped other people's bras open at work in horror-movie-quality supply closets lit by tenuous fluorescent bulbs. If it had happened to her friend, she'd be all over her to go to the clinic's HR department, or maybe even the police.

But here was the thing. Georgia didn't have any friends present when it happened, and her overriding concern in the moment—all she could think about—was getting out of that closet and down the hall and out of the building and up the stairs in the garage and into her car without anyone seeing her ripped shirt. She wasn't so much angry or frightened at first as she was in a state of disbelief. She could not accept the fact that this had just happened; it seemed surreal, nightmarish, totally unreal.

But, of course, it did happen. Pretending it didn't, or allowing her brain to warp reality into something a little more palatable than victimhood, wasn't helpful. By the time she could face it, though, it was no longer possible to do anything about it. She'd wrenched off the shirt the moment she entered her house, and it was now long gone, relegated to the middle of some festering heap in the Charleston County landfill. She didn't have any photographable injuries, and she didn't go crying to anyone else who could attest to her traumatized state. She didn't have any disgusting Donovan Wright DNA to offer up to a lab. Everyone knew what happened to women who claimed sexual assault when they could not prove it. Georgia wasn't entirely unsympathetic to skepticism; she preferred a logical world to an emotional one, and sometimes that meant crimes went unpunished. You couldn't convict someone based solely on someone else's word. She had absolutely nothing to back up any assertion she might make to anyone that this had ever happened.

And therefore she'd never said a word to anyone.

But there was another facet to this, one just beginning to make itself known to her. Perhaps this awful thing gave her the power to help Jonah. Donovan must harbor some worry she'd go public with this. He didn't know she hadn't told anyone. For all he knew she'd gone home, carefully scraped his skin cells from beneath her fingernails, and preserved them. Maybe his fingerprints were on the remaining buttons of the torn shirt she no longer possessed. Maybe, that evening, she had hit record on the cell phone in her pocket.

"I think I should go with Jonah to the next meeting with Donovan," she told Stewart.

"You don't have to do that."

"Not a chance," said Jonah, who still held her hand under the table. "There's no way I'm letting you do that."

"I take it there was an incident between the two of you," Stewart said, after a moment's pause. "And you believe it would offer some leverage in negotiations with Dr. Wright on behalf of Dr. Tsukada. Are you comfortable telling me the details?"

She wasn't, of course, but she did. And she was right; this time was easier. Stewart listened, his fingers steepled up in contemplative absorption, pausing every now and then to ask a question. By the time she finished, he'd filled several pages with notes.

"One thought," Stewart said. "You could take a polygraph. It doesn't commit you to any particular course of action, but in the absence of other evidence it could prove useful."

"A lie detector test?"

"Yes. It's a useful signifier of your veracity, or at least your perceived veracity."

"In English, though," Jonah said, and then, having evidently appointed himself as Stewart's legalese translator, "he's saying it will demonstrate you're telling the truth."

"No," said Stewart. He tilted his head slightly, addressing his comment to Georgia. "Let us make the assumption that you are not a psychopath."

"Allow me to stipulate," said Jonah. "She's not psycho."

"Excellent," said Stewart. He turned back to her. "If you pass a polygraph, it indicates your physiological reactions may be compatible with honest responses to the questions. As you probably know, polygraphs are not admissible in court, but that doesn't matter to us, because this is not a court. What matters is your willingness to take the test; it indicates you believe your story to be true."

"My story *is* true."

Stewart slid his glasses down the considerable length of his nose, peering over them at her. "The truth—whether or not this happened, and whether or not it happened in the manner you describe—is of very little consequence to us in the absence of a witness, or a recording device, or something similar."

"The truth doesn't matter?"

"Not really," Stewart said gently. He gave her time, waiting until she processed this statement. "We cannot prove it happened, and I certainly hope Dr. Wright cannot disprove it happened. Forget about the truth. What matters are the optics."

She felt her spine straighten. "The optics?"

"If I were representing you," he continued, "and you intended to pursue a claim against Dr. Wright, there are certain things I'd advise you. It matters who comes across as more credible in a situation like this. Does your story make sense in the context of what is known about both you and the man you accuse? Is there any corroborating material: evidence that both parties were present at the time? Or is there someone to whom you may have contemporaneously relayed the events from your perspective? In this case, no. Are both parties willing to submit to a polygraph examination? Is there anyone upon whom the accused may have inflicted similar traumas? Do you have a history of similar accusations against other men? Do you have any potential secondary gain from this accusation? Have either of the parties lied about anything significant before? And that last one relates to our biggest concern: if either of you could be proven to be lying—about anything relating to this accusation, no matter how minor or seemingly irrelevant—it's game over, no matter what actually happened. The other person wins."

Somewhere in the building, an air-conditioning unit kicked on. Recessed within the floor at her feet, a brass vent rattled faintly and, like magic, a cool stream of air entered the room. Georgia shivered—it was already cold in here—and then sat up straight. As if carried on the current, a little burst of clarity appeared, hovering with tantalizing promise just outside her grasp until, her heart racing, she lunged to pluck it from the air. *"Falsus in uno, falsus in omnibus,"* she said.

"That is correct," said Stewart. Eyebrows slightly raised, he tilted his head toward her in appreciation.

"What is correct?" said Jonah. "What did you say?"

"It's the Latin term for what Stewart was saying. It means *false in one thing, false in everything.* If they can show you got one thing wrong, even if it doesn't really matter, then no one will believe anything you say."

"Well, that's fine, because I never lie," said Jonah.

"Or exaggerate."

Jonah's eyes widened. "Does sarcasm count?" He put his head down on his crossed arms. "Oh, fuck, I'm doomed."

Stewart brought the train back to the station. "Dr. Brown," he said. "I take it you do not intend to pursue any legal options toward Dr. Wright?"

"That's right. And just so we're clear, I'm not planning to overtly threaten Donovan either." She thought back to his demeanor during the meeting when Jonah was fired; he'd seemed uneasy. "But I have no qualms about allowing him to make his own interpretation of my support of Jonah."

Jonah let go of her hand. "You can't let him get away with this, Georgia! You should sue him for harassment."

Stewart removed his reading glasses, folded them, and set them on the table. "Even if she sued," he said, in a gentler tone than she'd heard him use before, "she might be prevented from publicly commenting on anything that happened to her."

"Seriously?" said Jonah, dropping his head back into his hands.

She replayed the last portion of Stewart's sentence in her mind. "What about Jonah? I thought your entire strategy in Jonah's situation revolved around bringing this to the public's attention."

"Ah," said Stewart. "That's because they made a mistake. A big one." He paused. "Or rather, their attorneys did. There's a significant error in the original arbitration clause: it does not include a confidentiality provision."

A light switched on for Jonah. "You mean there's no rule saying I can't talk."

"That's correct. Because there was no provision regarding confidentiality in the original electronic document you signed, you're free to talk about what happened to you as much as you want."

Georgia was still puzzled. "That's the same thing I signed, though."

"Yes, but you can be sure now that they've seen the counter-letters Jonah has been sending to his patients, they're going to add a clause to the arbitration document stating one of the conditions is confidentiality— anyone who has a problem with the clinic may not be legally allowed to make public comments on their situation. One of the major goals for companies who require these agreements is to prevent the public, including other people in their employ, from knowing anything about cases against them. It was a big oversight to leave this out."

"Why would anyone agree to sign anything giving up their right to talk about their own circumstances?"

"They can force you to accept this provision the same way they made you sign the original agreement to use arbitration: it is a condition of your employment. They can fire you if you don't agree. I'd expect an amended arbitration agreement to go out to every employee of your clinic any day now."

"Well," she said, "it doesn't matter. Even if I thought I could win, I wouldn't sue—or arbitrate—anything. I don't want to keep reliving this."

"Even if you thought you'd win?" Jonah stared at her.

"Correct. But we all know I wouldn't win, so what choice do I have at this point? I can't prove it. If I bring it up and can't account for every single detail, I'll be branded as a liar. If I bring it up and cannot remember everything, I'll be branded as a liar. And if I bring it up and then drop it, I'll be branded as a liar." She stared past them, her gaze unfocused. "I probably should have kept my mouth shut in the first place."

"If you brought it up and then didn't pursue it," concurred Stewart, "Dr. Wright would almost certainly claim you slandered him. I doubt he'd pursue legal action; I'd advise him not to, if I were his attorney, given the same constraints you have: he cannot prove you are lying." He let loose with an irony-conveying *harrumph*. "Theoretically, if you made these claims and then dropped them, allowing him to proceed unchallenged in his characterization of them as untrue—then he'd have a case for slander. You spoke something negative and false about him, causing him substantial harm to his reputation."

Jonah leaned forward. "I wonder if he's consulted a lawyer. I mean, what could he be thinking?"

For a few seconds, she tried to imagine it: Donovan Wright in some hushed, upscale law office like this one: floor-to-ceiling bookcases; thick Persian rugs; a silver fox in a thousand-dollar suit gazing solemnly and wisely from behind a desk, discreetly offering a container of tissues when emotions got the better of someone. How would he bring it up? *One second I was trying to save a dying teenager, and the next this woman flung herself on me in a supply closet. What could I do?* It was hopeless; she could no more place herself inside Donovan's mind than she could fathom the motives of a tornado.

"I have no idea," she said.

15

～～～

A DEAL WITH THE DEVIL

The clinic contained two private areas for doctors: one, a space adjacent to the outpatient OR suite; and the other, a larger lounge on the first floor, complete with its own kitchen, a food bar, charting areas, and a television perpetually tuned to *SportsCenter*. It being a weekday morning, this space hummed with bodies. The usual suspects were in all the usual places: a scattering of bleary-eyed hospitalists—internal medicine doctors who ran the inpatient service—parked at computers along the back wall, entering notes from their shifts the night before; a clump of surgeons, awaiting the start times for their morning cases, seated on couches in front of the television; a swirl of people at the breakfast buffet surveying hot metal rectangles full of cheese grits and eggs. Georgia could say this for the ladies who ran the cafeteria: in the time-honored tradition of the South, they equated food with love. None of their doctors were ever going to starve.

Not quite a week had passed since the meeting with Stewart. It was maddening, waiting for word, but the clinic dragged their feet on every communication. All Jonah could do was hunker down and wait. He'd begun to fret about his patients, texting Georgia frequently to see if any of them had reached out to her. She checked her phone now and then slid it back into her pocket.

One of the partners in her urology practice, McLean Andersen, sidled up, his round cheeks puffed out as he munched. Waving a red strip of meat, he unleashed a grin. "Want some bacon?"

This had become their ritual: in reference to the *Pulp Fiction* character who didn't dig on swine, McLean cheerfully offered her bacon almost every morning, and, in keeping with the character, she refused to accept it. Like Georgia, McLean possessed a near-encyclopedic ability to regurgitate eighties and nineties movie lines, which, surely everyone would agree, was a desirable trait in a urologist. Or in anyone, really.

After belting out her lines (*No man, I don't eat pork*) Georgia nodded politely to her carnivorous colleague and plodded over to the coffee machine. Despite the fact that it took foam cups five hundred years to decompose, the clinic insisted on purchasing them, so Georgia kept her own mug squirreled away under the sink. At first she'd used a charming handmade pottery mug, but after weeks of walking into the lounge to find other people drinking from it, she'd eventually switched to one emblazoned with the words *DR. BROWN: URINE GOOD HANDS*. Now no one touched it.

McLean had drifted over to the end of the counter to speak to an ancient, bristly spine surgeon named Rooney Greeley and a bookish anesthesiologist whose name Georgia couldn't remember. She joined them, guzzling from *URINE GOOD HANDS*.

". . . heard they're making us all take a urine test," McLean said. "They don't need to bother in my case. My wife would castrate me if I was messing with drugs."

Rooney, who'd been standing with the immobile passivity of a turtle, suddenly stirred, clapping McLean on the back hard enough to cause him to take a step forward. "Huh," he harrumphed. "Sounds like your wife rules the roost."

Georgia rolled her eyes at McLean, who, despite his ire about the drug testing, managed a grin in her direction. Rooney was about a thousand years old and still regarded women through a prehistoric filter where you told them the way it was going to be and they said "Yes, dear" and went to iron some socks. He'd only barely managed to adjust to the newfangled idea of female surgeons, and now a bunch of evil administrators were swooping in to force him to pee in a cup. She almost felt sorry for the guy.

McLean diplomatically ignored Rooney's spousal assessment. "Does anyone know any specifics about the drug theft?"

"The administrators do," said the anesthesiologist. "The executive committee met about it last night. Claude Reiner, Dan Tolbert from internal medicine"—he gestured across the room—"Judd Sluder from cardiology, Donovan Wright. John Beezon, of course. The hospital's lawyers were there too."

Georgia snorted. "So basically a bunch of old white dudes."

"Don't start that PC stuff with us, Georgia," McLean said, winking at her. Next to him, Rooney, breathing heavily, appeared to have fallen asleep standing up. Georgia stared, fascinated, as his nose hairs ruffled with each prodigious exhalation.

The anesthesiologist sidestepped the issue of representation on the committee. "I heard it's been a mixture of drugs," he said, "not just opiates. Ketamine, some benzos."

Rooney roused himself; apparently he was listening with his eyes closed. "Why in God's name would anyone steal ketamine? It puts you to sleep."

"Technically, it doesn't," said the anesthesiologist. His nose twitched in a rabbity fashion and he absently rubbed it with his sleeve. "It's a dissociative anesthetic. It detaches you from reality."

"And why, oh why, would anyone ever want to detach from reality?" said McLean, grinning.

Georgia drifted a few feet away to slurp her coffee. Rooney and McLean and the anesthesiologist, still talking, had moved from the counter to a clump of chairs in front of the television, with several other people joining them. Marianna Aiken, a plastic surgeon, passed behind the couch, pausing and squatting in her block-heeled pumps to bestow an air-kiss on the anesthesiologist's face, whose name, Georgia now remembered, was Tom Aiken.

Georgia eased toward the group. ". . . Jonah Tsukada's the one suspected of the medication theft," a pediatrician, Gretchen Nease, was saying. "So maybe that's why he was fired."

"What? That didn't happen." Georgia had spoken more loudly than she'd intended; across the room, a couple of the bleary hospitalists turned their heads.

"I'm certain Jonah wouldn't steal medications," offered someone. Georgia swung her head around to note Darby Gibbes standing next to the Aikens. If Georgia's tone had caused everyone to tense, Darby's had the opposite reaction: Gretchen Nease was smiling at her, and so was Tom Aiken. Even old Rooney Greeley had softened.

She tried again with Gretchen, this time trying to imitate Darby's soft accent. "Where did you hear that?"

"From one of the PAs. In fact, I've heard lots of people talking about it since it was on the news the other day." People nodded; over the weekend, both the local newspaper and the local TV stations had carried the story, framed as a dispute with a troubled employee. "The first thing they said was that he'd been engaging in questionable medical practices"—Gretchen answered the question before Georgia could get it out—"specifically, I think they were talking about hormone therapy for transgender people."

"That's not—"

"I'm just telling you what they said. Or that's what I think they said; they weren't talking to me. But they moved on from that right away to the missing drugs."

"Could they point to anything to indicate he did it?"

"Yes, actually," Gretchen said. "I heard they found a bottle of fentanyl in a coat pocket hanging outside the procedure room. Around the time Jonah was fired."

"Whose coat?" Georgia asked, her mouth suddenly dry.

A very slight smile appeared on Gretchen's face. "Jonah's," she said.

Darby placed a hand on Georgia's arm before she could respond. "This is only speculation, y'all. We shouldn't repeat it."

"They were right to kick him out," said Rooney. "And any other drug users along with him."

Darby's voice took on a faint quiver. "People who abuse drugs need treatment, not condemnation."

"Listen," Georgia said, "I was in the meeting when Jonah got fired. They fired him because he treats queer people. Not because of medication in a coat pocket, which they didn't say a thing about and which anyone could have placed there. If they'd been able to prove he did it, they'd have fired him for that when it happened. He didn't do it."

She looked around: at the word *queer*, everyone's eyes had shifted away. Only McLean and Darby were still looking at her. "Please, you guys. We've got to band together to fight this idea that the hospital can dictate who we treat. I'm going to put together a petition and I hope y'all will get behind it."

Silence. Even the hospitalists across the room had stopped clacking at their computer keys; in the back of the room, a couple people just outside Georgia's visual field slipped outside into the hall. Rooney Greeley lumbered up to his feet, wearing an expression that looked suspiciously like amusement. "OR," he grunted, pointing in the direction of the operating rooms. He left.

Well, fine. The odds of Rooney Greeley supporting someone he considered to be a fancy-pants homosexual were obviously nil. But the others . . . Georgia rotated her head around the circle. Marianna and Tom and Gretchen and two other guys Georgia didn't know had all developed a sudden passionate interest in a *SportsCenter* debate between two blockheaded behemoths over whether or not there should be a fifteen-yard no-blocking zone in front of the kickoff team. "Well," said Tom Aiken, with an ostentatious fake stretch, "I better hit it."

"Me too," Gretchen and Marianna said simultaneously. One of

them giggled. The other guys didn't say anything at all as they drifted off. The hospitalists resumed their weary typing.

Only McLean and Darby were left. "I'll sign your petition, honey," said Darby softly. She straightened the gold chain at her neck; it was tiny, with a pearl cross looped at the end.

Georgia looked at McLean. He shrugged, his smooth, boyish face blank. Then he smiled. "Sure, I'll sign it." Before Georgia could thank him, he leveled a finger at her. "But if your boy turns out to be a junkie, you owe me dinner."

～～～～～

Georgia stepped into the OR hallway. Her first case didn't start for another ten minutes; she should've been using the time to review the schedule for the day, but a gnawing sensation had invaded her gut.

Amsterdam aside, Jonah had never been a drug user. He flirted on the boundary of inappropriate alcohol use, perhaps, but had never quite crossed the line. He didn't drink on a daily basis or upon awakening or during professional hours. He didn't reach for the bottle as a crutch. Had he gotten hammered and said something regrettable on Grindr? Yes. But, really, who hadn't?

She was certain Jonah could never hide a drug habit from her. Physicians who stole opiates, however, were a stealthy bunch. They wargamed their strategies; they took precautions. They performed their duties at work with clear-eyed competence, going the extra mile to be a hard worker, to treat their patients with care, to perform their duties with collegial integrity. Read any profile of a physician addict and you'd invariably read this line: *She's the last one I'd have ever suspected.* They steered their ships along without a hint of distress, until finally and inevitably the habit rose up from their sea of deceit, foaming and monstrous, to swallow them whole.

But apparently, she was the only one who'd have a problem believing that Jonah was a druggie who stole from the hospital. Why was it so easy for everyone else to assume he'd break the ultimate taboo for a physician?

"Dr. Brown."

She looked up and found herself only a few feet away from Donovan Wright. Without thinking, she whirled on one heel, but he reached for her arm, clamping it in the same iron grip he'd displayed in the hall the other day. She wrenched it away.

"I need a moment," he said.

This was not the first time they'd encountered each other since the afternoon in the closet, obviously, but it was the first time they'd been alone. Or virtually alone, anyway: a few people traipsed along the hall a bit farther down, outside hearing range. Georgia weighed whether it would cause a noticeable commotion if she refused to speak to him. But then she thought of her discussion with Stewart and Donovan's strange silence when Jonah had been fired. Slowly and deliberately, she met his gaze.

"I can help him," he said, his pale eyes strangely intense.

She didn't know what she'd been expecting, but it wasn't this. "What do you mean?"

"I think it's a mistake, firing Dr. Tsukada, and it's an even bigger mistake to dismiss his patients."

"You do?"

"I do. We shouldn't discriminate on the basis of the morality or immorality of our patients."

At the word *immorality* the blue light of a flame switched on in the recesses of her skull. "Because we are all immoral in some fashion?"

"We are," he agreed, not taking the bait. "I don't have to approve of the behavior, but it isn't a good idea to exclude a group of patients from the clinic on the basis of lifestyle choices."

"When you say choices—" she began, but he interrupted.

"Look, I'm sure you and I might have certain disagreements when it comes to social issues," he said. "But I heard what you said in the lounge just now, and I wanted to tell you I don't think the clinic should get rid of Dr. Tsukada or his patients. From everything I've heard, his patient care is excellent. What these people do on their own time is none of the clinic's business."

She rolled her eyes.

His tone was restrained. "Look, I'm offering to help. If he doesn't want it . . ."

She stared at him; to her surprise, he looked sincere. If this was a chance to aid Jonah, she'd better swallow her revulsion and obtain whatever inside information she could. "You're on the executive committee. Did they really find fentanyl in his coat pocket?"

"They did," he said, his expression unreadable.

"But they didn't use that as a rationale for firing him," she said, remembering that during the meeting Beezon had alluded to something else they had on Jonah.

"That's right. I convinced them not to."

She couldn't hide her surprise. "*You* did?"

"Like you said, anyone could have placed it there. A hundred people go in and out of the vestibule in front of the procedure room. Sometimes extra coats hang there for weeks."

"So how are you proposing you'd help him?"

"I haven't figured out the most effective approach," he said, glancing in the direction of the lounge. "The clinic is already seeking stronger ammunition for having fired him. John Beezon really hates him." He paused. "He hates you too."

"You're right," she said. "Beezon's a lost cause, obviously, in terms of whatever the arbitration yields. It would be better for everyone if the clinic rethinks things before the arbitration process."

"I agree."

The idea of aligning herself with Donovan, for any reason, was repugnant. Even standing here next to him now, she had to fight the urge to flee, or better yet, to apply the searing flame of her anger onto him. And yet, the possibility that Jonah could have his job back—even at the cost of making a deal with the devil—was too alluring to bypass.

Perhaps he was even sorry for what he'd done, and this offer represented a form of atonement, but more likely, he'd finally started to wake up to the fact that Georgia posed a threat to his reputation.

Donovan was still talking. "Back to your original question: it will probably come down to a discussion between the five docs on the committee, plus John Beezon and the lawyers and whoever shows up from the administration. You're not going to persuade John or Claude. But Judd was always opposed to telling those patients to leave. And I think I could sway Dan. He's a good guy."

Georgia questioned whether she and Donovan would have the same definition of *good guy*, but she wasn't about to argue the point. "So . . . you're saying you'll talk to him before the meeting."

"Yes."

She waited, but that was it. This vague reparation was the closest thing she was going to get to an acknowledgment of the wrong he'd done to her. He deserved revenge, not forgiveness. In a perfect world, he'd have been taken down, first with a nasty shaming via the HR department. She pictured him cringing his way down the clinic corridors. Then, when he'd achieved maximum public humiliation, she'd have appeared and kicked him in the balls. Did that make her a bad urologist? Possibly. But she could live with that.

"Okay," she said, so forcefully Donovan took a step back. "Okay. Make it happen."

~~~~~~

As soon as she closed the exam-room door on her last patient, Georgia raced to her car and called Jonah. "Something happened," she said, accelerating to pass a slow car, and then cursed herself for being cryptic. Predictably, Jonah started yelping and she had to raise her voice to power over him. "Hey! Calm down. I have to tell you: Donovan said he needed to talk to me today."

He fell silent. For about a second. *"What?"*

"He came up to me outside the lounge this morning. He said he wants to help you."

This time, he was slower to answer. "He did?"

She filled him in, speaking quickly. She expected him to be furious about the fentanyl and exultant about the possibility of avoiding arbitration, but his response was uncharacteristically muted. "Do you believe him?"

"I—yes. I guess I do. I'm sure the last thing he wants is to get into a big *he-said, she-said* knockout with me. This will sidestep all that. And it's the right thing to do."

Jonah ignored the last part of her sentence, since neither of them truly believed Donovan would be motivated by anything less than an ulterior motive. "Can you live with this?"

"I can," she said, her voice soft. "What about that fentanyl bottle?"

"I have no freaking clue. It wasn't me."

"Okay. Well, we'll see what Donovan can do with the committee."

"No, we won't. I'm not accepting any assistance from that asshole. And I'm certainly not okay with him thinking he's off the hook for what he did to you just because he says he wants to help me."

"Jones," she said, dismayed, "I already told him to go for it."

"Well, you should have asked my opinion first." Jonah's breath echoed down the phone line. "Can we please, please report him?"

"No," she said. "I just—no."

He sighed. "I will never say a word to anyone if that's what you want, George. But I'd rather stay fired than have that arrogant son of a bitch sticking up for me."

"Okay," she said. "We need to talk some more, clearly. Want to meet me and Dobby for a walk?"

Even now, his voice brightened at the thought of company. "How about a drink? I'm not really down with exercise right now."

"Nope," she said. "We're walking. I'll see you in front of the pineapple statue in Waterfront Park in an hour."

~~~~~~

16

MELATONIN IS OKAY BUT BOURBON WORKS BETTER

Just beyond the iconic fountain lay the glimmering water of the Charleston Harbor, a natural inlet formed by the junction of the Ashley and Cooper rivers. A row of symmetrical palm trees stretched away in both directions at the path's edge, backlit by a cluster of blazing pink and orange clouds. Georgia could just make out Jonah's silhouette, standing with his back to her, looking out over the water. Something about the stillness of his posture moved her; his head cocked, his hands in his pockets, he looked like a statue of a man frozen in eternal contemplation.

This illusion was dispelled as he turned and caught sight of her. "On time," he crowed, thumping his chest. He moved closer, scratching Dobby's head. "The Bible says punctuality is next to godliness."

"First of all, it's not punctuality—it's cleanliness that's next to godliness—and it's not from the Bible, it's from a sermon by John Wesley. In any case, you are almost never punctual." Georgia paused, adding kindly, "You are clean, though."

He glowered at her. "What is wrong with you?"

Taking that question as rhetorical, she moved on. "I need to say something. I was so shocked by Donovan approaching me and offering to help that I didn't even think about what you wanted. Sometimes I try too hard to control everything."

"Sometimes?" he said archly.

"I'm sorry."

"You are forgiven, you bossy bitch. But Dr. Wrong can go fuck himself. I'm not about to truck with Satan just to try to save my own skin."

She dug her fingers into her thighs to keep herself from arguing. Jonah might not like to admit it but he was every bit as stubborn as she was. "I meant to ask you earlier, what have you been doing all week?"

"I've been using this time to better myself," he said piously. "Podcasts, TED talks, maybe an online course or two. Some bodily fitness things."

"Oh my God. You've been lying around all day watching old episodes of *Nailed It*." She smacked him lightly. "Jonah! Your brain is going to rot!"

"I find inspiration in the failures of others, George. Don't get all judgey."

She could feel her lips compressing in worry but hastily rearranged them into a neutral line. Instead of answering, she stopped and pulled Dobby in for a pat. He obliged happily, shaking his bottom so hard he almost smacked her in the face with his tail. "Good boy," she said.

Jonah turned toward the sea and waited, hands back in his pockets. She released Dobby from her embrace and he lunged forward, nearly taking off her arm. They started down the path again, walking into the wind.

"How's Mark?"

"He's good. He's coming to visit."

Jonah's pace increased. "Yes! I'll plan some sightseeing for him. For, ah, when you're at work."

She gave him a fond smile. "He'd like that."

"We need him to think about moving here. You'll have to upgrade your house, obviously."

Georgia knew from experience it would be better not to try to interject logic into this discussion. "Sure, right," she said, and listened for a few minutes to Jonah burble instructions on how not to lose a man.

"It was so strange not having to go to work this week," he said, finally getting back to her question. "For the last ten years, I've bitched and moaned every single morning about waking up early, or staying up all night, or missing whatever fun thing I wanted to do because of work, but now I don't have work anymore and all I want to do is go to work."

"What *did* you do all week?"

"At first I did nothing. I couldn't get on social media because of the thing, and I couldn't read the newspaper because of the thing, and now the local TV stations are covering the thing, so I can't watch them either. I can't go to the gym or the grocery or the bar because I think people are looking at me."

"You seem . . . strong, though," she said cautiously.

He brightened at the compliment. "As it turns out, George, I am remarkably resilient. This week, the thing that bothered me the most was not the fear of the future or financial worries or even the injustice of it all. I'm waking up in the morning and it hits me like a bitchslap; I just can't get over my loneliness. I miss the people at work, even the shitty ones who haven't reached out, and most of all, I miss my patients. Being up in my house all by myself feels like I'm the only survivor of an apocalypse."

Georgia nodded.

"But then," he went on, "I decided to man up. When you come right down to it, the only solution when things go wrong is to think of yourself as a badass survivor."

"Have people from work been supportive?"

He ran a hand though his hair, the end of his sleeve falling back a bit to expose his wrist. "Actually, I haven't heard from many work people."

"Jonah, I am so sorry."

He tried a smile. "My office has a large Onion population, if you know what I mean. I wasn't expecting them to organize a crusade."

"Fine. We'll organize our own crusade."

"Yes." He brightened, then deflated. "Uh-oh."

"No, you're right that Donovan can't be trusted. I've been giving it some thought, what Stewie said about optics," she said. "And I think there's an opportunity there."

"What do you mean?"

"We are not being nearly proactive enough. I mean, what's the goal here?"

Jonah raised an eyebrow. "Our goal? We want our patients back. And we want them to have access to the immeasurable blessing of my brilliance without some hypocritical Onion bellowing that they're sinners."

"And who decides what happens?"

"The arbitrators. Unless the HR department and the executive committee come to their senses first."

"But most of those guys are Onions. Right?"

He considered this. "Yes. Pretty Oniony group."

"So you're setting yourself up for failure."

A breeze blew in off the ocean and ruffled his hair. "So what are you saying? I give up?"

"No." She stopped walking and faced him. "I think, somehow, we have to get people on your side."

"Okay," he said. "Then I have an idea."

~~~~~~

The concept, he said, was uncomplicated. They didn't have to do anything special to paint Beezon in a negative light; they'd simply allow him to speak and then use his words against him.

"I thought," Jonah said, "we could request a private meeting and then wait for him to say something atrocious, which he undoubtedly will; and then, later, we'd threaten to tell the press."

"You mean . . . leveraging public opinion to embarrass the clinic. Like Stewart said."

"Yes. I think most people, no matter where they fall politically, are not okay with banning medical care to an entire population of people. The clinic might genuinely believe this is the right thing, but I think we can count on Beezon to show an uglier side."

"That's fine," said Georgia, "but I don't know if you can be the one to do this. Even if you did manage to get him to say anything outrageous, why would anyone believe you? Beezon would just deny he ever said it and the committee would believe him."

"He can't deny it," Jonah said, wearing a delighted grin, "because we'd record him. With drones!"

No doubt he was picturing them skulking around in disguise as they activated a nest of insect-shaped recorders. "Ah," she said. "Do we need to go that high-tech? How about a cell phone in a coat pocket?"

"Oh," he said. A tiny vertical line appeared between his eyebrows. "I suppose that could work too."

"He might be less suspicious of me than you."

"George," he said, "Beezon thinks you're as much of a monstrosity as me." He considered this, grinning. "Bigger, even."

"Fine," she conceded, pursing her lips in thought. "It would be better if it were someone he likes. What about Darby? I'm going to run with her at her house on Sunday."

"No way," Jonah said. "Darby Gibbes is a sweetheart. I'm not dragging her into this."

"Well," Georgia said, dismissive. "It's a moot point. She would probably never agree to do it. But that's the problem: we need a person who'd never be suspected of an ulterior motive. She'd bounce in there, talk to Beezon about her church or whatever, and you're right, he'd be bound to say something godawful. We could hoist him with his own petard."

Jonah cocked his head, a shock of his hair falling into his eyes. He pushed it back with an aggrieved motion. "I know I'm going to be sorry for wondering, but what—"

"'Hoist him with his own petard' is from Shakespeare. *Hamlet*, I think. A petard was a bomb or an explosive device, and in this case, it blows up its maker. Poetic justice."

"I knew I'd be sorry I asked."

"Forget the petard." Georgia paused, thinking out loud. "What if the person goes in there and vehemently defends you? Beezon will argue."

He stared at her. "You've lost your mind."

"No, I haven't," she said, becoming fired up as she considered this idea. "She'll rhapsodize about how you were the highest-ranked resident in your family medicine program, how you killed your board scores, how many grateful letters you get from patients. She'll talk about all the volunteer stuff you do. By the time she's done, she might even convince Beezon you're a saint."

"This is never gonna work, George, but damn, I am *melting*."

They walked the length of the park and turned off onto East Bay Street toward the Battery, and as the wind blew toward them Georgia caught another whiff of Jonah, who smelled like a brewery. Abruptly, she stopped walking. "I actually had another idea. Earlier. But I've been afraid to bring it up."

"The petard reminded you of this idea?"

It floated in front of her; something about . . . Beezon and his computer. She tried to focus on it, but it eluded her; then, suddenly it coalesced.

"Yes. I want to check with Mark's IT guy, but I have an idea. Let me think about it, okay? Maybe we won't need to record anybody."

"Okay," he said, raising his eyebrows. "This better be good."

"Speaking of being good, behave while you're off work, okay?"

He bristled. "How about you behave? You're not the most diplomatic human being. And I can't always be with you to keep you in line."

"Exactly. So you cannot move away, Jones. I need you."

She could feel his eyes shifting toward her. When he spoke, his voice was uncharacteristically gentle. "You know I don't want to move.

But I have to be honest: I'm not sure how much I want to fight for the prize of going back to a place that scorns my people."

"But I'm here."

His hands rose, fingers fluttering, but he didn't say anything. After a minute, she swayed to a stop, leaning against a pole so Jonah wouldn't see her face.

"Let's do lots of brunch this weekend, okay?" he offered. "We can meet for breakfast at The Daily on Saturday and then Sunday we can go to Husk. We'll talk more."

She forced an upbeat note into her voice. "I can do Saturday, but on Sunday I'm running with Darby at Isle of Palms."

"No problem. I could pick you up from Isle of Palms in the boat!" Jonah loved any excuse to hit the water on the weekends.

"Sure. You can actually walk to Darby's house from the marina if you want. I'll text you the address."

"Look." He walked a few feet away, staring across the shimmering expanse of water at a solitary boat, bobbing in the distance. Behind it, the lights had come on over the distinctive filaments of the Ravenel Bridge, glowing silver against the deepening sky. "You need to temper your expectations. I know I'm the one who suggested this, but I'm not sure we can rewrite history with an iPhone in our pockets. A clinic administrator saying he doesn't approve of queer people probably isn't going to move the needle much."

"But—"

"Listen to me, Georgia." As soon as the words left his mouth she braced herself; all the flippancy was gone from his tone.

"I don't want to go through hell for the privilege of working for a group who sees my patients as an atrocity. If they don't take them back, then I'm going to move no matter what happens with my job."

She tried to interject but he locked his eyes on hers. "You're the closest thing to family I have, and I know you want to help. I love you for it, but you're never going to know what this is like."

Stung, she took a step backward.

"Don't get me wrong," he went on. "I know your job is at risk too. I know how much you care about your patients and I know how pissed you are about the freaking travesty of being told you can't treat them. That's all legit. But you'll never be forced to endure the things they endure. Or the things I endure."

"I know, I—"

"Still," he said, in the same gentle tone, "I know you mean well." He moved toward her and smiled, determined, apparently, to lessen the blow of his implied rebuke. "But I have to say . . . I'm a little bit afraid of the way your mind works. Try to tone down the crazy."

~~~~~

Saturday morning, Georgia met Jonah for breakfast and a vigorous discussion of his situation. After that, granted a rare respite from work, she spent most of the day in her backyard workshop, tinkering with the hidden compartment in a cabinet she was building. At sundown, she curled up in bed with a book, trying to curb her anxiety about what Jonah might be doing. She flicked the pages until midnight, when she found herself in a fitful daze, not quite asleep but not quite awake. Exhaustion hung over her, but she could not rest; some corner of her brain buzzed with worry. She set down the novel she'd been reading and picked up her Bible, reading until she fell into a restless sleep.

The next morning, Sunday, she met Darby for an early run.

After, she watched through a window of the back deck of Darby's home as Darby went indoors and stretched. She looked up as Georgia came in and plopped down at the kitchen table. "So I can be more productive and more intentional with my time," Darby said, jerking her head toward her phone, which she'd just tucked away in a drawer.

"Excellent idea," said Georgia, even though she'd sooner stab herself in the eyeball than separate from her phone. Hiding their phones was the sort of thing overscheduled married people did, along with employing phrases like *more intentional with my time*. "Jonah should be here before long to pick me up. Thanks again for the run."

"Don't thank me," Darby said. "Stick around for a little while. Jonah too. Last night I told the kids we'd have some company this morning, and they can't wait. They love to have visitors." As if to illustrate this, they heard an excited squeal and an answering adult voice in a distant part of the house. Matt and the girls were up.

"We have about five minutes before they descend and eat us alive," she said now, grinning at Georgia as if Georgia were doing her a favor. "Let's hide."

Before she could answer, Darby carried her cup of coffee outdoors onto the deck. After a moment, Georgia followed her outside, where bright tendrils of sunlight shot from beneath a cloud onto the glinting waters of the marsh.

"You okay?" Darby leaned, stiff-armed, against the railing next to her.

Before she could respond, two small blurs raced past her, doubled back, and exploded onto her lap. "Mommy!"

Darby pulled her older two daughters into her arms. They looked like Darby: small and lithe with spindly limbs and big sleepy green eyes. No one would ever mistake them for anything other than her daughters.

The younger child of the two turned to Georgia. "Hi," she said. "Can I sit on your lap?"

"Sure," said Georgia, nonplussed. She sat down on a deck chair, and to her surprise, both girls piled into her lap, looking at her expectantly. Now what? "Hey there, varmints," she said, after a moment's pause, thumping her knees up and down so they bounced. "What's shaking?"

The little one giggled. "Fleur backfired on me this morning." She pinched her nose and waved a small, dimpled hand around.

From Fleur, in a scandalized whisper: "Backfires are private, Brin."

Darby attempted a diplomatic change of subject. "How did you sleep, Brinnie?"

"I sleeped pretty good," she said, and then considered further. "Except my nose drooled a lot."

A second later, Darby's husband, Matt, bounded onto the porch, holding a baby in the crook of his elbow. "Morning, ladies," he said, wrapping his free arm around Darby. He twisted a hip so the baby faced Georgia. "This is Clover."

Brin hopped off Georgia's lap to tickle Clover's foot. "Baby Clove, looky here," she said. "It's Sissy!" Clover laughed, flopping her small body toward her sister. "Dababababa," she cried joyously. Georgia, feeling an unaccountable prick of warmth behind her eyes, redirected her gaze to the marsh.

"Honey?" said Darby to Matt, her hand on the playroom door. "Do you mind if we hide on the porch while you get the kids dressed for church? Georgia's friend is coming to pick her up and I thought we'd hang out on the patio for a bit."

Matt remained chipper. "I don't mind one bit!"

Right on cue the doorbell rang: Jonah, his face hidden behind an enormous basket of muffins. From a couple prior pit stops here after running, Georgia knew perfectly well Darby and Matt didn't dig on junk food, especially for the children, but they both made sincere-sounding murmurs of appreciation as Matt accepted the basket. As Jonah lowered it, Georgia couldn't suppress a gasp: his nose, normally straight and short, had ballooned to twice its size, and thin half-moon bruises had formed in the creases under his eyes, almost perfectly mirroring the arch of his black brows. From a distance it looked as if he were wearing dark round spectacles. He jerked his head at her in silent instruction: *Don't ask in front of them.* "Gather round, young'uns! Muffins are here!" he bellowed, prompting an excited stampede of little feet down the hall.

Although he was definitely the sort to rile them up to fever pitch before handing them off to someone else, and despite his bachelor status, Jonah had a way with kids. After a few galumphing shoulder rides and the doling out of sugary muffins, Jonah thanked Matt for letting him play with the girls, and Matt thanked Jonah, a bit too heartily, for the muffins; and then Matt whisked the overstimulated children back to the playroom.

"We should get going," said Georgia, anxious to talk with Jonah.

"Oh!" said Darby, in a disappointed tone. "Why don't you sit for a minute?"

"We'd hate to impose," said Georgia at the exact moment that Jonah said, "We'd love to, thanks."

They traipsed out to the deck, settling, side by side, on three fat-cushioned chaises overlooking the marsh. Georgia tried to catch Jonah's eye but he ignored her, turning to Darby. "How was the run?"

She responded softly. "It was fine, Jonah, how are *you*?"

He shrugged. "I'm better than I look."

Hopefully this was true, because his face was an unmitigated catastrophe, his fine features marred by swelling, his voice distorted by the lack of airflow through his nose. What could have happened? When they'd met yesterday for breakfast, he'd appeared normal.

She motioned toward his nose. "What . . ."

Jonah cast a sideways glance at Darby, but apparently decided to proceed. "There was an unfortunate incident with my neighbor. I might have lost my temper and said something rash. It turns out he objects to my love life and so I objected to his being a slovenly, pea-brained warthog and then he said, 'Oh yeah? Well, I object to your face.'"

"Oh no! How did this happen?"

"Somehow he got ahold of a newspaper and apparently he was able to sound out enough words to realize the subject of an article was his gay neighbor. So he did what any decent citizen would do and marched over to investigate whether or not there were any strange men lurking about."

"Which of course there weren't."

Jonah shook his head. "Well, actually," he said, "Jace and Tucker were over."

Tucker, an accountant, was a fitness junkie with an obsession with extreme endurance sports—ultramarathons or open-water swimming or something—and therefore paradoxically resembled death. Thirtyish and balding, he had a bony skull and sunken eyes and razor-sharp, emaciated limbs. Every time Georgia had ever seen him, he'd been decked out in a racing shirt and Lycra shorts so adherent they left nothing to the imagination. His partner, a sidesplittingly funny graphic designer named Jace, represented the opposite extreme: he personified the term *couch potato*. They lived down the street from Jonah.

Appalled, she said, "The guy has an objection to you having friends?"

"In his eyes, the only thing three gay men could possibly be doing together is some kind of unholy *ménage à trois*, and obviously he couldn't let that shit go unchallenged. He punched me in the face and Tuck called the police."

Georgia glanced at Darby to see how she was handling all this. She sat, wide-eyed, between the two of them, her mouth frozen in a little O, reaching up for the dainty cross at her throat.

So: Darby was literally clutching her pearls. She looked so uncomfortable Georgia would have laughed if her anger at the situation hadn't already alchemized into something physical, burning her face in a red-hot flare. After a brief glance at her, Jonah buried his head in the crook of an elbow. "Talk about something else, please," he said. "And look away. I'm hideous."

"You really are," Georgia agreed in a thick voice. "I'm not sure we can be friends any longer."

Darby went with a different tactic, one doomed to fail. "Oh, honey. Nobody cares how you look."

"*Everyone* cares how I look. It's the *only* thing people care about. There's *nothing* else—"

Georgia jumped in before the rest of the morning devolved into a discussion of Jonah's physical beauty, or current lack thereof. He would feel better if they could distract him. "Did you get any sleep last night?"

"Yes. With a bit of help from pharmaceuticals."

Darby looked up. "Have you tried melatonin?"

"Melatonin is okay but bourbon works better."

"Oh, Jonah—"

"Joke. I'm kidding! Actually, bourbon is crap compared to oxy."

Darby fanned herself.

He shot her an evil grin. "Just kidding again. Let's move on and dissect Georgia's life for a while."

"I'm the boring one here."

"Please," said Darby. "I'm the boring one. You and Jonah are so . . . vivid."

"*Vivid* being code for unwholesome," Jonah said.

"No," Darby protested but her cheeks had gone pink.

"Well, I'm certainly not unwholesome," Georgia said.

"Hmm," said Jonah. He grinned. "How are things going with the Dutchman?"

She couldn't help smiling. "I'd say pretty well. We talk every day. And he's definitely coming to visit."

"Yeah!" The glee in Jonah's voice was unmistakable. "When?"

"Next week."

She knew she was setting herself up for Jonah to have fun with this, but Darby changed the subject. "Hey, I've been wanting to ask you." She shot a nervous glance at Georgia. "Have you seen any of those surgeons again? Or Donovan Wright?"

Jonah stiffened. "What happened with Donovan Wright?"

"Nothing," Georgia said. "Some resident got all hostile with Darby for no reason."

"Somebody got all hostile with *Darby*?"

Darby looked from Georgia to Jonah. "Donovan defended me. It was sweet."

"You know what?" Georgia said, before Jonah could react to Darby's statement. "Darby, I'd love more coffee."

Darby jumped up. A breeze blew in over the marsh, rustling the palm fronds in a skeletal rattle as Georgia leveled a murderous glare at Jonah. He mimed an apology and she mimed an acceptance. This wordless communication over, she felt herself relax. She still had no desire to share the story with Darby or anyone else, but in recent days, the specter of Donovan Wright seemed to be losing its power over her.

Jonah must have been thinking something along the same lines, because he leaned toward her, speaking in an exaggerated whisper that was almost louder than regular speech. "We have to talk."

"I know." In hopes that he'd take the hint, she made her whisper nearly inaudible.

He didn't. "I did it," he said, at normal volume. "I did the thing we planned. Last night."

She was torn between the urge to ask him to shush and the urge to pry information from him. "How did it g—"

The glass door grated along its tracks and Darby reappeared with a fresh pot of coffee to refill their cups, her bangled wrists flashing crazy fireflies of morning sunlight onto the surface of the porch as she flitted around. Darby appeared not to notice the sudden tension in Georgia and Jonah, both of whom sipped their coffee, mute, as they stared out over the marsh.

"Jonah," Darby said, in a tentative voice. "I was wondering. Did the police arrest your neighbor?"

"No. I asked them not to."

Georgia sprang forward in her chair. "Jonah! Why?"

"Because," he said, "once I calmed down, I figured having the guy thrown in jail was not going to be the best way to reestablish neighborly relations."

Darby was staring at Jonah, a contemplative look on her face. "You didn't want him to pay for hurting you?"

"I did. I have to say, the idea of seeing that guy perp-walking with his hands behind his back to a cop car sounded pretty sweet. But I got a look at his wife's face, and"—he shrugged—"I let it go. And you know what? This morning, before I left to come here, I found some roses from her garden on my front porch."

Darby placed a hand on Jonah's chair, a few inches from his shoulder. "I hope everything will work out for you," she said. Georgia looked at her, surprised at the worry in her voice.

"I appreciate the sentiment, Darby, but sometimes things don't work out. Sometimes there's no antidote for what's wrong."

"There's an antidote for everything," Darby said, optimism written all over her face. "Sometimes you just have to figure out what it is."

Jonah's eyes cut back to the marsh, where something large under the surface sent a concentric ring of ripples cascading across the water. "Maybe," he said. "But you know what they say: sometimes the cure is worse than the poison."

PART

THREE

~~~

17

PLAUSIBLE DENIABILITY

Georgia stepped out of the parking garage and squinted into the morning sun, which cast its rays not just over the tropical stucco buildings and the still-exuberant fall flower beds and the neat little crushed-pebble pathways, but also over a massive conflagration of people milling around the clinic's grounds. She stopped and gaped.

In the week or so since the conversation at Darby's house, the clinic had exploded in controversy. Some of the commotion came from news trucks spilling camera-toting men and sound booms and various pieces of unrecognizable equipment; along with them came the talent, who tended to be young, attractive women with bright lipstick and massive amounts of hair.

Then there were various groups of screamers.

Along the left side of the clinic bobbed chanting people carrying lots of clever, rainbow-themed signs, and these people seemed to have attracted several other loosely affiliated groups who marched with the seasoned appearance of near-professional protestors; and these in turn had spawned a group of outraged counterprotestors waving signs and placards of the fire-and-brimstone variety, indiscriminately hollering at anyone who went by wearing scrubs. One of them churned the handle of his sign up and down as he loped alongside a hospital worker trying to make it to the door. "God hates fags!" he blared.

Georgia joined a cluster of three other hospital workers preparing to walk the gauntlet. Keeping their heads down, they took deep breaths and hustled toward the epicenter. "God hates fags," explained the protestor, transferring his attention to them. Apparently *God hates fags* was the extent of his oratorical repertoire.

Two people—a man and a woman—detached themselves from the sidelines and appeared at Georgia's side, both dressed in the flowing black vestments of the clergy. They linked their arms with hers, angling their bodies as a sort of human shield to protect Georgia from the waving signs and the snarling lips. They passed by the spot where they'd been standing and Georgia realized they were with a church group, standing quietly behind a banner reading

GOD IS LOVE
ALL ARE WELCOME

"Bless you, my dear," said one of them as she and her colleague deposited Georgia at the door of the clinic. They turned back to escort the next wave of employees flooding from the parking area behind them.

The clinic had posted a guard at the doors. Georgia flashed her badge and the guard motioned her in. The doors swung shut, cutting off the shrieks and the tumult from outside, prompting a little cloud of simultaneous exhalations from the people standing in the lobby. A nearby lab guy rubbed his hands together. "Did y'all read the paper?"

The woman beside him shook her head. "Did it say anything about this?"

"It was about that doc who got fired. He says it's discrimination, they said he did some kind of malpractice."

"I hope he knows what a mess he's brought down on us," said the woman. "I don't see why those people were mad at us. The hospital's been sticking up for traditional values."

"The paper pointed out the doctor who got fired has supporters here," said the man. "Those guys outside must've taken offense."

Georgia had read the article this morning, after her run. Stewart had been quoted, and a couple of Jonah's patients. But there had also been a quote from Beezon.

> "We value all people," stated John Beezon, 49, the chief human resources officer overlooking Tsukada's practice. "Personally, I know several gay people. However, Dr. Tsukada's conduct, and the conduct of his patients, is of concern to us. We reserve the right to require a certain moral standard in our employees. And our employees should not be forced to condone practices contrary to their dearly held religious beliefs. More importantly, in Dr. Tsukada's case, we have other, more immediate concerns about his fitness as a physician, and those are being looked into at this time."
>
> Mr. Beezon declined to specify the nature of the other concerns, stating he would provide an update once the clinic's investigation is complete.

Trying to put the newspaper out of her mind, Georgia reviewed her day. Today was all-office—no operating—meaning she'd be home well before Mark arrived in Charleston tonight to visit her. Normally she'd swing by the lounge, but today, especially after the harrowing walk from the garage, she wanted to avoid the gossip.

In contrast to outdoors, the halls were quiet. She'd almost reached the turnoff to the back entrance to her private office when she heard an unmistakable voice echo down the hall; Donovan Wright was standing down a side corridor, chatting with someone. After wrapping up his conversation, he turned the corner with a tight, drawn face and a sheen of sweat dotting his forehead. As he passed by, Georgia stepped forward, catching the fabric of his blue suit jacket. For a brief second his pale eyes were quizzical and then she saw something else flare behind them. Was that . . . sadness?

"Donovan," she said. "Got a minute?"

"I'm on the way to the OR."

"I think we should discuss something." She stepped even closer, invading his personal space and throwing an arm up to the wall to hem him in. "It won't take long."

He sidestepped her arm. "It's not a great time."

"It's about Jonah," she said, moving alongside him as he began to walk. "I read that article in the *Post and Courier* this morning. There's a quote from John Beezon insinuating Jonah was fired because he's a bad doctor. What do you know about that?"

There was a brief, almost unnoticeable, hitch in his gait. "I haven't read that yet."

"That's crap, Donovan. You said yourself he's an excellent doctor."

"As I said, I haven't read it yet."

"What about our conversation? You told me last week that you knew he wasn't a drug thief, that you'd talk to Dan."

"I know."

She stopped walking.

"Look." He'd taken another step or two and swung to face her. "Something really strange is going on. I don't understand it. Tell your friend Jonah it would be better if he would talk with me."

She studied his face. He blanched under her gaze, turning his head to the side.

"Donovan. I have real concerns that someone, maybe Beezon, is manipulating you here. If there were anything negative about Jonah's medical skills, you'd have all known it."

"I didn't say it was anything about his medical skills."

"Beezon did, in the article."

"Did he? I'm surprised."

She tried, and failed, to recall the exact wording of the quote. "It was something like that," she said, uncertainty creeping into her voice.

"Well, I suppose you could say there are elements of his job performance, in a way, relating more to his decisions than his skills."

"What are you talking about?"

"For one thing"—Donovan raised a finger, as if he were ticking off a list of offenses—"he's been treating transgender patients with hormone therapy. Testosterone therapy to masculinize women who think they're men, and vice versa."

"So? That's the worst they could come up with, after all these *investigations*? Y'all knew that already. People with gender dysphoria can be treated with hormone therapy according to the Endocrine Society. It's hardly unusual."

"The hospital believes facilitating an unnatural physical state is inappropriate."

"We do breast augmentations here, don't we?"

"That's not the same thing."

"Why not? We're already allowing people to make changes to their bodies if it pleases them. Because guess what? It's *their* body. It's their life and it's their decision. Who the hell are we to tell them what they should and should not be allowed to do?"

He raised his hands. "Hey. There's no need for foul language."

The last vestige of her distress at what Donovan had done in the supply closet rose up, cycloning in the air until it re-formed as pure resolve. Georgia perched on her toes, suddenly twenty pounds lighter. She put her hands on her hips and leaned in. "Really? If this calamity isn't a call for cursing, I don't know what is."

Donovan scuttled backward, pinned in by the wall behind him and Georgia in front of him. He cast his eyes around for the cavalry. "Uh, the hospital believes changing gender is different."

"It's not done lightly," she said. "There are guidelines based on research and extensive interaction. The clinic shouldn't dictate how a physician and his patients make decisions, especially when the doctor is following accepted medical practices."

"Of course the clinic can dictate what kind of medical care is provided. It's a privately run, for-profit business."

Georgia thought of Frieda Myers Delacroix: her bright, alert eyes, and the grace in her expression. "I don't get it," she said. "Why does anyone care what's right for another person physically and psychologically? And doesn't this bother you as a physician? A nonmedical person like Beezon dictating medical decisions to doctors on the basis of *his* personal beliefs? What's to stop him from banning birth control? Or cosmetic surgery? Or anything we do? This is our fight too, Donovan. Ignore it, and one day you're going to wake up and find yourself living in a theocracy where you have to get permission from a religious ruler to provide any medical care at all."

Donovan looked stunned by this onslaught. "I'm sorry, Georgia," he said finally. He paused. "But Beezon has something else on him. And it goes considerably beyond a question of medical judgment."

Here it came: the clinic was finally going to announce what they had on Jonah. She'd been waiting, convinced each day that this would be the time. Instead of shadowboxing in the dark, they'd be able to fight in the open.

"What? That empty bottle of fentanyl? Someone tried to frame him."

"No. Ask Jonah. He'll know."

She knew, of course, what Jonah had done, but she couldn't let Donovan know that she knew. "Donovan—"

He held up his hands. "Georgia, I'll still do what I can to help save your job, but I don't think I'm going to be able to help Jonah anymore, and I can't tell you more than that. You should have a talk with him."

Reeling, she stepped back, but recovered quickly. Perhaps Donovan didn't know the specifics. And why would he bother mentioning her job? Did he think that would make up for the past?

There was one good thing that would come of Donovan refusing to help: at least it freed her from this unholy alliance. "Fine," she snapped.

"Jonah didn't want your help anyway. I should never have discussed it with you."

He reached the bank of elevators and stepped onto one as it opened, directing his last comment to her just before the doors closed. "Georgia." On his face was a look of terrible blankness. "Maybe you're right."

~~~~~~~

By the time she reached home, nine hours later, apprehension had frayed the edges of her stamina. Even though Mark would be arriving in a couple hours, she found herself longing to shut down, to crawl into her loft bed and cocoon herself under the covers. For over a week, she'd been expecting a development in Jonah's case that hadn't come. Surely *something* would change before the day was out. For the millionth time, she checked her phone to see if the clinic had released any information: nothing.

She sat in the car for a moment, drained, before dragging herself out. Dobby's head bobbed excitedly around in the window as he barked at the car to lure her indoors, and despite her mood, she couldn't suppress a grin. As always, Dobby's unconditional love cheered her. Where would she be without her boy?

Inside the house, she took one step and came to a dead stop. On her way out the door this morning, she'd noticed a bad smell, but hadn't had time to investigate. Now, the smell in the kitchen had intensified. *Intensified* wasn't quite the right word: it had grown so foul she almost vomited. Gagging, she made her way into the kitchen, where she discovered the problem to be a malfunctioning garbage disposal. A quick investigation revealed the culprit: a bunch of half-disintegrated shrimp peels refluxing up from the pipe beneath the sink, an unwelcome reminder of her dinner a couple nights ago.

After removing her shirt and donning the denim coveralls she kept for such situations, she eased herself under the sink and instantly regretted not tying a protective cloth over her nose. Dobby, who found the putrid smell invigorating, suddenly stuck his head next to hers and drooled on her face. "Out!" she yowled, yanking her head straight up, hard, into the S-shaped plumbing fitting. Whimpering, she reached up to feel a lump rising on her forehead. For a moment she considered abandoning the project long enough to apply ice to what felt like a huge, burgeoning hematoma, but then reconsidered: she didn't know if it was possible to die solely from inhaling a disgusting aroma, but if it was, she was toast. She figured she had ten more minutes before the smell disabled her completely. This was enough to spur her back into action; breathing through her mouth, she grasped her wrench and attacked the pipe. Just as she successfully disconnected the slip-nut fittings on the drain trap, the realization struck: she'd forgotten to place the catch bucket within reach.

"Shit!" she screamed, as a cascade of rotting shrimp peels poured onto her face.

The doorbell rang. It was still too early for Mark, so she ignored it, thinking nothing could possibly be more urgent than ridding her hair of rotting shrimp, but it rang again and again, so finally, gasping, she tottered away from the sink to open the door.

Jonah's eyes bugged as he took in her appearance: hair askew, shirtless, injured, and covered in filth. "Wha—" he managed, pointing at her.

"I got hit by some shrimp," she muttered. "Come in."

He took a tentative step forward. As the smell hit him, he staggered backward toward the porch swing, one hand waving in circles, propeller-like, and the other covering his nose. "Maybe I'll just wait out here," he said.

"Suit yourself," she said, trying to summon up some dignity. "I'll be as quick as I can."

Back inside, she discovered Dobby merrily rooting around in the pool of foul water, wearing a tiara of shrimp peels and a look of profound canine joy. She managed to throw him in the backyard, get the clog cleared, replace the fitting, clean the kitchen floor, clean the sink, clean the inside of the cabinet, fling her despoiled coveralls in the washing machine, and get herself in and out of the shower in under fifteen minutes. All that remained was to spray Dobby with the hose a few times in lieu of a full-blown bath. She trudged out to the back, armed with a spray canister of dog shampoo in one hand, scooping up the hose nozzle in the other. Dobby, correctly concluding that she planned to rob him of his newfound *eau de shrimp*, bolted for the back of the shed. With her last burst of strength she lunged forward to grab his collar. He fought the good fight, soaking both of them, but she won: never underestimate the power of opposable thumbs and superior intelligence.

She should have showered again but she didn't think she could handle even one more thing. Feeble and heaving, she toweled Dobby dry and shuffled out to the front porch to join Jonah on the swing.

He eyed her warily. "Everything okay?"

She grabbed a lock of her hair and sniffed it. "Mark's coming soon," she reminded him.

"Oh yeah! I forgot. I should go."

"Of course you shouldn't go. He'll be happy to see you."

"You sure? I can come back later."

"No, no. You're here. Wait; why are you here? Anything on the news?"

Mournfully: "Not yet. I just didn't want to be alone."

"You want to come inside?"

He gave a cautious sniff. "Ten minutes ago, I'd have said yes."

She opened her arms. "*Mi casa, su casa, amigo.* Plus, I think it will smell better in about fifteen minutes. Especially since I opened all the doors and windows."

He sighed theatrically. "I don't even want to know."

"You're right, you don't."

Dobby moseyed onto the front porch, aiming a baleful look in her direction, but forgave her ten seconds later when she scratched him behind the ears. Jonah scratched him too, even though Georgia knew he was repulsed by the smell of wet dog. She rested her head against his

shoulder. "Tell me about your day. I've been out of my mind, worrying about everything."

His phone pinged and he glanced at it. "Stewart. Nothing new."
He set it down. "I need to talk to you, but first, as your romantic advi-
sor, I feel compelled to tell you that you need to shower again. Or at
least throw on strong perfume and a sexier outfit. The man is crossing
a continent to be with you, you know?"

She glanced down at herself: her wet hair had created two damp
trails across her T-shirt and her pants were equally soaked, having
fallen victim to her battle with Dobby. "It's okay. I think he loves me
for my mind."

Jonah shoved her off the porch swing. "Trust me, he doesn't."

She flung open the door to the porch fifteen minutes later, having
dried her hair and donned an orange minidress and boots. "Better?"

Jonah stood and applauded, but he wasn't alone: next to him, Mark
stood as well. Georgia goggled at them for a moment until Mark
stepped forward and swung her up into an embrace. "Hi," he said into
her clean hair.

"Hi," she murmured back, inhaling the scent of him in a long
greedy gulp. What was this? Had she been struck dumb? Mark set her
down and she stood rooted on the porch, grinning, for a long moment
before recovering herself. She gestured at the swing. "Please, have a
seat."

Mark aimed a questioning glance toward the door, no doubt wondering why he wasn't being invited inside after his daylong transatlantic journey. Since Georgia seemed to be malfunctioning, Jonah helped
her out: "We're decontaminating for a few more minutes before we go
inside."

"Wha—"

Suddenly Jonah let out a yelp. He stared at his phone and then
waved it in an arc above his head, pacing around the porch. "Stewart!"

~~~

18

ILLITERATE, BELLIGERENT SOCIOPATHS

MARK

"Who's Stewart?" asked Mark.

"His lawyer," Georgia said. She turned to Jonah. "What? What did he say?"

"He said"—Jonah's eyes had gone wide—"after an internal investigation, the clinic is planning to report me to the police."

"The police?" Mark couldn't hide his shock. "For what?"

Jonah stopped walking, turning to search Mark's face. Not finding whatever he sought, he spun on one foot to face Georgia. "For stealing drugs."

The sentence reverberated between the three of them, the air rippling away in concentric rings from the conversational stone of Jonah's pronouncement. Mark blinked. He opened his mouth and abruptly closed it again.

Jonah took pity on him. "We have an automated medication storage system in our procedure room," he said. "It's full of narcotics and other dangerous drugs."

Mark listened as Jonah explained. As a family medicine doc, Jonah did dozens of small procedures a year, most of them performed under local anesthesia. But some cases required stronger medicine—narcotics, or even a kind of twilight anesthesia called moderate sedation, where the patient was not unconscious but was rendered so drowsy and out of it that he could not register pain or form memories. Rather than send these patients to a full-blown operating room, the clinic offered a shared procedure room, used by multiple specialties. The room was sometimes staffed by a nurse anesthetist, who could monitor the patient's vital signs and breathing as the drugs were administered, freeing up the doctor to perform the procedure more safely. The medicine storage system in this room, called a Pyxis, contained valuable and often abused drugs such as Dilaudid and ketamine. It required a code to open and the contents were carefully monitored by the nursing staff; Jonah, as a doctor, did not have access to the cabinet.

After a pointed glance at Georgia, Jonah began pacing again. Mark's head swiveled back and forth between them.

"Jones," said Georgia in a voice pregnant with subtext. "How exactly did they phrase it?"

Jonah shook his head. "It's very specific. They're saying I stole someone's access code and siphoned out little bits of various drugs and then replaced the missing cc's with saline."

"What?" she said. She put her hand on his arm, her face a frozen mask.

He shook it off. "It gets worse. They're saying I stole the opiates—fentanyl, all that stuff—to get high, but some of it, like the ketamine, they're theorizing I kept to sell to people at parties. Who knows where they'll go from there? Tomorrow are they going to say I molested half of Charleston?"

He stared at her again, his eyes boring into hers, before they both flicked their eyes toward Mark.

After a moment of this impasse, Jonah pushed open the door to the house. "I need to call Stewart back," he said, walking inside. Mark remained silent as they waited for Jonah to return, trying to gauge the undercurrents. Something was going on here beneath the surface; something he didn't quite understand.

Through the door they could hear snippets of Jonah's voice, alternating up and down the scale as he reacted to whatever Stewart was saying. Near the end of the conversation he said very little, responding in a series of monosyllabic grunts until finally he let loose with what was clearly a stream of animated curses.

He returned to the porch, his shoulders set. Whatever the lawyer had said seemed to have transformed his alarm to ferocity. He paced in wide circles, forcing Georgia and Mark to rotate their necks in synchronized circles to keep him in sight.

"Jonah? What did Stewart say?"

He stopped dead in his tracks and let out an evil bark. "Oh, the clinic is absolutely loving this one, George. They're loving it! If there's one thing I regret in all this, it's that I've lived my life in a way maximally guaranteed to reinforce every dumbass gay stereotype." He thrust a hand straight up toward the ceiling and began to count on his fingers as he spoke. "One, I have an extravagant personality AND a fabulous best girlfriend. Can't get more clichéd than that, am I right? Two, you could make a case that I'm overly fond of certain pop divas. Three, sometimes I wear leather, and when I do, I'm smoking hot. Four, I dance well. Five, as you know, I'm a straight-up sexy beast."

"Jonah," said Mark, still bewildered. "Why does the clinic think you did this?"

"There've been rumors for a long time," Georgia said, "that Jonah might have been the one to steal drugs from the clinic. It's not true, of course."

Jonah shot Georgia a loaded glance. "Stewart said they have evidence, but he says he doesn't know what it is yet." He turned back to Mark. "No one is going to believe I'm innocent, and who could blame them?" He ran a hand through his hair. His eyes were huge, wild.

Mark reached for Jonah's shoulder. "I believe you."

"Me too." Georgia looked straight at Jonah. "Of course you didn't—of course—there's no way on earth you'd have taken the medicines." But Mark could see it in her eyes, and so, presumably, could Jonah: for a second, she'd wondered whether he had.

"This is it, though, George. Even if Stewart gets me off, no matter how many people believe me, some people never will. I'm done. Why did I—"

She interrupted. "You didn't steal drugs, Jonah, and they won't have any evidence to show you did."

"Well," he said. Again, his eyes flitted toward Mark and then back to her. "Stewart says they've got *something* making me look guilty. *He* just doesn't know what it is."

Mark's head ping-ponged back and forth between Georgia and Jonah.

"Okay," Georgia said. She appeared to be choosing her words with care. "Okay. There will be an actual investigation—an impartial police investigation. The police won't just take the clinic's word for this. That's what you want."

Jonah flung his head down onto his arms and moaned something incoherent.

"Listen," she said. A touch of panic seeped into her voice. "Stay here tonight." She threw a quick quizzical look at Mark, and he nodded: *Of course.* "We knew something like this was coming, and you're right; it's going to be awful until they clear you. Try to lay low. Stewart will take care of this."

Jonah raised his head. "I thought about going on the lam"—here, for one shining second, his face returned to normal as he uttered the words *going on the lam*—"but you forget: I don't have any income anymore. I've been in practice for three years and I owe an amount the size of the national debt from med school and for my Nana's medical care and I have barely any savings, and what savings I do have, Stewart is going to suck up in about a minute. I can't leave town. I'm done."

"Let me pay for it," Georgia said. He started to protest but she kept speaking. "I have more money than I need, Jones. I love you. If you love me back, you'll do this. You'll get away from this. Promise me."

"I—"

"Please. Don't say no."

"Okay," he said, sounding defeated. "I'll stay here tonight and then I'll go out of town."

She got up and stood behind him, breathing deeply into his hair. Even from his distance, Mark could make out its faint evergreen scent. Georgia wrapped her arms around his thin torso and he leaned against her; despite their dramatically different coloring, for a moment, with their eyes closed and their cheeks pressed together, they looked like siblings. "This is all going to be okay. You'll go back and work out whatever Stewart needs you to do. As soon as he says it's okay, you'll go somewhere safe and you'll take a big stack of beautiful books. Or you can binge-watch every old episode of *Mad Men*, or you can learn to knit. I don't care what you do, as long as it's soothing and mindless, and I know—I know—this will work out."

"Okay," he said again. A shudder went through him. "Okay."

~~~~~~

As romantic evenings went, tonight was not shaping up to be what Mark had had in mind, but witnessing Jonah's distress had eclipsed whatever disappointment he might have felt. As Jonah went inside again to answer yet another call from Stewart, Mark pulled Georgia into his arms. He kissed the top of her head, gently, with all the passion of somebody's old grandpa. "I'll get a hotel," he said.

"Mark, you don't have to. We can all stay here." She paused, glancing through the open door to the tiny house beyond. "My bed's on a loft and there's not much in the way of privacy, but of course you can stay."

"No worries," he said. He should have been irritated to be thrown over for another man, but somehow Georgia's devotion to her friend only served to heighten his admiration for her. "I don't mind. I'll get a good night's sleep—which I'm certain I wouldn't have gotten here, even under the best of circumstances. I have to go up to New York tomorrow, but I can be back in a few days and we'll catch up then."

Her eyes were full of guilt. "I'll make you a reservation at a nice hotel nearby."

"Don't feel bad. I admire your commitment to your friend. Obviously he needs you tonight."

"He does," she agreed, as the sound of Jonah's conversation with Stewart drifted out to their ears. "Say what?" he was shouting.

Jonah returned to the porch, running his hands through his hair so it stood straight up in back. "Stewart," he said, "just told me he knows why they think I stole drugs." Again he looked at Mark and again Mark had the sense Jonah was dancing around something he and Georgia knew but he, Mark, did not.

"What—specifically—did they say?" she asked.

"Specifically"—he looked up, directing a pointed look at her—"he said they have a video that shows me accessing the Pyxis."

He flung up a hand, interrupting her before she could get out any words. "Of course I told him immediately it's a fake. Stewart hasn't actually seen it yet. He asked me about a hundred times if there is anything I want to tell him, George, and he isn't accepting 'no.' I think he suspects me of actually stealing these drugs."

"Don't lie about anything. You didn't steal any drugs." She hesitated. "Isn't there a law saying they have to show the evidence to you? Stewart should be able to view it soon, right? He'll prove it's a fake."

He sighed. "I think they have to show it to us if I'm charged with a crime. Which will probably happen any day now. But honestly, whether or not I get arrested is not my only worry right now. I came home today to find this on my door." He shifted his hip to root around in his pocket, eventually pulling out a tattered piece of paper, which he handed to Georgia, who glanced at it, blanched, and thrust it into Mark's hand as if it had bitten her. He looked down at it. On one side a picture of Jonah had been printed: dressed in a pink bowtie and a pale lavender shirt, he was smiling broadly, showing all his teeth. It looked like a headshot, possibly from the clinic's family practice website; either they hadn't yet taken it down, or someone had printed it prior to him being fired.

The other side of the paper was a printout of a definition from Urban Dictionary: the term *Colombian bow tie*. It took him all of five seconds to scan it: it referred to slitting someone's throat and pulling their tongue through the opening in the neck. Next to it someone had printed the words *Faggot fashion*.

Georgia looked as though she could not speak.

"Jonah," Mark breathed, appalled. "Did you take this to the police?"

"No."

They stared at him.

"This is a drop in the bucket. Look at my Twitter account."

Georgia found her voice. "Twitter! Who cares about Twitter? Half those people aren't even people and the other half are illiterate belligerent sociopaths. This is someone local who knows where you live and took the trouble to deliver an actual threat to your doorstep. You have to report this."

"I'm avoiding the police, remember? The last thing I want to do is present myself to them."

"But—"

"That's part of why I came over. Stewart said not to go back to my house yet." He slumped back against the slats of the swing, sending a fine, twanging tremor through the chains suspending it.

"What?" Her voice rose. "How will we keep you safe?"

"Right? I seem to be racking up hostile communications from my fellow citizens on an hourly basis." He refolded the paper and shoved it back in his pocket. "Exhibit A. In the meantime, Stewart's arranging for me to have a bodyguard."

"So he's taking these threats seriously."

He shrugged, flicking at a firefly by his head. "It's serious enough, I guess. Plenty of people have reached out to make it clear they think I should be mauled in some form. By far the most common suggestion is to have me emasculated, so to speak. I'm sure ninety-nine percent of them are just mouthing off, but Stewart says better safe than sorry. And I'm in so much debt now, the expense of a bodyguard hardly matters."

Georgia's throat worked, but nothing came out. Jonah reached out and laid a finger across her mouth. "Shush," he said tenderly, almost whispering. "I already know everything you want to say. I freaked out there for a second, but I'm okay, I promise." He turned to Mark. "I am so sorry about ruining y'all's time together. Again."

"No apology needed, my friend," said Mark, feeling hopelessly inadequate. He pulled his phone out of his pants pocket and pecked at his travel app. "I'll catch a Lyft to a nearby hotel," he said to Georgia, and then: "I'll call you in the morning."

"I'm sorry," she mouthed to him. She put her hand to her heart and tilted her head toward him. Even in her current state, her face was compelling: some sort of sizzling energy arcing out of her pores, bolding the lines of her features, giving the impression that she was more visible than other people. He drank her in, a long last glimpse, and then walked to the curb to wait for his car.

~~~~~

19

A NEW AND TRIPPIER REALM

Georgia and Jonah sat together in silence, rocking, as the light grew dimmer. It became harder and harder to hold her head up; finally she surrendered and nestled against Jonah. She'd entered that state of suspended reality right before you fall asleep, where everything was slowed and dreamy and you couldn't tell reality from the feverish, hypnagogic imaginations of your brain. A dense rumbly sound and a higher-pitched tinkling sound echoed around her head; after listening to them for an indeterminate period of time, she realized the sounds were words, and they were coming from Jonah and someone else. Blearily, she opened an eye.

"I think I need to get you to bed," said Jonah, looking down at her.

"Yes," she said, and then startled at the sight of a man's large form, standing stock-still with his legs parted and arms crossed, ten feet away on the sidewalk. Jonah followed her gaze and gestured to the man. "This is Edwin. He's with the security company."

Edwin stood somewhere in the vicinity of six five—Mark's height—but with at least a hundred extra pounds of muscle on his frame. Clearly the long-lost brother of Arnold Schwarzenegger and Howie Long, he had a giant square head topped with buzzed blond hair—*de rigueur* for a bodyguard, Georgia imagined—and an expressionless expression. He wore a short-sleeved black T-shirt and black pants of some synthetic material, neither of which did anything to hide the monstrous circumference of his arms and legs. He also wore sunglasses, despite the fact that the sky was darkening by the second. He was perfect.

"Ma'am," said Edwin, nodding his huge head. A biceps bulged as he moved a hand to his hip.

"Omigod," breathed Jonah in her ear. He elbowed her in the ribs, grinning stupidly.

"Do y'all want to go inside?" Georgia offered, belatedly remembering her manners.

"Yes, thank you," said Jonah.

They looked at Edwin.

"I'd appreciate assessing the interior," he said. "Then I'll be most comfortable waiting out here."

"Of course," she said, then added, "Please don't assess the smell as a threat. It should be dissipating rapidly."

"Yes, ma'am," said Edwin, after a slightly confused pause. They all trooped inside.

After Edwin assessed the interior—a short process, given that almost every inch of her home was visible from the doorway—he went back outside to guard them, and Georgia and Jonah collapsed on the futon. "So what do you think of Edwin?" he asked.

"He's mega-hot. Straight, though."

"*Au contraire.* I picked up a vibe."

A half laugh, half snort erupted through her nose, and suddenly she found herself seized with helpless laughter. She bent forward at the waist, fanning her face for air. Jonah looked up, startled, and then he began to laugh too, hard enough that tears came to his eyes. "Poor Edwin," she wheezed. "He has no idea what kind of mess he's gotten himself into by accepting this job."

"None," Jonah agreed. "Zero."

"He *is* cute."

"Delectable. My assessment: *très bien monté*."

She clutched Jonah's arm. His face looked the way hers felt: flushed and maniacal and utterly out of control. Together they slid to the floor, pressing their cheeks against the cool stone tile until finally their laughter subsided into hitchy gulps and then, eventually, into silence.

~~~~~~~

Georgia fell asleep as soon as they crawled upstairs but woke a short time later. No matter what she tried, she couldn't relax. She'd urged Jonah to spend the night on the loft with her, even though she knew from prior experience this was a mistake; he had a habit of going horizontal in his sleep, edging out anyone unlucky enough to share a bed with him. By one o'clock in the morning, he'd hogged so much of the mattress that she found herself half out of the low bed, one buttock suspended an inch above the planked floor by a hammock of twisted sheet. She started to poke him in the side when she caught a glimpse of his face in the moonlight. He was crying, silently, in his sleep.

She pressed her palm against his cheek until the silvery snail track of his tears disappeared. Moving her hand, she cupped the back of his head. The tension in his face fell away and she felt her own face relax too. She'd have thought he'd have woken, but he only shuddered in his sleep, his mouth falling open to produce a small snore. She untangled herself from the sheet and rolled onto the floor.

Creeping down the tiny staircase from the loft, she was careful not to make noise. Dobby raised his head from his nest behind the futon and, ridiculously, Georgia put a finger to her lips in a preemptive bid for quiet. He seemed to understand, though; after one cautious thump of his tail, he raised himself up and pattered over to her, his backside wiggling in silent joy at the unexpected nocturnal visit. Beckoning at him to follow her, she grabbed her phone and crept outside to the courtyard behind the house.

Her courtyard: this was where your average Charlestonian would place lawn furniture and maybe a nice fountain. She'd gone in a different direction. Although she did keep a small garden back here, she'd converted the majority of the space to an open-air workshop. The end of the yard housed a shed enclosing a worktable and all her tools, and scattered across the pebbled ground rested a sawhorse and a trestle and multiple industrial containers she used during her various projects. Tiptoeing around a bucket of pneumatic tubes, she regarded the one outdoor chair—an old metal tractor seat she'd soldered onto a rusty tripod—and turned on her phone.

Scrolling through Jonah's social media profiles, she tried to channel her horror into stronger resolve instead of picking up a sledgehammer and smashing her phone into a million pieces. These people . . . where did these people come from? They yearned for a return to a more moral America, for a return to the days of criminalized homosexuality, for a time when they weren't confronted with the horror of gay people insisting on living their lives in public. And those were just the politicians.

From there on Jonah's feed, it was just a hop, skip, and jump from the well-meaning hate-the-sin-love-the-sinner types to those urging stoning and beheadings. What was it about someone else being gay that consumed so much attention from the rest of humanity? Couldn't these people find an actual sin to rage against?

Georgia didn't realize it was raining until a fat drop splatted onto the phone's screen, blurring the Twitter profile of a snarling brunette in a red hat who had just accused Jonah of bestiality. She turned the phone off, stood up, paced the yard, and sat back down. Screw the rain.

Mark answered her FaceTime on the second ring; behind him in the dark she could just make out an expanse of headboard.

"Georgia."

"I'm so sorry to wake you up. I know you're exhausted."

"Please. It's okay." He angled his head to the side and clicked on a bedside lamp. They both blinked. "You're tired," he said, studying her face. "I hoped you'd have fallen asleep."

She started to answer but stopped as she regarded Mark's face; his warm eyes, his brow furrowed in concern that she wasn't sleeping. The concept that someone cared whether or not she slept was so novel her smart-ass comment died on her lips.

"I can't sleep," she said finally.

"Do you want me to come back over?"

"No. I mean, yes, of course, I want you to, but no. Jonah's finally asleep. It's selfish of me to call you, I just . . ." She trailed off, defeated by her own neediness.

"You don't have to justify calling me."

"You've done so much for me already, Mark."

"I've done nothing."

"That's ridiculous," she said. "You've listened to my drama every night for over a month, you've crossed the ocean to visit me, and then you allowed Jonah to crash our night together. I think I love you."

She hadn't meant to say it. She didn't know she meant it. Or perhaps she meant it casually, the way she loved Michio Kaku's books or the way she loved new shoes or the way she loved that guy at Cane Rhum Bar who made the best mojito in Charleston. But as the words hung, crystallized, in the air, she realized she did mean it.

Mark, bless him, did not attempt feigned surprise or false modesty. He did not try to pass it off as a joke. His eyes never left hers. "I think I love you too," he whispered.

They stared at one another, their faces connected through the physics of cloud-based video streaming, and it was like he was right there. Like a toddler, she reached her palm out to the screen. He placed his palm against hers. "Can you come here?" he said.

~~~~~~

It only took her a few moments to reach Charleston Place. Mark had given her the room number, telling her it had a little balcony with a view of a winding street lined with palm trees and pastel buildings. As she skulked through the grand lobby, it dawned on her that if Mark had a balcony with a view of King Street, he was probably in a suite, which, combined with what she knew about his luxurious digs in Amsterdam, meant he was about a hundred times too posh to stay at her house. If this association continued, one of them was going to have to adjust their living standards.

She took the elevator to the top floor. The room did indeed turn out to be a suite, and, as promised, had a glorious view. She saw the glittery street below through a set of open double doors for perhaps ten seconds before Mark swept her up into his arms.

Twenty minutes earlier, she'd have sworn nothing could have distracted her from her worries, but clearly she'd have been wrong. Mark bent back her neck to kiss her throat, and her eyes drifted shut. She entered a realm of pure mindless sensation, shrinking and magnifying her perception at once, so the smallest things grew mighty. The rough graze of his cheek against hers, the warm hush of his breath, the grasp of his fingers against the back of her skull; they obscured everything. She became hyperaware of her own physiology; her breath, surging in and out of her lungs; the hot urgent thrum of the pulse in her neck; the fine erectile furze of hair along her arms. She felt everything and thought nothing.

If only it could have lasted.

After, his fingers drifting through her hair, her leg tossed over his, they listened to the hushed nighttime sounds of the street below. She thought he didn't want to break the spell by speaking, and neither did she, but the words rasped out anyway: "It's awful."

His hand stilled. "I know."

"No, you don't know. You think I mean what's happening to Jonah. And of course; that is awful. But I meant something else."

He waited.

"I mean my reaction."

She'd spoken in a tone so low she thought he might not have heard—and maybe he hadn't, because the next thing he said was the last thing she expected. "But I do know," he said. "I know exactly."

She rose onto an elbow, unable to hide the skepticism in her voice. "You do?"

He remained on his back, staring at the ceiling. "I do. You're upset because you think you'll lose him."

She stared down at him.

"And," he went on, "that upsets you further because you know the correct thing—the dominant thing—you should be feeling is distress and anger at what's happening to him, not concern for what your life will be like if he leaves."

"Yes," she whispered. "How do you know?"

He lifted his torso so their faces were level. "I lost someone."

"Who?"

"My mother," he said.

She'd known his mother had died when he was young, but as he recounted the details, she found herself aching for the bewildered boy he'd been, stuck in a house with a father who vacillated between angry and absent and a brother only marginally more equipped to cope than he was. She stroked his arm as he talked.

"I lost my mother too," she said, when he was quiet.

"Tell me about her," he said.

She started to talk and immediately the ache burned at the edges of her heart, consuming a little more of her in a flickering smolder she could never quite manage to put out. The thought of her early childhood evoked a weird contradictory blend of feelings: anger and hurt for sure; but also a deep, uncontrollable yearning for her mother's voice and a sharp, bittersweet pang of nostalgia.

In retrospect, it became clear her mother must have suffered some form of mental illness. Why else would she have left, without a word, when Georgia had been so young? Later on, when it was just Georgia and her dad, they chose to spend most of their time on campus, where he alternated the afternoon hours between his office, his classrooms, and the small chapel where his closest friend served as the college minister. Spending time on campus was enchanting: Georgia discovered a new and trippier realm in the pages of books. She spent almost every day after school in the college library or holed up in one of the dozens of hiding places she'd fashioned in odd corners of the campus. To her father's delight, she developed a fascination with physics and mechanics; to his bewilderment, she also developed a fascination with the glittery fashion of the disco era, as unlike her mother's sartorial style as it was possible to be.

In all the years since Georgia's mother left, she had never once reached out.

But if Georgia lacked closure, at least she could comfort herself with the possibility, no matter how remote, that her mother might not have wanted to leave. Her father seemed to believe she'd left willingly—she'd often threatened to take off, claiming to feel trapped by the idea of a house, a job, a rooted existence. But perhaps something had happened to her. No one really knew.

"So all three of us—you, me, and Jonah—are, essentially, orphans," she said to Mark. Mark's mother had certainly not wanted to leave him, and Georgia's might not have, but Jonah had no such reassurance. His parents had disowned him when he came out at age eighteen. He didn't like to talk about it, and Georgia didn't know the particulars of how it had all gone down. But she knew he no longer communicated with his parents or with any of his three older brothers.

"We're all each other have," she said. "Me and Jonah. If he has to move away, I can't stand losing him for myself, for the hole it would leave in my life, but I also can't stand what it would mean for him. He has nobody else either."

Mark, wisely, didn't try to argue about car trips and vacations and video chats. He pulled her into him.

Eventually, she slept.

~~~~~~

She awoke to cool air and the bluish effervescent light of a predawn day, and despite being awake most of the night, she felt oddly refreshed.

Something about her confession had bled the worry out of her. In their sleep, she and Mark had knotted together in the center of the large bed, and as she gently untangled herself, he stirred but didn't fully wake. She kissed him, scribbled a note promising to call him, walked the short distance home, then crawled back up the ladder to the loft and burrowed beside Jonah.

She'd dozed off again, but Jonah must have risen, because now, at six thirty, the space next to her was empty. She stretched and sat up but then closed her eyes again, thinking of Mark, and a huge ridiculous grin split her face. She didn't know where this was going—obviously Mark was geographically undesirable—but at the moment she didn't care. She had, finally, broken her string of dysfunctional men. No more excruciating blind dates with men who couldn't shut up about their drug problems or their bitchy ex-wife or—surprise!—their bitchy current wife. No more relationships with men who turned out to be closet racists or passive-aggressive humorless workaholics or pretentious wine snobs. No more dates with men who thought Islam was a country or that the term *absolute zero* referred to "ugly chicks."

It occurred to her this was an inherently negative way of looking at the situation. It was fine to feel celebratory about the absence of bad relationships but it was better to bask in the glow of a good one. She thought of Mark's handsome face, his intelligent eyes, his repertoire of attentive, sincere expressions. Part of his appeal might have been related to the memory of him in bed, where his good-guy status devolved into something a bit edgier; their time together last night had burned up her brain to the point where the world had gone soft, reduced to an undulating hush, a wordless, formless ocean of haze and ecstasy. But it wasn't all lust; every conversation they'd had reinforced her impression of his intellect and his sense of humor and the Markness of him: every moment with him seemed a little shinier, a little more real than the moments without him.

But yeah: the lust was pretty freaking magnificent too.

A small sound—a shuffle, a snort—tickled her eardrums, and gradually she became aware she'd been hearing it for some time. Reluctantly, she opened her eyes and saw something perched at the top of the ladder to her loft that initially she mistook for a raccoon or a cat or some sort of small, malevolent creature. Black and fluffy, it trembled in an odd way, almost as if it were vibrating. Then it lifted up a fraction and she realized it was Jonah's head, bent forward as he shook with laughter.

"Here's you just now," he crowed, and his face took on a dreamy, demented cast: fluttering eyelashes and parted lips and a solidly stupid grin. "I almost fell off the ladder."

"Yes, well," Georgia said crankily, "I *was* having happy thoughts. Until you barged up."

He crawled forward on one hand, brandishing a steaming mug in the other. "Thought I'd bring you coffee, princess. Unless you need some private time."

"No, gimme," she said.

Jonah handed over the cup and clambered back down the ladder, reappearing a moment later with his own steaming mug. He settled in beside her, rearranging the pillows to prop himself up, and began clicking through his phone. She stretched, wishing she could stay in this cozy nest under her skylight with Jonah instead of getting up to get dressed for work, but she could hear Dobby whimpering at the base of the ladder. She'd already shed her sweatpants when a thought struck. "Hey," she said. "Where's Howie?"

"Who?"

"Howie? Arnold? I mean Edwin. Your bodyguard. I didn't see him. Surely he didn't stay outside all night?"

Jonah clapped his hands to his mouth and scrambled to the ladder. He returned perhaps five minutes later, wearing a chagrined look. "I have to go," he mumbled.

"Wait! Did Edwin stand outside all night?"

"No, he said he came in for a while when you left. He said it rather pointedly, in fact. I think he was mad we forgot to lock the door."

"You are the worst bodyguardee ever."

"I know."

"Well, maybe you can make it up to him when you get out of town. Buy him some good dinners or something. What's the etiquette in that situation?"

"George, I am not taking a bodyguard with me when I flee the law. I can't afford it."

"I'm paying, Jones."

He sniffed. "Not open for discussion."

Above their heads, a tiny bird swooped in graceful arcs above the skylight, at one point gliding so close to the tempered glass they could see the downy fluff adorning its breast. They watched it until something else caught its attention and it vanished from view. Georgia turned to Jonah, planning her words carefully, but his phone chirped again and he was already thumbing through it. She thought of taking it away—her mind filling with the monstrous image tacked to his door last night—but she was too late: just then he let out a sound like someone had kicked him, hard, in the kidney. "What?" she said, instantly on alert. "Something nasty online?"

"No," he managed. "Worse."

He'd gone still. Without touching him or looking over, she could sense his horror on a cellular level, as if he'd suffered a cataclysmic rearrangement of atoms that changed him from Jonah into a not-quite-right clone, as if his scent or his shape or some fundamental essence had changed. She reached out to touch him and encountered a wall of ice. "What is it?" she asked, her voice gone hoarse.

He passed the phone to her. "Look," he said.

20

~~~~~~

HYSTERICAL, SELF-RIGHTEOUS HYPERBOLE

She took the phone from his hand. For a moment she wasn't certain what she was reading; whoever had screenshotted the article had zoomed in too close. Then her eyes adjusted and she realized she was looking at an obituary. She flung the phone away. "Frieda Myers is dead? What happened?"

There was a pause before Jonah answered. "I don't know," he said finally. "The last I heard from Andreas, they'd tried a half a dozen doctors and no one could see a new patient."

She froze.

His tone was awful; heavy and dull. "I should have done more."

"It's not your fault, Jonah. We don't even know what happened."

"Does it matter? The last thing she knew is that no one wanted to take care of her."

"Oh, Jones, I'm—"

He crawled away from her, already halfway down the ladder before she could finish.

~~~~~~

She followed him. "Jonah," she yelled as he ran out into the street toward his car. After a brief hesitation caused by the fact she was wearing nothing but a T-shirt and underwear, she tore out of the house after him. Edwin, alerted by her frantic hollering, assumed a defensive stance that blocked her from reaching the car. At the same time, it must have dawned on him that Jonah was in the midst of a getaway. He leapt backward in the direction of the car, his eyes trained on her.

"I'm not a threat," she said, keeping her hands in the air. "I don't have any weapons. I don't even have pants."

Edwin's eyes dropped to her underwear—which was not, luckily, a thong—then hovered with brief but discernible focus on her thin T-shirt. His brow furrowed. The shirt was her favorite, a present from Jonah, with a drawing of the symbol for atomic power—a bunch of overlapping ellipses—and some blocky lettering:

YOU MATTER

Unless you multiply yourself by the speed of light squared

. . . THEN YOU ENERGY

"Sir?" said Edwin over his shoulder to Jonah. "I'm going to need to come with you if you're leaving."

"Shotgun," Georgia boomed, realizing as soon as the word left her mouth that this was a poor choice of phrase to use in front of a confused bodyguard.

"You can't come with me, George," said Jonah. "You have to go to work. And, you know"—he gestured—"you're naked."

"Give me a second to get dressed," she begged. Tentatively, her eyes on Edwin, she reached for Jonah's shoulder. "I can call in to work. I don't want to leave you alone."

"You are not calling in to work. You've never called in to work and you're not starting now. Let me go."

She let out an inarticulate whimper and he softened. "I'll be fine. I have Edwin, and he'll make sure I'm fine. Right, Edwin?"

"Yes, sir."

Jonah crossed around to the driver's side of the car. "Go inside," he said. "You're causing a spectacle. I promise I'll call you as soon as I've talked to Andreas. And after that, I do want to get away." He looked at Edwin. "I won't need a bodyguard if I'm not here."

"Promise me you won't go to your house alone," said Georgia, her heart hammering. "Okay? Edwin goes with you until you leave town. Promise me."

"I promise," he said, and then they were gone.

~~~~~~

She met Jonah and Edwin at Jonah's house as soon as she could get there after work. When she arrived, he handed her a sparkling water and an empty travel case, directing her to pack his toiletries while he gathered his clothes and books. A bit surprised by this request, she employed a kitchen-sink approach, sweeping up an armful of grooming products and dumping them en masse into various zippered pockets. Jonah, normally a meticulous packer, seemed to be following in her footsteps as he packed, haphazardly flinging items into his suitcase.

All of them were jumpy. Jonah refused to discuss Frieda Myers, other than to say Andreas had been too distraught to talk much. He also didn't want to stay at home long, in case the cops showed up: according to Stewart, they could issue a warrant at any time. This worried Georgia too, but even with Edwin present, she was less concerned about the threat of Jonah getting arrested than she was about how they'd handle a knock at the door if it turned out to be a herd of homicidal neighbors.

Still, after Jonah had finished packing, she was reluctant to leave. She wandered outside and he followed her, Edwin remaining discreetly behind on the other side of the sliding door. They stood silently on his ocean-facing porch, their hair whipping in the wind. The sky had gone darker as a bank of clouds rolled in off the sea, carrying with them the mysterious tinge of electricity preceding an imminent storm. Georgia watched as a beach umbrella raced along the shoreline, somersaulting and vaulting on the updrafts like a crazed gymnast.

"Where are you going?" she asked Jonah. He seemed to have regained a tiny bit of his equilibrium at the thought of evading the authorities; he'd always had a thing for old spy movies.

"North Carolina. Brevard, which is a little town outside Asheville. Tucker recommended it."

"I've heard of it. They have more than two hundred and fifty waterfalls there and you can ride horses."

Now he looked dubious. "Sounds kind of outdoorsy."

She thought fast. "I think it's where they filmed *The Hunger Games*."

He brightened. "Really?"

"Yes. And *The Last of the Mohicans*."

She leaned against him. "I wish I could go with you."

The wind kicked up again, sending a groan through the floor joists and rattling a row of flowerpots against the back wall of the porch. The first drops of rain, turbulent and fat, slashed into her face at a nearly sideways angle, and she ducked, whirling toward the closed sliding door to the house. In the few seconds before she made it indoors, the rain intensified, consolidating from discrete drops into a solid sheet, drenching the floorboards and the porch chairs, turning everything sheeny and dark. Inside, she blotted her eyes with her hands, turning to Jonah to see if he'd gotten as wet as she had. But Jonah wasn't there. Squinting through the downpour, she could just make him out: he stood, still facing the ocean, his hands at his sides and his head bowed as the skies rained their anger all around him.

<hr/>

Everyone said newspapers were a dying industry. With the press of a button, you could access news apps and twenty-four-hour cable news channels, not to mention the ability to hop on social media to glean invective-laden opinion from your high school best friend's barely literate stepbrother. In the midst of all this instant gratification, who had the patience to wait for someone to deliver to your door a giant wad of pressed cellulose pulp studded with inkblots?

Georgia, that was who. She hated the hysterical, self-righteous hyperbole of the cable news channels, and while she did read various stories from her aggregated news apps, she was mindful of the necessity to be wary; half these things were fueled by bias masquerading as genuine journalism. It had become acceptable in this country to stretch the truth, or even invent a story out of whole cloth, as long as it suited your ideological preferences.

The newspapers were—literally—a different story. Aside from the opinion pages, which were clearly marked as opinion, not fact, newspapers still believed in journalistic purity. They had to back up their assertions with evidence or they could be sued for libel. They were, in their ideal form, the result of meticulous research, sometimes occurring over weeks or months, and consequently they boasted a heft and depth you could never find in a twenty-sentence news app article.

Normally, Georgia liked reading the paper. She had a ritual on her front porch, involving coffee and Dobby and her swinging chair, that she tried to enact whenever time allowed. But this morning, she'd awoken beset by a flurry of nervous energy. It had taken an extra three miles tacked on to the end of her run before she'd been confident she could face the day with anything approaching calm. She'd left the house late, arrived at work late, and been forced to play catch-up all day. Now, as people streamed from the clinic at the end of the workday, she dangled in the swinging chair in her office, kicking against the wall again and again to propel herself in a loop. The motion was soothing, but she eased the paper from its plastic sleeve with no small amount of dread.

It didn't make the front page, but instead had landed as a prominent, above-the-fold story on page two: *Local Physician Accused of Drug Theft*. She skimmed it quickly and then read it again more slowly. The reporter had done her homework, turning what could have been a two-paragraph nothing of a story into a nuanced human interest piece. She touched on Jonah's backstory, briefly mentioning his childhood as a biracial boy in the Deep South. She didn't mention the rift with his family, but of course she was aware of his recent firing before the current scandal broke, since the paper had already run a couple stories on it. All of this was fine; favorable, even. But as the piece took a deeper dive into the allegations against Jonah, things got ugly.

Yesterday, the video had leaked online. To say it had gone viral would be an understatement; you'd be hard-pressed to find a sentient creature anywhere in the greater Charleston area who hadn't seen it. Georgia had watched it on her computer at work. Even though she'd known what to expect, she pressed her hands to the sides of her head, breathing in short bursts as she read the comments beneath. After she'd seen it once, she made herself watch it again, imagining the experience through the eyes of someone who didn't know Jonah.

She'd known, of course, that it would appear damning. Taken from a vantage point about ten feet from the entrance to the medication area, it showed a male figure, dressed in black, hovering at the keypad of the Pyxis. At first only the back of his head was visible, but then he shifted, revealing three quarters of his face: a short nose, one high cheekbone, the contours of an eye marred by a resolving bruise. His hair, too, was recognizably Jonah's; spiky and dark. He looked in the direction of the camera for a long moment with an expression of unbearable sadness, almost as if he knew it was there. Finally, he shifted back to the keypad, shoulders curving inward as he hunched forward to punch in the code.

The video didn't actually show him removing any medications, but it didn't matter: the intent was clear. The newspaper article described the video in detail, following with a paragraph of responses from people at the clinic. Several of them caught her by surprise: blinking hard, she read the words of people she knew and liked, people she knew to be smart and generous, as they sucker-punched Jonah in the face. Or no, it wasn't a sucker-punch, exactly; more like a thin-bladed knife sliding between the ribs, so subtle you were halfway through your day before you realized you were bleeding to death. She had to hand it to this reporter. Physicians were a notoriously tight-lipped group when it came to judging their own. But here there wasn't much restraint.

Reading the article for a third time, she realized she was probably giving the reporter too much credit. The comfort in speaking freely had undoubtedly filtered down from the leadership of the clinic; if they were outspoken in their certainty and condemnation, what was to stop someone else? She pulled out her phone and checked the comments section of the paper's online version. A few people cautioned against a rush to judgment, but most people fell all over themselves as they rushed to judge. It *was* an awful accusation: if true, not only was it thievery for the worst of motives—debauchery and money—but it also raised the specter of a clinic patient suffering through a procedure, awake and feeling pain, because the bulk of his anesthesia was comprised of useless salt water. And then the hapless anesthetist, believing the patient to have a high tolerance to medication, might have administered more—this time from an unadulterated batch—and the patient could have overdosed.

And sure enough, halfway down the comments section: *I had a knee replacement there in August and I could feel everything! I knew something was wrong but no one would listen.*

Okay, this was bullshit. Joint replacements were performed in the OR, an entirely separate entity from the moderate sedation room. There was zero chance this person had been affected by these events, even if they had been true. But how long would it be before someone who had had a legitimate procedure performed in that room alleged the same thing?

Thirty seconds: that was how long. She hit refresh on the browser and an astonishing number of new comments came up. Things had gone downhill in this crop: the words *faggot* and *homo* figured prominently, and those were the gentler epithets. There was a lot of concern for the children, and how they might have been corrupted. Devastated parents of Jonah's teenaged patients relayed how, even if he hadn't molested their children, he'd probably tried to turn them gay. One man, who identified himself as Jonah's neighbor, insisted he'd frequently heard the loathsome sounds of orgies drifting down the street.

She turned off the phone and set the newspaper aside. Jonah had been gone for three days, and in that time, thanks to the video, the story had exploded. The local TV stations had it, as did a few national media outlets. Every time she hit the news app button on her phone, she'd run across his face. Most of the news sites used Jonah's professional headshot when they needed a photo of him, which they must have downloaded before it had finally been scrubbed from the clinic's website. Some of the dodgier sites, however, featured a blurry full-length shot of Jonah leaving Stewart's office. Wearing a baseball cap and a furtive expression, he looked every inch the felonious pervert your mother always warned you to avoid. It was only a matter of time before he became a meme.

He should have been blowing up her phone. He had to be aware of these news stories and the mounting outrage over the clinic's allegations and he should have been calling and texting about it, but she'd heard nothing other than one message saying he'd arrived at the rental house, and a peevish follow-up the next day complaining about the quality of the sheets. The last twenty-four hours: nothing. Not for the first time, she wondered if it had been a bad idea for him to go out of town. Isolated in the mountains far from home, watching helplessly as his life imploded—who knew how he'd react? He'd borne up remarkably well throughout all of this so far, but a shudder went through her as she thought of the handful of times in the past when he'd stumbled across the depression trip wires hidden in his brain. What if that happened again and he was alone?

She tried calling him and got his voicemail. *Jonah Tsukada's phone,* his voice sang. *Do it!*

She did it. "Hey, it's me," she said. "I'm getting nervous that I haven't heard from you . . . Call me."

"Hey," someone said.

She spun in her chair, aiming for the direction of the door so she could see who it was, but overshot a bit. She twirled in a brief, dizzying circle before she managed to get a boot on the floor to halt her motion.

"McLean," she said.

McLean shut the door behind him. "Sweet Georgia Brown," he said. "Sorry for busting in. You have a moment?"

"Sure."

"The committee is meeting tonight."

Georgia raised an eyebrow; she hadn't heard this.

"Listen, Georgia. They found a box in a locked drawer when they searched the room that used to be Jonah's office." McLean's round face had twisted up in discomfort. "It had a stack of syringes and a tourniquet in it. Some alcohol wipes. And . . . an empty bottle of fentanyl."

Her hand flew to her mouth to stifle a cry. "Jonah didn't take those medications," she said.

He looked at her with unmistakable pity. "I don't want to believe he did either. But I've seen the video and when I heard this . . . I thought you should hear it from a friend."

His words blurred in Georgia's ears as she tried to make sense of this. Jonah had not stolen any medications. She thought again of the drugs named in the article: ketamine, Ativan, fentanyl. The last one, fentanyl, was one of the deadliest drugs in America, accounting for a third of all overdose deaths.

"McLean," she said, leaping to her feet. "I have to go. Thank you for telling me. I'm very grateful, I . . ." She was out the door in two steps, waiting for McLean to make his way out so she could lock it. "It was kind of you to tell me."

"Georgia, can I do anyth—"

"Nothing!" she shouted over her shoulder, already halfway down the hall. "No. But thank you!"

21

~~~

A STEEL HUMMINGBIRD IN FLIGHT

He didn't answer the phone. She tried him repeatedly on the drive home and again every thirty minutes. Nada.

She called Mark. "I can't get in touch with Jonah."

"I'll be back tomorrow," he told her. "It'll be okay; I'm sure he just has bad cell phone reception."

It was the same in the morning. No answer. After checking again to make sure her ringer was on, she set down the phone. Normally at this time on Saturday morning, she'd have gone for her run, read the paper, and changed into her coveralls in preparation for whatever project she had going in the backyard. Today, none of that mattered. She should have tried to burn off her angst by exercising, but a paradoxical electricity had taken over her brain, leaving her hyped and jittery but also unable to take any concrete action. At the least she could have tidied the house: Mark would be here soon and he'd never seen her home; he hadn't even made it through the front door during his aborted earlier visit. But instead of running or working or cleaning, she paced the house, Dobby by her side, until he couldn't take it anymore and started barking.

She knelt and gathered up his big blocky head, scratching behind his ears. "You're right, you're right, we need to get out of here," she told him. He panted in agreement, the sunlight streaming in through the window behind him transforming the ruffled frieze on the back of his head into a halo. "You're a good boy. I love you," she said. He drooled happily, batting his head under her hands the instant she tried to stop scratching.

Across the room on the kitchen counter, her phone buzzed. Instead of walking around the futon like a sane person, she hurdled it like a track star, only just missing hooking her foot into a cushion. She made it to the counter and snatched up the phone midway through the second ring, hoping, of course, it was Jonah. It wasn't.

"Georgia."

Mark's voice: she basked in it for a second, caught in the brief respite from stress. Then she realized she should be paying attention to his actual words, not just the tone of them.

"Say that last part again?"

"I'm here."

"You're already here?"

"Yes, I'm here in Charleston. I switched flights for one last night but it got delayed. I actually got in last night around two o'clock but I didn't want to wake you."

"That's wonderful. You should have gotten me up." In the background of the call she could hear the murmur of television. "Where exactly are you?"

"Just waking up." He sounded sheepish. "I got a hotel last night. Same place I stayed earlier. It's lovely, actually."

"Perfect," she said. "I can pick you up in five minutes."

~~~~~~

Mark had an hour before he had to check out of his room, so she met him upstairs. In happier circumstances, greeting your lover in a beautiful hotel suite in a beautiful city on a beautiful weekend morning would lead to a lust-addled frenzy, but today, after one look at her, Mark seemed to recognize that any romantic action was off the table. He sat down on the bed and patted a space beside him. She sat down, leaning into his arms.

"What's the latest?" he asked.

"I still can't reach Jonah."

"He's in the mountains?"

"Yes. As far as I know."

"The media . . ."

"Yes," she said again. "Brutal."

Softly: "I've seen it."

She said, "He gets depressed. Not often. It's been a while since the last time." She thought back to a few years ago, when his antidepressant medication had stopped working, coinciding with a bad breakup with a fierce-eyed M&A banker named William. "He gets quieter and quieter and stops going out and then he stops answering texts. He functions, but he functions at about twenty percent of normal—everything nonessential shuts down. He goes from crazypants to normal to dull, and then he dips below that and becomes some sort of automaton. It's terrifying, like part of his mind's been sucked out."

The room in which they sat was white-walled, very bright, with a huge sleigh bed and silvery brocaded chairs, light streaming in from the open balcony doors. Here amid all this serenity, the black rot of depression seemed to be an alien concoction. You could grasp the concept intellectually, but it felt mythical, otherworldly. Still, Mark made a valiant effort: "Given what he's going through, anyone would feel situational depression. But you think it's more than that?"

"He's done so well," she said. "Through all of this. He's been upset, but he's been himself. But now, I don't know. It's one thing to be stressed and anxious, but if he becomes depressed, he won't fight back. Or—" She couldn't bring herself to state aloud the other way in which he might decide to opt out. She rolled toward Mark and clutched his arm. "I think it's a mistake for him to be alone. I should drive to the mountains."

"I'll go with you," he said instantly.

Gratitude flooded her. "I need to know he's okay."

A buzzing sound from inside her bag reached her ears. She'd dropped her handbag just inside the door, and so for the second time today, she hurtled across a room to reach her phone before it quit ringing. *Jonah,* she prayed, *let it be Jonah.*

But it wasn't Jonah this time either. It was Stewart, asking where he was.

"I haven't seen him in a couple days," she said truthfully.

Stewart, no stranger to evasive tactics, followed up strong. "Do you know where he is?"

"I hope so," she said, honestly enough. "Why?"

A clipped puff of air, Stewart's version of a sigh: "I'm afraid there's a warrant for his arrest."

She made the same noise you'd make if someone whirled around and punched you in the stomach. Across the room, Mark's head rose; stricken, he mouthed, "What happened?"

She shook her head at him, and then, realizing how he might interpret this conversation, she put her hand over the phone and whispered, "They're going to arrest him."

"Please tell me he didn't leave the county," Stewart was saying. "I can voluntarily surrender him, but he'll have to do it soon. Otherwise, they'll come after him."

"You can't let them arrest him, Stewart. He didn't do this!"

"Submitting to an arrest is not an admission of guilt. But evading arrest is a crime in and of itself. We don't need to make this any more complicated than it is. Jonah needs to come to my office."

"Is he evading if he doesn't know he's supposed to be arrested?"

"They've asked him to come in today, Georgia. Is that going to be possible? He hasn't been returning my calls."

"I don't know. He hasn't been returning mine either."

"Have him call me as soon as you hear from him."

She ended the call and smoothed out her dress, a maxi, studded throughout with small mirrored discs sewn on with embroidery thread; it was light orange at the top, deepening to a dusky blood-orange at the bottom. It was a dress that screamed *Happy!* You'd wear it to a festival or a groovy concert or a day of browsing the Charleston markets. You wouldn't wear it to fetch your best friend so he could be arrested. "We should go, right now," she told Mark, slipping the phone back into her bag.

He stood and started dressing, his back to her as he pulled a long-sleeved gray shirt over his head and tucked it into a pair of jeans so worn they'd softened to a velvety blue-white. His hair had grown an infinitesimal amount since she'd last seen him, enough to trigger a small curl at his neckline. Even with a houndstooth-patterned old blazer thrown over the top, this was as casual as she'd ever seen him; she realized she'd become used to the sight of him in a suit. In all, he looked relaxed but elegant, like a glossy magazine ad for good scotch or expensive men's watches. Even in the midst of her worry, she felt a small stab of amazement that she'd met him, that she liked him, that she wanted him here, and, most of all, that he wanted to be here too. "Thank you," she told him. "Thank you for coming."

He paused, one foot suspended above a battered leather shoe. "I'm glad I came."

"I'm sorry it isn't going to be a fun trip for you."

He waved a hand as if to say this wasn't worth consideration. "Did you call the place Jonah's staying?"

"It's an Airbnb. There wouldn't be anyone there."

"But you could try the owners," he said. "Maybe someone could go check on him."

She was already thumbing through her phone in search of the details. "Good idea."

"I mean, he's probably just let his phone battery die. Or there's no reception there. But getting a message to him would be a lot faster than driving to the mountains, yeah?"

She found the information and dialed the number. It rang five times before a woman's voice came on the line.

She explained she was a friend of Jonah's who needed to reach him urgently; was there any way she could get a message to him in person? She was in the midst of apologizing for the inconvenience when the woman interrupted.

"Oh, honey," she said. "He's already checked out. The day before yesterday, I think it was."

She froze. "What?"

Her voice hovered somewhere between defensive and apologetic. "We have to keep the payment, you know. There's no time to rent it to someone else."

"That's fine," Georgia said. "Did he say where he was headed?"

The woman hesitated, as if searching her recollection. Georgia bit her tongue to keep from crying out for her to hurry.

"I don't think he said where he was going," she offered finally. "But he said he had to leave right then because he had something that couldn't wait."

~~~~~~

Mark drove Georgia's car so she could keep trying Jonah. Since he wasn't familiar with Charleston, he'd activated the GPS on his phone, which issued its instructions in an efficient English-accented voice, directing them out of the city and down Highway 171 toward Jonah's house at Folly Beach. As the miles ticked by, Georgia tried to stay calm, placing her flushed cheek against the cool glass of the window and taking big, slow, regulated breaths. She didn't dare vocalize her thoughts, or even allow them to take form in her mind, but even so, unspoken and unarticulated, they battered around in the hollows of her skull like demon-driven bumper cars, flattening any attempt at rational thought.

Wisely, Mark didn't try to talk to her. His face grim, he gripped the wheel tightly at ten o'clock and two o'clock as if he were an old lady, deftly whipping the car around the actual old ladies clogging up the road. They made good time; the roads were sparsely populated at this hour on a weekend morning. Even so, by the time they reached Jonah's house, Georgia had aged a million years. Like the character in the Stephen King story who stays awake during a galactic journey lasting eons, she expected to emerge from the car with a shock of pure white hair and an auto-cannibalized brain, driven mad by her own thoughts.

They raced up the long flight of stairs to Jonah's front door. Mark rang the doorbell and Georgia pounded, but there was no answer. Even from up here they could make out the edge of Jonah's front bumper through the slats in the garage wall below them; at some point, he'd come back. Georgia peered through the panes of glass on the side of the door into Jonah's foyer, and beyond that, his living room, finding both in a state of unviolated order.

"Key?" said Mark. Even on this, the lee side of the house, a strong wind off the sea riffled his dark hair. He thrust a hand through it, pushing it off his face.

"In back," she panted.

Mark followed her as she galloped down the stairs, through a gate, and around a narrow path between the houses to Jonah's back porch. Just beyond the house a little dune rose up, encrusted with an undulating row of sea oats, their spiky tops dusted with wavy green florets. A battered old walkway of silvery wood wound through a break in the dune, leading out to the beach in one direction and to Jonah's patio in the other.

Georgia rushed up the creaky back steps to his upper deck, where she retrieved a spare key from the mouth of a copper statue guarding one corner. With an unsteady hand she inserted it into the lock on the patio door, remembering to jiggle the key a little as she lifted the door slightly off its tracks. With a creak, the door slid open.

They stepped into Jonah's living room, a tidy space dominated by a blocky sectional sofa printed in a geometric pattern. Jonah had chosen to forgo the typical beach house decor for an edgier, more industrial look; there weren't any seashell motifs or rope-twined lamps or plump navy-and-white club chairs. The room held an eerie air of desertion. Despite the sunshine pouring in from the patio doors, all the lights were on, pooling onto the chrome and leather surfaces from recessed LED pockets in the ceilings; the only sound, a faint mechanical hum, came from somewhere in the adjacent kitchen. A galaxy of dust motes caught in a shaft of light glittered benignly in one corner of the room.

"He's not here," said Mark.

Georgia hooked a finger in the air, as if testing it for the presence of human life. "Wait," she said.

Mark followed her to the front of the house, where she performed a cursory check of the guest bedroom and a little study. She didn't expect to find anything, and she didn't; even Jonah's computer in the study had been fully powered off. Next, they hit the kitchen. It too was clean, but in contrast to the perfectly ordered living room, the kitchen showed signs of human habitation. A junk drawer had been left open, its contents askew. On the buffed concrete counter rested a silver bottle opener, one end dangling perilously over the edge. The bottom shelf of the liquor cabinet was in disarray, bottles turned every which way, with one even lying on its side. An empty ice cube tray lay glistening in the sink.

They exchanged a glance.

Beyond the kitchen, the door to Jonah's bedroom hung slightly ajar. No light emanated from within, not even daylight from the large bay of windows facing the sea; he must have pulled the blackout shades. Georgia eased into the room quietly, listening for the sound of breathing as her eyes adjusted to the darkness. After a moment she thrust a hand to the wall beside it where she knew there to be a light switch.

After she flicked it the change was startling, like a strobe or a crack of lightning had gone off, dousing the room in supersonic whiteness. She blinked. Mark came up behind her, his hand wrapping around her waist just as the shapes in the room resumed their form and color.

Jonah was on the bed.

He lay on his back, his mouth gaping. Georgia ran to him, her breath coming in desperate little hitches. His eyes were shut but not all the way; she could make out a little rim of white between his lids as she pressed her hands to his face. He lay still, nonreactive, one leg folded under him in an odd way, but his skin was not cold; not yet, anyway. She felt for a carotid pulse, her fingertips digging into his neck too deeply. She forced herself to lighten her touch, but she couldn't tell if the faint pulsation she felt was from Jonah's artery or the violent trembling of her own hands. Lowering her ear to his chest, she allowed her cheek to brush against the soft cotton of his T-shirt; through it, she could feel the indentation of his ribs. After a moment of holding her own breath she heard his: a harsh but shallow inhalation.

She lifted her head and looked at Mark, scarcely able to force out the words. "He's alive."

Mark's face had gone dead white. "They can pump his stomach, right? He'll be okay?"

"Call nine-one-one," she said, lifting her head from Jonah's chest. Gripping his shoulder blades, she rolled him onto his side on top of the crisply made bed, in case he were to vomit, propping him into position with a pillow. Even with her maneuvering, his slight form barely made an indentation on the smooth coverlet on which he lay. Next to him, on his bedside table, two shapes caught her attention: the gleam of a cocktail glass and the tall silhouette of a bottle. An empty pill container lolled next to them, its label obscured. She picked it up and read it: Clonazepam. A benzodiazepine; a sedative. He'd used the alcohol and the pills to knock himself out, to wallop his pain into oblivion, maybe even to try to die. But Mark was right; this was survivable, as long as they could get him to the hospital and as long as he hadn't spent any significant time without oxygen. She felt again for his pulse.

Her own heart was hammering so hard it could have escaped her chest, a steel hummingbird in flight. Still, she managed to scoop the pill bottle into her pocket; the ER docs would need it to try to determine how much he could have taken. She swept her hand across the table as she listened to Mark giving the details to an emergency services dispatcher on the phone: *Overdose, yes, he's breathing; no, he's not conscious; no, he's not seizing or vomiting.* Mark tilted his head toward her. "Is he a known addict? Do you have any Narcan?"

"He's not and I don't," she answered, recognizing the name of the broadly used antidote for opiate overdoses. "And I don't think this is an opiate overdose."

Mark listened to the dispatcher and turned to her again. "She wants you to check for other pill bottles."

"Of course," she said. "But I don't think—"

She froze and Mark broke off his conversation with the dispatcher to look at her. Alarmed, he set down the phone. "Georgia? What is it?"

Pointing at Jonah's table, she tried to speak, but all she could manage was an awful inhuman rasp.

~~~~~~

22

HER PARTICULAR DOOM

Mark strode over to the table and picked up a second bottle, this one giant and white. "Acetaminophen?" he asked, confused. "That's just generic Tylenol, right?"

She nodded, still unable to speak. She felt herself folding in the middle, like her spine had given way. The floor rushed toward her, a loud whooshing noise between her ears.

Mark jumped to her, pulling her into him before she could hit the floor. "Hey, hey, easy there," he said. He lifted her away from Jonah's inert form, away from the bed and the table of horrors beside it, easing her onto the only chair in the room, a low-slung steel and black leather contraption that had been exiled from the living room because no one ever wanted to sit in it. She had a fleeting memory of mocking that chair, calling Jonah's bedroom *the dungeon* because of it. He'd played along with good grace, but in truth his bedroom was the least sexy room in the house, since there were at least five photos of his beloved Nana Midori, his maternal grandmother, by the bed. Additionally, one whole wall of the room had been devoted to shelving containing his childhood collection of Star Wars toys and books.

Mark waited for her to speak, his eyes flitting back and forth between her and Jonah, still sprawled on his side on the bed with a terrible vacancy on his face. "Can you open the shades?" she managed finally, gesturing at the heavy blackout drapes.

"Of course," he said, moving smoothly to the window. In an instant, natural light flooded the room, subsuming the ugly brilliance of the track LEDs. Mark moved back to her. "Tell me," he said.

"Acetaminophen poisoning is . . . bad," she said, forcing herself to speak. "It's especially bad when combined with alcohol."

He gestured to Jonah. "*Tylenol* did this to him?"

"It didn't make him unconscious. The benzos and the booze did that," she said, trying to calculate the maximum length of time that could have passed since Jonah had taken the pills. At some point he'd likely have been vomiting profusely; he was lucky he hadn't choked and died in his sleep. She heaved herself out of the S&M chair and crossed to Jonah, peeling up one of his eyelids. The sclera—the white part of the eye—was bloodshot but still white; not yellow, thank God. Next she pried open his mouth and lifted his tongue, inspecting the bottom of the mouth. Pink, not yellow. She felt herself sag in relief: maybe he hadn't been this way for long.

"What are you doing?"

"Checking for jaundice," she said. She closed Jonah's mouth, but kept her hand on his face, stroking along the angle of his jaw up to his cheekbone. He did not respond. "Tylenol eats your liver. It's a slow, nasty death, and once it reaches a certain point, it's irreversible."

"There's nothing they can do? They can't pump his stomach?"

They both startled as the wail of a siren reached them. "Not unless he just took it, and even then . . . There's an antidote, but it's time- and dose-dependent. If he took too much too long ago . . ."

She could not bring herself to finish the sentence. If he'd taken too much too long ago, there was no way to save him. He'd die.

Jonah would die.

"He'll be okay." Mark crossed to her and took her in his arms, wiping away a deluge of tears she hadn't known were there. "He'll be okay, Georgia."

~~~~~~

The family space adjacent to the ICU was standard-issue Hospital Waiting Room; crammed with fusty people, it contained angular pleather couches and a whole host of AARP magazines from the early 2000s, along with the mandatory wall-mounted television set tuned to Fox News. With bleary incomprehension, Georgia stared at the TV; a Barbie-esque blond woman stared heatedly back, her mouth moving and moving and moving.

They'd been in this room for hours, in a big downtown Charleston hospital less than an hour away from the hospital where Georgia and Jonah worked. She buzzed the ICU nurse yet again, and this time she was told someone would be out to talk with them shortly. She returned to Mark, who looked at her with new energy. "Did she say anything?"

She shook her head. "But soon, I hope."

They waited. Neither of them wanted to eat, but every hour or so Mark had gone on a coffee run, traipsing down to the cafeteria and returning with yet another steaming cardboard cup. Georgia hadn't been able to bring herself to leave the waiting area for a bathroom break, fearful she'd miss an update, so by now she was nearing a state of profound discomfort.

Doubling over, she made her way out of the room in a gait that could only be described as a speedy hobble. She flung herself out into the hall and into the doorway of the nearest restroom. It turned out to be a men's bathroom, with several startled men standing at urinals, but no matter. This was an emergency.

When she emerged from the stall, feeling infinitely more comfortable, the men had fled. She washed her hands at length, splashing water onto her face in an attempt to ward off the desire to curl up and weep. She rubbed the cold water into her skin until her hands had gone numb and her cheeks stung. Looking in the mirror, she saw the face of a stranger staring back. She had Georgia's dark red hair and her arched eyebrows and her stubby nose, but her eyes were hollow coals set in a mottled patchwork of pink and white, with nothing recognizable behind them. For a moment reality had suspended itself; Georgia had the impression she didn't exist anymore, that she'd been replaced by someone else.

This—this feeling of extreme disorientation—had happened to her before. Her dad died in a hospital when she was seventeen, hardly more than a child. After her mother disappeared, Georgia and her father had forged their own little family unit of two, just her and him, preparing the food they liked, reading their books together at night by a fire, working on projects together in their workshop out back. After he died and she'd moved to Charleston, she'd worked for weeks to re-create their workshop in her little backyard, designing and building and curating the structure to match the original as best she could from her memories and the one photo she had of their backyard in Kentucky. All her dad's things, including his tools and books, had been sold by her guardian at an auction to raise money for her care; it was one of her greatest regrets that she hadn't had the foresight to snag and hide a few of his favorite items for herself. She'd give anything to be able to hold his beloved old calculator, to turn it over in her hands and see the numbers, encased in blurry circles from the oil of his fingerprints. Or the one ancient army jacket he'd worn every day in the fall, winter, and early spring; she could picture herself wrapped in it, inhaling his scent, resurrecting a momentary feeling of safety, of being loved by someone above all others.

Perhaps it was her special burden, her particular doom, that everyone she ever loved would leave her.

~~~~~~

When she made it back to the waiting room, a slender woman with lustrous black hair stood with her back to the door, talking to Mark. From the confidence of her stance, Georgia immediately pegged her as the admitting ICU doctor, or possibly a toxicologist. She used her hands for emphasis, fluttering them in front of her like two brown birds as she spoke. Georgia rushed up, catching the tail end of her sentence: ". . . perhaps by tomorrow."

"Georgia Brown. Like the song," Georgia said, thrusting her hand toward the woman and then retracting it when she remembered that for obvious reasons ICU docs weren't big on shaking hands. She nodded instead. "I'm Jonah's friend, the one who brought him in."

"Of course," she said. She had a lovely accent, as if she were speaking in cursive. "I'm Stephanie Levin. Thank you for the information you provided to the ER doctors. Do you know how to reach Dr. Tsukada's family?"

"Jonah isn't close with his family; I don't know how to contact them. I'll work on it." She hesitated. "But I can help you. I'm Jonah's healthcare power of attorney."

She and Jonah had each designated the other to make medical decisions on their behalf if the worst happened; as every doctor could attest, you wanted someone who knew you extremely well to do that.

"Thank you for everything you're doing for him." Georgia could barely contain her anxiety. "How is he?"

"I was just telling your friend here"—Dr. Levin nodded to Mark—"that it's going to be a while before we know." She angled the tablet she was carrying so Georgia could see it. "You're a doctor at another hospital, correct?"

"Yes. A urologist."

Dr. Levin tapped on the screen of the tablet. "Do you remember what this is?"

Georgia looked at the screen. It contained a graph with a horizontal axis plotting the plasma concentration of the drug and a vertical axis for the time elapsed since ingestion.

"It's been a while," she admitted. "But I think I remember you use this to determine how effective the acetaminophen antidote might be?"

"You're close," said Dr. Levin. "The name of the antidote is N-acetylcysteine, but we call it NAC. In certain situations, the nomogram allows us to figure out if liver toxicity is likely; in this case, how-ever, it's not as useful because we don't know the time of ingestion."

Georgia slumped. "Jonah is still unconscious, then."

"Yes," Dr. Levin said. "We've had to intubate him to protect his airway from aspiration."

Georgia nodded, and then, remembering Mark was likely to be bewildered, she translated. "She's worried he'll throw up and suck the vomit into his lungs. So they put in a breathing tube."

"I got that much," he said. "But does that mean he can't wake up? Or you're giving him more medicine to keep him unconscious?"

"It's a good question. Right now we are not giving him any addi-tional sedation, so we're certainly hoping he'll wake up once the drugs and alcohol wear off." A tiny frown puckered Dr. Levin's lips as she turned to Georgia. "What can you tell me about his drinking habits?"

Georgia knew where she was going with this. Chronic alcohol use and acute acetaminophen could be a bad mix. Not so much in the short term, but heavy consumers of alcohol faced more of a problem when their livers were suddenly called upon to detoxify large quantities of poi-son: they'd already depleted their stores of natural antioxidants, meaning a smaller amount of acetaminophen could take them down. She couldn't suppress a wince. Jonah had always been a social drinker, but he'd upped his game in the wake of his firing, occasionally even to the point of slur-ring words. To Dr. Levin she said simply, "I think he's been drinking more than usual lately. He's been facing some difficulties."

She could tell from Dr. Levin's expression that she was aware of Jonah's specific difficulties. Before she could even formulate an inter-nal worry that Dr. Levin would find him distasteful because of them, she placed a gentle hand on Georgia's forearm. "I can see how much he means to you," she said.

"You need to know—he doesn't regularly use drugs," Georgia said. She could feel a flush warm her cheeks at the thought of Amsterdam. "He drinks and he had that benzo prescription, I know, but he didn't steal drugs, like you've probably heard. Test him."

"We already sent a tox screen and we'll follow up," she promised.

"His other labs," she asked. "What do they show?"

"Since we don't know what time he did this, or even what day, we're assuming the worst-case scenario based on the timeline you gave us." Georgia nodded again; she'd added four and a half hours of drive time to estimate the earliest possible time Jonah could have overdosed if he'd sped home and immediately chugged an entire bottle of Tylenol after talking to the Airbnb woman. But now it struck her: Jonah could have taken the Tylenol while still in the mountains. She struggled to contain her expression.

"Liver enzyme levels don't correlate with the severity of a Tylenol overdose," the doctor went on, "but we have to consider the possibility of significant, possibly even fatal, liver damage. But at this point we don't really know. We're also waiting on our second blood draw to retest his level."

"How do his liver function tests look?"

Dr. Levin clicked on the screen and a different image came up: a list of Jonah's labs. She took Georgia and Mark through them one by one, patiently explaining to Mark what each of them meant. Georgia tried to focus on her words, but it had taken only one glance to know: they were bad.

Dr. Levin read Georgia's expression correctly, again placing a strong, slim-fingered hand on her arm. "You should go home and rest," she said softly. "It will be a long time before we know how he'll do. Go home and sleep and pray or meditate—or whatever you can do to gain strength—and come back tomorrow. I promise I'll call you if anything changes, and I'll make sure the next physician does too. We'll take care of him, just like you would."

Through rubbery lips Georgia said, "I will, but first . . . can I see him?"

Dr. Levin increased the pressure of her grasp on Georgia's arm, her gaze soft and strong at once. "Come with me," she said.

~~~~~~~

She'd seen a billion people in a state of unconsciousness before, including, at the end of his life, her own father; but nothing could have prepared her for the sight of Jonah in the ICU. He looked so small and helpless; a child caught in some monstrous alien contraption.

All physicians employ some degree of dissociation when viewing their most vulnerable patients; you had to master the trick of simultaneously thinking of them as fully human but also as a kind of disembodied technical challenge to master. This trick didn't negate compassion or empathy, but it smoothed over your reaction, allowing you to process the worst of it later.

Here, though, Georgia couldn't think of Jonah as a patient to be fixed, or as anything other than Jonah. Even with all the gadgets and tubes, even with the dull, insentient face of unconsciousness, he was so fully himself. His features were dear; his shock of black hair was dear; his thin, wiry shoulders and scrawny chest were dear. She wanted so badly to kiss him, to rattle him awake, that it caused actual physical pain: a searing sensation in her chest.

She gulped in air and looked away. By force of habit, her eyes drifted to the monitor above Jonah's bed: his vital signs were normal and his ventilator-regulated breaths were measured and even. By machine standards, he was doing fine.

She picked up his hand, gripping it tightly, and leaned down to his ear.

"Come back," she whispered. "Please come back."

23

VINDICATION

MARK

The next day—Sunday—passed without much change. Mark had been scheduled to go to Raleigh for a meeting, but he quietly canceled, opting to stay another day or two in Charleston with Georgia. He couldn't bring himself to leave her in the midst of her terror for her friend. The more time he had spent with her, the more he'd begun to admire her character. She was so honest, so authentic and open; even though she'd made it clear she cared a thousand times more about what happened to Jonah than she did about her budding relationship with him, it only served to deepen his respect for her. That kind of integrity was uncommon.

The word about Jonah leaked out: Georgia had told Stewart, who told the police, who told the clinic administrators, who told the press, who, naturally, told the entire world. Not the details, not that Jonah had overdosed. But within a day, everyone in Charleston had access to the knowledge that he'd been hospitalized for something serious enough to land him in the ICU.

As the long, torturous hours of Sunday bled into Monday, he remained by Georgia's side. She refused to leave the hospital, so they spent the night in the waiting room. He couldn't sleep, of course, sitting upright in a hard chair. Moonlight sliced into the room, falling through the blinds and across the floors in silvery stripes. Across the room, a discarded white hospital blanket on a chair trembled as air blew up from vents in the floor, its edges ghostly and ephemeral. An image of Mark's mother appeared in his mind, her face eternally young and kind and full of comfort. He often did this when he was stressed or concerned: conjured up his mother's features and held them as long as he could, allowing the unconditional acceptance in her gaze to warm him. Perhaps this was juvenile and maudlin, but he didn't care. If you didn't have anyone in the world to offer you unconditional love, the next best thing was the memory of someone who had once done so.

He would've sworn he hadn't slept at all, but the next thing he knew the room was bright with sunlight. Fragments of the night returned to him: restless shifting in his chair; his attempts to bore himself to sleep by naming, in alphabetical order, all the states in America, then all the state capitals, and then, in desperation when that hadn't worked, all the countries in Africa and Asia. (He'd always been a bit of a geography buff.) He thought he'd gotten through them all, but at some point in the process he must have drifted off.

Beside him Georgia still slept, her full lips parted enough to reveal the glint of her top two teeth, her hair tumbling all over the back of the seat like a paint spill. Perhaps she sensed his stare in her sleep, because suddenly she opened her eyes. For a glorious moment there was pleasure in her gaze at the sight of him. Then the pleasure turned to confusion as she caught sight of her surroundings, and then, horribly, her face contorted in pain as she remembered why she was here.

They spent the day at Jonah's bedside, whenever they were allowed. His condition did not improve.

In the afternoon, Georgia began to obsess about whether or not they'd locked the door to Jonah's house after the departure of the EMTs, and he agreed to drive her back to check. As he drove, Mark registered the glowing cloudless sky and the ever-present lure of the sea, casting its brisk winds into the city. It was a gorgeous afternoon, almost evening.

They sailed through the city in her quiet car, the only sound the whooshing of the wheels on the road. Mark reached for the dial of the radio, flipping through the preset stations until he landed on NPR. Keeping the volume low, he drifted in the cultured murmur of the voices, a comforting and reassuring background sound even though for all he knew, they could have been discussing a massacre in South Sudan or the corruption of a treasury cabinet member or the erosion of the Arctic ice. As a single person, he often used the radio as a reminder of human connection, a way of eating silence, even when he didn't want to know the news. He'd almost forgotten the radio was on when Georgia suddenly tensed and reached for the dial.

"They're talking about him."

They caught the tail end of the local news segment: it was indeed about Jonah. For a moment, Mark flinched, thinking they were going to report that he'd died, but this was something else: the reporter sounded upbeat, even intrigued.

". . . certain to be more to this developing story," she said. "In the meantime, though, we'll continue to try to reach out to his place of employment for comment on the allegations against them."

"Did she say allegations against *him*?" asked Georgia, echoing Mark's thoughts as the story ended and the anchor began talking about white supremacists. "Or allegations against *them*? As in, allegations against the clinic?"

"It sounded like *them*," he said. Georgia bent forward, searching for something on her phone. After a moment of frustrated tapping, she set the phone down. "I can't find anything on the news sites."

"What about Jonah's lawyer?" Mark suggested. "Maybe he'd know."

She cocked a finger at him. "Brilliant."

She put the phone on speaker so Mark could hear. "How is he?" barked the lawyer as soon as she identified herself. "Any improvement?"

"No. Stewart, I just heard them mention Jonah on NPR," she began, but the guy, sounding revved up, interrupted.

"I can't talk," he said. "I'm on the phone about it now."

"Can you just—"

"I don't know quite how to tell you this," Stewart said. "But it looks like someone at the clinic may have framed him. I'll be in touch." He hung up before Georgia could say another word.

Mark tried to take in Georgia's face from the corner of his eye, but all he could make out was that she was staring dead ahead. "He said 'framed,' right?" he asked. "I can't believe it!"

She still didn't react and so he took his eyes off the road, briefly, to swing his head in her direction. Why wasn't she more surprised? She caught his movement. "If Jonah dies and then he's exonerated, it won't matter one bit. I get why Stewart's worked up, but . . ."

"Hard to blame him for being excited about that if it's true, though," Mark pointed out. "Not only an innocent client, but somebody actually framed by the other side? It's every trial lawyer's dream."

"I don't give a damn about what makes trial lawyers happy. I only want him to be okay."

"It's absolutely crazy, isn't it? That someone would do something so dishonest as to manufacture evidence against someone they wanted to be fired? If it's proven to be true, the clinic is going to get crucified in the press."

"Yes," she said dully. "It would be utter vindication. His patients would have their doctor back. If he'd only hung on another day or two, everything would have been fine."

～～～～～

It turned out to be a good thing they'd gone back: Jonah's patio door was not only unlocked but also open a crack. Mark entered with trepidation, wary that the house could have been burglarized but also cringing from the awful memory of having found Jonah here near death. He went first, his body tense, standing directly in front of Georgia.

"It's okay," he said, after a moment. "No one's here. I don't see anything out of place, but maybe you want to look around? You know his stuff."

"I don't know," she said. "I'm not sure I want to look through his stuff."

Mark accepted this without comment. He turned toward the glass door of the patio, through which they could see the ocean sloshing around in majestic indifference. The color of the sky had deepened; it was almost navy at the horizon.

Georgia started toward the door but Mark spoke before she could open it. "Hey," he said quietly. "We should probably check for a note."

She startled, as if this had not occurred to her.

"If he expected to die, he might have left you something." He kept his voice soft. "Don't people often do that? Leave instructions for their things or a list of goodbyes or . . . an explanation?"

She blew out a shaky breath. "Okay," she said. "Will you . . . will you check around for me? I'm going to step out on the porch."

Mark nodded assent and she eased out of the room, leaving him standing alone in the dark living room. He flicked on a light. The junk drawer, still open, sat in a state of disarray, the neat little divider within it separating a mishmash of pens and pieces of paper and batteries and all the extraneous crap that accumulated, as if by magic, in a household. Given what he knew about the man's extravagant personality, he might have assumed a certain wanton disregard for order on Jonah's part had Georgia not told him Jonah possessed a meticulous nature when it came to his environment. According to her, he was tidy, almost fastidious, at home. He color-coded his drawers, arranged the contents of his closets on identical custom hangers. He made his bed daily. He had a standing appointment, every three weeks, for haircuts.

He left the kitchen and stepped into the bedroom. Here, again, was evidence of Jonah's neat nature: aside from the messy bedside table, still littered with the remnants of Jonah's overdose, everything seemed to be in place. Idly, he poked his head into a closet and he peered onto a shelf. Nothing. He exited and returned to the bed, lifting up Jonah's pillow.

Jackpot.

Footsteps sounded close by and he turned to see Georgia standing behind him. He shifted from one leg to the other, his hand behind his back.

"You found something," she said.

He brought his hand forward. "It's a note. To you."

"A note?" Terror slashed across her face. "Did you read it?"

"I did."

"Oh," she said, the word coming slowly. "Can you—will you read it to me?"

Mark extracted the reading glasses he'd just returned to his pocket and put them on. "It's for you," he said, again, moronically, as if she could have missed that. He cleared his throat and began to read.

Dear George,

It's midnight and I'm back. You're going to be pissed but I left the mountains. Turns out it is not as exciting as you'd think to be an outlaw. It's not exciting at all, actually. It's . . . excruciatingly lonely.

I've been giving a lot of thought to my situation and the only thing I am sure of is that I don't want to think any more about my situation. I don't want you to have to think about it anymore either.

And I'm sick of my demons.

I thought I'd go home, get stupidly drunk, pass out, and wake up with new insight but the only thing I've achieved so far is getting stupidly drunk.

So . . . I am making a list of my favorite things about you, just in case I forget to tell you in person.

Top Ten Things I Love About Georgia
10. Angry hair
9. Smarter than Wikipedia
8. Has way more facial expressions than other people

7. Sings like an angel on crack

6. Knows how to make vodka from potatoes

5. Extravagant kindness

4. Adds extra money to group tips when she thinks no one's looking

2. Thinks I don't know about my Christmas gift this year

1. Is the only person I've ever loved

Georgia sucked in a breath and turned away from him so he could not see her face. "There's no number three."

Mark flipped the paper.

"On the back. It says: *Fuck. I forgot to write number three.*"

"Ah," she said, and then folded, jackknifing her chin toward her knees so violently that for a second he thought she'd cracked herself in the jaw. After a startled moment he rushed to her, pulling her onto his lap. A great tide of pain distorted her features before she buried her face in his shoulder. Her body felt so tense it might have been made of iron.

"Georgia," he said, helplessly, once she'd managed to dial it down to a series of dull hiccups. Gently dislodging her from his lap, he rose, went to the kitchen, and returned with a paper towel, which he used to dab at her face. She eased under his arm and together they lay down, flat on their backs, staring up at Jonah's bedroom ceiling.

"You okay?" Mark asked finally.

"I'm better."

"I wondered . . ." Mark hesitated, wary of following the spectacularly stupid question he'd just asked with another one. "What did he mean by his demons? Do you think he wishes he weren't gay?"

"Oh!" she said, surprise in her tone. "No. Even before this, Jonah's been through plenty of crap as a result of being gay—his family, various teenaged torments—but he *likes* who he is. He doesn't want to be something he's not."

"Then what did he mean?"

"He means his depression," she said simply.

"Ah," said Mark again, adding, "I understand depression."

"When your mother . . ."

He nodded, feeling a dull, familiar tug in his chest. He'd been depressed when his mother died—of that, there was no question—but depression had sought him out at other times as well. As with Jonah, sometimes it struck him without warning, rising up from some unknowable neurochemical wasteland in his brain.

The wind kicked up outside. It was fully dark now, the last traces of purple gone from the sky. He slid his arm under her neck, brushing his hand against the side of her still-damp face.

"I know you sing well," he said. "I've heard you in the shower. I know you overtip. I didn't know you could brew vodka but I'm not all that surprised. But what did he mean about the Christmas gift? It's not even Thanksgiving."

Her voice held a hint of a smile. "I don't know how he found out. They promised me they wouldn't say a word."

"Who did?"

"The people at the medical college. I made a donation to have an area in the research lab named in honor of Jonah's Nana."

"That sounds . . . substantial."

"It's hard to get anything for Jonah," she said. "We try to outdo each other every year. His Nana is the one who encouraged his interest in medicine. I wanted to do something he'd truly love."

"I'd say you succeeded. I've never known anyone with so many photos of their grandmother by their bed." He was quiet a moment, then added, "I don't know if I should mention this, but there's more."

"More what? Another note?"

"No. A postscript." He could hear the sheepish tone in his voice. "I'm a little hesitant to read it . . ."

"Just do it."

His other arm still pinned down by her head, Mark struggled to get the letter out of his pocket, where he'd tucked it during her meltdown. Eventually he managed it and held it straight up in front of his face.

"*P.S.*" he read, *"Promise me you won't screw it up with Mark."*

"Mark . . ."

"I swear, I'm not making it up. He actually wrote that." He thrust the letter into her line of sight so she could see for herself. She almost, but not quite, managed a smile. "Well," she said, "I finally have proof: Jonah would micromanage my love life from beyond the grave if he could."

24

THE CELESTIAL DISCHARGE

She sat up. "Do you mind giving me a moment?" She staggered to her feet and waited, pushing the door shut as soon as Mark left Jonah's bedroom. She'd been in here a thousand times, but never alone. She surveyed the room as if she'd never seen it before.

Jonah was one of those people who cast a larger-than-life vibe. Even when he was quiet—which wasn't often—he drew your attention. His facial expressions, his body language—even his thoughts— seemed to broadcast themselves on some dominant frequency, pulling your attention toward him. The room without him was shaded and dull. His things were just things. For the first time, it struck her how little of his personality was reflected in this room. A nondescript bed. The S&M chair, which he never sat in. Even the pictures of his Nana were colorless and generic, as if they'd been selected on the basis of the photographic quality, rather than as a representation of the person within.

She sat on his bed, avoiding the side where they'd found him, and ran her hand along the edge of the bedside table, which had already accumulated the tiniest film of dust. She looked across to his shelves— the one area of the room that captured an element of his personality—

and scanned the books: mostly nonfiction—biographies and military history—which she knew he liked. But one volume was different: a slim, fabric-bound tome, light blue, with a faint ingrained pattern woven into the cloth. She crossed the room and plucked it out.

A journal.

Again, she was surprised. For all that she loved reading, she'd never kept a diary, believing it to be an introspective waste of time. And it required creativity: even the most basic recounting of one's day had to be embellished with interesting language, so as not to bore the reader, even if the readership was limited to the author. Thumbing through it, she saw Jonah had taken this sentiment to heart; his journal was lengthy, with multiple pages per entry and little drawings in some of the margins. She started to read it, then shut it abruptly. What right did she have to spy on Jonah?

But then she opened it again. Yes, it would be a breach of his privacy to read it, but what if he died? Someone would go through his things. It would probably be her, but she knew the hospital would reach out to Jonah's family as soon as they tracked down the contact information. Even if he didn't die, his family might come to his house, they might search his belongings, and they might take this journal. It might contain exculpatory evidence as far as the drug theft was concerned, but it could contain other material too, things Jonah would never want them to read. For that matter, it could contain things she'd never want them to read either.

She opened the cover and began to riffle through the pages without actually diving into any individual entry. Jonah had been an erratic chronicler of his own life, skipping weeks or months at a time before sinking into frenzies of what appeared to be near-obsessive detailing. He employed various methods of capturing his thoughts: occasionally straightforward narration, but more often verse, poetry, or even drawing. Consequently, the diary looked to be more of a reflection of his moods than a recounting of events.

The writing, what little she allowed herself to read, was shockingly good. She'd had no idea Jonah was capable of writing a grocery list, let alone an exquisite verse. She turned to the last page and, abruptly, her gaze sharpened. She read and reread the words on the page, analyzing each one with the fervor of a scholar, tracing her finger along them until she'd committed them to memory. Carefully, she creased the bound edge of the page and tore it from the corner until it ripped from the book, folding it into a small square, which she placed in her pocket.

Lifting the edge of Jonah's mattress, she slid the journal between it and the box spring. If he died, she'd return and retrieve it before anyone found it. She stood for a moment at Jonah's window, bathed in moonlight, watching the surf as it drifted and receded in an endless loop, and then she turned and went back to the living room.

~~~~~~

Tuesday also passed without a change in Jonah's condition. Or at least it passed without a positive change; his liver enzymes continued to worsen. After a conversation with Dr. Levin, Georgia walked back to the waiting room to talk with Mark. She watched him for a moment before he saw her. He sat, his back straight, on one of the uncomfortable plastic couches, reading a newspaper. Even seated, his head loomed a good six inches higher than the heads of the other people in the room, who, like her, all looked wrecked.

By now Georgia recognized some of the other families in the ICU waiting room, including a large group containing at least six or seven weepy adults and several oblivious small children. The children's mother occupied the bed next to Jonah, and, like him, she was unconscious and on a ventilator. Georgia didn't know what had happened to her.

Mark looked up, searching her face. Immediately he tucked the newspaper under his arm and crossed to her. "C'mon," he said, taking her by the elbow. "I'm taking you to the cafeteria. We need to move a little and you need to eat."

Despite its subterranean location, the cafeteria was bright and appealing, with clean white-tiled floors and blond wood tables. Georgia didn't want food, but she also didn't want to disgrace herself by fainting, so she choked down some yogurt once they'd settled at a table at the back of the room.

"What did Dr. Levin say?" Mark asked.

She told him about the liver enzymes.

"But didn't she say those labs don't correlate with the ultimate outcome?" Mark asked. "Even if they get very high, he could still recover, right?"

She pulled her spoon in a listless path through the half-eaten yogurt. "That's true, but there's more. Some of his other labs are starting to tank as well."

"Like what?"

"His kidneys are failing."

Mark frowned. She explained: in the hours immediately following his ingestion of the drugs and alcohol, Jonah had apparently passed out so deeply he hadn't moved at all. When they'd found him he'd been in an awkward position, with one leg folded under the other in a manner eventually compromising the blood supply to that leg. Because of that, Jonah's muscles had started to break down, releasing large amounts of protein and metabolites into his bloodstream. This in turn had begun to fry Jonah's kidneys.

"Can they fix that?"

"They're giving him massive amounts of fluid to try to flush out the metabolites. And he may need dialysis." She hesitated, trying to think of a way to describe Jonah's appearance right now. "If he wakes up today, he's going to be pissed," she said, finally. "He looks like a swollen tick."

Mark smiled at this, but in truth, despite her attempt at a joke, she was barely holding it together. There were times—many times—in life where ignorance was bliss. She thought of the happy tots darting around in the ICU family waiting area, clueless of the tectonic shift in their lives as their mother clung to life in the next room. Once you grew up, you never again enjoyed that level of protection from reality, but when things went badly in a hospital, most people were at least somewhat shielded by their lack of medical knowledge. They held on to hope when there was no hope. Not Georgia; she'd taken one look at Jonah's labs today and she knew it meant his organs were shutting down like falling dominoes. *The Celestial Discharge, The Eternal Care Unit, Hailing the Jesus Bus*—all examples of the bluff posturing doctors employed to mask the antagonism they felt toward the Grim Reaper. It turned out, despite all their euphemisms for death, doctors weren't any less gutted than anyone else when it was their person circling the drain.

And yet. This wasn't her area of expertise. She knew a crappy renal function test when she saw one, but how much did she know, really, about toxicology? Maybe you could fry your kidneys and poison your liver and shred your muscles and marinate your brain in a high-quality vodka and still come out of it okay. Maybe she was being too grim. Maybe she was overanalyzing. Maybe she should leave this infernal hospital and try to get a little distance.

Mark was on board with this idea. He'd be leaving in the morning for meetings in North Carolina, and although he offered to cancel to stay with her, she refused. She'd have to go to work in the morning too. She could call in again, legitimately claiming an emergency, but she'd always been loath to cancel surgeries. It caused disruption for her patients and created a headache for the OR and the schedulers. Plus, she knew sometime soon, for one reason or another, she'd need to be off again: either Jonah would recover, and she'd need to help him; or he would not recover. As far as tomorrow went, she could come back if anything changed; so far, Dr. Levin had been true to her word in keeping her informed.

Stewart's behavior, on the other hand, had been mysterious. They'd exchanged voicemails, but his was short and cryptic, stating he was trying to verify some final information and he'd be in touch when he could.

She motioned to Mark's newspaper, which he'd lain on the table, both hoping and not hoping there would be a story in it about Jonah. "Can I see that?"

"Wait," he said. "There's Jonah."

There was a confused pause as she tried to figure out how Jonah could have been miraculously resurrected in the moments since she'd left the ICU. Then she followed Mark's gaze and realized Jonah's image was on a TV screen across the room, just as the picture changed and went to a commercial. They'd been too far away to make out the caption under the photo or to hear the accompanying narrative, and in any case, the sound on the TV was muted. Georgia jumped up but Mark pulled her back down.

"That was a teaser," he said. "The story's coming up and I bet we can stream it. What channel is that?"

They huddled over Mark's phone. Georgia watched with ill-concealed impatience as the news show resumed with an interminable weather report on rain that might or might not be imminent, followed by a sports story about a team that might or might not have a winning season. Finally, after another commercial, they got back to the story on Jonah.

"And now for an update in the case of the local physician accused of drug theft," said a beautiful female anchor, "we turn to reporter Ashley Evans."

The screen changed to show an equally beautiful reporter with big brown eyes and a pert expression. She was standing in front of a sign reading EMERGENCY, which Georgia recognized as the entrance to the emergency department of the building in which they now sat.

"Thanks, Molly," said the reporter. "Dr. Jonah Tsukada, a family practice physician, has been under a cloud of suspicion after accusations that he stole powerful medications meant for surgeries." The screen switched again, this time demonstrating a generic stock shot of a syringe dripping a clear liquid from its tip. The syringe rested in front of a bunch of glass vials labeled POTASSIUM CHLORIDE. This, of course, was not what Jonah had been accused of taking: you wouldn't steal potassium chloride to inject at a party unless your idea of partying entailed instant cardiac arrest. Nonetheless, the photo did its job: it was creepy and vaguely ominous.

"Now, however, there have been significant developments. Dr. Tsukada has reportedly been hospitalized and is in critical condition. It is not known whether this is related to the theft of the drugs, but Dr. Tsukada's attorney, Stewart Hessenheffer, issued a statement earlier today asking for privacy regarding Dr. Tsukada's condition. He also discussed a startling announcement: he contends Dr. Tsukada is not only innocent of the charges against him, but that he was framed by someone at the medical clinic where he works."

Now a prerecorded segment with Stewart came on the screen. In contrast to the reporter, Stewart did not radiate a wholesome telegenic look. He'd been interviewed standing outside his office in what appeared to be a major gust of wind, and he kept blinking. His cautious oratorical style did not translate well to TV either; he had a tendency to use qualifiers in every sentence, so as not to overcommit. Even so, he managed to get his point across.

"We've asked the police to reexamine the investigation of the potential misappropriation of these drugs." He paused, eyes fluttering. "New evidence suggests it was an unknown individual entering the medication storage area, not Dr. Tsukada."

The cameras cut back to the reporter outside the hospital. "Molly," she said, "Dr. Tsukada's attorney says he will have more information soon. As you know, Dr. Tsukada was in the news earlier for discrimination claims against his employer. Could this be related? Right now we have more questions than answers."

The view switched back to the anchor in the studio. "It certainly sounds like it," she said. "Thank you. Keep us posted, Ashley."

25

A DOWNWARD SPIRAL

Not much had changed at the clinic in the days since Georgia had been away from work. The protestors and the counterprotestors still lined up outside the clinic lobbing spit bombs at one another, still flanked by news crews and gawkers. She avoided them all, hustling by with her eyes down. It burned her: Jonah lay unconscious, his liver slowly dissolving in the indolent grip of poison, and the universe had the gall to grant some of these dipshits perfect health? Why?

In the doctors' lounge, the conversational buzz fizzled as she made her way through the room. People who'd been speaking normally a second ago clamped their lips shut as she passed them. It was as if she possessed repellent superpowers: she could stifle speech and force people to avert their gazes, even send them spinning in the opposite direction.

Only McLean approached. "Hey there," he said, thrusting something in his hand toward her. To her surprise, it was *URINE GOOD HANDS*, already filled with hot coffee. Gratefully, she gulped it. McLean's small act of kindness had the paradoxical effect of strangling her; she wanted to thank him but couldn't get any words out. If he recognized she was suffering from social paralysis, he didn't let on; in an easy tone, he began to chat about an upcoming case, asking simple yes-or-no questions until she'd recovered enough to sound normal. Ignoring the stares, they walked from the lounge to the OR hall, still talking, where they set up to scrub at their respective sinks. Letting the water run over her hands, Georgia tried to banish everything from her mind except the surgery she was about to perform.

By the time she reached the physician's parking garage, many hours later, it had taken on a look of eerie desolation, the remaining cars casting long shadows from the overhead fluorescent lights. A parking garage in a medical facility was never empty, but this was as close as it got; her floor contained a handful of nice SUVs, a minivan plastered with soccer and lacrosse stickers, and Donovan Wright's stupid Ferrari, parked as usual across two spaces in a prime spot near the exit. Shuddering at the sight of it, she hurried to her Prius, which she'd left around a corner just as the floor began to slope upward to the next level. Rounding the last concrete wall, she almost swallowed her tongue in fright as she spied someone lurking at the door of her car.

Recovering, she nodded at Darby, who handed Georgia a small quilted bag.

"What's this?"

"It's a care bag," said Darby. Briefly, she clasped Georgia's arm. "I figured you've been living at the hospital for the last few days."

"Oh, Darby," she said. She peeked inside the bag: on top were homemade energy bars, wrapped in cellophane and tied with a gingham bow. "That's so kind."

"I was wondering . . ." Darby's hand curled around the strap of her shoulder bag. "I know this is out of the blue. But I was wondering— could I go with you? To visit him?"

Before Georgia could answer, Darby preemptively answered her own question. "Of course not," she said. "What an intrusion. I'm sorry."

"Why do you want to go?"

Her eyes closed. "I've been thinking about him."

Unbidden, a lump asserted itself in the middle of Georgia's throat.

She worked to swallow around it. "Sure," she said finally. "I bet he'd appreciate that."

～～～～～

Georgia started the car, angling the Prius around and around the twisty expanse of concrete leading to the bottom floor of the garage. It occurred to her the path to the exit was a pretty good metaphor for her life right now: a downward spiral. When was the last time things had been normal?

"I should have told you this before," Darby said, after miles of silence. "He called me."

Georgia's hands left the steering wheel, flying into the air toward her face, and just as quickly returned to the wheel as the car began to drift into the adjacent lane. A BMW careened past at high speed, the pitch of its horn receding as it Dopplered into the distance. Georgia must have lifted her foot from the gas pedal; hastily she returned it, and the car leapt forward.

"He called *you*? When?" she asked.

"Before . . ." Darby faltered. "I guess it must have been shortly before whatever happened. His voice sounded off, like he was confused."

A flash sizzled behind Georgia's eyes. "You knew he was messed up?"

Even in her peripheral vision, she could sense the shame in Darby's body language. "I thought he'd been drinking," she said, her words almost inaudible.

"What did he say?"

"He said . . . he said he wanted to tell me how much he'd enjoyed the morning at my house. How he thought I was a . . . good person. I thought: *Okay, this is goofy,* but it was also sweet. But then it got stranger."

"In what way?"

"He told me he'd done something bad, something he wanted to take back but he couldn't."

Regret choked Georgia into silence. A chain of cars passed them on the right. Georgia put on her turn signal and eased back into the right lane, resolving to pay attention to her driving, no matter what Darby said next.

"I know I should have done something, because he sounded so . . . off. But I thought he'd finish drinking and sleep it off and then maybe he'd be embarrassed if I showed up."

Georgia waited.

"Here's what was strange: he said again he'd done something wrong, and of course at the time, I'd just heard he'd taken those medicines and I thought he was talking about that. But now, I think he meant something else."

Georgia could barely swallow. "Why?"

"'I had to help her,' he said, 'that's why I did it; it was for her.' That makes no sense if he was talking about a suicide attempt, obviously, and it doesn't make sense if he was talking about stealing medicines from the clinic, either. Why would a woman want him to steal medicines? As far as I know, Jonah isn't close with any woman besides you, and you'd never want him to steal anything, let alone dangerous drugs. I have no idea what he was talking about."

By now, they'd almost reached the hospital. Georgia gripped the wheel tightly as she turned into the vast visitor's lot, inching up and down the crowded rows of cars until she found a space. Darby waited as she guided the car between an enormous black pickup truck and an enormous black SUV. Cutting off the engine, Georgia angled her torso toward the center console, taking care to speak in measured tones.

"Is that it? Did he say anything else?"

Darby shook her head. "I don't think so. I've tried to remember but I was driving the girls when he called and he was on the speakerphone and I worried he'd say something they shouldn't hear. I took him off it and held the phone, but I hate driving that way, especially with the kids in the car; it makes me nervous. So I was distracted."

The parking lot seemed to ripple and buckle for a second as they exited the car, everything slightly, subtly off before Georgia blinked and it went back to normal. She waited for Darby to cross around the car. "Come on," she said, taking Darby's arm. "Let's go see him."

~~~~~~

They crowded on the elevator along with a group of others, alighting in front of the doors to the ICU. Across from the elevator, a few doors down the hall, Georgia could hear sounds from the waiting room as they drifted out of the open doorway: someone crying quietly, the background buzz of the TV, several murmured conversations. A little black-haired child stuck his head out of the door, laughed at nothing, and popped his head back in. Above her head, a fluorescent bulb spat and fizzled.

She pressed the buzzer to the ICU. The doors clicked and Georgia motioned to Darby to follow her past a long central counter dotted with computers. The patients' rooms ringed the perimeter of the space, granting each of them access to natural light from a window. She sped up as they neared Jonah's room; even before they approached the door, Georgia could tell something was wrong. There were at least five people visible through the glass of the interior window and all of them were moving.

She burst through the door, Darby on her heels, and came to a stop.

~~~~~~

It was a scene from a slaughterhouse, dominated by red. Soaked sponges; packets of viscous ruby liquid; and everywhere lines of crimson from Jonah's nasogastric tube and IVs and catheters. Dr. Levin, a blur at the foot of the bed, was issuing orders to a nurse and a respiratory therapist and several others Georgia couldn't immediately identify. Alarms beeped and voices blurred into a cacophony of sound. For an indistinguishable period of time none of them noticed Georgia until finally Dr. Levin looked over her shoulder and acknowledged her. "Coagulopathy," she said.

Georgia felt her face contort. She knew what this meant: Jonah's liver, stressed beyond redemption, was giving up. His blood couldn't clot—or sometimes in these cases, the body developed a ghastly condition where uncontrolled clotting and uncontrolled bleeding occurred at the same time. Often signaling the end game in liver failure, it was a nightmare to treat.

"Acidosis?" she barked, trying to mask her terror with doctor terminology. "Encephalopathy?"

Dr. Levin threw her a look of profound sympathy instead of answering, her smooth forehead knotting up. "There's hope. He's still on the transplant list."

"Will they . . . will they consider him to be a good transplant candidate? Because of what he did?"

Although she could tell Dr. Levin knew what she meant, she didn't answer right away.

This was terrible news, not only because of the obvious—Jonah was dying—but also because if his only hope was a liver transplant— even a partial liver transplant—the odds were grim. On average, twenty people a day in the United States died needlessly, waiting for an organ donation that would never come. And while many transplant lists prioritized the sickest patients first, there were ethical issues associated with choosing people as organ recipients who had attempted to take their own life. What if they did it again? The last thing anyone wanted was to undertake the immense cost and effort of saving a life with a surgery that could have saved someone else, only to have the recipient kill themselves afterward. There was also the issue of alcohol abuse: for obvious reasons, it was less than ideal to get a new liver and drown it in booze. Georgia raced through a mental catalogue in her mind, trying to remember what she might have said to Dr. Levin about Jonah's alcohol use that could have wound up in his chart.

"This was situational," she blurted. "He's young and he wants to live, I know he does. He's healthy otherwise. He's not an alcoholic, he's not chronically depressed." Was this a lie? He'd certainly battled depression on and off, but that didn't preclude saving his life, did it?

Given the circumstances, Dr. Levin's voice was calm. "We'll talk to you about it as soon as we can. We've got to get him stabilized."

Nodding her understanding, Georgia took a step backward and bumped against Darby. In the shock of Jonah's deterioration, she'd forgotten she was in the room. She'd pressed herself against the window looking out into the hall, watching in glassy silence as the team caring for Jonah buzzed around him, hanging blood and drawing labs and adjusting his ventilator settings. Georgia grabbed Darby's elbow and steered her into the hall, where they both leaned, speechless, against a wall.

Darby broke the silence. "I didn't know it was this bad."

A passel of student nurses went by, their voices cheery.

"I know I don't have any right to ask," she went on. "But will you tell me what happened?"

Of course: Darby didn't know for sure what Jonah had done. She remembered the odd looks people had given her in the lounge this morning and grimaced. "What exactly have you heard?"

Darby closed her eyes. "The word at the hospital is that he overdosed on the medicines he'd taken from the Pyxis."

"He overdosed on Tylenol. He didn't steal those medicines, Darby."

"But the video," she said uncertainly. "It shows him taking them."

"It doesn't, though," Georgia said. "It only shows him standing at the door. The clinic was desperate to get rid of him and didn't want to risk a big discrimination lawsuit. So maybe faking the video was their way out."

"I can't believe it," Darby said. She closed her eyes. "How could anyone do that?"

Georgia started moving toward the door when it occurred to her, suddenly, that if she walked through the exit from the ICU, it might be the last time she ever did so. This might have been the last time she'd see Jonah alive. She hadn't touched him, hadn't whispered encouragement to him, hadn't fixed his face in her memory as anything other than an unfolding medical catastrophe. She slowed, feeling pulled by some deep-seated force to go back and fling her arms around him, to tell him she loved him.

To tell him goodbye.

She kept walking, knowing they couldn't disrupt the medical team again. Something in her chest sharpened until it hurt to breathe, but she continued to put one foot in front of the other, making her way toward the exit and then the stairwell and then down the stairs. Both she and Darby were in excellent physical shape, but you'd never know it to hear them descending the stairs; they were breathing so heavily they sounded like they'd both been shot in the chest. They passed through the main floor toward the main entrance. Georgia took a few more steps before realizing Darby had stopped behind her.

"Georgia," she said, "I have an idea. Will you come with me?"

Georgia turned. She wasn't overly familiar with this hospital, but Darby, who'd gone to medical school here, probably knew every inch. She followed Darby outside and down the length of Ashley Avenue until they reached the corner of Bee Street. Darby stopped.

"Do you know where you are?"

"Sure," Georgia said, baffled. She might not know every corner of the medical center, but she knew her way around this section of Charleston.

"I mean," said Darby patiently, "do you know what that is?" She gestured toward the building on the corner: steep, narrow gables, warm bricks, a courtyard framed with palm trees and old oaks dripping Spanish moss.

"A church."

"Right," she said. "St. Luke's Chapel."

"Darby, I don't—"

Darby interrupted, her eyes intent. "You know who St. Luke was, right?"

"He wrote the Gospel that's named for him."

"What else?"

Georgia considered for a moment. "Also, I think he's the author of the Acts of the Apostles. He was Greek, maybe; educated for sure. They called him . . ." She trailed off. "Oh."

Darby nodded. "They called him the physician. He's the patron saint of doctors."

They walked closer. Darby made her way to a side door and turned the handle.

The lights were off but Georgia could see it was a narrow, lovely room, with dark-stained pews and rafters. Three simple stained-glass windows graced the wall behind the pulpit, casting streams of colored light onto the floor. Darby knelt at the entrance to a pew and then seated herself, making a space next to her. She plucked a Bible from its slot in the pew in front of her and fluttered its pages.

"But God has shown me," she read, *"that I should not call any man impure or unclean."* She reached for Georgia's hand. "So says the writer of Acts."

Behind Darby glowed an arched window made of elongated hexagonal panes of red and yellow and blue glass. Georgia wondered how old it was: decades? Centuries? So much of Charleston was ancient by American standards, the city having been founded in the early 1600s. Then she remembered this church had been nearly demolished in Hurricane Hugo. It had been rebuilt on the same foundation, but with stronger, more enduring beams and beautiful new windows. Maybe this was a metaphor, both for the church and for humanity: as they aged, they should hope to grow stronger and more enlightened.

"Darby," Georgia said. Her heart pounded, almost audibly. "He did mean me."

Darby released her hand, startled. "He stole those drugs for you?"

"No! No, I promise, that's not what happened. But I did ask him to do something else for me." She stopped, honesty compelling her to add, "I did more than ask. I may have manipulated him a little bit."

Darby regarded Georgia for a moment, her face solemn and contemplative in the blue light from the window. Finally, she said, "Do you want to tell me?"

"It's better if you don't know."

"Is it . . . are you saying this was something illegal?"

"Jonah did nothing illegal, no." Georgia ran a hand along the back of the pew, feeling the smooth solidity of the wood. "But I think I made a terrible decision."

Darby bowed her head. After a beat, Georgia bowed hers too. Darby reached for her hand again without speaking aloud, but Georgia knew what she was doing: praying, in this church named for a healer, for God to spare the life of her friend.

26

I DON'T WAVE

Georgia rolled out of bed, already awake when her alarm went off. She made herself run, sticking to her routine, pounding the predawn pavement of the city. This was the only tolerable part of the day, where focusing on the repetitive thrum of her footfalls and the rhythmic hush of her breathing sent her into a mindless trance.

The last week since the chapel with Darby had passed in a haze. It was the week before Thanksgiving—a holiday she normally spent with Jonah—and everyone around her was preoccupied. She went to work. She went to the hospital. She spoke, every night, to Mark, who'd left for North Carolina. She slept, barely. She kept it together, taking care of her patients, fulfilling her responsibilities.

Jonah did not wake up.

Back at the house after her run, she unleashed Dobby and gave him his breakfast, which he gobbled with delighted abandon. She showered, standing under the hot water until she pruned up, then staggered out and discovered there were no clean towels in the bathroom. There were no towels of any kind in the bathroom, actually, so after a moment of hesitation, she dried herself off with a small, ratty washcloth. Her hygiene had deteriorated significantly since Jonah's hospitalization: she was out of both deodorant and toothpaste, but between work and ICU visits there was no time to shop, and she kept forgetting to order anything online. She brushed her teeth with baking soda, and after a moment's consideration, spritzed perfume onto her armpits.

She'd gotten into a pattern of waking an hour earlier than usual so she could swing by the ICU before heading to the clinic. Today the ICU doc, a guy named Augustine Blitzer, called her name as she passed the workstation. She'd gotten to know most of the intensivists a bit. Each of them texted her from time to time; whether they were driven by a sense of professional courtesy or whether they extended this level of compassion to all the families of their patients, she didn't know. Dr. Blitzer, who was finishing up the late shift, was a stout guy who looked like he'd sprout a full beard the instant he finished shaving. He sat hunched forward on his round stool, his chin resting in both huge hands, staring at the computer screen in front of him. A dart of fear pierced her at his blank expression. Was he going to tell her Jonah had died?

"No, no," he said, looking up and correctly reading her face. "Jonah's okay." He caught himself. "Not okay; you know what I mean. He hasn't changed." He waved a tired hand at himself. "Bad night."

"I'm sorry," she said, with genuine sympathy. When an ICU doctor said he'd had a bad night, it usually referred to a mighty effort to save someone who died anyway. Or sometimes, it was just an unending cascade of misery: complex new patient after complex new patient, all of them requiring urgent intervention and careful thought.

"I stopped you because he's not here. He went to the scanner. Just left."

"Oh," she said, flooded with disappointment. She'd miss him this morning.

"They were supposed to scan him last night but emergencies kept rolling in. We're checking for any new cerebral edema."

She nodded; they were looking for brain swelling. Being on a transplant list was a delicate balancing act; the sicker you were the more you moved up the list, but eventually you crossed a line and became irre-deemable. At some point in the last few days, she'd stopped wearing her doctor hat around Jonah, afraid that if she probed the status of his labs and his tests too extensively, she'd recognize that final line as it receded in the rearview mirror. She no longer asked questions; if any decisions needed to be made, they'd ask her. Instead, she'd started fo-cusing on the gift of time. She stroked his hands and whispered in his ears. She skimmed his cheeks with the backs of her hands and brushed his floppy hair from his face. She told and retold all the funniest and most beloved stories from their friendship, emphasizing all the things that made him vain: his handsomeness, his wit, his bright mind.

His kindness.

He never responded to any of this. No movement, no change in his vital signs, no flash of sentience behind the mask. But she talked to him anyway.

"Who's coming on today?" she asked Dr. Blitzer.

"Stephanie," he said, referring to Dr. Levin. "I know she'll call you the minute there's anything new to tell."

"Thank you," she told him.

She made her way back through the hospital to the parking lot and to her car, which, like her, had grown grimy and disheveled during the crisis, littered with empty water bottles and discarded changes of cloth-ing. As she hit the highway, she rolled the window down in time to feel the warmth of the sun on her arms as it cracked the horizon over the ocean.

~~~~~~

Stewart called en route. "Anything?" he inquired, unable to hide his hope.

He'd taken to checking in with Georgia every day. She was touched by his anxiety. Surely some of it related to the increasingly likely con-clusion that he'd been gifted that most elusive of clients—a truly innocent man, martyred by villains—but it also stemmed from an appreciable personal concern. He liked Jonah.

"Nothing," she said. "They were scanning him again. I should hear more later."

"Keep me posted."

"What's new on your end?" she asked. Strangely, the sicker Jonah had become, the less she'd cared about the public developments in his case.

Stewart's voice kicked up a notch. "Quite a bit, actually. Have you seen the paper today?"

"Not yet. I'm in the car."

"Read it as soon as you get wherever you're going. And call me." He hung up.

She hadn't bothered to grab her copy of the paper when she'd left home, so as soon as she parked the car at work she scurried inside to snag the copy from the lounge. She was earlier than she'd expected to be, and she was in luck: the paper was lying unmolested in its plastic sleeve on a table. No one looked up as she scooped it up and bolted.

Skulking down the hall to the clinical wing of the compound, she let herself into her still-dark practice and then into her office. There it was: an article on the third page. The headline read *Developments in Physician Discrimination Case*, which she took as a positive: they were no longer framing the story as something Jonah might have done wrong, but as something that had been done wrong to him. She scanned it hungrily, absorbing the gist, and then read it again more slowly to focus on the nuances. The reporter made note of the fact that Jonah had been hospitalized but didn't out him as an overdose, either out of some sense of decorum or, more likely, because she didn't know. Or maybe it violated privacy laws to report medical information. In any case, she mentioned he was said to be lingering in critical condition but didn't provide any specifics. Unlike the TV station, however, this time there was no speculation regarding alleged drug use as the cause of his malady.

Over the last few days, more information had come out. First, and most interesting, Stewart claimed he could prove the original evidence—the video showing Jonah accessing the medicine storage area—had been doctored. Computer experts, he said, had examined it and concurred: it had been altered to show Jonah's face.

Second, Stewart said, the clinic had been unable to provide any corroborating evidence to bolster their claim to the police that Jonah had been using drugs. No one else had made similar allegations. No one reported Jonah having sold them drugs. No one reported any wild parties. Even after all the speculation and trollish comments online, no one had come forth with any declarations that they'd been abused or harmed as a patient. And, in fact, patients of Jonah's had started contacting Stewart with their support.

Georgia called him. "This is stunning."

"There's more." He made a small hacking sound, somewhere between a laugh and a cough. In the background, she could make out a hum of voices and a clattery sound like a printer.

"Stewart? Are you at work?"

He made the sound again. "Excuse me. No, I'm at a TV station. There are some people—hold on, I'm just about to—okay, hold on." He must have placed his hand over the phone or put it in his pocket, because for the next moment or two she could only make out a dull *woh-wah* sound. Then the sound cleared and his voice returned. "I'm waiting to go on the show and they just showed me on the air in some sort of holding area and they wanted me to wave at the camera." He cleared his throat again. "I don't *wave*."

"What channel are you on? I'll watch you."

He told her the channel, adding: "I'm on in the next five minutes." His voice dropped. "Georgia, you're going to be shocked by some of the things I've uncovered. We need to talk after I'm finished here."

"Of course," she said. She swallowed. "I'll call you before I step into the OR."

She hung up. She booted up her desktop computer and clicked onto the livestreaming morning news show. Not a minute too soon: the newsfeed came up with a video of Stewart, sitting in a studio in front of a big fake window displaying an image of the Ravenel Bridge at dawn. He faced a smooth-skinned female reporter in a pale blue suit.

". . . can you tell us about the new evidence in the case?" she was saying.

Stewart nodded. He looked much better—more dignified and lawyerly—on camera today than he had the day they'd interviewed him outside. "My office received an anonymous communication instructing us to review the image captured by the video camera."

The reporter interjected, her voice audible over a series of still images from the video, showing Jonah's face just before he punched a code into the keypad. "These are the images from the video showing Dr. Tsukada entering the medication area?"

"Correction," said Stewart. "They *appear* to show Dr. Tsukada entering the medication area. This isn't a high-quality image, but in any case, his face is clearly identifiable."

"So if his face is identifiable, how does it only 'appear' to show him?"

"Because the images have been altered," said Stewart. "Or rather, the video itself was altered. When we had it examined by computer forensic experts, they determined Dr. Tsukada's features had been superimposed on someone else's form. It wasn't a particularly sophisticated attempt either: it took the forensics people only a quick glance to determine the video had been doctored." Stewart paused, as if examining the irony of this last bit of terminology, adding, "So to speak."

"Did the clinic have their own experts perform a similar analysis?"

"Not to my knowledge. But I'm sure they will now."

"But it is their video, correct?"

"Actually, no," said Stewart. He looked directly at the camera and then immediately looked away, as if remembering he'd been instructed to avoid it. A buoyant glow lit his face. "The clinic does not have surveillance cameras in any location that would capture the entrance to the medication room. This was probably filmed on an individual's phone."

"How did the clinic become aware of it?"

"I've inquired as to that but haven't received a reply yet."

"And in any case, you are convinced the video was altered?"

"I am convinced."

The reporter leaned forward, the picture of animation. "If it wasn't Dr. Tsukada, were these experts able to determine who was actually in the video? And how they did it?"

"We can't tell who was in the video," said Stewart. "I have an idea as to who is responsible but I can't share it publicly yet. But it's no mystery how it was done: through a digital video-editing program."

"Does that require special skills?"

"Not in this case," said Stewart. "Anyone could do it. The way these programs work is interesting. They utilize artificial intelligence algorithms by training the machine to recognize an image—say, a person's face—by showing it hundreds of images of that face. Then the program is able to transfer the face to a video image of someone else. It's the same technology that allows people on Reddit to make fake porn movies of celebrities, or to portray politicians saying things they've never actually said."

"What they call deepfakes," said the reporter.

"That's correct. We live in a time where it's very difficult to discern what's real and what isn't."

"So whoever did this would need hundreds of images of Dr. Tsukada?"

"That's a very good question. Yes. Dr. Tsukada's phone—and maybe his computer—would contain a digital file like that. There'd be hundreds of his own images, assuming he kept pictures of himself. Regular photo apps have facial recognition software that automatically groups images of a particular person together."

"So," said the reporter, "who would have had access to Dr. Tsukada's phone?"

~~~~~~

Georgia called him as soon as the interview was over. "Stewart," she said. "If Jonah—if Jonah survives, they would have to offer him his job back, wouldn't they? Nothing could possibly support firing him now."

"I would hope so," said Stewart. "Especially as there was more information than I could share on the air."

A dramatic pause.

"Yes?"

"The clinic was able to determine the code used to access the room. The machine time-stamps them, so it was a matter of looking at all the recordings from after-hours access. Then we asked the clinic to identify the individual to whom the code belonged."

"And?"

With the air of someone imparting a blow Stewart said, "Jeannie Solomon."

Georgia had no idea what to make of this. "Jeannie Solomon? She's a nurse anesthetist, is that right?"

"Correct," said Stewart. "So my first action was to ask the clinic if Ms. Solomon could be the person responsible for the drug theft. But the clinic had already checked their records and she was on vacation that day. So someone—presumably someone close to Ms. Solomon—used her access code."

"Oh," Georgia said slowly. This made no sense at all. "What do you think?"

"I couldn't say this on the air, obviously," said Stewart, "but my first thought was to wonder if it may have been Dr. Wright who entered the room. He oversees Ms. Solomon."

A flash of unease jolted through her at this speculation. Much as she'd have loved it to be Donovan who'd broken into the room, she couldn't picture anyone believing a scenario in which he was using or selling ketamine. She just couldn't. She detested the guy, but he was as vanilla and pedestrian as they came, aside from his nasty little habit of molesting coworkers. If he was going to develop a drug habit, Special K was an unlikely candidate. Opioids were different—everyone knew opioids could hook anyone, even the least likely people—but none of it made much sense in Donovan's case.

Another thought occurred to her. "Why did you tell the reporter you had an idea who was behind it? Did you mean Donovan?"

"Not exactly," said Stewart, "But I know how the clinic obtained the video."

"You do?"

"Oh yes," said Stewart. She could hear footsteps over the line, as if he was clomping down a stone hall. "Thank you," he called to someone. To her he said, "Let me correct that statement. I'm not certain, but I have a good idea how they obtained the video."

"How?"

"They stole it from Jonah," he said.

27

AN INFINITE FRACTAL OF SMALLER DROPLETS

There was a pause as she tried to collect her thoughts. "What do you mean?"

"Jonah's work email account is still active—it has an automated reply that he's left the clinic. But he also had a habit of checking his personal email on his work computer, and it looks like someone at the clinic was accessing that account too. And continued to do so after he was fired."

"Okay . . ."

"Someone emailed Jonah the video in what seemed like a crude attempt at blackmail."

"So," she said, "you're saying whoever was reading his private email correspondence saw the video too and decided to use it."

"That's what it looks like."

"You think it was the clinic who faked the video?"

"No," said Stewart, "I don't think the clinic faked it, unless it was a rogue individual. There would be no reason for them to manufacture a video clip and then email it to him if their intention was to use it to justify his firing." He paused. "Unless they hoped to scare him into dropping his attempts at arbitration."

Before she could reply, Stewart went on. "I don't have independent confirmation of this, so it has to remain confidential. But I'm hearing something compromising was found on John Beezon's computer. I'm wondering if it could be the video-editing software."

Georgia's breath escaped in a whoosh. "What?"

She could hear the slam of a car door, then the muted sound of an engine catching. "Hang on," said Stewart, "I'm transferring to Bluetooth." A pause, and then his voice resumed, slightly echoey. "Can you hear me?"

"Yes," she said. "How do you know the clinic was monitoring Jonah's private email?"

"An anonymous tip." She could feel Stewart's smile through the phone line. "Apparently Dr. Tsukada has a friend or two at the clinic. And now that we've had access to the video, we were able to tell that it has been altered."

"So why didn't you say all that on the show just now?"

"An abundance of caution," said Stewart. "I want to be able to tie all of this together before making a public allegation against the clinic. Once we know more, I'm planning a press conference to lay out the whole situation."

Georgia sat up straight. "Can you make them offer Jonah his job back?"

There was a pause. "Perhaps," said Stewart. "I don't think Jonah ever wanted to go to court. Initially I'd hoped to persuade him to pursue it to the fullest legal extent, but I've changed my mind."

An inarticulate noise escaped her: did this mean Stewart thought Jonah had no chance of recovery?

Correctly interpreting this, Stewart answered her unspoken question. "Yes," he said gently, "I know he can't make decisions. First, I want to honor his wishes, and I know Jonah had no real desire to be a legal pioneer. If he doesn't recover, the only thing left will be his reputation. Salvaging it in the media as quickly as possible is the best gift I can offer him now, but I don't want to jump to conclusions. We need to wait a little longer."

Her phone had been steadily beeping for the last five minutes, but she didn't take it away from her ear to look at it. She knew what it was: the OR calling and texting, wondering why she hadn't shown up to scrub for her first case.

"What's the second reason?"

"What?"

"You said 'first.' *First*, you wanted to respect Jonah's wishes."

"Oh. Yes." A slight whistling sound issued through the phone: Stewart was sighing. "The second reason. As much as I'd love to see all laws allowing people to refuse basic human services to others over-turned, it's probably a futile effort."

"But people are becoming more accepting," said Georgia. "This isn't the 1950s."

"Maybe," said Stewart, "but at the same time the judiciary is chang-ing. Even if social acceptance of a gay person's right to obtain housing or a job is increasing, the legal climate of the country is changing with every new federally appointed judge. Religious freedom laws are in-creasing in many places, not decreasing." He paused, adding in a softer tone, "Last year, the government stopped enforcing nondiscrimination protections for transgender people who've been denied healthcare."

"Stewart, I . . ." She stalled out. What could she possibly say to a gay man who'd had to battle his whole life for the things she took for granted?

"We'll get there, Georgia," he said. "Someday, we'll get there."

～～～

As soon as she left her office, she encountered a swarm of men in suits heading in the direction of the clinic's main administrative hallway. Striding alongside them in stony-faced silence was the CEO of the main hospital, a leonine man in his sixties whom she recognized from various frowny photographs in the media.

The men passed without making eye contact. She'd have liked to have followed them, but she was now late for her first case. She took off in a brisk trot. As soon as she entered the OR suite, a wall of gossip nearly knocked her off her feet, echoing up from the halls and central scheduling desk, where several separate knots of people stood arguing.

"—heard they placed the Cheerio on administrative leave—"

"—haven't seen it myself but—"

"—told you the first time I heard it there was no way that guy could've—"

Rumors abounded: an arrest—or multiple arrests—were imminent. The person entering the medication area on the video had been John Beezon. No, it had been an anesthesiologist. There had never been any medication missing at all. The medications had been stolen by a drug ring consisting of administrators. No, the ring consisted of gay anesthesiologists. An enraged union of gay patients was planning a mass lawsuit against the clinic and soon everyone would be working for them.

Bypassing the sound and fury, Georgia set up at the scrub sink in front of the OR. She whaled at her hands and arms with frenetic determination, elbows flying, as if she were a character in a sped-up old film. Holding her dripping hands aloft, she bumped her way into the OR butt-first.

All conversation in the room ceased. She looked from the circulator to the scrub nurse to the nurse anesthetist, all of whom wore similarly guilty expressions and all of whom she'd heard chatting a moment ago. "Was it something I said?" she asked.

"Hah!" honked the scrub tech, a guy named Chuck. Great beauty had been bestowed upon Chuck by whichever deity handed out physical appearance, granting him soulful black-rimmed green eyes and an exquisitely carved jawline and waves of thick black hair. Unfortunately, however, as she'd discovered after one date with him five years ago, the same deity had skimped when it came to brainpower. Beautiful Chuck was as dumb as a bag of hammers. "Hah! Hah!"

She looked at the nurse anesthetist, her friend Debra. She peered back at Georgia though her thick glasses, blinking. She shrugged her shoulders in apology. "We were talking about Jonah."

"As chief surgeon in the room," Georgia said, thrusting her arms into the billowing blue gown Beautiful Chuck held in front of her, "I'm setting conversational limits today. No talking about Jonah or the clinic or anything related to any of that."

"Yes, ma'am," said Beautiful Chuck. "What should we talk about?"

"Whether Damien Hirst should have won that Turner Prize way back when," she said firmly. "How to best flood-proof urban areas in advance of escalating weather events. The decimation of honeybees. The second revolution of quantum mechanics. Anything of cultural or historical or scientific significance; use your imagination. Take it away." She waved a gloved hand expansively in Beautiful Chuck's direction.

Total silence.

She glanced at the table, where her patient lay sleeping, his eyelids taped to his cheeks to prevent his corneas from drying out during the operation. He looked like an angel.

She sighed. "Okay, then." She nodded to Nancy, the circulator. "How about some Led Zeppelin?"

~~~~~~

By the time she made it to her car that evening, it was obvious a profound shift had occurred. Levers rose and cogs churned and mysterious machine parts whirred in the great mechanical beast of public opinion until a critical mass had been achieved. Suddenly, everyone was convinced Jonah had been done wrong. As Georgia exited the clinic, Gretchen Nease, a pediatrician who a few days ago had sidled out of her path as if she were a leper, now fell all over herself to throw her glances of warm sympathy. The radio opened the hourly news broadcast with a story of possible malfeasance on the part of the clinic. Several coworkers were quoted, claiming close friendship as they praised Jonah's personality and medical skills. Georgia felt her eyebrows shoot skyward; she could have sworn at least one of them had been dissing Jonah in the newspaper mere days ago.

The entrance to Jonah's hospital across town was abuzz with reporters talking earnestly into handheld microphones. Fragments of their sentences drifted into her ears as she barreled past: *wrongfully accused . . . issued an apology . . . fired not for his job performance but for his . . .*

The ICU nurses buzzed her in with their usual brisk cheer. Georgia thought she detected curiosity on the face of the ward clerk, but no one flagged her down as she made her way down the hall to Jonah's room.

Aside from Jonah, immobile on his puffy mattress, the room was empty. She pumped hand sanitizer from a dispenser on the wall, applying it to her already-roughed hands and arms as hums and beeps filled the air from the machines tasked with keeping Jonah alive. She listened to each surge from the ventilator, sending oxygen in and ushering carbon dioxide out in its alien, monotonous rhythm. Yellow fluid fell, one drop at a time, from a bag on an IV pole through a transparent polyvinyl tube and into a large central vein on the side of Jonah's neck. A blink, and the numbers on his monitor updated: heart rate, respiratory rate, oxygen level, blood pressure.

She dragged a chair to Jonah's bedside and picked up his hand. "Hey, babe, it's me," she said softly.

No response.

She leaned forward and forced her voice into a ridiculously upbeat tone. "Big news today, Jones: you're a celebrity. If—if you were feeling better, you'd probably be fielding calls from screenwriters and Hollywood agents. I'm serious. I even saw your picture on CNN this afternoon." A wry smile creased her face at the thought of the photo CNN had shown. Jonah would have considered it a full-blown catastrophe: an old black-and-white of him in which he'd been laughing so hard you could see straight up his nose. He'd also been rocking a flippy Bieberesque haircut, à la the mid-2000s. He looked about twelve.

Now for the hard part. Even though they were alone in the glass-walled room, she glanced over her shoulder. Outside, at the long central counter, people typed on computers and talked; no one was looking in her direction. She leaned in farther.

"And the clinic: it's a mess. People are sorry about what happened to you, Jones. Everyone wants you to come back. They want—" She stopped; she couldn't keep the positive tone going. Her throat felt like it was filled with sand. "They just want you to be okay," she whispered.

In a movie, this would be the moment. She'd close her eyes and hang her head, overcome with grief and the terrible futility of it all as a single tear rolled from her eye, tracked by the cameras on a close-up slo-mo of its path over the soft downy fuzz of her cheek and out into the immensity of space. It would land, finally, on the rise of Jonah's cheekbone, splashing into an infinite fractal of smaller droplets before it vanished. Her shoulders would heave. She'd turn away.

And Jonah's eyes would open.

She waited, full of perverse hope, as her eye obligingly discharged a tear, but Jonah did not play his part. His eyes remained stubbornly shut; his face did not twitch in the throes of imminent consciousness. His chest rose and fell, steadily, evenly, in the measured breaths allotted to him by the machine.

Her vision blurred and, blindly, she reached for her handbag. Her packet of tissues must have settled in a crevice at the bottom of the bag; despite pawing through its contents two or three times, she couldn't find them. She'd just resigned herself to a trip to the bathroom, when her fingers curled around a piece of paper. She pulled it out, sending the bag skittering to the floor.

Ignoring her damp face, she ran her fingers along one edge of the paper, soft and fringy where she'd torn it from Jonah's journal. The words were hard to distinguish through the film of her tears, little clumps of black against the moon-white glow of the page, but once she squinted and blinked a few times she could make them out. She blotted her face in the crook of her elbow, thinking of Jonah alone in his house the night he'd taken the pills, his brain bubbling and boiling until he'd grabbed pencil and paper and produced the words on this paper.

THE WRAITH

I know I knew I went I came
I turned the corner and called your name
I searched for fire, for love, for life
I heard your voice through blackest ice

I looked for you in grime and grit
through heaping hills of counterfeit

I hunted hope on VR screens
in fairy tales and cryptic dreams
through desert sand and arctic floes
on eyelashes of embryos
in dying stars and Georgian clay
atomic dust and cabernet

I thrust my soul toward sweet vibration
not you, they said: Abomination
and still I bowed before the noble
ever wandering ever hopeful

through circuit boards and dazzling towers
I tracked your scent for countless hours
I scoured the earth till it degraded
wizened wretched sick and aged

and all the while I could not see
you are whole; the wraith is me.

She closed her eyes again, defeated, and eased her face down to his chest. She rubbed it against the rough fabric of his hospital-issued gown until she could feel the pulsation of Jonah's heart, like a hyper little frog under his skin. "Jones," she whispered through the clog in her throat. "I'm so sorry about what I suggested you do."

"Georgia."

Her eyes flew open. It wasn't Jonah, of course; people on ventilators could not speak. She leapt back from him, ashamed of her heedlessness of the germs she could be transferring. "I'm sorry," she squawked to Dr. Levin. "I just . . ."

The doctor moved swiftly toward Georgia just as she stood up. She turned from Dr. Levin, trying to swipe her face on her sleeve without being obvious about it. She turned back, and for a hideous moment, she thought the doctor was coming to slap her away from her patient.

"Ah, there, now," Dr. Levin said and opened her arms. Georgia fell into them, trying not to smear her scrubs with her tears. Everything fell away: Jonah, the room, the hospital, the universe. She clung to the back of Dr. Levin's slight shoulders, swaying feebly, until a semblance of self-possession returned. "Oh shit," she said, wiping away a last rogue tear. "Getting slimed by distraught urologists is surely not in your job description."

Dr. Levin laughed: a beautiful light tinkle. "He's lucky to have you. I've seldom seen as devoted a friend."

"We made a vow," Georgia said, "a long time ago, that we'd be each other's families."

"Yes, well," she said, "from my perspective, I'm awfully glad you followed up that vow with legal power-of-attorney paperwork."

Georgia smiled, surprised she'd attempted a joke. "I am too. I can't imagine visiting every day and not being allowed to hear any information. Although you may have noticed I'm trying not to focus on the labs anymore."

"I have noticed," she said. "Do you want to hear anything today?"

They looked at Jonah's bed. From this perspective, they couldn't see his face; he could be anyone, any wasted form in a hospital bed. "No," Georgia said. "I mean, yes. Is there anything good?"

Dr. Levin hesitated too long. "We seem to be caught in a one-step-forward, two-steps-back pattern. He weathers one crisis and another develops: acidosis, renal failure, rhabdomyolysis. Still, though, he's survived the most dangerous period, I think. Liver enzymes are actually a bit improved."

Tactfully, she left unsaid the thing they were both thinking: he had not woken up. Georgia thought Dr. Levin would say more about his presumptive encephalopathy but she changed the subject. "I have been seeing my patient all over the news today."

"Oh. Yeah. Things have changed rather significantly." Georgia felt the knot in her throat start to collect again. "I wish he could know about it."

"Perhaps he will," said Dr. Levin. They stood quietly for a moment, looking at him, and then she extracted a piece of paper from her pocket. "I almost forgot. Have you turned off your phone ringer?"

"Yes," Georgia said, remembering she'd switched it off as she entered the ICU. "I have. Why?"

"Someone is trying to reach you." She handed over a piece of paper. In unfamiliar handwriting someone had penned:

Message for Dr. Brown (Jonah Tsukada, bed 8). Call Mark McInniss as soon as possible.

"Thank you," Georgia told her. They walked out of the room together and, in the hall, after a brief clasp of her shoulder, Dr. Levin left her. She dialed Mark immediately.

"Georgia," he said. "How are you holding up?"

"I'm okay. I'm at the ICU." Before he could ask she added, "Nothing new. His labs are a bit better but he hasn't woken up."

Directly across from where she stood, she could see into the room of the young mother through the slatted shades on the interior window. Her family stood clustered around her bed, holding hands, their heads bowed. Georgia could not discern the words, but she could make out the cadence of the prayer from an older man at her bedside; his voice, rich and deep, might as well have been singing.

"I've been following the news," he said. "It's crazy. I even caught it on the TV in my hotel."

"Yeah," she said.

"Do you want to talk about it?"

"I don't. I don't want to, at all."

"Then I'll do my best to take your mind off it."

"Where are you?"

"I'm here. I came back."

She felt her eyes widen. "You're in the hospital?"

"I'm on my way to Charleston. I finished in Raleigh."

"Can you—where are you going to stay?"

"I was hoping I could stay with you," he said.

Across the hall, the prayer had ended. There was a momentary silence and then the siren of a single wail went up. The sob—it sounded like it came from a woman—cut off abruptly after a few seconds, replaced by a many-voiced symphony of grief. Georgia squinted; the monitor above the woman's bed displayed a flat line in place of the tracing of her heartbeats. A young black-haired man stared sightlessly at the wall, each of his hands clasped by a tiny, bewildered child. Georgia began to walk, very fast, down the hall away from them.

"I'll see you soon," she told Mark.

28

∼∼∼∼

CAVALIER ABOUT ETHICS

MARK

All during the drive, Mark burned with anticipation. In North Carolina, he'd had an epiphany: despite the relatively short time he'd known Georgia—okay, the extremely short time he'd known Georgia—he knew for certain he loved her. He wanted to be with her. Even in these few days he'd been apart from her, he'd missed her, he'd thought about her, he'd had the sensation of missing something elemental. This was an experience entirely new to him; in all his forty years, and especially in the twenty-five years since his mother had died, he'd never felt as drawn to another human being.

His mother, he felt certain, would have loved Georgia. Not only because of her lovable qualities but also because his mother had been his advocate—his only advocate—for the things he wanted.

In a roundabout way, these last couple months with Georgia had allowed him to forgive his mother for the deception she'd employed to keep her illness from him. She'd run herself ragged, trying to hide doctor visits and chemo appointments, all the while giving him the impression her world was stable and secure. Much later, when he realized the lengths to which she'd gone, he'd become convinced her death had been his fault. For one thing, in the midst of what must have been the worst time in her life, she'd taken a part-time job solely because he'd been invited to Washington, D.C., to compete in a math tournament. There were all kinds of costs: entry fees, travel and hotel charges, meals. His father, predictably, had balked: he had minimal interest in anything his younger son might be doing, let alone an interest in funding a trip with a bunch of math nerds, and in any case, money was tight.

"We pay for Todd's baseball expenses," his mother had said, her voice low and hopeful. They'd been standing in the kitchen—a tiny, hideous alcove dominated by mustard-yellow appliances—while his father rooted through the refrigerator and then the cabinets with increasing irritation. He'd probably run out of beer, which meant this was the worst possible time to bring up a non-sports-related financial request.

"That's baseball," his father grunted.

"Mark never asks for anything," his mother pointed out. This was untrue; of the four of them, Early was the only one who never asked for anything. But in comparison to Todd, who suffered from an excess of first-child narcissism, Mark asked for relatively little.

"No." His father pivoted, heading for the rickety table in the dining room where he kept his keys in a bowl.

"Ed, I'd be happy to—"

"No," said his father again. This apparently concluded the debate in his mind, because he extracted his keys from the bowl and banged open the front door without another word. Mark and his mother watched him huff down the sidewalk to his truck and open the door, heaving his bad leg up into the vehicle in a straight-legged arc.

Mark's mother ruffled his hair. "We'll figure out a way," she said.

The way, once she announced it, involved her earning the extra money for the tournament by working a part-time job in a massive industrial bakery. This led to a spectacular fight between his parents, but in the end, Early emerged victorious: she departed three mornings a week at the same time as her boys, returning an hour before they arrived home from school. Tension began to simmer in the evenings—

more tension than usual, rather—as the quality of dinner and house-keeping began to slip. Mark experienced a surge of guilt each time his father pointed out with a kind of righteous pleasure each small infrac-tion: they'd run out of toilet paper upstairs, again. Canned soup for dinner, again. An unforgivable omission: no one had signed Todd's permission form to ride the bus to an away game in Blue Ash.

The day she died, she'd been supposed to attend an after-school meeting about the math tournament. He hadn't been worried at first, figuring she'd gotten delayed leaving work, as had happened a few times in the past. When she missed the entire meeting, however, he did grow concerned. His teacher, Mr. Worlitzer, offered to wait with him to be sure he had a ride, but the idea of trying to make small talk with Mr. Worlitzer, who could not have more fully embodied the math geek stereotype if he'd been working from a checklist, was ex-cruciating at the best of times. Mark turned him down. Eventually he walked the four miles home.

No one was home. He waited, getting hungrier. By the time his father's truck pulled into the driveway, close to midnight, he'd worked himself up into a state of rabbity anxiety. Unable to stand still, he'd worn a groove in the tufty orange shag carpeting in their living room, and his hair was damp with sweat. He flew out of the house and down to the curb, stopping abruptly as he caught sight of his father's face.

His father stumped past him. Reaching the house, he turned enough to take in his gangly, awkward son, and for possibly the first time ever, there was tenderness and pity in his gaze. "She's gone," he said.

~~~~~~~

It would be a ridiculous exaggeration to say he'd never recovered from that moment. He had; of course he had. But his grief, all tangled up with shock and betrayal at everything that had been kept from him, had taken years to ebb. Now, though: this excitement, this anticipation, this joy he felt in Georgia's presence—he wished he could share that with his mother. She'd have been so happy for him.

He bounded up the walkway to Georgia's little house. She flung open the door for him and embraced him with her eyes closed. He knew there had been no change with Jonah—she'd have told him instantly if there had been—and he hugged her harder. Because of his height he was accustomed to stooping a bit when he hugged anyone, but Georgia was tall enough that when she stood on her tiptoes, they made a good fit.

"Wow," he said, opening his eyes and taking in the tiny kitchenette and the vaulted ceiling of the living area and the ladder to the loft. After the soulless grandeur he was used to in hotels, Georgia's home was charming: a patchwork quilt thrown over the back of the futon; a collage of old music posters and photos on the wall behind the couch; a bedraggled stream of Swedish ivy snaking down the wall behind the futon.

Georgia followed his gaze to the old posters. "You're probably wondering if you've fallen into a relationship with a person whose psychosocial development was arrested in college," she said.

"I like it."

"It's home," she said. Before she could say more they heard the telltale swish of the dog door. Georgia appeared to brace herself. "Incoming," she gasped as Dobby barreled toward Mark, nearly taking him out at the knees. Recovering, Mark sank down and scratched Dobby's head. "Oh, hello, hello; that's a good boy," he said, laughing. He looked at Georgia. "He's smiling." He'd always heard that dogs often resembled the humans who owned them, and if this was true, then Dobby fit the bill perfectly. He had one of those big wide-jawed dog heads with a mouth that turned up at the corners, giving him the appearance of a permanent grin. Georgia was the human equivalent: her lively features aligned themselves into a kind of Resting Happy Face.

"Georgia," he said, the crook of his elbow over his face as he tried to shield himself from Dobby's enthusiastic slobber. "Why . . . did . . . you . . . select . . . such . . . a . . . large . . . dog?"

"He was a rescue," she explained. "Anyway, it's just me here and I thought maybe a big dog would be good protection." They eyed Dobby as he flung himself down on his forelegs, smiling, his butt in the air, his entire form quivering with joy. "He wouldn't do that with a criminal," she added defensively.

"Okay, right," said Mark. He raised himself to a standing position and glanced at the kitchen, dubious. "Am I going to fit under there?"

"It'll be close but you'll make it," she assured him. "The ceiling height under the loft is seven feet."

"This place is wonderful."

"I'm glad you like it. I worried you might not since it's obviously a bit of a step down from the accommodations you're used to."

"I'll have to take you to Cincinnati sometime," he said, "to show you the place I grew up in. It was a typical tract house—living room, kitchen, and two bedrooms, one of which I shared with my brother, and one bathroom, which I shared with everyone, which was normal at the time. It was fine—I'm not complaining—but it lacked all pretense at charm or individuality. If you lined up a million people, any one of them could have lived there. Your place is infinitely better."

"Thanks. Let's go out back and I'll show you my tools," she said.

"Well, that's a come-on if I've ever heard one. Try to restrain yourself, please. Or"—he grinned and gestured to the loft—"why don't you show me whatever's up there first?"

He could read the desire in her eyes. He swept her off her feet and lowered her gently to the futon. "I don't think there's any way I can carry you up that ladder," he whispered. "How about we stay right here?"

"Not a good idea," she said.

He felt his eyes widen. "Why not?"

Dobby's head appeared and stuck itself between them, panting.

"That's why."

~~~~~~~

They lolled on her low platform bed, her head on Mark's shoulder, watching a battalion of purple clouds float past the skylight. "Are you hungry?" she asked.

"Strangely, I'm not. But I'm going to hit the bathroom. Don't go anywhere."

She smiled lazily. "I won't."

He scooped up his boxers and tugged them on from a seated position, as the loft ceiling was far too low for a regular person to stand in, let alone him. He could hear a phone ringing downstairs as he eased himself down the loft ladder. His phone, not hers: he must have left it in his jacket. He snagged it on his way to the small bathroom, taking his time washing his hands and face after he'd finished with the toilet, regarding himself in the oval mirror with unfocused eyes.

His phone buzzed again. He almost didn't answer it. It was Olin, the head of IT for his company, and while he liked Olin, he was so weird that talking with him could be disorienting. But at the last second, he hit the green answer button on the phone.

The majority of the conversation turned out to be fairly mundane. It wasn't until the end of it that Olin dropped the bomb, and when he did, he appeared to have no idea of the impact of what he'd said. After ending the call, Mark stood completely still for some period of time—one minute; two minutes; five?—and then he walked from the bathroom and climbed the ladder.

Georgia lay on her side, facing him, the swell of one hip outlined by a thin sheet. "Tell me what you did in North Carolina," she said.

A deep sadness was etching its way through his skin down to his core. He tried to push it back, to sound normal, to enjoy these last few moments of idle conversation before he had to confront her. "There's no chance I'm going to do that," he said, "because that would bore you to sleep."

She raised herself up onto an elbow. "Can you stay longer than one night?"

"I've been summoned back to Amsterdam, unfortunately."

"Is everything okay?"

"My boss generally careens from one disaster to another, so no, probably not. He's one of those people whose unconventional way of thinking first startles you, then intrigues you, and finally stuns you with its brilliance, which is wonderful for humanity but doesn't always make for an easy job on my end. I have to clean up after a lot of misfires. But it's worth it, because Rolly—the guy I work for—is innovative beyond anything I could possibly describe. Oh, and he's married to a doctor."

"You haven't told me much about what your company does."

"Basically, I've told you everything I can. We invest in start-ups working on certain biotechnological advances. Genetic stuff, mainly."

"That's . . . vague."

"Yeah." He sat up, leaning against the planked wall behind the platform bed. "I had to sign an NDA."

She sat up too. "You had to sign a nondisclosure agreement? Now I'm really interested."

"Well, I actually know very little of what happens on the scientific side. But maybe sometime you can come out to California and tour the mothership facility. It's extremely trippy. Lots of VR integrations, so you're never really sure if what you're seeing at any given time is real or not. Rolly loves toys."

"I'd love to see it," she said. "Sounds super nerdy and computer-y."

"Speaking of which," said Mark, "that was Olin on the phone just now."

She blinked. "Olin? The IT guy at your work?"

"That's right. The guy who does all our cybersecurity. He's the one whose number I gave you when you said you had a computer question."

"Of course." Her face had gone blank.

"He said to tell you hello," said Mark, his tone expressionless, "and he asked how you were doing with your black hat."

"My . . . what?"

"Georgia." Mark swung around so they faced one another. He felt his heart kick up into a harsh, jolting rhythm. "He said you asked him to give you the name of a black hat hacker. And I was trying to figure out why you'd specifically ask for the one type of hacker known to be, shall we say, somewhat cavalier about ethics."

"You want to know why I needed a hacker."

"There's no innocent reason anyone would need the name of a black hat."

"To be specific," she mumbled, "I asked for the name of a gray hat, not a full-on black hat."

Mark looked at her. "Georgia," he said, "what did you do?"

29

∼∼∼∼∼

FALSE IN ONE THING,
FALSE IN EVERYTHING

The pressure of Mark's gaze was unrelenting. Georgia caved and looked away first. It had gotten fully dark in the time since he left to go to the bathroom, so she leaned across him and switched on a lamp she'd fashioned herself from an interesting piece of driftwood. The yellow light washed across him and she studied his expression: there was characteristic calm but also an element of resigned knowledge. He'd figured out what she'd done, or he thought he had. What she couldn't discern was how he was taking it. She reached for his hand and he allowed her to pick it up, curling it back into hers.

"So?"

"Mala in se," she said, reverting to the language that had bonded them in the first place. Sometimes there was no good equivalent in English for the original Latin.

He got it: "Inherently wrong. Universally wrong. An act evil in itself, even aside from any laws that might prohibit it."

"Yes," she said. "Exactly. An act almost all people would consider to be immoral. Murder. Rape. Unjustified theft."

He nodded, but aside from his understanding of the phrase, she'd puzzled him. "This," she said, waving her hand to represent the situation, "was a clear case of *mala in se*. It is inherently wrong—inherently evil—to refuse to provide medical care to a group of people because of their sexual orientation. It is inherently wrong to fire someone from a job because they refuse to discriminate against their patients. It is cruel and harmful and indefensible to place someone else in a true existential crisis—where they cannot have a means of supporting themselves or maintaining their health in order to stay alive."

"Yes; okay. I'm with you so far."

"So," she said. "What we did was manipulative. But it"—she thought for a moment, choosing her words carefully—"it wouldn't have been our first choice or second choice or even third choice of how to handle the clinic's actions. This fell more into the court of last resort. If we'd been able to think of any other way . . ."

He waited her out.

". . . but we couldn't. And eventually we came to realize that none of it was going to work. The president and the judges and the courts in this country are on the hospital administration's side."

"But you didn't need to publicize anything beyond what actually happened. The truth is enough to persuade people that Jonah shouldn't have been—"

She was already shaking her head. "No, I wish it were enough, but it isn't. Someone got fired because they treat transgender people? To most people, that isn't particularly noteworthy. It isn't *memorable*. It isn't even illegal."

She sat back, out of breath. Mark was still regarding her closely, his attention focused on her face. As unnerving as this was, it gave her pause to think. Prior to Jonah being fired, if you had asked her to identify the most useless personal characteristic, she'd have said introspection. She had never been one to turn her mind inward, and consequently she might be unfamiliar with how other people viewed her as well. She didn't really care how other people viewed her, in fact. She was what she was, and other people were what they were, and the whole idea that there was something to be gained by a preening, self-absorbed, exhaustive study of inner motivations—or whatever—struck her as a waste of time. Few people were that important.

But she did know this about herself: she was honest. Or—and this was the key—she used to be honest. In the past, it would never have occurred to her to mislead someone else, and if she had misled someone, she'd have been ashamed to lie about it further. Not anymore.

Now she saw she was living in a house of cards. You'd have to have a hard-core commitment to the philosophy of *The ends justify the means* in order to absolve her, but it was now her most intense hope that Mark would do exactly that: absolve her for the choices she'd made.

"Think about it," she said. "We live in a society where our wrong-doers immediately shift the conversation: blaming the victim, lying, delegitimizing those who are outraged, so the crime becomes condemning the crime, not committing the crime."

Mark nodded; he was still trying to understand. "I can't even tell sometimes," he said, "what's reality and what is fiction."

"Yes," she said. "We live in an age of normalized lying."

It began during the time she'd been waiting for Beezon, when she'd commandeered his empty office. She noticed he'd enabled a program on his computer to auto-populate his password, or maybe he hadn't had a password at all. At first, it only served to illustrate Beezon's hypocrisy: protecting confidential information was a perennial favorite topic featured in the *Bulletin*, right up there with an insipid monthly "inspirational quote" and generic advice on how to plan for retirement.

Of course, she had no way of knowing at the time how consequential this would turn out to be. Over the next few weeks she tried to believe reasonable people would overcome unreasonable people and good decisions would outweigh bad ones. This, of course, did not happen. The clinic doubled down on their justification for firing Jonah and turning away certain patients.

"Listen," she'd told Jonah; it was a Saturday, the morning after they'd met for their walk at Waterfront Park. They were huddled in a coffee shop near her house, watching an apocalyptic rain sluice against the cafe windows. It was coming down in contiguous sheets, as if some wrathful weather poltergeist were upending a series of cosmically huge buckets of water against the glass. Neither of them wanted to brave the outdoors, so they just kept ordering more lattes until it got to the point where they were so keyed up they almost couldn't function. Georgia rattled her nails along the table; Jonah was doing some kind of sinuous upper-body dance to the music playing over the cafe's speakers. They probably looked like a couple of cokeheads.

"Can you be still for a second? You're distracting me and I need to focus."

"Negative," he said. "This beat is *poppin'*."

"Okay, fine. Whatever." She considered the beat for a moment; it actually was pretty good. "Here's the thing, Jonah: I've been giving a lot of thought to the question of what influences public opinion. And it's unfortunate, but I've come to the conclusion facts don't matter."

"So what does matter?"

"It's like we said: Spin. Perception. Making it look like the other guy is unfairly attacking us."

"The other guy *is* unfairly attacking us. Mainly me."

"Yes, but no one cares. We need to make this be about Beezon."

"How?"

"We need *kompromat* on him."

"You're not seriously thinking of investigating Beezon, are you? What are you going to do? Blackmail him?"

"No. I'm thinking a video of you. Of something extremely questionable."

"Geez, Georgia, that is definitely going to be NSFW."

"No, no; I don't mean whatever sordid nonsense you're thinking of. I mean something at work."

"I don't do anything sordid at work. Or anything questionable." He stopped swaying and sat very straight. "I'd never do anything to compromise my patients' care."

"I understand that. The video is going to be fake. Or rather, it will be real, but it will be a double-fake."

"I have no idea what you're talking about."

"It's not going to show something you'd actually do; it's going to show something you'd never do. And actually, it's not going to be you in the video at all."

His mouth opened slightly. "Why?"

She leaned forward. "There've been plenty of rumors that you're the person behind the drug theft at work. Someone even put that empty bottle of fentanyl in your coat pocket."

He stared at the table. "I didn't do that."

"Of course you didn't! But the clinic is using that to gain sympathy for firing you, and we need to expose that you've been framed. So what if we were to film a video that makes it look like I am the person who's been breaking into the med room?"

His jaw dropped further. Before he could ask the obvious question, she hurried on.

"Listen. We'll start with whatever it shows—let's say it's me breaking into the Pyxis to steal drugs. I won't actually steal the drugs, of course, but there will be this video of me trying to enter the med room or whatever. The first thing that will happen is the clinic will be forced to acknowledge it wasn't you stealing the drugs."

"That still doesn't help my patients. It won't even get me my job back, plus you'll lose yours and be disgraced." His face was the epitome of confusion. "What am I missing here?"

"I'm not done. We'll give it a little time. And yes, there will be an uncomfortable few days for me, but I'm okay with that. Because the next thing to happen is that we will prove the video was faked."

"I still don't get it."

"The clinic will run with that video. They'll love it—they want to fire me anyway; this is the perfect chance to paint the two of us as degenerates. They'll say: *See? These people condone an unnatural lifestyle and they're criminal drug thieves.* They'll conflate the two things and they'll conflate the two of us and they'll be very vocal about it. We'll give them a chance to bring it up to a boil—and then we'll out them as liars."

She went on: "We'll be able to show, convincingly, that someone edited the face on the video. I'll remove my real face from the video and replace it with digitized images of my face, taken from photos. They'll look real enough at first glance, but it won't take a genius to uncover that's it's altered—people in fake videos don't blink, for one thing, because the hundreds of images you use to generate the video don't usually show the person with their eyes closed. It will look like someone framed me. And because the clinic said I'd committed a crime I didn't commit, they'll be toxic. It won't matter what they say after that. Even the most hard-core homophobes out there will back off, because there will be a public outcry. The clinic will be pure poison. They'll have to acknowledge they were wrong about both of us."

Jonah sat, stunned. Finally he angled his head and mumbled something.

"What?" she asked.

"It's that thing; the Latin thing you said in the meeting with Stewart. *Falsus in uno, falsus in*—whatever the rest of it was. *False in one thing, false in everything.* That's where you got the idea."

"Oh," she said, impressed.

"Georgia, I—" He stopped and closed his eyes. When he opened them, he didn't look at her. "We can't lie like this. That makes us no better than them. And it could ruin someone's life if they get blamed for changing it."

"I know."

"A thing like that?" he said. "Someone could burn for it."

"Well—"

"And there's always the chance they figure it out. This has to— sheesh, this could be breaking the law. You could go to jail for real. No way; this is not happening. I won't let you do it."

"Jonah, please," she said. "Please consider it."

"No. You are not doing this."

She had a flash of inspiration. "Don't say no right now. There's always the possibility I could go back to Donovan and threaten him if he doesn't help."

Jonah's face paled. "Georgia, no," he said. "Don't do that."

"That's the only other thing I can think of."

He stood up, walking past the table to the exterior door. Startled, she threw tip money on the table and gritted her teeth as she walked out into the deluge. It hadn't been raining when they'd walked here; neither of them had so much as a raincoat. She was soaked to the skin in under a second, her hair molded to the sides of her head like a couple of sodden towels. She flipped her hair back, sending two great arcing sprays to the street behind her. "Jonah, wait," she called just as a huge crack of thunder boomed in her ear. The lightning strike must have been incredibly close to sound that loud—it physically hurt her ears—but she hadn't seen a strike through the dense rain. Involuntarily, she doubled over, clapping her hands to her head.

She sensed a presence next to her: Jonah. He'd appeared out of nowhere, also holding his hands to his head. She straightened up and they fell into one another, so wet and traumatized by the ringing in their ears that they didn't notice they were standing in the middle of the street until a car horn blared. The car passed inches from them, kicking up a gargantuan spray of water. Demoralized and half-drowned, they inched to the sidewalk, clutching one another.

"I'm in for the plan. The video thing. I'd rather do that than ever have you face that guy again." Jonah took a huge shuddering breath.

"Jones, that's—"

He cut her off. "On one condition. No, two conditions. I'm the one in the video. It's going to be me, not you, in case we get caught."

"No way." In truth, she'd thought of this—it would be better, in some ways, because it would lead to a more direct exoneration of Jonah—but she'd nixed the idea on the grounds that Jonah would have to tolerate the public shaming that would ensue before the video was revealed to be a fake.

"Not negotiable," he said, his face taking on a mulish cast she knew well. "We do it that way or we don't do it. I'd never put you at risk."

"Jonah," she said.

"And the other thing," he said, ignoring her beseeching look, "we don't frame anyone. Period. I'll make the video and I'll email it to myself. They'll only see it if they're monitoring my email."

"What if they don't?"

"Then, nothing. It doesn't happen. But I'm pretty sure Beezon reads my personal emails."

Another crack of thunder: this one farther away. Suddenly Jonah threw his head back and whooped, a hard-edged, long laugh that ended with him wiping his nose on his already-soaked sleeve. He turned to her. "I love you."

"I love you more."

"Also," he said, "you're not meeting me to do this. I'll set up a camera and do it myself. I can figure out how to make the deepfake. They can't see the underlying image, right?"

"Right, I think, but I'm coming too."

He gripped her shoulders. "You're not understanding me. I'm not involving you. I'll do this for two reasons and two reasons only: for my patients and to keep Donovan Wright away from you."

She shut her eyes, already assaulted by misgivings. The plan had seemed so clear-cut when she'd pictured herself doing it, but the thought of Jonah at risk cast things in a whole new light.

"Maybe we should think things over a little," she mumbled.

"Too late." Jonah flashed her a parody of an evil smile. "You already unleashed the genie, sweetheart."

~~~~~

Mark listened without a word. In the twenty minutes or so it had taken her to recount what she'd done, he'd basically become a still life; he hadn't budged at Dobby's impassioned whining from downstairs or the frequent buzzing from both their phones or at any facet of her story, even the most shameful parts. She held nothing back, telling him exactly what had transpired up until the point where Jonah agreed to film the video.

"He drove to the clinic that night," she said, "and then I guess he went home and altered it right away."

Mark finally stirred. "How did he film it by himself?"

Georgia tried to infer how he was taking this, but his voice gave nothing away. "I don't know. Maybe he used a selfie stick taped to the wall."

"So he sent the video clip to himself?"

"He did. From a fake account on the dark web to his regular email account, along with a note making it sound like someone was trying to blackmail him."

"So how did the clinic see it?" His face: still carefully neutral. She mimicked his neutrality, hiding her desperation to know what he was thinking.

"The HR guy at work—John Beezon—was spying on everyone's computers, even their home email if they'd ever checked it from a work computer."

"How did you know that?"

"Jonah guessed it ages ago, when Beezon made some snarky comment about his personal life."

"So he figured Beezon would see this?"

Georgia nodded. "When he sent the video, Jonah put *PERSONAL & CONFIDENTIAL* in the subject line, which pretty much guaranteed anyone monitoring the computer would read it. Or at least we hoped he would. It took him longer than we thought. And then—it was out of our hands."

Mark didn't say anything. After a long moment, he rolled to the side. "Do you mind if I get something to drink?"

"Of course! I mean, of course not."

They both crawled to the ladder and descended. Mark stayed at the base of the ladder, patting Dobby, while Georgia retrieved two hand-blown glasses from the kitchen shelf, along with a bottle of small-batch bourbon. Mark's eyes widened at the sight of the bottle. "I was thinking water," he said, "but this is probably a better call."

It didn't seem like an auspicious moment for a toast, so she took a hard swig of the bourbon, letting it burn against the back of her throat before swallowing it. Mark sipped at his, gazing absently at the photo of Jonah on the wall behind them. "It wasn't really out of your hands at that point, though," he said, "was it?"

"I—"

"Why did you need the name of a hacker from Olin?"

"I needed advice."

"Because," he said, "despite what you promised Jonah, you did wind up framing someone. You made it look like it was that guy John Beezon who altered the video."

"No," she said.

"Georgia."

"Okay," she admitted. "I considered doing that." Her tongue felt strange; heavy and reluctant. She had to force the words out. "It would have tied things up so neatly. And there was something I didn't know at the time that actually made everything much worse."

"What? What could possibly justify that?"

She tossed back the entire contents of her glass and let the warmth of the whiskey flood through her. Liquid courage: what a cheap ploy. It did help, though: she wiped her lips and faced Mark, going for broke with her next words.

"Because," she said, nearly choking on the words, "I think Jonah really did steal the drugs."

30

A VICTIMLESS PLAN

"None of it happened the way I thought it would." Georgia paced the small room. "I thought we'd be guilty of making a false video with the intent to deceive the clinic. But it was a more or less victimless plan: no one specific person would be blamed for it, and giving the clinic a black eye shouldn't matter at all, since someone had tried to frame Jonah in the first place. The biggest risk was they'd figure out the video was a trick and somehow trace it back to Jonah, which would have been catastrophic."

"That didn't happen."

"No, thank God. But, obviously, things went wrong in an even more terrible way." She turned away from him. "He hated the idea of lying, even to expose a lie."

"Why would he steal the drugs? That doesn't make any sense."

"I don't know."

"Are you sure he did?"

"They searched his old office and found a box of supplies. My partner McLean told me."

"Couldn't the real thief have hidden it there?"

"I guess, theoretically. But there have always been rumors that Jonah had a drug issue. I never believed them, but when they found the stuff in his office, it shook me. What if he'd been in a situation of unbearable temptation?"

"Why did Jonah overdose?"

She stared at the image of Jonah on her wall; he'd been sitting on her futon when Dobby had reared up behind him and licked his ear. She'd happened to have her phone in her hand and snapped a shot of him as he shrieked in surprise. It was her favorite photograph of him. "I don't know. I don't know if he meant to do it. I don't know if I will ever know."

"So you heard the drug theft was real, and then what happened?"

"I panicked. Jonah was already out of town and I couldn't reach him."

"This was the night before I came into town. The night before we found him."

"Yes. That's right. I didn't know he'd tried—I didn't know, at that point, that he wasn't coming back. All I could think about was protecting him."

"So you snuck into John Beezon's office and uploaded the photoediting software and the files with the pictures of Jonah onto his computer. So it would look like the clinic hadn't just *found* an edited video of Jonah stealing drugs and believed it to be real; it would look as if they'd framed him by filming the video. As if John Beezon himself had framed Jonah."

She stared at him, numb. "No. I didn't do that."

He shook his head. "But, Georgia," he said, "if that is the case, why did you ask me for my IT guy's number? You asked me for it a long time before you found out about Jonah taking the drugs."

The question hovered in the air between them, an unexploded bomb. This was it for her and Mark, she realized. Even if he believed her about the IT guy—even if he believed her about her motivations for any of it—who would want to be in a relationship with someone who had proven herself to be a liar?

"I want to know. Were you lying to me?"

She raised her head. "I planned it. But I couldn't bring myself to do it. Faking a video that the clinic would only see if they were spying on Jonah was one thing. Framing an innocent guy—even a guy as loathsome as Beezon—would have been a totally different thing. But yes, I lied to you. And to everyone else. This whole thing was a lie."

She hadn't realized how stiffly he'd been standing until his back loosened, taking at least an inch off his height. "I—I need some time with this."

She wanted to go to him, to bury her head in his shoulder, but she hung back, afraid he'd rebuff her.

He raised his glass to his lips and took a long swallow. "What would you have had the hacker do?"

"Remember: this was something I considered, not something I actually did." Mark was looking at her with a strange expression, so she looked away. She couldn't tell if he believed her. "If I had gone ahead with it, I would not have needed help getting the stuff onto Beezon's computer. I researched video-editing software programs; I had a billion photos of Jonah. If I could figure out a way into Beezon's office, I'd be golden since his computer was accessible."

"Wouldn't they have been able to tell who'd gone into his office? Aren't there surveillance cameras?"

"I don't think the clinic uses surveillance cameras, or at least they don't use them there. But if I'd done it, I'd have had to use my badge to get into the office wing. It would have been stupid."

Mark frowned. "Is that why you didn't do it?"

"No. I told you: my conscience attacked me. And Jonah would never have agreed."

"So why did you ask Olin for the name of a black hat?"

"I knew enough about how to get the material onto Beezon's computer, but I didn't know how to cover my tracks. The computer would keep a time-stamped log of when the files and the editing software were added, and that would obviously be well after the video had been made. I didn't know how to change that."

Mark's face was horrified. "I don't know what to say."

"Mark . . . I know it was a terrible thing to contemplate." She could see him slipping away, but this realization only served to infuse her voice with an unattractive panic. "But I did not frame anyone. Does thinking about doing something count the same as doing it?"

Above them, on the loft, she heard one of their phones skittering across the floor as it buzzed. It occurred to her she'd been hearing that sound repeatedly over the last little while; time had gone elastic as she'd been confessing to Mark. He stood now by the back door, staring into the garden, where she'd placed a little row of solar-powered path lights. They twinkled like a miniature landing strip, illuminating the stone walkway she'd painstakingly installed last month.

"You want to go outside?" she offered. "Take some time?"

He swiveled. She searched his face: no anger, none of the horror he'd displayed a few moments before. Just a sad resignation. "I should go."

"To a hotel, or . . ." She trailed off, unable to finish the idiotic sentence. Of course he'd go to a hotel. What was he going to do? Make a friend at a bar? Spend the night at the airport? "Mark, I am so sorry."

He nodded toward the ladder. "I guess I'm going to need to retrieve my pants."

"Oh! Let me get your stuff." She waved a hand toward the other end of the house. "There's the bathroom if you need to . . . freshen up, or whatever. I'll just—" She stopped because Mark had reached for her wrist.

"Georgia," he said quietly. "I want you to know I'm not going to say anything. About any of it."

"Oh!" she said again. Her brain didn't seem to be computing properly. She realized for the first time that by telling Mark her story, she'd not only put herself and Jonah at risk, but she'd made Mark complicit. Either he protected them, possibly breaking the law in the process, or he outed his lover and a dying man for manipulating the truth. She thought of the time he'd told her he could tolerate anything but dishonesty, and she hung her head.

"Mark," she said. But there didn't seem to be any more words.

His beautiful hazel eyes met hers, just before he stooped and kissed the top of her head. "Goodbye, Georgia," he said.

~~~~~~~

She went outside as he dressed. She took Dobby with her and opened the painted wooden gate at the back of her property, following the dog into the alley and then out to the main street. Clouds scuttled across the black sky, alight from the glow of the city so they looked almost to be a dusty gray-orange. Somewhere down the street she could hear the sounds of a party: people talking, strains of music spilling out of a house, a man's voice roaring in laughter.

She walked and walked until she found herself at the edge of the water. Strangely, she didn't feel upset; a cold, numb peace had settled over her. The worst had happened: Jonah was gone, or would be soon. Mark was gone. In the end, her efforts to wrest control of a situation had resulted in ruin. She might or might not be found out and she might or might not suffer the personal consequences associated with that, but it didn't matter. It was refreshing to reach a stage where she no longer cared what happened.

The water, black and endless, stretched away from her. She reached out a hand toward it, wondering what it would be like to slip below the surface and remain there forever. Dobby, mistaking her gesture for an invitation to be petted, thrust his head under her hand and yipped once. For a long moment, she didn't move, staring at the sea. Dobby nudged her hand again and she patted his head, turned away from the water, and began the walk home.

~~~~~~~

By the time she reached the house, she'd made a decision. She could not salvage things for Jonah or for herself. But there was one small thing she could do, something Jonah had wanted: she could confront Donovan, and if he was unwilling to accept responsibility for what he'd done, she could report him.

Jonah, so full of grace when it came to forgiving transgressions against him, had wanted Donovan's head on a pike after he'd hurt her. But she'd come to realize she didn't care about revenge against him any longer. She wanted an acknowledgment of the harm he'd caused, a sincere apology, and a guarantee that he'd never again touch another woman without consent.

Jonah had urged her not to tolerate what Donovan had done. He had not wanted her to stage an elaborate ruse to manipulate public opinion. And he most definitely had not wanted her to align with Donovan on his behalf.

He'd done it because she'd wanted him to.

It took only a second to find Donovan's contact information in the physician directory. She stared at the number for a good two minutes, steeling herself, and then she picked up the phone.

She had expected to leave a message. But he answered on the first ring, almost as if he'd been waiting for the call. He surprised her again when she told him who she was; instead of the hostility she had anticipated, his voice was subdued, almost resigned.

"I've been thinking we should talk," he said.

"Really?" she said, unable to hide her skepticism. Perhaps he'd planned some kind of countermeasure against the possibility that she might report him. But no: his voice. It was so dull, so . . . full of pain.

"I know it's late," he said. "But is there any way you could meet now? Any place you'd like. I promise it won't take long."

~~~~~

They made plans to meet at a late-night dive not far from Georgia's house. She arrived first and sipped a beer. The atmosphere in the bar, an homage to working-class Americana, was about as far from Donovan's comfort zone as she could envision. Despite her misgivings, she had to suppress a grin as she surveyed the scene: two burly dudes at the pool table, their jaws working at wads of chewing tobacco as they contemplated their shots. A big Budweiser sign glowed in the background. Perfect.

With a start, she sensed a presence next to her. Silently, Donovan slid into the chair opposite her, wearing a pale pink button-down and khakis, his fair hair carefully combed. She regarded him silently as well, trying to figure out how to begin. What was the etiquette one should employ when confronting a sexual assailant in public?

Donovan broke the silence, an uneasy tone in his voice. "Can I get you anything?"

She motioned to her beer. "I'm good."

"Good, good."

They sat. Georgia had just resolved to lay into it—no holds barred—when Donovan leaned across the table toward her. His pale eyes fixed on her like two disembodied marbles hovering in midair against the shady dimness of the bar.

"I'm sorry," he croaked.

These were the words she'd wanted to hear, but before she could formulate a response, he got up, scooting his chair next to hers across the square cocktail table so he could lean in even farther. Even so, his voice was barely audible when he spoke again.

"I'm going to tell you everything," he said.

31

~~~~

WASTE

DONOVAN

Donovan hazarded a glance at Georgia as he launched into his story. Dressed in unusually circumspect clothing—a yellow T-shirt and bell-bottomed jeans with some sort of flower appliqué crawling along the leg—she wore no makeup and had piled her hair into a messy bun. Were it not for a deeply etched set of circles under her eyes, she'd have resembled a college kid pulling an all-nighter.

He had wanted to gauge her reaction as he spoke, but now that the moment was upon him, he found he couldn't bear to meet her eyes for more than a second. He could glean nothing from her expression; it was neither encouraging nor discouraging. Still, even after only one sentence, and even though this confession was going to mean the end of everything he'd worked for his entire life—his job, his reputation, his dignity—he knew this was the only thing he could do to try to salvage some shred of self-worth. He'd passed the point of no return a long time ago.

"Do you remember," he asked, "an OR tech named Keely?"

~~~~

It began, as these things often do, with alcohol. One night after work he went out with some guys and got to flirting with a feisty, freckled twenty-nine-year-old OR tech named Keely who was known among the male doctors for her magnificent cleavage and for the fact that she was one of a set of female triplets, all of whom worked at the hospital. It had been a long day and everyone was a little drunk—not bad, just enough to blur the edges—and the next thing you knew, everyone was making stupid decisions. In Donovan's case, his bad decision took the form of screwing this chick, this girl he barely knew, in an alley outside the bar. It was sordid and uncharacteristic of him and the hottest thing he'd ever experienced. It was also over in three minutes. He thought he'd never talk to her again.

But of course: his wife found out instantly. Marissa, never the warmest woman to begin with, decided it would become her singular mission to make his life hell. Most of it was petty bullshit he could have tolerated, but she figured out almost immediately the way to hurt him most was to turn his boys against him. Within two months, none of them, not even his youngest, his pride and joy, his son William, would speak to him. In disgrace, he moved out.

Meanwhile, he encountered Keely again at work, and this time he allowed himself to talk to her. He knew it was a mistake, but he was lonely and horny, and Keely had an infectious laugh and a rocking body and no demands whatsoever.

As it turned out, she also had a bit of a drug problem.

He was shocked the first time he realized she was shooting fentanyl. She didn't get it from the clinic—at least he didn't think she did—and she assured him she wasn't addicted, she just did it because it "chilled her out" and made her happy. Keely *was* happy; there was no denying it. She seemed to have no troubles. By contrast, he couldn't remember what happiness felt like.

And so, one day in the OR, after a bad morning and a particularly vicious phone call from his wife, he found himself thinking, *What the hell?* The call with Marissa had left him trembling with rage. Surely he deserved just one chill moment, as Keely would say, just one moment without stress and anger. Oh, his unrelenting, all-consuming anger! If he'd happened to be holding a gun just then, he'd have blasted a hole in the wall, or possibly in whichever unlucky human was closest.

But he wasn't holding a gun. Instead, he found himself holding a syringe with a smidge of leftover fentanyl in it.

He looked around; no one was watching him. He slipped the syringe into his scrubs pocket and edged to the table behind him. He picked up an empty syringe, and, holding it aloft in front of a container on the wall, called "Waste! Fifty micrograms." The nurse barely glanced up. "Got it," she said.

He waited until he got home that night. Home; that was a laugh. Completely ignorant of all domestic matters, he'd accidentally signed a lease on a crappy apartment that looked nothing like the stylish showroom apartment he'd viewed. All day the syringe of fentanyl in his pocket had generated this little surge of anticipatory excitement, a spark of fear and vitality that was the best thing he'd felt in months. He hadn't even tried the drug yet and already he felt better.

And yet. When he found himself on the floor of his bathroom, having actually withdrawn the syringe and rolled down his sock to expose the soft blue rope of the vein on the side of his ankle, all the positive feelings vanished. They were replaced by a tide of shame so strong he literally could not hold his head up. He bent forward to the grimy, cold floor. What was he doing? The action he was about to take constituted a disgusting betrayal of his profession.

But everyone knows how this kind of story ends. He shot the fentanyl, a minuscule amount, into his ankle vein. The relief was instant and immense. A rush of well-being suffused him. It was golden, gorgeous, a swell of orgiastic glory. His misery receded and vanished in a puff of cool smoke.

He felt happy.

The thing about fentanyl: you habituate to it quickly. When you start, a relatively small amount can kill you, but your body develops a rapid tolerance. By the end of the month, Donovan's usage had ramped up to the point where the glow would wear off within a few hours, and now it took him three times, four times, five times the original dosage to get it back. Even though he didn't use during work hours, this level of theft was not sustainable. Rather, it wasn't sustainable from his cases alone: he began sneaking into the Pyxis of the med room, using some-one else's code. He started drawing up more painkillers than were nec-essary for a given patient and stopping into ORs staffed by other providers, under the guise of his supervisory capacity as head of the department. All of this upped the level of risk to another stratosphere, but by then, he was desperate. He could barely make it through the day, and the only thing sustaining him was the thought of the relief he'd have after his last case finished.

The clinic began to take notice that someone was stealing opiates. Fortunately for Donovan, a nurse's assistant or a tech or some lower-level employee had OD'd last year, which tended to direct suspicion away from the doctors. People were much more likely to accept the idea of a twenty-something tattooed dude as a junkie than they were the head of the anesthesia department. They should have been think-ing the opposite, of course, but they weren't. Work-wise, he kept it together. He took excellent care of his patients; he kept his mind sharp. He didn't use until he got home.

Mostly.

But he did get crankier. The later the day grew, the more he yearned for release, and the more he yearned, the more his personality soured. People began to be a little afraid of him. Then, several months into his new life of loneliness and debauchery, he hit a low point.

Keely was out of the picture: her parents had yanked her from her job after she'd passed out in a Food Lion, and one of her siblings had narced on her, after which they sent her away. Donovan didn't know where: rehab, presumably. He started hitting on women at work, or in bars, emboldened by his loneliness and the drug use. He'd begun to confide, a little, in a woman at work, a quirky urologist named Georgia, who wasn't his usual type. She was sexy, in her weird way. She dressed in shiny clothes and she had a nose ring, and something about that combination screamed *Wild in bed!* to him. He could tell she wanted him.

One afternoon he'd been on his way to a pain management consult when he passed a commotion in the rehab wing. When he stuck his head in the room it was apparent in an instant that no one knew what the fuck they were doing. Codes weren't common in the rehab unit—people that sick were supposed to be in the hospital proper—and the room was a cluster. No one was doing the two things that needed to be done immediately: defibrillating the patient and securing an airway. Georgia, the hot urologist, stood at the head of the bed with an expression of terror. This was his wheelhouse; he sprang into action, taking the laryngoscope from her and barking orders.

Within short order, he got the patient tubed and lined and shocked and vasoconstricted. It was a futile effort—she died—but at least they'd done what they could. He looked for Georgia, expecting admiration for his competence, but she'd left without even discussing it. As the adrenaline from the procedure wore off, the yearning kicked back in with the force of a gut-punch. He found himself suddenly shaky. The urge was so bad he could have clawed out the eyes of a baby, assuming the baby in question had access to opiates, of course.

He had nothing. The well was going dry; he hadn't dared try to palm any meds from the OR today in the one case he'd had the chance, because the nurse had been watching him like a hawk. Did she suspect?

He felt his blood pressure rise. He almost yelled at a nurse's aide who brushed by him, but caught himself just in time, forcing himself into a courteous comment when what he really wanted to do was backhand her. And then he saw it: a syringe sticking out of a pocket.

The pocket in question belonged to a nurse, who must have been en route to inject someone when she was drafted into service during the code. She stood by the counter, jawing with the unit secretary in the kind of low, intense voice people use after a tragedy. They were caught up in the conversation.

He pulled out his phone and leaned against the work counter as if answering a page. In a move that he'd question for the rest of his life, he snaked out a hand toward the nurse, extracting the syringe from her pocket. She didn't feel a thing.

He hustled to a bathroom. For a moment it seemed his audacity would be rewarded; the syringe was labeled HYDROMORPHONE, a narcotic. But then he held it up and realized it was empty. Or almost empty; a minuscule amount remained, which he heedlessly shot straight into the antecubital vein in the crook of his elbow. It barely touched the urge. Then, lowering his head to the same elbow, he began to cry.

〰〰〰

Five minutes later, he stumbled out into the hall, turned a corner, and there she was: Georgia, the red-headed urologist.

She looked like she was crying too, and for some reason that touched him. She felt bad about the teenager, or, more likely, she felt guilty that she couldn't have saved the girl without him. (The fact that they hadn't saved the girl was irrelevant, obviously.) For a moment, the urge receded, replaced by tenderness.

He lifted her from her sad crouch and embraced her. She was shaking and flushed. He took in her long fluttering eyelashes, the metallic glint of her hair, the confluence of her tan freckles, and an altogether different kind of urge possessed him. He swept her down the hall until some sort of closet presented itself, reminding him of the encounter with Keely in the street. He kissed Georgia's neck and pulled her shirt aside and squeezed her breast. She moaned and writhed and this excited him further. She pushed him away and this fanned the flames to an extreme. It might not be a drug, but this feeling was pretty fucking close. He reached for her again and suddenly found himself tumbling away.

She'd shoved him. Or maybe she'd slapped him. He felt his mouth open and close uselessly, like a fish. She said something and he said something and then he floundered out of there, every cell in his body burning with shame and anger.

It was the worst he'd ever felt.

~~~~~~

He didn't tell Georgia all of this, of course. He omitted any mention of his absurd belief that she had wanted him, or of his conviction that their conversations in the surgeon's lounge had meant something significant. In retrospect, they'd apparently barely registered to her, and this realization, even in light of his current utter debasement, was too humiliating to speak aloud. But he told her about his addiction and about stealing the syringe from the nurse right before their encounter in the closet.

By now, he'd been able to bring himself to watch her as he spoke. At first her face had been guarded. But the deeper into the story he went, the more her shield fell away. Her warm brown eyes had widened and her mouth had parted, just a little, so the tips of her two front teeth were visible.

"It was you," she whispered. "Jonah never touched the drugs."

He nodded, closing his eyes.

It took her a minute, but she figured out the rest of it. "And you planted that empty bottle of fentanyl in his coat pocket, so people would think it was him."

His head, which had begun to nod, abruptly switched to a shake. "I didn't know it was his coat at the time," he said. "I almost got caught with it in my hand."

He could see the wheels turning. "That's why you asked the board not to fire him for drug theft. You knew—you were the only person who knew for sure—that it wasn't him. That's why you came to me, offering to help him."

He slumped back in his chair. "I owed both of you. I didn't agree with what Jonah was doing with his practice, but I didn't want him to be fired for something I'd done either."

"But—the box in his office—"

He nodded again.

"But why? Why him? I thought you said you'd help him."

Here it was: the most shameful of the shameful things he'd done. "I started to be afraid he'd turn me in."

"He *knew*? Jonah knew it was you?" She paled; even the brown of her freckles went dormant.

"He saw me. He was in the clinic after-hours one night after he'd been fired, hanging outside the med room door. I was inside, and didn't know he was there. I thought, actually, that he was there for the same reason I was, when I came out and saw him. But he confronted me, about the drugs, and about what—what I did to you, and he said he was calling the administrators."

"Why didn't he?"

"Because," he said, "I told him I could save your job."

32

~~~~~~

STATUS DRAMATICUS

This was the last thing Georgia expected him to say. "What?"

"It wasn't an idle threat from the administrators," said Donovan. "They would have fired you next. They're cleaning house." He cleared his throat. "They've been combing through your charts, looking for anything they can use against you."

She thought of the patient death that had haunted her, and her face flamed.

"You've had medical errors. You've had disagreements with cowork-ers," Donovan went on. "You've been a thorn in their side for years."

Georgia sat back, hard, against her seat. "I didn't realize it had gone that far."

"When Jonah caught me," said Donovan, "I begged him not to turn me in. He wouldn't have listened, but then I told him I'd help you." He looked down. "From that point on, he only cared about protecting you; whatever happened to him was secondary. I kept my word to him: I convinced Claude and Beezon and the rest of those guys it would be a mistake to fire you. They're not going after you anymore, or at least, they aren't as of right now. My ability to protect anyone from this point forward"—he allowed himself a tight, painful smile—"is obviously going to be limited."

"Jonah agreed to let you go," said Georgia, in a broken voice, "because he thought you'd help me?"

Donovan straightened, his trim form projecting a sudden intensity. "He didn't agree to let me go. He made me call my primary care doctor to start Suboxone and he made me agree to take a leave of absence from clinical work until I enter a treatment facility when a spot opens up. I've only been at the clinic for meetings since then."

"He helped you. How could you put that box in his office?" At a sound near her feet, Georgia looked down; she was trembling hard enough to rattle the legs of her stool.

"I couldn't understand what was happening," Donovan said. He rocked forward on his stool. "I'd already gotten a firm commitment from Dan to vote to reinstate Jonah back to the clinic. I even had Claude on board; we were on the verge of canceling the arbitration. We'd already drafted letters to send to some of Jonah's patients, inviting them back. And then . . . and then that video came out."

She heard herself make a small sound, like a kitten mewing, almost inaudible over an enormous rushing in her ears. Leaning forward, she gripped the counter with both hands to brace herself.

Donovan's voice filtered in, dimly, over the noise in her head. "That video ruined everything," he said. "Claude reneged immediately on his support, and even Dan said no. They got investigators involved. I was baffled—I knew Jonah hadn't been stealing drugs, so I couldn't understand what in the world the video meant. I thought he had to be involved, but I couldn't figure out why. Maybe he intended it as some kind of threat to me? Or maybe he really had been there that night for the same reason I'd been there. By the time I realized the video had been faked, it was too late; he was in the hospital and I heard he was going to die. And I also realized"—he took a breath—"I realized that gave me an opportunity."

"It gave you an opportunity to pin your crime on someone else,"

Georgia said in a voice so low and vicious that Donovan glanced at her, startled, and then lowered his eyes to the black-and-white-checkered floor.

"Right," said Georgia. She stood, sending her chair scooting backward with a screech. "You did it when he couldn't defend himself. We're done here."

"Georgia, wait," said Donovan. He reached for her arm, and she recoiled, so violently it flung him backward. "Please," he said. "I came here to tell you all this before I go to the board to resign. My spot in a treatment facility opens up next week."

"What do you expect, a medal?" she hissed.

Alerted by the tension between the two of them, people were starting to look over. The pool-playing dudes paused their game, one of them slowly raising his cue in the air as he took her in. "You need help, miss?" he said.

"No, thank you," said Georgia. "I'm just leaving. But I appreciate it."

The pool dude nodded. She could tell Donovan wanted to follow her out; the desperation in his gaze could have seared a hole in the wall. But he wouldn't risk it, not with the whole bar watching. He leaned toward her, making one last effort before she got away. "I want you to know," he said, "I'm sorry."

~~~~~~~~

The ride home was agony. Her heart hurt, her brain hurt. Everything hurt, more than she could have believed was possible. There was no denying the significance of what Donovan had said—with her absurd confidence that she could swoop in and fix things for Jonah, their plan had devastated him. She replayed Donovan's words: they'd been on the verge of canceling the arbitration. Of inviting Jonah's patients back. All while he was still whole and alive and in a reasonable frame of mind.

And then she'd suggested they film that video.

As soon as she entered her home, she heard it: the buzzing of her phone, abandoned on the couch. After so many days of checking it obsessively, it felt odd to have left it behind and not even noticed. She scrambled up the ladder and grabbed it, scrolling through all the notifications. Missed calls from Jonah's hospital. Missed calls from Stewart, two of them. Texts from Dr. Levin. She opened the texts from the doctor to find they contained a summons: the hospital needed her to come in as soon as possible.

～～～～～

The shroud coating her brain fell away as she raced to the hospital. Never had she covered any ground in such a short period of time; she sped, cut corners, and startled passersby on her rampage from the house to the hospital and then from the hospital entrance to the ICU. Too impatient to wait for an elevator, she barreled up the stairs two at a time, so by the time she reached the doors to the unit, she was breathing so hard she probably looked as if she required admission herself.

Dr. Levin's final text had been short and to the point: He's awake. Georgia's imagination carried her all over the place: he was conscious, briefly, but in the final throes of organ failure and wanted to tell her goodbye. He'd had a miraculous recovery and would be fine. He was awake but altered, never to regain the essential spark of whatever it was that made him Jonah. This last vision terrified her beyond all others: a shell Jonah, a husk, someone who would live without living, only dimly aware of what he'd lost. She charged past the central work space of the ICU, not registering who might be sitting at the counters or what was happening in any of the other rooms, until she reached the open door to Jonah's room.

A swelling, soaring gush of wonder almost brought her to her knees.

She could tell at a glance: they must have just finished extubating him sometime in the preceding seconds. Free of the tube connecting him to the ventilator, he seemed to take a moment to readjust to the sensation of moving air through his lungs on his own. His breathing was shallow and punctuated with small hitches, giving him the appearance of someone shuddering after a momentous cry. Automatically her eyes went to the monitor above his head to check his oxygen level: perfect.

A respiratory therapist on the far side of the bed tossed the discarded breathing tube into a bag. In front of her, Dr. Levin and another physician, Dr. Wasserman, one of the toxicologists, turned at her entrance. "Ah," said Dr. Levin, beaming. "I was just about to text you again. Look who is breathing on his own."

She stated the obvious. "You've been weaning him off the vent."

"It didn't take long," Dr. Levin said. "He woke up and started fighting it."

She and Dr. Wasserman shifted positions, allowing a space to open up at the bedside so Georgia could move closer. She eased into the gap, not taking her eyes off Jonah. His hair hung in clotted strands, and his lips, ridged and cracked, had turned so pale they were almost white. His skin, too, was abnormally drained, flecked with pepperish dots of stubble that for Jonah constituted a substantial period of beard growth. His cheeks had cratered into hollows. But his eyes, black and aware, locked on to hers.

"Give us a minute with him?" someone said. Georgia looked over her shoulder: the toxicologist. In contrast to delicate Dr. Levin, everything about Dr. Wasserman radiated solidity: the Paul Bunyan of women, she probably stood over six feet tall, with a build that looked as if it could withstand hurricane-force winds. "We'll come find you in a few."

Georgia pointed at a chair in the corner. "I'll stay there," she said. "I won't speak or get in the way. I promise."

Dr. Wasserman nodded, and Georgia watched them as they examined him, conferring over labs on their tablets and ordering new ones. The respiratory therapist drew a blood gas from his arterial line; somebody came with a new bag of fluids to hang. One of the nurse's assistants, a sweet-faced older woman named Karla, came with a comb and a spray bottle of water and fixed Jonah's hair. Throughout all this, he slept, occasionally opening his eyes to take in the hubbub around him. It was clear to all of them, though: barring some new deterioration, Jonah would live.

She stayed until they made her leave. She drifted through the ICU and out onto the regular floor, up and down the stairs, pacing aimlessly, unable to convince herself that this miracle was real. It was nearly dawn when Dr. Levin buzzed her again. She didn't bother answering the page; instead she ran for the stairwell, bounding up the same flights of stairs and into the ICU and into his room, where she skidded to a stop beside his bed.

Jonah opened his eyes. She picked up his hand and in a voice sounding nothing like herself she said, "Jonah."

His cracked lips formed a smile. With some difficulty because of the IV tethering him to a pole, he lifted his arm weakly and pointed to himself. *"Status . . . Dramaticus,"* he croaked.

She clamped her lips together so hard she wound up making a weird whinnying noise though her nose. *Status Dramaticus* was one of her nicknames for him, a play on *status asthmaticus*, the medical term for a severe, unrelenting asthma attack. It was also a snarky slang term used by doctors for patients who magnify their symptoms to get more attention. "I love you," she told him, not caring that she'd begun openly weeping.

He shut his eyes and she thought he might have drifted off, but then he opened them again. "I'm sorry," he mouthed. She shook her head, her vision distorted by tears. A machine-like sound filled her head, louder and louder; her knees began to buckle. Quickly, she leaned forward with her arms extended, placing both her hands on Jonah's bed and dropping her head to her chest. Dr. Levin, recognizing her instability, took a small step forward and placed a hand on her back. "Hey there. You okay?"

Georgia took a few shuddering breaths of her own. "His labs?"

"We just got the last round back and they're better," she said. "We're not there yet. He's still sick. But—"

She cut off, and Georgia looked up to see she had a few tears of her own. "I can't tell you how much I hoped for this," Dr. Levin said.

Jonah had closed his eyes again; his face was peaceful.

~~~~~~

Georgia called her scheduler and told her she wasn't coming in for the next few days. She spent much of the next day and night on the chair in the corner; when they made her leave, she dozed on the hard plastic couch in the waiting room. The following day, Jonah was in and out of it, spending a long time sleeping. When he did speak, it was in brief bursts and short phrases and she couldn't tell how much he understood. They kept it light; Georgia read to him or they listened to music or they just sat, him in the bed and her in a bedside chair, holding hands and dozing.

She tried not to let her hope run away with her as she entered the ICU on the third day after he'd regained consciousness. The team had just wrapped up their morning rounds, with various medical staff streaming in and out of rooms to carry out the business of the day before the new admissions started rolling in. Entering Jonah's room, she braced herself for confusion or mental dullness. But *Status Dramaticus* had been a positive sign; how addled could you be and still come up with that one?

It was bright in here; someone had fully opened the shade on Jonah's window, allowing a cheery blaze of sunshine to bounce off the reflective surface of a faceted metal washbasin by the bed, creating a crazy disco-ball effect on the ceiling. The bright light washed out Jonah's face, making it look even paler than it was. They still hadn't shaved him, probably worried about causing bleeding or an infection. His stubble had progressed from peppery to whiskery, granting him a rakish air despite his pallor. He caught her staring at his whiskers and grinned, and immediately she could tell: he was back.

"Manly?" he rasped.

"Very," she said. "I didn't know you were capable of such masculinity."

He smiled. "Don't mock me, woman."

He wasn't alone. Sitting next to his bed were Jonah's neighbors, Jace and Tucker. She'd seen them in here once since Jonah had been hospitalized; they'd shown up early in the course of Jonah's illness and she'd offered to bring them into the ICU with her, which had not gone well. They'd stood, frozen, at the end of the bed, staring at Jonah's inert form. Even Jace, so loquacious that Tucker claimed he talked nonstop in his sleep, couldn't manage a single word as he took in the tubes and the drips and the ceaseless, monotonous gush of Jonah's ventilator. Afterward, they'd continued to stop by the hospital on occasion, but confined themselves to the waiting room, where they barraged Georgia with piles of magazines and French macaroons and once, memorably, a coupon for something called Restorative Facial Filler. ("What the fuck?" she'd said, laughing, at which Tucker had turned to Jace and snapped, "I told you she wouldn't want that.")

Today Jace beamed at Georgia, his blue eyes alight. "We asked if we could come in, and look what we found. He looks marvelous!"

"I look like five kinds of shit," said Jonah, working the controls of his motorized bed to sit up more fully. "But I'm here."

"Luckily he was never all that pretty," added Tucker, the acerbity of his voice belied by the doting manner in which he leaned toward the bed.

"You need anything?" Jace asked Jonah. "We've been bringing Georgia all the essentials."

"Thank you for taking care of her," said Jonah, at the same time that Georgia said, "Maybe he'd like the facial filler."

Seeming to sense that Georgia wanted to see Jonah alone, Jace and Tuck visited for a few more moments before making a gracious exit.

"You sound good," she told Jonah. "Like yourself."

"I feel . . . with it, actually. Must have knocked out the cobwebs yesterday."

"You were still snowed all day yesterday. I read you seven chapters of *Gates of Fire: An Epic Novel of the Battle of Thermopylae*"—this was Jonah's favorite book—"and all you said was 'Neato.'"

"Must have . . . needed downtime."

She'd been smiling back at him but now the smile vanished. "Oh, Jonah . . ."

They were both silent, caught in their individual reflections. She wanted to ask him so much: what were his memories and his understanding of what had happened; what had that last evening alone been like; in what frame of mind had he been to think this solution was the one? She didn't even know for sure when he had done it. But most of all: why had he tried to kill himself? It was all too much; she couldn't ask any of it.

His thoughts must have paralleled hers, because he reached for her hand and said, "You must have been through hell."

"How did . . . how did you get to that point? You seemed okay. Not okay, but you know what I mean: not despairing. Not suicidal."

"It's happened to me before, but this was so much more powerful than the other times. I don't know how to describe it."

"Try. Please."

"It's like a demon swept through me and ate all my hope," he said. "I can't get it into words right: it's not that I'd had hope and it was gone; it's more like I didn't realize anything had ever been good. All that was good was gone—not just gone from the present and the future but the memory of it gone too."

She nodded slowly. It had always been a fear in the back of her mind—sometimes in the front of her mind—that one day, this blackness would appear in him again and progress, sweeping through until there was nothing left. What would that be like: to believe, with every ounce of your being, that the only thing existing was misery and the only thing that had ever existed was misery and the only thing that would ever exist is misery?

He went on: "I was still in the mountains when Andreas called. He'd seen Freida Myers's will. He said she'd left some things for me and started reading me this list and I realized that every single item on it was something I'd once complimented her on. She'd remembered everything. There was this brooch—I told her my Nana would love it . . ." His voice twisted and trailed away.

She waited for him to continue.

"Andreas said every time I'd admire something, she'd go home and take it off and put it in a box marked *Dr. Tsukada*. Most of it was stuff I wouldn't even want, but you know how it is: I was trying to find something nice to say."

She picked up his hand.

"I didn't help her."

"Jonah," she said, her voice thin. "Did you mean to take the Tylenol?"

"I don't know," he said. "I don't even remember. I drove home and decided to get hammered and I think I wrote you a letter and that's the last thing I remember."

"You did write me a letter."

He turned to her, interested. "Ah, okay; yes. I thought I had done that but I wasn't sure it was a real memory. I told you not to let Mark go."

Her gaze shifted to the side, briefly, but Jonah caught it. "Wait," he said. "You did it? You dumped him?"

She shut her eyes against the memory of Mark's face, Mark's scent, Mark's voice. "Not exactly."

"You're ghosting him. Because of all this—because of me?"

"No," she admitted, feeling the same stab of loss she experienced every time she thought of Mark. "He left. I told him—about what I had planned to do."

He took this in, mulling it over with a blank look. She wondered if he even remembered the details. Her understanding of the human psyche was as limited as anyone's, but she could imagine the trauma that would result as your brain slowly unearthed a memory upending everything you believed about yourself.

"We can talk about this later, Jones," she said. "I don't want to wear you out."

"Yeah," he said. "Maybe I need to rest."

33

〜〜〜

THE COUP DE GRÂCE

One nice thing about spending ninety percent of her time trekking back and forth between a hospital room, a waiting room, and a cafeteria, all in the same massive building, was that it effectively shielded her from reality. She slept in the waiting room, dodging phone calls and emails and texts. She ignored TV and news apps and social media. She saw none of her work colleagues. She stayed in a bubble, catching a glimpse of others from time to time; Dr. Levin or Karla the nurse's assistant or any of the capable and kind RNs who cared for Jonah. But mainly she tuned the world out.

This avoidance came to an end a week later as she approached the waiting room of the ICU after visiting with Jonah. Before she could dodge, a silver-haired man in a bespoke suit accosted her. "Dr. Brown!"

"Stewart."

"You haven't been returning messages. But you're here, so Dr. Tsukada must be in somewhat the same condition? He hasn't . . . worsened?"

Poor anxious Stewart: he had clearly been worried Jonah had died. Since he was a nonrelative, she was his only source of medical updates. She'd completely neglected him.

"He's better, Stewart," she said apologetically. "He's awake. They took the breathing tube out and his liver and kidney function have improved."

Stewart faltered, coming to a halt just outside the doors to the waiting room. "He's awake?"

The look of wonder on his face: it just about destroyed her. "He's awake. He's talking."

"Is he . . . is he . . ."

He could not bring himself to complete the sentence.

"It took a couple days, but his cognition is good," she said, punctuating this news with her hands clasped in front of her chest. "Excellent, even. He has gaps in his memory but he's sharp. So far, anyway. They had a neurologist in to look at him this morning, and I haven't heard the results, but I can't imagine they'll be bad. And a psychiatrist assessed him as well. He's okay."

This might be an overly rosy assessment, but she still found herself in the grip of a profound astonishment that Jonah had recovered to the degree he had. The liver, remarkable and unique when it came to the human body, was the only visceral organ known to have the capacity to regenerate. Jonah's seemed to have risen from the ashes. At the same time, she knew it was likely to be a long road: spending significant time in an ICU could have long-term consequences. But having his brain back: that was a boundless gift.

"Can I see him?" Stewart peered over his round, nearly frameless glasses. "Does he want to see me?"

"I'll ask." She should have asked this already, she knew, but the urge to protect Jonah from his recent past had seemed too important. "Stewart." She waved a hand in the air, a vague moue of apology. "I should have called you right away."

He nodded, turning toward the elevators, dragging her, reluctant, in his wake. "Where are you going?"

"We need a more private place," said Stewart. The elevator opened and he stepped on, presuming she would follow. They reached the ground floor and she expected him to head for the exit, but instead he stopped at a row of chairs at the far end of the atrium, at least ten feet away from anyone else. "This will do," he said.

"Okay," she said, and sat, childlike, before she was instructed to do so. Suddenly it was the most enormous relief to have someone else handling the problems. She listened to Stewart talk about Jonah's case and the developments that had occurred since she'd gone dark. The words, couched in Stewart's prudent legalese, flitted in and out of her head. It wasn't until the name John Beezon floated by that she straightened up and began to pay attention.

"Say that last part again?"

"I said, it seems in the course of the investigation into Dr. Tsukada, the clinic uncovered damaging information about Mr. Beezon as well."

"Why were they looking into John Beezon?"

"Someone asked them to review Mr. Beezon's handling of Dr. Tsukada's firing."

"Who?"

"A physician named . . ." Stewart cast his eyes to the side, as if reviewing a mental database. ". . . Darby Gibbes."

Georgia's mouth fell open. "Darby?"

Stewart cleared his throat. "Dr. Gibbes organized a campaign to have the hospital issue an apology to Jonah's former patients, along with an offer for them to return to the clinic to see any physician of their choice. During this process, Dr. Gibbes reported to the executive committee some concerns about Mr. Beezon's judgment. He was investigated and now it seems he's being discharged from his position here."

"Why? Because he read everyone's email?"

"Not quite." Stewart smiled. "Because of material found on *his* computer."

"Which was . . . ?"

"Ah," said Stewart. He hesitated and then delivered the coup de grâce. "A trove of photographs of female coworkers at the clinic."

Georgia tried to process this. "Are you saying John Beezon is a Peeping Tom?"

"The photos appear to have been shot at the clinic, and they aren't pornographic or compromising. But"—here Stewart's lips stretched into a wide, satisfied smile; the closest thing to schadenfreude she'd seen him express—"they're fairly creepy. Close-ups of a woman licking her lips, for example. A zoomed-in shot of someone's décolletage or someone's derrière. All of coworkers who were technically subordinate to him."

She still wasn't processing this. "Beezon took pervy pictures at the clinic? So they're firing him?"

Stewart's smile dissipated. "Well, not quite. He is voluntarily resigning from his position."

She dreaded asking, but she had to know if Stewart suspected. "Who do you think shot the video of Jonah?"

Stewart shifted in his seat, averting his gaze. He reminded her of a gentleman from another era with his precise speech and his immaculate grooming, but in the bright light of the exterior window behind them, she could see the tender sheen of his scalp between the carefully combed strands of his hair. It softened him somehow.

"It's interesting about that," he said. "I don't know who sent the video. John Beezon monitored usage of many of the employees' computers, which is allowable. But he did more than note what websites they accessed; he went into their personal email accounts and took screenshots. He also ignored several complaints about inappropriate behavior on the part of certain doctors from their female coworkers."

"He certainly didn't ignore any complaints about Jonah."

"No," Stewart agreed. "He seemed to focus much of his attention on Dr. Tsukada. I wonder if he's the one who actually faked the video." He met her eyes. "But there is no evidence to indicate that."

Georgia's heart clanged; a jittery little beat. "They're pushing him out, so that has to be good."

"Well, perhaps," he said. "It's my understanding he's being transferred to a very nice facility a few counties over. We'll see what
happens."

"Stewart," she said. "Thank you for everything. For everything
you've done for Jonah. Do you think once he's recovered, the clinic
will give him his job back?"

Stewart turned and looked directly at her. "Do you think he'll want
it?" he asked.

~~~~~~~

The next day, they moved Jonah from the ICU to a step-down unit,
and then, two days after that, to the regular medical floor. He started
physical therapy to regain his strength and did well, rapidly progressing
to the point of complaining about the hospital food.

This evening Georgia was bringing him his favorite noodle bowl
from Jack of Cups, an überhip restaurant near his house in Folly
Beach, along with a bag of things he'd requested from his house. It had
taken her far longer than she'd thought to get out to Folly and back, so
it was considerably past dinnertime by the time she got to his room.
She strode in after a cursory knock and halted in her tracks at the sight
of a large figure leaning over Jonah's bed. For a moment she thought
someone had sent in an assassin: the person, dressed in various shades
of black, looked as if he'd eaten Jack Reacher for lunch. It took her a
minute: overinflated biceps . . . giant flat-topped head . . . expressionless gaze . . .

"Edwin?" she said, her voice rising to a squeak.

"Ma'am," said Edwin, nodding his big head.

Her confusion must have shown on her face, because Edwin spoke
up. "I'm here in a personal capacity, ma'am."

"Oh," she said, "how nice."

"I regret that I did not keep Dr. Tsukada safe."

"Jonah," said Jonah. "Not Dr. Tsukada. Please."

Georgia cast a sidelong glance at Jonah, who looked moony. "Jonah wasn't, uh, attacked," she said, uncertain of what Edwin thought had happened. "You must not blame yourself."

A slow flush crept up Edwin's neck. "I do blame myself," he said.

What in the world was going on here? She looked back and forth between the two of them and noticed for the first time a batch of half-wilted dyed-blue daisies in a cellophane wrapper on the little wheeled table by Jonah's bed. She set the shiitake bowl down beside the flowers and a thick creamy envelope, upon which the words *DR. JONAH TSUKADA* had been penned in a neat, militaristic hand.

"Ohhh," she said, accidentally out loud, adding, after a moment: "Huh."

"Thanks for dropping off the food, Georgia," said Jonah, his gaze on Edwin.

"Well, yeah, I'm going to bop down to the cafeteria for a bit, so . . ." She edged toward the door. Jonah waved a careless hand in her direction, but neither Jonah nor Edwin actually looked away from one another as she backed slowly through the doorway and into the hall.

〜〜〜〜

By the time she got back to Jonah's room, Edwin had departed and Jonah had fallen asleep, his black lashes casting tiny fuzzy shadows across his cheeks. She stared at the *DR. JONAH TSUKADA* envelope. It brought to mind another item; under the strap of her handbag, her shoulder sagged as if the weight of its contents had suddenly become too much. She placed the bag in her lap and dug through it, shoving aside a glob of loose receipts, an emergency pair of underwear, and a tiny, broken umbrella before unearthing the thing she sought.

Jonah's journal.

She'd been steadfast in not retrieving it from his house since the day she had found it and removed the poem. But tonight, as she'd been trucking out to Folly for Jonah's food and the items he'd requested, it occurred to her that this might be the kindest way to ease him into the memory of exactly what had happened. If he'd written about it in his journal, he'd learn about it in his own words, rather than her having to tell him. But also: he'd be in the hospital, in a safe place if it disturbed him. He wouldn't be home alone.

Once again, in the hours since she'd fetched it, she'd had to resist the urge to open it and read it, even though every time she opened her bag it glowed in the bottom like a radioactive coal. Suddenly, uncertainty assailed her. What if he'd written something awful, something that would tear open the tenuously stitched wound of his mental recovery? Maybe she should look through it, just to be sure it wouldn't harm him, before she gave it to him. After all, she'd already read—and stolen—the poem from the last page.

She dithered, watching Jonah sleep. Finally, she lowered the journal from her chest, where she'd been clutching it with the passion of a child holding a favored book, and placed the journal on his bedside table.

A hand snaked out from Jonah's bed, clutching her wrist in an icy grip.

34

A FULL-ON HEAVING MONSOON

She let out a small scream. "Jonah! You scared me." She traced the path of his gaze to the diary.

"Did you read it?"

The shame in her voice was obvious to both of them. "I took the last page. The poem."

"That's it?"

"Mostly. I skimmed it a little when I first found it," she said.

His eyes glittered. "Do you know about Donovan?"

"I do. But not because I read your diary. He told me."

Jonah's eyes went wide.

"Jones," she said. "There are things I don't know if you remember. And things that have happened since you got sick."

He listened, completely still. She talked him through the things he'd missed: the discovery of the box in his office, the reactions of people at the clinic, Stewart's maneuvering, Darby's prayers for him, Donovan's self-implosion, Beezon's disgrace, and her own shame at what she'd done. She also mentioned the media coverage. A faint smile appeared when she brought up all the rights organizations to whom he'd become a hero, and an even bigger one blossomed when she let him know he'd been in *People* magazine. "I kept a file of all your media appearances," she told him. "I'll bring it in tomorrow."

He shook his head a little, as if amazed, but his face went anxious again with his next question. "What happened with Beezon? Are they firing him?"

"No," she said. "Stewart just told me Beezon's probably getting transferred to another part of the state."

To her surprise, Jonah laughed. "That's perfect," he said. "That's about what I would have expected."

"No bad deed goes unrewarded."

"Speaking of that," he said, "what are you going to do about Donovan? Now that you know everything."

"You didn't have to protect me, you know. I could have fought for my job on my own."

"That's pretty rich," he said, "coming from you."

"Touché," she said. "I deserve that."

He nodded, almost absently. "I wasn't thinking clearly that night; it had already been a terrible day. I got into that fight with my neighbor, who smashed up my nose, and then I had to psych myself up to go to the hospital to make the video. I got there and I walked inside and I leaned against the wall, and I just couldn't do it. Every time I started toward the med room, I thought, *You liar. How does this make you any better than them?* So I left and went back to my car."

"But—" said Georgia, baffled.

"Wait," he said. "I'd almost driven away when I saw another car drive up and park in the doctors' lot. It was two o'clock in the morning on a Saturday, and this is the clinic, not the main hospital, so nobody was there. Plus, I recognized the Ferrari. I didn't know what he was doing there, but I thought about what he'd done to you and I got so pissed I got out of the car and I followed him into the clinic. I was about to storm up and confront his ass when all of a sudden he just sat down against a wall outside the procedure room and put his head in his hands."

He motioned to a glass by his bedside table and Georgia handed it to him. He took a long sip.

"He sat there for I don't know how long and then he got up and started walking, very fast, down to the entrance to the med room. I followed him."

"I still can't believe it was him," Georgia said, in a tone of wonder.

"There are physicians who have substance abuse issues, just like anybody else," said Jonah. "Look at all these programs the state medical board has for troubled doctors. It's been known to happen." He raised his eyebrows. "Even with straight rich white guys."

"I'm sorry. Of course," she said, adding, "But why didn't you tell me?"

Jonah, who had started to nod again at the beginning of her sentence, abruptly shook his head. "Oh hell, no," he said. "They had a hit list. Donovan told me how hard they were going to go after you. They were going to use the case you had last year"—he tilted his head to indicate he understood the impact the case in question had had on Georgia—"they were going to use it against you."

She had to force herself to breathe. "It must have been awful, trying to decide what to do."

Jonah looked down at the bedsheet, gliding his hand along the top of it until every wrinkle had disappeared. "Yes, well." He exhaled. "There was no way I was letting them take you down too. I told Donovan if he called off the dogs and never touched the drugs again, I'd keep my mouth shut about what I'd seen."

"You still should have told me. We could have turned him in together. How could they go after either of us after that?"

"Who was the clinic going to believe: the head of the anesthesia department, a member of their board, a respectable married guy; or you and me? In this day and age, people believe whatever fits with their worldview, no matter how strong the evidence against it is. They see me as a fag and you as a belligerent mutant with a nose ring. All I cared about"—his voice cracked a little—"was protecting you."

"You protected me," she said, "and my grand plan nearly killed you."

She sank back into the chair and buried her head in his chest. He played with her hair, twirling it around a finger. "I'm so sorry for what I put you through."

She tried to smile. "Thank God you didn't have a gun."

"I'd never shoot myself, George. Depressed or not, I'd still want to be a beautiful corpse."

She reached a finger to his lips. "Don't."

He pushed the button on his remote and sat up even more. "Here's the thing, George. Even though Donovan promised me your job was safe, I couldn't stand what I'd become. A liar; a blackmailer. To say nothing of the fact that if he wound up harming a patient, I'd be complicit. But I couldn't figure a way out. If I blew the whistle on him, I knew it would hurt you."

"You did help me," she said quietly. "They didn't fire me."

"Are you kidding? I screwed up everything."

"No," she said. "You're not the one who screwed up anything. I'm the one who tried to outsmart the universe. You are the most fundamentally honest person I know and I convinced you to lie."

He tried to say something and she held up her hand. "Let me finish. I wanted to protect you and protect our patients, but in the process I sacrificed whatever virtue I possessed. I was wrong. The only thing that matters—the only antidote for discrimination and corruption and every other evil that plagues our society—is integrity. Behaving with honor. Shining a light on the truth. Not gaming the system to suit your . . . aims."

Inexplicably, Jonah had gone shaky with excitement as she spoke, causing her to trail off at the end of her sentence. He looked as if he'd like to leap from the bed, but instead he turned and fumbled in his nightstand, producing his cell phone, which he jabbed at her. Before she could take it, he snatched it back, reading aloud the words on the screen.

Lux, Honoris, Veritas

She stared at him. "*Light, Honor, Truth.* That's . . . Latin."

"Right," he crowed. "It's exactly what you just said. You said it! I didn't even tell you to say it."

"Yes," she agreed, bewildered. "Why . . . why do you know that phrase?"

Jonah placed the phone back in the drawer and trained his eyes on hers. She tried and failed to read them.

"Mark," she said. "Mark must have said that."

He nodded. "He's been calling me. Just to check up. And—to see how you are."

She caught her breath. "He wants to know how I am?"

"Yes. Yes! I know—I understand what happened with you two. He was trying to explain it to me and he used that phrase, the Latin thing I just showed you. I looked it up. And now you just said the exact same thing, without even knowing it." He beamed at her, delighted, his animation slowly fading at the expression on her face.

"He used those words because he wanted you to understand why he can't be with me again. Those things matter to him, more than anything else. He believed they mattered to me too."

"They do matter to you."

"*Ex post facto,*" she whispered. She didn't bother to provide the translation, but Jonah seemed to understand: *Realized in hindsight.*

Both of them went quiet. For a long time they lay, him flat with his head on a pillow, her with her head on his chest, listening to the hush of his breath and the steady thrum of his heart. The room grew darker, lit only by a sliver of yellow creeping in from under the door. Jonah wrapped an arm around her shoulders, and after an eternity, he whispered to her.

"Georgia?"

"Yes?"

"Your giant head is squashing what's left of my liver."

She sat up, blinking. "Oh. Sorry. I guess I should let you sleep."

Jonah flipped on a bedside light. It must have been intended as a reading lamp; a beam of white fluorescence glowed behind his head, giving him the backlit glow of an angel, or, depending on your perspective, a vampire. "Wait," he said. "Will you do something for me?"

"Of course."

"Call him."

"Call Mark?"

He made a dismissive flicking motion with his thumb and finger. "Yes, Mark, of course. Call him. Tell him everything."

"He doesn't want to talk to me, Jonah."

"Do it anyway."

"We just discussed this."

He sat up straighter, leaning forward. "Tell him everything you just told me. Do it for me, okay?"

"I . . ."

Jonah's face was unyielding.

"I'll think about it."

He slumped back against his pillow, his breathing accelerated. "Good. Thank you. You'll see; this is going to work out."

She squeezed his hand, knowing she'd never do it. If Mark had been inclined to forgive her, he'd have called her.

"You'll see, George. He'll come back."

She stood and slung her bag over her shoulder, turning as she reached the door. "Sleep well, Jones. I'll see you tomorrow evening."

He raised a hand to wave at her. "Love you, George."

"Love you too."

She shut his door gently and drifted past the nurse's station to the elevators, where she waited in silence with a group of four or five other people. At the hospital's main entrance, she walked past a giant holiday tree fashioned of poinsettias and through the front doors, which had been strung with yellow twinkling lights. Christmas, she realized, was under a month away.

Outside, in defiance of the holiday spirit, palm trees rustled in a warm gush of air. She walked through darkened rows of cars until she found the Prius. She retrieved her keys from her bag, belted herself into the car, and drove, slowly, toward home.

~~~~~~

After another few days, Jonah was released from the downtown hospital into, of all places, the rehab facility at the clinic. He'd lost a startling amount of weight, mostly muscle, and despite his overall mental clarity, he still experienced occasional periods of confusion. He did well in rehab under Darby's care, and after his eventual discharge, Georgia took a short leave of absence and moved into his house, bringing with her an overstuffed wardrobe bag, a giant stack of books, and one highly enthusiastic dog. If she'd owned Dobby before she purchased her city home, she'd have most likely moved to the beach from the get-go. There were few things in life as illustrative of crazed joy as a ninety-pound mutt loping down the shoreline to frolic in the surf.

Dobby's humans tended to move at a slower pace. Georgia made Jonah get outside and walk every single day, no matter the weather. When she'd been off work they'd gone at midday, typically walking somewhere for lunch, but now that she'd started back at the clinic they'd moved their walks to early morning or late afternoon.

Except today. Today she'd been off work to attend the funeral of her patient Leonard Fogelman. He'd succumbed peacefully, at home, his jolly Santa-like frame withered from the cancer that had stolen what should have been at least another decade or two of his life. After the service and the burial, his tiny wife had stood, glassy-eyed, at his gravesite before being led away by two robust but somber men in their forties—her sons, presumably—and Georgia hadn't had a chance to hug her or whisper what a fine man her husband had been. Still, his service had been comforting: so many people touched by such a warm life; so much love in that church for a good man.

Now, at the beach with Jonah, she shivered. She still wore her black dress, and today, in late January, it was uncharacteristically cold. They shuffled along the sand like an elderly couple, bitching about the frosty air. Earlier in the month, Charleston had boasted temperatures in the seventies and even the eighties, but now a cold wind had swooped down from Canada—or from wherever cold winds arose—instantly deep-freezing any Southerner foolish enough to venture outside without a balaclava and a substantial coat.

"I feel like we're those military guys who open the helicopter door in *The Day After Tomorrow*," said Jonah morosely, flicking at an imaginary flake of snow above his head. "The ones who ice over with a startled look on their faces after a fast-moving glacier hits England?"

"Truth. This is intolerable."

Jonah hauled his phone out of his pocket. "Oh Lordy, George, this says it's forty-one degrees. How can people live like this?"

"They can't," she declared. "I pronounce enough fresh air for today. Let's go back and make a fire."

"Okay!" said Jonah, adding, after a moment's reflection, "It would help if I had a fireplace, though."

Jonah moved slowly but gamely toward the house. Every day, he seemed to be regaining a little strength, as evidenced by their walks: today, despite the cold, they'd made it all the way to the wooden pier near the Tides hotel. It took them longer than usual to get back, though: they were now walking into the wind. Despite their joking, Georgia began to worry the cold could be affecting Jonah. She could hear the sharp intake of each of his breaths over the hiss of the wind.

Back at the house, he looked pale. She settled him on the couch and fussed around him for a minute with a blanket before heading to the guest room to grab her computer. When she returned, Jonah was on the phone.

"Yes," he said. "Yes, I understand. I'll let you know as soon as possible. I have to talk it over with my partner, but I'm optimistic." Georgia directed a bug-eyed stare at him at the word *partner*, but he only grinned. "Okay, yes. Thank you. You too. I'll be in touch."

"Who was that?" she demanded as soon as he hung up. "And since when do you have a partner? Have things progressed with Edwin?"

"Edwin's great," said Jonah, his face taking on the besotted look he always wore when talking about his bodyguard-turned-boyfriend, "but I was referring to someone else." He brandished his phone in her direction, like a laser pointer. "You. You are my partner."

"In what?"

"Just listen for a minute before you freak, okay?" This was not an encouraging start to a conversation, but Georgia resolved to remain calm as she eased down beside him on the couch. "I've been offered a job."

"At . . . at the clinic?"

"No." He smiled gently. "Not at the clinic. It's a bit farther away, actually."

"How much farther?"

Jonah set the phone down. "California."

"California?"

"Hold up. Just listen to me. There's an adolescent medicine clinic there, not far outside San Diego, and they're looking for someone who specializes in treating LGBTQ youth. They heard about me"—no doubt from the nonstop barrage of media attention he'd received since the clinic had been forced to issue a formal statement acknowledging his innocence—"and they feel I'd be uniquely qualified to treat these kids. They offered me the job."

"Without even an interview?"

"I've done several interviews," he said. "Video-conferencing."

"Oh," she said. She slid from the couch to the floor. "Oh. I thought— I thought the clinic here would offer you your job back."

In a still-gentle voice, he said, "They did. I turned it down."

"Oh," she said again. She couldn't manage more.

"Georgia, listen to me." He leaned forward, bringing their foreheads so close she could make out his individual eyebrow hairs. "I miss my patients, but at least I know that now they have the option of returning to the clinic. But I can't go back there."

She nodded miserably.

"Look." He picked up her hands. "This California job—it's perfect. It's what I've always wanted to do."

She stirred, squaring her shoulders. "Of course. Of course it is. It does sound perfect, Jonah."

"I don't know much about California, but how bad can it be? I'd miss the humidity, of course."

"And the heat."

"Southern politicians."

She rallied. "Mosquitos and chiggers and palmetto bugs. People saying *y'all.*"

"Oh, I'm totally still going to say y'all. It's the most useful word in the English language. And I like the mega-plural form even more: *all y'all.*"

Only one appropriate response there: "Well, bless your heart."

He still held her hands. "I'm going to miss Charleston so much. But California could be wonderful, you know."

She grasped at a straw. "What about Edwin?"

"I don't know. We'll have to see how it goes, but he offered to drive me out there. Help me move; all that stuff."

"Edwin already knows about this?"

"Yes. Don't be mad, George. I've been so afraid to tell you. I've started to bring it up a hundred times and chickened out."

"I could never be mad at you for doing what you're meant to do. You'll be starting a new, glorious life and you deserve it." Despite her best efforts, her voice broke a little at the word *new* and she quickly corralled it. "It's the right thing."

"Georgia. There's something else, but I don't want you to get pissed at me."

What could possibly be worse than losing him? She opted for honesty. "You got me at a vulnerable moment here, Jones. I can't think of anything that could make me mad at you."

"I'd better seize the moment, then. Here's the thing: I took some action."

She felt a glitch in her heartbeat. "What did you do?"

Jonah let go of her hands and stood. "You're acting like a damn fool. Your whole adult life, you've blundered through a string of lesser men, and finally you meet someone who could possibly be worthy of you, not to mention the fact that *I've* officially sanctioned him as acceptable, and you gave up on him the first time things got tough. What the hell? I know—I *know*—you don't want to go through the rest of your life hooking up with a series of subpar Tinder guys." At this last pronouncement, he leveled a meaningful stare.

Heat spread across her chest. "I don't even use Tinder."

"You do too, but whatever." Jonah waved a dismissive arm. "So I took matters into my own hands and discussed this with Mark."

"Jonah!" She jumped up. "What did you say?"

"We had a nice long talk, actually, the details of which are privileged due to male bonding. But here's the upshot: he wants you to call him."

"I . . ."

"Call him! George, he misses you. Yes, he was concerned at your Machiavellian machinations to bring down our enemies, but he admits he may have overreacted, especially since the plan basically relied on the clinic to hang themselves with their own . . . what was it?"

"Petard."

"Petard! Georgia, all you did was suggest the petard. You didn't even do that, really. We hid the petard and waited for a bunch of morons to steal it. And they did." He started to pace. "Yes, you weren't a pillar of honesty, but your remorse should count for something." He paused. "And maybe, in the future, you shouldn't feel the need to unburden yourself of all your *theoretical* misdeeds when you're confessing to people. Just stick to what you actually did."

"That's not what the Bible says, you know."

"The Good Lord will forgive you. And so will Mark."

She threw up her hands, the trace of a smile creeping across her face. "Okay. Okay, okay, I'll call him."

"Good. I told him you'd call him tonight. And since his company is in California, you can tell him about the job."

"Your job?"

"No, your job. Oh, did I forget that part?" His black eyes crinkled. "Here." He reached to the end table next to the sofa and thrust his laptop at her.

She opened it. A low cream-colored building with a wavy red roof; behind it, a hazy slash of blue. The sea. A glistening ribbon of sun streaming across the water. A man and a woman holding hands, walking away from the building, beatific looks on their faces.

"What's this?"

"It turns out there's a urology practice in Southern California—in sunny La Jolla—that's seeking a new doctor. It's California, so the pay is crappy, but it sounds like an awesome practice. I don't know, I just thought, I thought maybe . . ." He peered at her, suddenly assailed by doubt. "I thought maybe you would consider it."

"Me? Move to California?"

"You didn't think I'd do this without you?"

"Yes, I did," she said and found that she was crying. Not a dainty cry; not a few decorous tears highlighting the delicate contours of her cheekbones; but a full-on heaving monsoon, the kind with ugly gulping. Jonah stood for a brief moment, a stricken look on his face, and then his arms were around her. She grasped his back, her hands catching on the jutting ridges of his scapulae as if they were handles. He was still so thin.

Jonah detached himself from Georgia as soon as the storm began to subside. With a magnanimous flourish, he pulled off his shirt, a sumptuously soft charcoal tee with the words

Jude &
JB &
Willem &
Malcolm

printed in block letters. Georgia raised her teary face to stare at him. He flexed his chest muscles, and she snorted. "Are you trying to . . . dazzle me . . . into feeling better?"

"This," he explained, "is chivalry. You are in need of a hankie, and we don't have any sort of tissues handy, so"—he handed the shirt to her with another flourish—"I am willing to sacrifice myself. Or at least sacrifice this garment."

She took the shirt from him and wiped her face on it, at which his virtuous expression immediately devolved into a regretful wince. "Steady," Georgia said. "It's only a T-shirt."

"It brings back memories," he said. She gave him the eye and he had the grace to blush, since he'd bought the shirt for himself in an effort to establish his literary credentials with a hot, bookish server at Kudu Coffee he'd once fancied.

"So does this mean you'll do it?" he asked. "You'll apply for the job?"

"Yes, I will."

"Mark could move to California full-time, you know, since his business is there. I asked him."

"Of course you did."

"Go ahead," he said, motioning toward her phone, a few feet away. "No time like the present."

It would take only one push of a button to summon Mark; she'd never erased him from her favorites list. She took the phone, hooking it between her chin and her shoulder, and stepped back onto the frigid balcony for privacy. Inside, Jonah parked himself at the window end of the couch and gave her a thumbs-up.

She turned toward the sea, huddled in her coat against the cold. The phone rang and rang. Finally a click and a pause and then his voice on a recorded message, instructing her to leave her contact information and he'd get back to her. She hung up without leaving a message and turned back toward the house.

In her hand, the phone vibrated. She shut her eyes—just for a moment— as a wild flare of hope filled her and then, without looking at the words on the screen, clicked the green button to answer.

"Hello, Mark," she said.

AUTHOR'S NOTE

Dear Reader,

It was not my original intention to produce a book steeped in the currents of cultural upheaval. In the earliest versions, Georgia's big dilemma revolved around her reluctance to tell her best friend she'd been diagnosed with a fatal brain tumor. After some discussion with early readers about whether or not Georgia would die (I voted yes), I was encouraged to find a different story line.

By that point, I could not set Georgia and Jonah aside. I loved them, especially Jonah. He's a complete figment of my imagination, but in a weird twist, he reminds me of someone I met after I wrote the book, who has since become a beloved friend. I was still debating what fictional disaster should befall my two characters when a couple of things occurred to inspire the shift toward the topic of discrimination in healthcare.

First, my state passed a law forbidding communities from passing their own antidiscrimination laws, which piqued my curiosity. I wanted to know what these politicians think is legally and morally acceptable when it comes to refusing housing or a job or public services to another human being.

It turns out the laws are complicated. They also depend on where you live. At the time of this writing, it is still legal to discriminate in much of the country. Not against me, generally, because I'm protected by nondiscrimination clauses covering gender and race and religion. But if you are a gay man or a transgender woman, you are not always protected. Everyone pictures wedding cakes in these scenarios, but because our laws are such a patchwork of differing regulations, there are many places in America where not only can you be booted from a cake shop but you can also be fired from your job or evicted from your home or, in certain cases, refused medical care solely because you're a person who doesn't fit into someone else's definition of an acceptable identity.

In some ways, I'm not the ideal person to write a book about discrimination, given that I've never had to face the kind of institutional bias Jonah has. And for that matter, neither has the straight protagonist of the novel, Georgia.

However, as a physician (and as a person of faith), medical care is my lane. I took an oath to treat *all* patients. I'd like to believe that events such as the one depicted in my novel are entirely fictional, but it's not difficult to imagine a widespread scenario in which institutions are allowed to dictate whom physicians can and cannot treat, based on the personal beliefs of the powerful people who run these institutions.

As of this month—October 2019—the Affordable Care Act is supposed to prohibit most medical discrimination on the basis of sexual orientation and gender identity. However, the Department of Health and Human Services has already stopped enforcing protections for transgender people. They're also actively seeking to overturn these protections in the courts.

I don't want some corporate overlord telling me I cannot treat a particular group of patients because of who they are. I believe wholeheartedly that most Americans, no matter their political leanings or religious background, would not want that either.

By the time some of you read this book, however, the Supreme Court of the United States may have issued a ruling in a case related to employment discrimination against the LGBTQ community . . . and maybe we will have a better idea which way the country is headed regarding medical equality as well.

That brings me to the second event that sparked the idea for this novel. I know someone, a colleague, who was instructed to stop providing care for the transgender patients in their practice. They refused.

And they were fired.

I don't wish to end on a sad note. *The Antidote for Everything* is about equality, yes, but it's also an ode to friendship. I could never have written it without the inspiration provided by my own friends, who tolerate me despite hailing from many different backgrounds, ideologies, and experiences. Special gratitude goes out to my doctor friends, both for their unceasing determination to battle illness and injury on behalf of their patients and for the shining beneficence of their spirits. And, it must be said, also for their epic mastery of stupid humor, which seems to have infected the characters in this book. My apologies.

Or, as Georgia and Jonah would say: *mea culpa*.

ACKNOWLEDGMENTS

As I wrote this book, I relentlessly hassled friends, colleagues, and experts for assistance; they are in no way responsible for any flaws. Errors, misguided attempts at humor, and anything else you disliked is on me.

On the other hand, anything you loved was probably inspired by one of these guys:

The brilliant, caring, and witty female urologists who were kind enough to allow me a peek into their unique world: Helen L. Bernie, D.O.; Michelle T. Chang, M.D.; Kellen B. Choi, D.O.; Elizabeth K. Ferry, M.D.; Emma Jacobs, M.D.; Rena D. Malik, M.D.; Katherine Rinard, M.D.; Aldiana Soljic, M.D.; and Kristina D. Suson, M.D. I want to become a urologist after spending time with y'all. You ladies rock.

Ditto for the toxicologists and critical care specialists (Rachel Haroz, M.D.; Kelly Johnson-Arbor, M.D.; Yana Levin, M.D.; Laura Ryan, M.D.) who helped me with the meet-cute-on-the-plane scenario as well as the acetaminophen overdose. I took some creative license here and there to make the plot work (i.e., Mark's rapid recovery). Don't hold it against them.

In real life, I am beyond grateful to all the anesthesiologists who show up, every day, to save the day. I owe an apology to you (and all the HR dudes) out there; I needed villains with certain powers, and Beezon and Wright fit the bill. Their dastardly deeds in no way reflect on the rest of you.

A word about a character: The rehabilitation doctor Darby Gibbes in the novel was originally an important narrator who got axed during the editing process. If this disappoints you, don't fret: you may see her again in a future story. My heartfelt thanks to all the PM&R docs who helped me understand this vital, compassionate specialty, especially Bradeigh Godfrey, D.O., and Cheri Wiggins, M.D.

Charleston doctor peeps: Kate Herwig Harris, M.D.; Nicole Franklin, M.D.; and the rest of our fun FB group. Thanks for sharing a glimpse of your charming city with me. (Road trip soon!) And to the marvelous city of Charleston, please note I set the clinic in this novel *outside* your borders; the medical settings in the story are entirely fictional.

The spectacular city of Amsterdam: I'm sorry my characters got up to such shenanigans on their journey. (I'll do better the next time I visit!) Thank you especially to my bookish Dutch friends for the camaraderie over the last few years.

I am grateful for the guidance of the incredible ministers at First Presbyterian Church of Charlotte, especially the Reverend Pendleton Peery and the Reverend Katherine Kerr. Thank you for your bountiful grace every time I pester you with theological queries.

All my groups: Women's Fiction Writers Association, Physician Moms Book Club, Women Physician Writers, Charlotte Mecklenburg Library Fund, Ink Tank, Authors18 . . . your support has been invaluable. Thank you also to the kind people at Movement Advancement Project and Equality NC for helping me navigate the byzantine morass of our nation's antidiscrimination laws.

Many, many thanks to the lovely doctors in the worldwide Physician Moms Group who provided exuberant advice on everything from naming characters to urethral issues.

All the Instagram book nerds: love you guys. Special shout-out to @whatmeganreads, @kourtneysbookshelf, @prose_and_palate, @travel.with_a_book, sweet Kristy Barrett at A Novel Bee (Facebook), Ashley Spivey, and the inimitable Anne Bogel, aka Modern Mrs. Darcy . . . your dedication to literature inspires me.

Beta readers and sensitivity readers! Nicole Carrig; Betsy Thorpe; Joanna Drowos, D.O.; Bradeigh Godfrey, D.O.; Rachel Haroz, M.D.; Lara Lillibridge; Lisa Williams Kline; Luke Marlow; Rebecca Smith, M.D.; Jennifer Stever, D.O.; Philip Vernon, Ph.D.; and most especially, Bess Kercher. I owe you all a fine bourbon for plowing your way through those dreadful first drafts.

To my extraordinary editor, Kerry Donovan, my most profound gratitude for enduring all the nerdy words and tangents. And the panicked phone calls.

To my agent, Jane Dystel, all my love. You are the greatest.

To the team at Berkley—Sarah Blumenstock in editorial; Craig Burke, Lauren Burnstein, and Tara O'Connor in publicity; Fareeda Bullert in marketing; Colleen Reinhart in design—your skills are so appreciated. Plus, you are cool people and I heart you.

To Kathie Bennett: You're such a bright light. Thank you for introducing me to so many marvelous book people.

To my writing group, Bess Kercher, Tracy Curtis, and Trish Rohr: There would be no books without you. Also, life would be boring as all get-out. #WritingGroupInk

How many people would trek around the country to ensure at least one person shows up for their best friend's book tour? Heather Burkhart, I thank God each day for your friendship. And if something ever happens to me, you're now capable of telling all my stories.

My beloveds: my med school girlfriends, who inspire me daily; my sister, Shannan, who is perfect; my mother, Judy, who is the most invincible person I know; my children, Katie, Alex, and Annie, who are dear beyond all measure; and my husband, Jim, who embodies everything you'd want in a spouse: smart, handsome, supportive, and hilarious.

Finally, to my Dad and Rosanne: I wish you'd had the opportunity to know I became a writer. I miss you every day.